LYTTLETON SIREN

LYTTLETON
SIREN

J. Patrick Armstrong

The Book Guild

First published in Great Britain in 2025 by
The Book Guild Ltd
Unit E2 Airfield Business Park,
Harrison Road, Market Harborough,
Leicestershire. LE16 7UL
Tel: 0116 2792299
www.bookguild.co.uk
Email: info@bookguild.co.uk
X: @bookguild

This work is entirely fictitious and bears no resemblance to any persons living or dead.

Typeset in 11pt Adobe Garamond Pro

Printed and bound in Great Britain by 4edge Limited

ISBN 978 1835741 092

British Library Cataloguing in Publication Data.
A catalogue record for this book is available from the British Library.

For Dianne, Dexter and Mum

In loving memory of Keith Andrew Armstrong, 1946-2023

PART I

The Dead of Winter

MELVYN

Her face then his face. Hers first. Always. Then his above hers. Materialising out of the fog like ghosts. Bleached in the headlights. Eyes wide in sudden shock. Hands half raised. Mouths open. Silent screams. There then gone.

The Jaguar. So quiet it could creep up on you. Like a cat. Like a *jaguar* for Christ's sake. It had crept up on that girl earlier. Caroline. That was her name. I found out later. *Caroline.* She was there when we pulled up. Drunk already. Coat open even though it was freezing. Shiny green dress. Dazzled in the headlights. Giggling with her friend then turning and wobbling away.

Margret watched from the passenger seat. Fierce in the gloom, shadows under her eyes. Classic Margret. Angry in an instant, arbitrary and crushing.

"Might be fun," I said. "Not dead yet, you know."

I knew this would rankle. And sure enough, Margret climbed out, all bouffant and bluster, slamming the car door, marching up the path to the front of the house. I watched her in the light of the porch. Not a happy moment. Far from it. But I would do anything to return to it now. *Anything.* Just to be sitting there, watching Margret fix her fringe in her little compact make-up mirror, fuming at Geoff and Angie's front door.

It crossed my mind to beep the horn and call her back, go for dinner instead. I've had agonising daydreams where we do just that. I tap the horn, Margret's scowl turns into a smile, she trots back to the car, we kiss and drive away to a happy montage of dinner, wine and a pleasant drive home through the fog and flashing lights of Lyttleton at Christmas. But the front door opened and Geoff was there, all drunk and silly with a scarf of green tinsel like a feather boa, hugging Margret, dragging her inside, waving at me to hurry up. The moment to leave had passed.

I found Margret in the kitchen. She glared at me and poured herself more wine as I kissed Angie on the cheek. That was the way of it for the next few hours. We drank and chatted in separate huddles. Margret danced with one of Geoff's male stylists. I smiled but I was embarrassed. Then she disappeared. I found her in the downstairs spare bedroom, half beneath a pile of coats, slack-mouthed and snoring.

I drank more and wallowed. I tried to dance but felt old and fake, stiff and uncoordinated. People yelled and whooped, patting me on the back like some granddad at a wedding.

I chatted with Geoff. We were both drunk and made little sense. We shook each other's hands repeatedly, interrupted by young women hugging him, telling him he was the greatest boss in the world.

We'd done well, Geoff and I. He had three salons. My optician business was smaller in scale but still successful. Geoff had advised me to expand, but I'd stayed focused on the one unit above the Parade in the village centre. My client base had swelled. I'd taken on an assistant. Business was steady. I felt comfortable with its size, and I was content, most days, on the short walk home from work.

Geoff had stayed young, though. He was slim and he'd kept his hair. I'd slackened around the waist and thinned on top. His wife, Angie, was beautiful and fashionable, still youthful, like an ex-model or dancer. She glided around smoking thin brown cigarettes, flicking her thick wavy hair from her eyes. She was independent and positive about people. She spoke French, knew about jazz and the origins of rock 'n' roll before Elvis. Her vintage clothing business was also successful. Between them, they had become quite well-off. They were parents but looked ten years younger than us. They treated us like their older, squarer friends. Geoff would call me *old boy, old sod, old fart, old so 'n' so*. Margret and I would smirk or scoff at their moneyed bohemianism. But whenever we spent an evening in Geoff and Angie's company, we'd often drive home in silence, lost in introspection.

I went to check on Margret again. She had managed to wedge herself under the covers by shoving coats onto the floor. She was still snoring but softer, more regular, like a cat's purr now that she was deeper into her sleep. I touched her cheek and whispered her name. She whined but didn't wake. I tried to roll her over but she resisted. I sighed and gave up. I was drunk and tired. I wanted to leave but now Margret was asleep I knew we'd be there for hours, perhaps even until morning.

I found my coat and slipped out of the back door into the garden. Grass, trees and hedgerows all sparkly with frost. The bench under the kitchen window was icy. I sat anyway, smoking and sipping at my whisky, relieved to be outside, away from all the yelling and laughing. Inside was at full tilt. Everyone was singing "Don't You Want Me?" Screaming their heads off in the chorus.

The back door opened and I half hoped to see Geoff or Angie or even Margret. But instead, the girl in the shiny green dress appeared around the corner of the house. Stockinged feet, no heels, wobbling like a stringed puppet.

"Sorry," she slurred, half giggling. "Having a moment to yourself?"

I stood up, took my coat off and put it around her shoulders.

"Proper gentleman," she said.

I said nothing.

We sat down on the bench, and she swung her damp feet into my lap.

"That's better," she said.

The light from the kitchen window fell across her face. Her eyes were lazy with alcohol. She winced and eye-rolled while her head dipped and bobbed. But even through the slackening of booze, her face had a golden plumpness. Her blonde hair fell thick and leonine around her shoulders. I watched her while she battled her drunkenness.

"I'm Melvyn," I said, holding out my hand for her to shake.

"I know," she said, not noticing the gesture. "You're the bloke with the Jag and the scary wife."

"Yes," I said, taking back my hand, not knowing what else to say.

I should have stood up for Margret, but I placed my hand on the girl's shin and watched for her reaction. She began to fall asleep as I made small circular movements with my fingers. I remember thinking, *What the bloody hell are you doing, Melvyn*? But I didn't stop. I kept imagining Margret in the spare room as people were finding their coats to leave. *Get up*, I kept telling myself. *Go to her! Force her awake! Leave now!* I could see the words and hear them shouted by the sober half of my brain. But my fingers kept moving over the hard shin and soft curve of calf in my lap. I stared ahead into the dark garden, incredulous at the risk I was taking for such a cheap and piffling thrill.

The back door opened again and light poured into the garden, illuminating a frosty stone cherub by the pond. At a barbecue the previous summer, Margret had scoffed at the statue and whispered, "Talk about delusions of grandeur," drawing a hard stare from Angie.

Someone appeared around the corner of the house, another young woman.

"There you are," she said. "Been looking for you everywhere. *Caroline*!"

I realised I'd not even asked her name. Caroline swung her legs to the ground.

"What's up?" she said. She took my coat off her shoulders and gave it back to me. "This is Melvyn," she giggled.

Her friend gave me a disapproving look. I stood up and held out my hand.

"*I've* been trying to get us a taxi," she said, glancing at me as if I were to blame.

"Melvyn could take us in his big Jag," Caroline said, grinning and giving me a playful shove with her shoulder.

"Yes," I heard myself say. "Where to?"

Caroline's friend looked me up and down.

"Forrest Road," she said.

It was ten minutes away at most.

"Fine," I said, smiling at them both, doing my best to appear sober and nonchalant, as if women half my age asked me for rides home every weekend.

"Fine," she said, forcing a smile back.

Inside, the party had died a little. The volume was lower. Geoff was near the stereo, playing a Roxy Music song, doing his best Bryan Ferry, swaying and miming the words with his eyes half-shut, pointing at those who egged him on.

The girls began saying their goodbyes. I announced I'd take them home and come back for Margret. Geoff was too drunk to care but he nodded and shook my hand. Then he threw an arm round my shoulders.

"Melvyn, you old sod," he slurred, close enough to my ear for me to feel his spittle. "Nearly nineteen eighty-two. Our year for sure, mate. *Our year*!"

I wanted to tell him that every year was *his year*. But instead, we laughed and danced together, awkwardly, our arms around each other's shoulders until Caroline and her friend reappeared with their coats.

"Don't think your wife's gonna be up for a while," Caroline sneered.

"Probably a good thing," I answered.

Caroline laughed. I'd meant it was best for Margret to sleep it off, but the moment to retract or correct the comment had passed.

Again, my sober consciousness spoke to me. *Just tell them you've drunk too much to drive.* I ignored it, convinced that Caroline would engineer the situation for us to be alone again. Maybe she'd suggest dropping off her friend first. I hovered while they finished their goodbyes, endless hugs and kisses and Merry Christmases. I kept glancing towards the spare room, half-expecting to see Margret emerge at any moment, make-up smudged and hair all over the place. Part of me hoped she would appear. Put a stop to me making a fool of myself. But the other part, aroused and deluded, was thinking of quiet spots near Forrest Road.

As we left, I noticed Angie watching me. She'd changed into some floaty white linen trousers that tied at the waist. Leant against the kitchen door-frame, one heel resting yoga-style on the other knee, she looked like a film star – Ali McGraw or Jaqueline Bisset. I waved but she didn't wave back. My head was full of her as I stepped into the freezing night air of the front garden. *Angie and I on the deck of a yacht, soft focus, kissing amidst the aqua sparkle of the Mediterranean.* I was prone to these ridiculous musings about Angie. They were vivid and potent and always left me crestfallen.

"Come on, we're freezing," Caroline's friend said.

Caroline pulled her coat about herself and made a shivery face. Her friend regarded me as she might any taxi driver.

The car warmed quickly. The friend huffed and sighed while Caroline and I made small talk. She asked me how much I'd paid for the car. I told her I'd got a good deal. I asked her what it was like working for Geoff. She said it was great. Our eyes locked in the rearview mirror, and I read her expression for the smallest hint of sarcasm. There was none. Everyone, it seemed, really did love Geoff.

After driving for a few minutes, I noticed Caroline's friend was silent. I angled the rearview mirror so I could see her. She was taking deep breaths, opening and closing her eyes. I asked her if she was going to be sick, if she would like me to stop.

"She's fine," Caroline said.

"She doesn't look fine," I answered.

In the dim light of the car's interior, it was hard to tell. But she looked paler than before, a little yellow about the cheeks. She retched and put her hand to her mouth. I braked harder than I meant to and both of them were thrown forward against the back of the front seats.

"Jesus!" Caroline said. "Calm down!"

I apologised and checked they were okay.

Her friend sat back, straightening her dress over her thighs and taking mouthfuls of air. Then she vomited into her lap and over the back of the passenger seat.

"Christ," I shouted, and I told her to get out.

Caroline kicked the back of my seat and yelled at me again to calm down.

"She's sick," she said.

A gin-tinged, bilious smell filled the car.

"I can see that," I replied. "Get her out before she does it again."

Caroline opened her door and struggled out. I watched in the rearview as she pulled her friend across the back seat.

"Don't fuckin' help or anything, will you," she spat.

They staggered over some grass onto the pavement. Caroline's friend threw up again, hunched against a tall fence like a nocturnal animal cowering from the streetlight. Caroline rubbed her back and mumbled soft, soothing words I couldn't quite hear.

I stood with the driver's door open and leant on the roof. Guilt began to replace my anger. I asked if they still wanted me to take them the rest of the way.

"I think we'll walk, thanks," Caroline said without turning around.

I told her we could drop her friend off first. She didn't respond, but I thought I saw her shake her head.

I stayed there for a while, feeling stupid, wondering what to do. Caroline kept comforting her friend, ignoring me. I began to shiver a little with the cold. I slipped back into the driver's seat and sat for a few seconds, the whole evening flashing behind my eyes in hateful snippets. Margret slamming the car door. Her scowl as I kissed Angie's cheek. The smirking stone cherub in the back garden. Caroline's damp stockinged feet in my lap. Geoff's assurance that next year would be *our year*. Angie watching me from the kitchen door. Caroline's friend throwing up in the back seat. I tried to work out where I'd gone wrong, but the whole night seemed like a cruel joke at my expense.

I leant over to look out of the passenger window. Caroline had helped her friend up, and they were wobbling along in their heels. I hit the button to drop the window.

"Are you sure you don't want a lift?" I said.

I couldn't stand the thought of them talking about me the next day, *That old pervert with the Jag. Mervyn, Melvyn, whatever his name was*. Neither of them responded.

When I told them to get home safe, Caroline turned and silently mouthed the words, *Fuck off*. I sat there and watched them through the front windscreen, their arms around each other's shoulders, like injured soldiers hobbling to a field hospital.

When they'd disappeared into the fog, I swung the car in a wide arc and drove back to the Lyttleton roundabout, cursing myself, Margret, Caroline, her friend and the whole blasted night.

I took the exit for Lyttleton Village Centre. The automatic transmission sensed the steepness of the hill and dropped a gear. I squeezed the accelerator down and felt the leather seat grip my back. The car eased up the hill, picking up speed. The chassis gave a quick rise off its wheels at the crest before settling firm, squat and smooth onto the dark straight road ahead. I was still angry and confused but the loping speed of the car lifted my mood. I raced between dark hedgerows and shadows of farm buildings and giant greenhouses, my shame and anger disappearing, leaving only my enjoyment of the Jaguar's quiet speed.

The ancient Lyttleton Church loomed off to my left. I strained to make out its small spire set back from the road, ghostly in the fog. The car then bumped and hopped as the front left wheel caught the kerb, and I yanked the steering wheel back to the right as the tyres squealed and the car fish-tailed then straightened. I blew out a long sigh of relief and checked the rearview mirror and saw the church retreating into the fog like a phantom.

Then her face, then his face. That's how I saw them. Quick succession. Hers first. White in the headlights. Then his. Above hers. Bleached and shocked in the sudden glare, hands rising to protect their eyes.

They tumbled and banged over the long bonnet. Him up the middle, her just off to the right. Two or three quick bumps, fractured scream, loud crack, then gone. I stamped on the brake pedal, and the tyres squealed, long and agonising like a pig in an abattoir.

Then the car was still, idling by the kerb, as if waiting to pick up a friend. I squinted into the rearview mirror. Nothing at first. Just black road and wisps of drifting fog. But then, some distance back, their shapes. Two dark patches on the tarmac. Like clothes blown from a washing line. One in the gutter, draped over the kerb, one close to the white lines in the middle of the road. Both not moving. Both still as stones.

I forced myself as far back into the seat as I could and tried to think. My mind was blank. A sigh came out as a whimper. I smelt whisky on my breath. I checked the rearview mirror again. No change. No hint of movement. If the car had not still been running, I might have got out and gone back to check on them. But the engine was vibrating almost imperceptibly beneath the steady tick of the clock in the walnut dashboard, the bonnet still pointing the way home. I lifted my foot off the brake and accelerated away, checking the mirrors until the dark shapes of their bodies had gone, and all I could see was the road again, and the streetlamp coronas in the fog.

*

I turned the car too quickly onto our driveway and had to stop with a short skid that sounded like it might wake the whole village. I got out and went to the garage door, checking both ways up and down the lane for lights coming on or silhouettes in bedroom windows. Nothing but freezing fog and weak glows from streetlamps and Christmas lights. I turned the handle and lifted the garage door slowly, easing it through the metallic groan and rusty squeal it made if pulled too fast. Then I got back into the car and drove into the garage and turned off the ignition and lights. As the car ticked and cooled, I sat and concentrated on the darkness. I knew I had to act, but I needed a few moments of stillness and quiet.

White expressionless faces in full-beam headlights.

I got out of the car and went to the light switch by the door into the house. I flicked on the light, then stood for a while, staring at the car. The first thing that drew my attention was the jaguar. Not the car itself but the leaping chrome cat on the bonnet. It was bent and bloody with a flap of blue material wedged beneath it.

Again, their faces, his above hers. No detail or identity. Just faces and tumbling, bumping bodies.

Examining more closely, I saw that the blue flap of material was denim with a yellow seam. The blood on the chrome jaguar was still wet. I had the urge to touch it, taste it even, make sure it was real. But I didn't. I just stared and waited for my mind to catch up.

There was a large scar in the paintwork on the bonnet, more blood and some dents in the otherwise smooth metallic finish. The windscreen was almost intact, but there was a crack and some blood mess at the very top in the middle. I remembered the sound as their tumbling bodies disappeared over the car, the loud cracking sound as something clipped the top. I moved around to the side of the car and leant over to inspect it. My stomach leapt and rolled and I crumpled as if punched in the gut. I stayed there on my haunches until the nausea passed. I have no idea how long. Two minutes? Ten minutes? Crouched by the front wheel. I really don't know. Eventually, I steadied myself and stood up. I took an old greasy cloth and screwdriver from the workbench and went back to the windscreen. I wedged the flat head of the screwdriver behind a small piece of flesh caught where the cracked glass met the chrome rim at the roof. I managed to work it free, then held it closed in the cloth before I dared look. An earlobe, torn off, small gold stud still attached. I folded the cloth gently around it, as if swaddling a tiny, bloody and bejewelled newborn, and placed it on the workbench.

I needed to sit down, so I got back into the car. When my breathing was even again, I made a list with a notepad and pencil I kept in the glove compartment. It went like this:

clean car (quickly)

drive to G+A's

wake Margret

home and sleep

assess damage in morning

I found the list later and burnt it, shocked I'd needed one to order these few simple actions. But remarkably, at that moment, it helped.

I half-filled a bucket at the kitchen sink and squirted in some washing-up liquid. I looked at the clock but the time meant nothing to me. I could not work out a time frame for events. It must have been less than one hour since I'd left the party but it seemed like several hours had passed, the party itself an event from another lifetime.

I sponged the front of the car. The blood washed easily away. The mess at the top of the windscreen was thicker but was gone after a few hard scrubs. I opened the garage door, reversed the car out and went back inside to lock the kitchen door. I looked around the garage. Just the bucket and sponge and the cloth and screwdriver on the workbench. I took the bucket into the garden and emptied it into one of the flower-beds. Then I wiped the head of the screwdriver and slipped it into a drawer with some other tools. I put the cloth and sponge into the boot of the car and shut it as quietly as I could, looking both ways to see if anyone might be watching. Nothing but frost-white gardens beneath a layer of street-lit fog, the faintest sounds of music and laughter coming from down the lane near the corner. A Christmas party, I guessed, much like the one I'd left earlier.

I remembered Caroline's friend being sick, so I went back inside the house and filled the bucket again with hot soapy water. The reek caught in my nostrils as I opened the back door of the car. Most of the mess had gone onto the mat behind the front passenger seat, so I took it out, scrubbed it and threw it into the boot. But there was some on the carpet and on the seat itself. I rubbed at it a few times with the wet cloth, then emptied the bucket into the flower-bed again. I leant into the car and sniffed an unsavoury tang beneath the familiar dark green smell of Fairy Liquid. I decided to air the interior by driving back to Geoff and Angie's house with the windows down.

A siren sounded in the distance as I reversed down the driveway and into the road. I stopped and listened, trying to locate it on my mental map of the village. I couldn't be sure, but it sounded like it was coming from the direction of the Old Church Road. *A siren might mean they're alive*, I thought. Maybe one of them. Maybe both. It crossed my mind that it would be better for me, maybe even for them, if they were both dead. I buried the thought and smothered its accompanying shame. Then I drove and focused on the white lines and Catseyes on the road, my sole purpose to reach the party again and act like nothing out of the ordinary had happened.

When I arrived back at Geoff and Angie's, I searched the street for a dark spot where I might leave the car. Fronting the house next door was an old brick garden wall, bowed by a large leaning fir tree, forming a thicker darkness on the street. I eased the Jag beneath the branches, partially mounting the pavement to reach the darkest shadows. As a rule, I would never usually have parked beneath a tree for fear of paintwork damage from sap or bird droppings. But the deep gloom made the scars and dents on the bonnet and roof almost invisible to the ignorant passer-by.

Geoff and Angie's house was quieter than earlier. Fewer cars in the driveway, fainter music and voices from within. I'd always loved their house. I remember when they bought it. Geoff had told me it had been built in the twenties to an Italian modernist design. He was always saying things like that. "Look at this watch," he'd say. "It's an exact replica of the one Mario Andretti wears when he's racing." Somehow with Geoff it didn't come across as showing off, rather a genuine desire to show you something he was proud of buying and owning. The house was his pride and joy. It completed him and Angie. It was handsome and hip, masculine and feminine all at once. The large windows on three sides let light in and out, so at night the garden was draped in a warm yellowy glow that mirrored the rich contentedness of the lives inside. In the ten years Geoff and Angie had owned the house, they'd perfected it without changing its essential character. Paint, lights, interior fittings, furniture, and garden features had all been renewed or refurbished. But gradually, as if rushing would have been an offence to the design. As I stood in front of their home that night, shivering in the well-kept garden, I almost wept. If only the house were mine, I thought, none of this would be happening. I would be the one inside, entertaining my guests while my beautiful wife floated about the place, pleasing everyone with the sophisticated elegance of her presence.

I decided to go around to the back of the house to see if I could slip in unnoticed. I quietly opened the back door and stepped into the dark utility area next to the kitchen. The cold smell of damp coats was somehow reassuring. It reminded me of my own house. I could hear the remnants of the party now, just a few drunken-sounding voices and laughter, some much older music, jazz or blues or something. Geoff was working his way through his collection, no doubt, proudly showing off rarities he'd bought at record fairs and second-hand shops. He loved a small, devoted audience, and more often than not, his audience loved him. I tried the door to the kitchen and let it swing open. Light filled the small space I stood in. I froze for a moment, exposed, peering into the kitchen, steadying myself, working on the idea of looking and acting normal. But when I stepped inside, I was surprised by a voice.

"So, the late-night wanderer returns."

Angie was standing at the sink, rinsing glasses and looking at me in the reflection of the dark window. She spun around with pink rubber gloves on and caught me noticing them.

"I'm funny about my hands," she said, tired and a little slurry. "Part of the reason I gave up hairdressing. All that water and shampoo. Bloody terrible for the hands." She looked at me, expecting an answer. I had nothing to say, so she continued. "You should see some of the girls who work for Geoff. Seventeen. Hands like old hags. Poor things."

She shook her head and turned back to the sink.

I remained silent.

White faces blinded in headlights. Vomit in the back of the car. Caroline's face, drunk and hateful, mouthing obscenities.

Angie turned and faced me again.

"Girls," she said, laughing to herself. "They haven't got a clue."

She looked at me again in the dark reflection of the window, where I hovered behind her, an ethereal ghost in the light of the kitchen.

"You should stay away from girls, Melvyn. They're nothing but trouble. I should know. I used to be one."

She raised her eyebrows and turned her attention back to the sink. I stared at the back of her head, her thick curls and highlights, wondering if her comment had been loaded.

"Good advice," I said. "Mind if I make myself a drink?"

"Our house, your house, Melvyn," she said, smiling over her shoulder.

I told her I'd stopped off at home for a bottle of whisky but couldn't find one. She hadn't asked but I felt the need to explain where I'd been.

She peeled off her gloves and tossed them into the sink where they lay like two beached jellyfish, pink, limp and flaccid.

Bodies in the rearview mirror, low dark shapes on the road like puddles in the clearing fog.

"Come on," Angie said, offering the crook of her elbow to escort me into the lounge. Even now it's a moment difficult to let go of, a gesture of friendship, the last true one I can remember.

LISA

I woke up when I heard the car. It was still dark. The clock by my bed had those luminous hands. Like two little pale green ghosts. Quarter to five, they said. No one comes down the close at that time. Not even the milkman or postman. And anyway, it was a Sunday. Neither of them delivers on Sundays.

I knew something was wrong. I just lay there, listening to the car coming closer, willing it to stop outside someone else's house but somehow knowing it wouldn't. I could see my breath. I didn't keep the heating on at night. Too expensive. I heard the car stop and the door open. Then voices. A woman's and a man's. I couldn't hear what they were saying. They weren't whispering but their voices were quiet, respectful of the hour.

I got out of bed and went to the window and peeked out between the curtains. The police car was parked right in front of our house. *Shaun,* I thought. What else would it be? I hoped it might be something else or just a mistake. But I knew it was Shaun. He hadn't come home. And sometimes you just know. Even through your own denial, you know. The alarm bells go off stronger and shriller.

I grabbed my dressing gown off the chair and went downstairs and switched the hall light on. I could see PC Dreek through the glass in the front door. I knew it was him. He was so big. Impossible to mistake for someone else. We knew each other from back when Shaun was just a baby and Neil was away. Dreek would call round after his shift, bring biscuits and tea and sometimes a little toy. But we'd not seen each other much since then. I think the gossip had frightened him off. That and Neil being back home.

He must have seen the light come on. He didn't ring the bell or knock the door, which I was grateful for. Either of those sounds may have undone me. I stopped for a few seconds before opening the door. I tied my dressing gown tight and smoothed my hair down, as if these things would help hold me together.

Dreek and some policewoman. Pam, I think her name was. Can't remember. They came in, and I made them a cup of tea. Dreek sat down, big as ever, filling up the kitchen with his size and his uniform. Pam tried to help me with the tea. I told her to sit down, which she did after a nod from Dreek. It was habit. A leftover from Mum and Dad's time. Whoever came round got a cup of tea. Neighbour, relative, even the police telling you your son was dead.

Dreek waited until I was sat down, then told me. "Hit-and-run," he said. Shaun and Paula. Both at once. He took hold of my hands. I stared at the condensation on the window. A porthole below sea level, like I was drowning in my own kitchen.

Dreek told me I should call Neil. But it was so early, still dark outside.

"He needs to know, Lisa," he said in that gravelly Scottish voice of his. "If yae leave it too long, he could find out from someone else. Yae know what this place is like."

"Lyttleton by name," Pam started, but Dreek gave her a look and she didn't finish.

He told me he had to get back to the site of the accident. Speak to people. See if they'd seen or heard anything. He told me Pam would stay until I had company. Neil or a neighbour, he said. I told him I'd rather be on my own. No offence to Pam, whatever her name was. I didn't want a stranger lurking about the place. I needed some time to get myself together, run a bath, put some clothes on, have a meltdown. Then I'd call Neil. Dreek wasn't happy. Not what he'd planned. He looked at me closely, scrutinising me, I think, trying to work out if I was safe alone or a danger to myself.

When they were leaving, Pam went on ahead to the car. Dreek stopped in the little porch and turned to face me, his back stooped and his head bent forward to fit beneath the top of the doorway. He told me again to call Neil as soon as possible.

"He needs to hear it from you, Lisa," he said.

He gave a little shake of his big head and sighed. Then he said he'd be back later in the morning to check on me and update me with any developments. He told me he was sorry for what had happened. His eyes looked pinched and pained as if fighting off tears. His skin pale and grey from a night of little or no sleep. I think he wanted to embrace me. But I was in the hallway and he was already outside in the porch, too far away and too big in his police coat and hat to get back through the door without it being awkward and uncomfortable. So he nodded, tight-lipped, and left. I watched him go down the little path and squeeze into the driver's seat of the police car. Too small for him, as everything always seemed to be.

After they'd gone, I busied myself with things I would usually do on a Sunday morning. More tea, washing up, folding clothes, putting them away, and making my bed. When the house was tidy, I ran a bath, thinking that being clean would help. Instead, when I got into the hot water, I just lay there in a kind of limbo, the reality of the situation present but just out of reach. I lowered my head into the water and held my breath, watching the wobbly light above the surface. I wondered if I could just stay there and drown with little pain or fuss. The temptation was so fierce it sat me up with a gasp.

When I was out of the bath and dressed, I called Neil and told him the news. Then I made another pot of tea and sat and waited for him to arrive. Outside the kitchen window, another frozen day began, just like the one before.

KEVIN

My Sunday paper round finished near Colemans', where Apple Tree Lane met the Old Church Road. Sometimes, if it wasn't raining, I would buy ten JPS or Consulate and find somewhere quiet to smoke before heading home for breakfast. There were trees in the park and in the woods behind Lyttleton Hall that were perfect, easy to climb, with comfortable places to sit, though not so good in winter when the leaves had gone and the exposed branches were cold and slippery. As I got to Colemans' that morning, just before daylight, blue police lights flashed in the fog.

Inside the shop, I grabbed a Mars Bar and a can of Lilt and put them on the counter. Old Mr Coleman came out of the back, cardigan, shirt and tie, immaculate as always. I eyed the cigarette display but he shook his head and cut me off before I even asked.

"Better not," he said. "No wi' auld Dreeky aboot."

He seemed pleased with his Scottish accent, even though it sounded nothing like Dreek. I told him the fags were for my mum, which usually worked fine. Colemans' was renowned among the underage smokers of Lyttleton as the best place to buy cigarettes and the best shop to nick from when you were skint. I wasn't much of a shoplifter myself. My greatest success had been a Cornetto stuffed down the back of my shorts the previous summer. But

I knew kids who'd walked out of there with a week's supply of Chewits or Hubba Bubba in one hit. Some even claimed to have got behind the counter to steal cigarettes while old Coleman was out the back, but that was probably just bollocks.

Outside the shop, I sat on the green transformer box on the forecourt and watched the goings-on from there, eating my chocolate, sipping from my can, and belching tropical, pineapply burps. The police had closed the road by parking two cars crossways, sectioning off a fifty-yard stretch. A man was taking pictures of the ground. On the other side of the road, PC Dreek was talking to a small group of residents, gathered around him in their dressing gowns, coats, hats and scarves. Mrs Ryle waved at me. I went to school with her son, Christopher. Dreek turned and noticed me. He frowned and began to cross the road. My bladder tightened and complained as it often did when I was nervous. The damp freezing metal beneath me wasn't helping.

Dreek was huge, six and a half feet, I reckon, nearly seven in his hat. A giant lumbering through the fog. All the kids in Lyttleton were terrified of him. Even some of the bigger kids who already had motorbikes and scooters, none of them gave Dreek any lip. They'd call him all sorts behind his back, *big jock twat, Scotch cunt, McFuzz,* giving it the big I am. But to his face, no chance. I wanted to leave and avoid him speaking to me, but I didn't want to appear rude or guilty in some way. He made me feel like a midget. I was small for my age. Fourteen and five foot one. I had not developed yet. That's what everyone at school called it. *Developed.* The boys who *had* developed had fluffy moustaches, bad skin and hairy legs. They were proud of their newly enlarged genitals. In PE, before and after football or rugby or athletics, they would parade around the changing rooms with their hairy cocks and balls on show, whipping smaller boys' arses with wet towels, making fun of their pristine, *un*developed bodies.

Dreek stood in front of me, took his big hands out of his coat pockets and blew steamy breath into them and rubbed them. He looked pale, tired and very serious. He tried to smile. Then in his thick Scottish accent, he said, "Yae didnae ought tae be sat in the cold like that, son. Yae'll end up in yer bed for Christmas."

"Yes, Mr Dreek," I said. "I'm just going home."

Then I asked him what had happened.

He made a grimacing kind of toothache face and sucked cold air through his lips and moved his tongue around the front of his mouth.

"Ach, Christ," he said. "You'll find oot soon enough, son." He shook his big head and sighed a great cloud of warm coffee-smelling breath into the cold air. "I take it yae werenae here aboot three thirty this morning."

"No, Mr Dreek," I said. "I was in bed."

"Aye," he said. "Good job, too."

Dreek was usually stern and hard. His steely stare made you feel guilty whether you'd done anything or not. On this morning, however, he was gentle and sad, and he hardly made eye contact at all. I wanted to stay longer and have him call me *son* again, but the cold fizzy drink and the cold metal I was sat on had caused my bladder to ache with an urgent need to urinate. I hopped off the box and fetched my bike from where it was leant against the shop window.

"Yae should have lights for this fog, son," he said.

I apologised and told him I'd left them in the shed.

"Aye," he scoffed, "course yae did."

Then he sighed again and headed back across the road to the gaggle of neighbours, who stood rubbing their hands against the cold and shaking their heads about whatever it was that had happened.

I rode back through the fog towards home, desperate for the toilet. My bladder throbbed and I thought about stopping and going behind a hedge somewhere. But it was all neat gardens and kitchen lights coming on, people waking up and making their Sunday morning teas and coffees to take back to bed. I knew paperboys who'd been fired for taking a sneaky slash in a posh garden, so I just pedalled faster for home.

Mum was still in bed when I got back, so I legged it straight into the downstairs loo and pissed for England. Upstairs in my room, the bed was stripped. I'd awoken in the early hours, mid-piss, thinking I was dreaming. This was a common sensation for me, an almost pleasurable warmth before the wet jolt of realisation and shame. I'd stuffed my sheet in the washing machine and manoeuvred my mattress in front of the window. It wasn't dry but it had aired and didn't smell too bad. I rubbed talc into the damp area, just to make sure. Then I put the mattress back on the bed with the damp side facing down towards the carpet.

Dad's leaving had apparently aggravated my nocturnal enuresis. I'd taken to calling it by its medical name after hearing a doctor explain it to Mum. The phrase *wetting the bed* made me feel childish and ashamed. Enuresis, on the other hand, sounded like a proper disease, like I was sick and it wasn't my fault. It had been cured the previous summer with the help of an alarm, a brass-coloured metal box attached to a rubber undersheet that registered the slightest drop of liquid with a single loud robotic tone. Mum said it worked on a similar principle to Pavlov's dogs, creating a mental link between a full bladder, the alarm, and the need to wake up. I hated the thing. It had been the final resort of several years of visits to doctors and hospitals, having my penis and testicles inspected, charts with gold stars for dry, green for wet and blue for very wet nights, my liver and kidneys tested, my blood taken, and dye injected into me so that my pulsing guts were visible on a TV monitor while I was wedged between two giant radioactive cameras. The final diagnosis was that I was a very deep sleeper with a short urethra. Nocturnal enuresis was therefore inevitable but curable with time, persistence and the machine. Tea, coffee and fizzy drinks should be avoided, especially after six o'clock in the evening. Diurnal incontinence, or the sudden desperate need to piss, might accompany nervous or stressful episodes but could be controlled with muscle contractions. I had become an expert at these, often wincing away the last twenty minutes of classes, crossing and uncrossing my legs and playing an imaginary upside-down piano on the bottom of the desk before racing out the door at the bell, haring into the boys' toilets and sighing with immense relief as the tension and fear of embarrassment drained from my body with every fluid ounce of urine that ran down the porcelain and bubbled in the trough. Some of the happiest moments of my school life had been spent alone in the toilets, breathing in the mixed scent of urine and urinal cubes through the tingle of relief, pondering that strange name, *Armitage Shanks*, stamped in ceramic blue.

The curing of my affliction had been a personal triumph for Mum's dogged persistence. It had been her nemesis for years. Its return had caused her great consternation, convinced as she was that hers and Dad's separation was to blame. The wet nights this time round, however, were only sporadic, and there had not yet been the need to pull the alarm out of its box in the attic. Some nights before falling asleep I imagined it there, stuffed away in the spidery dark with the Subbuteo, Scalextric and Christmas decorations, waiting for the permanent return of my problem. The machine had been my cure and it should have been my friend. Yet I saw it as my enemy, with its industrial lie-detector-cum-shock-therapy design and blood-brown, copper-wired, hospital-rubber undersheet that pricked and scratched my back in the night. More like an instrument of torture than the key to the freedom of school trips and sleep-overs.

When Dad arrived to take me to his football match, Mum was still in her room getting dressed. He rang the front doorbell, as he had taken to doing, like the pools man or milkman when the bill was due. He was shifting and shivering on the step and rubbing his hands against the cold when I opened the door. I asked him why he didn't just come around the back and let himself in, but he ignored the question and followed me inside, telling me to hurry or I'd let all the heat out. The cost of the central heating was an obsession, especially since he'd moved out and the money he spent on it wasn't even keeping him warm.

"Yer mum up?" he whispered.

"Yeah," I said. "She'll be down in a minute."

"I need to speak to her," he said. "Something's happened."

"What?" I said.

"I'll wait till Daph's up," he said.

Dad only called Mum Daphne when they argued. Otherwise it was Daph or darlin' or yer mum to me.

I asked him if it was about the Old Church Road.

"How d'you know about it?" he said.

"I don't," I said, but I told him about Dreek, the police cars and the man taking pictures of the road.

Dad looked uncomfortable and scratched behind his ear.

"Dreek didn't tell you what happened then?"

"What's happened?" Mum said.

She was halfway down the stairs in jeans and the thick purple jumper Dad had bought for her for Christmas the year before. *A good sign*, I thought. She looked clean and fresh. Her skin was peachy at the cheeks and her hair was all big and blow-dried. I noticed Dad appreciating her.

"Daph." He sighed and met her at the bottom of the stairs and held her while she looked worriedly over his shoulder at me.

"What's wrong?" she said. "Brian, what is it?"

He let her go and stood back and sighed again. Mum asked him again what was wrong and he told us. Shaun Terridge and his girlfriend were dead, killed on the Old Church Road. Hit-and-run.

Mum's eyes went all big and shocked-looking. She opened her mouth as if to say something, then put her hand over it instead. Dad looked at both of us and kept shaking his head.

Shaun was a bit of a local star. He'd played for Dad's team on Sundays, even though he was only seventeen. He was considered by many the best young player in Lyttleton and was already in the first team for Hareham Town in the Saturday league, and they were semi-professional.

"I knew it was something really bad," I said, but Dad's hard stare stopped me from continuing.

Mum turned away and cried silently with her hand over her eyes; her shoulders jerking was a giveaway. She gave a big sniff and moaned, "Oh God."

Dad made a face at me and raised his eyes towards the ceiling, so I slipped between him and Mum and went back upstairs to my room. Their low voices murmured wordlessly up the stairwell, Mum's tearful and sad, Dad's deeper and soothing.

I sat on my bed and tried to think about Shaun Terridge. I'd never seen his girlfriend. I could only picture him in his football kit, the way I'd seen him at the Rec. He was tall and his hair was crew cut. He had a big grin, freckles and a gold stud earring. I tried to imagine him cold and white, like a vampire, black around the eyes and staring, zombified. I wondered if I should cry. I didn't feel like crying. I felt excited, like something important had happened, and I'd been a witness. Well, almost. The timing seemed unfair though, the first weekend of the Christmas holidays. By the time school started again, there'd be nothing to tell that wasn't already known. I wanted to call my mates and tell them about my early morning conversation with Dreek, but Mum and Dad were talking in the hallway, right next to the little telephone table by the front door. And anyway, the bill was itemised and I was limited to one call a day.

Dad shouted up the stairs.

"Five minutes, mate."

"Okay!" I shouted back.

I finished making my bed and put my coat back on. I was happy to be going to football with Dad, away from the awkward discomfort of Mum's tears. I'd seen her cry before, once when she'd found our old tabby cat Milly dead under the front hedge, and once after an argument with Dad. Both times I'd felt useless and helpless in equal measure, selfishly desperate to be somewhere else. I was excited also by the prospect of further talk with Dad about the news. He was something of an expert on road accidents. He'd been a fireman before switching to lorry driving. He would have stayed on but for the *crap wages before the big strike*, as he often grumbled. I hoped I'd have the chance to fully recount my meeting with Dreek.

I didn't see Mum before we left. Dad said she and Shaun's mum, Lisa, had known each other a long time, and Mum needed a while for the news to sink in. We drove the short distance to Lyttleton Rec, and he explained what he knew. Both Shaun and his girlfriend Paula had been killed almost instantly. The driver had stopped, apparently, and then driven away. I wondered how long *almost instantly* meant.

"What a fuckin' bastard!" Dad said, and he banged the butt of his hand against the steering wheel. The horn gave a quick and angry blare and Dad apologised.

I was shocked. I'd hardly heard him swear before. My friends and I were swearing like soldiers at the time. Everything was *fuck this, fuck that, fuckin' twat, fuck me and fuck you.* It was just habit, and no doubt we thought it made us seem grown-up, like smoking and spitting through the gaps in our front teeth. But for some reason it still stunned me when my parents swore. Mum never swore, apart from the occasional time she lost her temper. She had dropped a whole saucepan of cooked spaghetti on the floor once, just as she was about to serve it onto warmed plates. It sat there on the green tile-patterned kitchen lino in a big, wormy, steaming pile. Dad and I were sitting at the table waiting for tea. It must have been a Friday because Friday was spaghetti night. Mum got down on her knees to clean up the mess but instead she started beating the floor with the empty pan, shouting, *fucking stupid fucking spaghetti fucking bolognese every fucking stupid fucking Friday fucking night!* I had been very impressed with the swearing but troubled by the possibility that Mum didn't want to cook spaghetti bolognese on Fridays for me and Dad anymore. Then later, when Mum and Dad had their problems, I worried that perhaps she never really had.

We reached the car park at Lyttleton Rec. A small group of men stood smoking and talking by one of the cars. A couple of them waved and nodded as they noticed Dad pulling up.

"Just wait here a second, Kev," he said.

He got out of the car and walked over to the group. Several of them were hunched and rubbing their hands against the cold. They looked more like tramps around an oil drum fire than half a football team.

I watched Dad. He nodded, shook hands and patted several of the men on their shoulders. The smiles and reactions were muted, and they shook their heads in disbelief and appreciation of the terrible news. Dave Knight put his arm around Dad's shoulder and walked him away a little. The other men paid no attention and continued to talk and smoke. Dave noticed me and waved. He was talking to Dad, and Dad was nodding and shaking his head. I watched them through the windscreen as I stole two cigarettes from a box of Number 6 in the glove compartment.

Dad opened the car door and stuck his head inside.

"Yep," he said. "The game's on. Minute's silence for Shaun before kick-off." He shook his head and sighed. "I need to tell the ref and sort it with the Barmush lads."

Everyone observed the silence. Dog walkers stopped and shushed their dogs. Mums and dads briefly ignored their kids and watched the group of cold men shivering in the centre of the frosty pitch, breathing into their hands, jigging in their shorts from one foot to the other to keep warm. Only the crows and rooks ignored the ritual, but their incessant plaintive cawing from the foggy treetops sounded fittingly mournful, like the wordless croaky dirge of a hundred voices.

I watched one of them take off and fly diagonally over the football pitch before landing on the fence of the telephone exchange with an angry squawk. Close by, at a railing in front of a gap in the old park wall, a man was standing, watching the silent footballers on the pitch. He leant forward and spewed onto the grass before wiping his face and disappearing through the gap in the wall, as if I'd imagined him and he'd never been there. But he had. Because the crow flapped the short distance from the fence to the patch of steaming grass by the railing and strutted around like a camp commandant, inspecting the ground and looking in all directions for a competitor, stabbing at the puke with lightning jabs of its big black beak.

MELVYN

I woke up on Geoff and Angie's couch. Everything looked soft and warm, whisky glazed. I must have still been drunk. I turned and someone else groaned. Another person on the couch. A head was nestled between my backside and a plump purple cushion. I sat up and flexed my feet on the soft Persian rug. Then I stood and my brain seemed to empty of blood, leaving nothing but a headache like cracked glass. *Two white faces rolled and bumped in the foggy darkness.* I put my hand to my mouth to stifle a short wail. The other person on the couch moaned and shifted. I could see now it was Janet, Geoff's manageress from the Lyttleton salon. I stood for a few seconds watching her, squeezing the bridge of my nose, realisation pumping through me, an ache at my left elbow and a fizzing in my ears. Janet did not wake. I went through to the kitchen, ran the cold tap and took a glass from the drainer. I remembered Angie from the night before, standing where I was standing now. *So, the late-night wanderer returns.* She'd said it playfully, drunk, but would she remember me creeping in the back door? Guilty. I gulped down three glasses of water and stood wiping my mouth with the back of my hand, looking around as if some kitchen appliance or utensil would tell me what to do. Something at the back of my head stabbed and I winced. I drank more water. *Blank white faces stricken in the dark, his above hers, rolling and bumping over the bonnet, up the windscreen, then gone.* Another stab in the back of the head as I stood at the sink with my hand on the tap. Their faces again, and then again, paused, rewound and replayed like VHS or Betamax, but for my eyes only.

In the spare bedroom Margret looked peaceful. Her drunken coma from the night before had eased itself into real sleep, and her expression was benign. Margret was a sleeper. Sleep was her healer. I'd known her to get home at four a.m. and sleep for twelve hours, only to get up for a few hours before going back to bed for another eight. I was the opposite. Something always drove me from my bed too early. Then my tiredness would follow me around all day like a cloud or heavy shadow, pulling at my patience and making me indecisive as I faded in the afternoons.

"Margret," I whispered. "Margret." She opened one eye. "We should go. It's morning. I'll wait for you in the lounge."

Back in the lounge, Janet was stirring. There were noises from upstairs. Someone padding to the bathroom. A few moments later, a toilet flushing. I listened, watching invisible footfalls on the ceiling, willing whoever it was back to bed.

I noticed Janet watching me.

"Morning," I said. "Waiting for Margret."

She croaked, uninterested, and buried her face back into the large, purple, velvet cushion.

I went back to the spare bedroom. Margret was still sleeping.

"Margret," I whispered. "We should go. It's morning."

I peeked through the curtains. It was lighter now but only twenty yards of garden were visible. Then a wall of freezing fog. I was thankful for the weather. Fewer people around to see the car. I willed the fog to stay and shroud everything, including me.

Then their rolling faces again, the hint of a broken scream, the same loud crack as they disappeared over the roof of the car.

"What time is it?" Margret said.

I looked at my watch.

"Eight thirty," I said. "Almost."

"Oh, God," she said, and rolled over with a groan. "So early. It's Sunday. Just get in and cuddle up."

Her foul mood from the night before had evaporated. She was playful, flirty even. She gave me a twinkly smile from her pillow.

"I'd like to leave before they're up."

"Why?" she asked.

Her voice was whiney, like a tired child's.

"I'm hungover," I said. "I want to get home, relax."

I didn't want to see Geoff or Angie, particularly Angie. I could imagine her asking me insinuating questions in front of Margret.

"Come on, darling," I said. "We can relax all day once we're home."

Margret let out a long sigh and rolled the covers back.

"Give me a minute," she said. "Wait for me in the lounge or something."

"I'll be in the kitchen," I said.

"Fine," she said, beginning to get cross, "whatever."

In the kitchen I began to make tea, thinking it might appease Margret. I filled the kettle and raised the roller blind and stared into the garden. The fog and frost made it otherworldly, the shapes of the little statues by the pond just visible, bushes and small trees like hunched Narnian beasts. I plugged in the kettle, then stood listening for sounds from upstairs. Nothing but the electric hum of the fridge and the hiss of heating water.

I tried to think about my situation, put it in some kind of order. But it poured in like floodwater through a breached dam. *Their faces and twisted bodies on the road, screaming faceless parents and relatives, funerals, police, shame, Margret leaving, the business collapsing, my friends, Geoff and Angie, all turning away in disgust, and me, rotting in a cell, with only a life of exile to look forward to on release*. The urgent bubble of the kettle brought me back to the present. Too much to confront all at once. I needed time to unpack and separate all the elements. The kettle clicked off and billowed steam.

"Oh, you're making tea," Margret said from the doorway.

I turned around and looked at her. She had brushed her hair and reapplied some make-up. A huge thump gonged somewhere in my blood. I wanted it to be love but suspected it was guilt. She sat at the kitchen table and looked at me.

"I'll be fine after a cup of tea," she said.

I turned back to making the tea and squeezed my eyes shut and held myself with every muscle to stifle a huge rising sob. It could have been a perfect Sunday. I could have driven Margret home, smooth and quiet in the Jag, perhaps made us some morning drinks, Bloody Marys or gin and tonics, a cold, bracing walk in the park, maybe, an afternoon film on the television, a Chinese takeaway for dinner before bed. But it was dawning on me that this Sunday, and every subsequent Sunday, had been ruined forever, swallowed by the open mouths of those faces as they rolled and bumped and disappeared over the top of the car again and again. All the days of every week to come, for that matter, smashed and broken like the bodies I'd left on the cold road.

What were they doing there at that time of night in the freezing cold? Why couldn't they have been somewhere else? At home. Still at their party. On another road. Stood on the fucking pavement, for Christ's sake.

I could hear Margret breathing behind me. I thought she might be watching me, not knowing I'd ruined our lives the previous night while she slept, unaware I'd slipped out in the drunken hope of a dirty little tryst in our car with a girl half my age, ignorant of the two people I'd smashed to pieces on the road. *The earlobe in the boot of the car, cold and congealed in the soiled rag.* My blood began to burn from the feet up. It fizzed around my ankles. My legs felt like they would char into twigs and snap where I stood. I looked in the cupboard for teabags. I wanted to rip the cupboard door from its hinges and use it to beat myself to death. Then none of this would matter. Instead, I put the teabags in the cups and poured the water. *Maybe tea would help.* The thought was so preposterous I almost laughed.

On the way home Margret said the cold fog made her feel *Christmassy*. She wanted to stop in the village centre and get a newspaper. I told her I wanted to get home. She said it would only take a minute. I told her I'd walk to the shop once we were back. She said that didn't make sense. I said I needed a walk. She looked at me. I could feel her looking as I drove. I glanced at her and attempted to smile.

"What's wrong with you?" she said.

"Nothing," I said.

"Are you sure?"

"Yes," I said. "Just hungover."

"I thought you wanted to lie down," she said.

"I do," I said. "The fresh air'll do me good, though. First, I mean."

"Shall I come with you?" she asked.

"No, it's fine," I said.

"I'll make some breakfast," she said. "We can have a huge breakfast then loll about like teenagers all day."

She smiled and looked at me for a response. Again, I could feel her looking at me, trying to read my thoughts. This time I couldn't bear to look back. I was convinced she would see it in my face, see *their* faces rolling and bumping and screaming behind my eyes, a perfect repeating image of my crime in my expression. I looked at the bonnet and saw the large scratch up the centre. I glanced at Margret to see if she'd noticed. She had leant back against the headrest and was looking out of the passenger window. My hands tightened on the wheel. I craved her oblivion for myself. It was probably my hangover, but I swear I could feel her unawareness, its sweet innocence, its idle, happy thoughts of Christmas and shopping and the lazy day ahead. Another giant sob rose in me like a huge air bubble from a sinking ship. I stuck the soft butt of my thumb in my mouth and bit so hard I could focus on nothing but the pain.

When we arrived home, I got out of the car and opened the garage. There was a dog walker on the other side of the road, but I didn't recognise him or his dog. I got back in the car and eased it into the garage. I sighed, and Margret noticed.

"What's wrong?" she said.

"I told you," I said. "Just a hangover."

"You're usually more fun when you're hungover," she said.

Right then, the urge to tell her was huge. A wall of words ready to roll out and crush her. I wanted to confess and cry at her feet, have her hold my head against her waist and forgive me.

We got out of the car and faced each other over the roof. She had still not noticed the scratches in the paint. I glanced at the bonnet and the bent leaping jaguar, remembering the blood and denim from the night before, the gold-studded earlobe wedged in the cracked rim of the windscreen. *The twisted white faces rolled again and bumped and disappeared.*

"Are you sure you're okay?" she said.

"Yes," I said. "Just queasy. A walk'll do me good."

I made as if to walk out of the garage.

"Can you wait, darling?" she said. "I'll see if we need anything."

That word, *darling*, a hot needle in the ulcer of my guilt. Every second, the betrayal grew while the likelihood of telling her shrank.

She disappeared inside the house but left the door open. I could hear her in the kitchen, opening cupboards and looking in the fridge. I began to flex my fingers and toes while I waited. I looked at the tools on the workbench. An axe hung between two nails in the breeze block wall. I pictured myself hacking up the car in a frenzy, destroying the evidence and giving myself away at the same time. Margret appeared at the door.

"Just more milk," she said. "Lots of tea today, I think."

"Right," I said. "Another paper?"

"Yes," she said, smiling. "Christmas telly." She rubbed her hands together in pleased anticipation. "I'm going to change. I'll make us some breakfast when you're back."

She disappeared again inside the house, humming something jolly as she went. I leant on the workbench and listened to the ticks and creaks of the car cooling, the soft thuds of Margret's feet on the stairs.

I could have killed myself before Margret finished changing. Her bare feet on the soft carpet of our bedroom as I opened my wrist with a Stanley knife or sat in the car with the engine running and a hosepipe through the window. These thoughts were vivid and tempting. I switched on the light and inspected the bonnet and radiator. There was still some blood in the grill. I chided myself for having missed it the night before. I wiped at the stain with a rag and stuffed it in my jacket pocket. I bent close to the scratches and dents on the bonnet, checking for more blood. There was none. I checked the top of the windshield. Nothing. I ran my hands over the cold roof and looked at them. Just wet dirt from the melted ice. I walked around the car twice, inspecting the paintwork, the wheels and the garage floor. Nothing. I opened the boot of the car and took out the rag with the earlobe inside and put it with the other rag in my coat pocket. Then I walked out of the garage and pulled the door down. I looked both ways. Fifty yards of visibility, then fog. Everything hidden. Again, I willed it to stay that way.

The newsagent's was a walk of maybe a quarter mile around the loop of Cornerfield Lane, past the corner of the park, the telephone exchange, the doctor's surgery and the Brownies' and Girl Guides' hut. If the weather had been less severe, I could have expected to meet one or two neighbours on the way. But there was nobody out in the freezing fog.

When I arrived at the shop, the interior was stifling from a hot air blower on the floor. The brick-coloured linoleum was wet, gritty and slimy from the feet of paperboys and customers who'd been walking in the slush of local roads and pavements. I picked up a fat Sunday paper and a *Radio Times* from a large pile and took a carton of milk from the glass fridge.

A woman at the counter was talking to Barbara, the co-owner of the shop. I smiled at the woman but she didn't smile back.

"Morning, Barbara," I said.

"Morning, Mr Pettifer," she said.

I'd asked her to call me Melvyn many times. She never had, so I'd given up.

"Just these, thanks," I said. "And forty Dunhill."

Barbara turned and took my cigarettes from the display unit behind the counter.

Warm air blew around the shop, and it was hard to breathe.

The old woman at the counter sighed and shook her head. I looked at her. Barbara also looked at her and said, "I know. It's just too awful for words."

The woman forced her lips together and nodded. She had on a purple headscarf and a thick cream woollen coat.

"I suppose you've not heard," said Barbara.

"No," I said, steeling myself for what was coming. "What?"

"The accident," the woman said. She was looking up at me, shaking her head, her face round and squashed by the scarf. "It's just terrible," she said. "Those poor families."

My throat began to feel like it was closing. The warm air from the blower was in my nostrils. I became aware of the bulge in my jacket pocket, the earlobe in the rag, fibres stuck and crusted with dried blood.

The woman at the counter dabbed at the corners of her eyes with an old Paisley handkerchief. Barbara leant over and placed a hand on her shoulder and squeezed. My legs were cold below the knees, the small hairs there rising on goose bumps and touching the inside of my trousers. I could feel sweat forming on the backs of my knees. I gave Barbara a damp and crumpled five-pound note. She looked at me and shook her head, then opened the till.

"The Old Church Road," she said. "Young Shaun Terridge and his girlfriend. Both of them, dear God!"

Their faces rolled and bumped again in the darkness. Only this time I recognised them. My throat growled, but I kept my teeth clenched.

"Hit-and-run," Barbara continued. "Some people." She shook her head again and gave me my change. "Probably drunk, this time of year."

The old woman at the counter nodded and tutted like some disapproving toy or ornament on a shelf.

I could see his face. Shaun Terridge's. Handsome. His girlfriend. Much smaller. Very pretty, like Cheryl Ladd from *Charlie's Angels*. I'd seen them just a month or so before, arm in arm somewhere. Greetings gift shop on the Parade. That was it. I had been looking at boxes of Christmas cards. They'd both smiled at me. I had tested Shaun's eyes once in the past. Perfect vision. *Like a hawk*, I'd told him. But he'd been much younger then, twelve or thirteen perhaps.

Barbara continued with the details, shaking her head all the while, her voice droning along with the hot air blower on the floor. The woman in the headscarf dabbed at the corners of her eyes with her handkerchief as Barbara wittered on in a low incredulous whisper. A mother came to the counter with a whining child in tow, and I took the brief window of opportunity to escape.

Then I was outside, walking towards home, not knowing what to do, not really knowing anything at all. I kept my fist clenched around the rags in my pocket, for fear of them falling out and being discovered. I should have been sick or tearful but I wasn't. Instead, my mind, my power to think and feel had been sucked out of me, leaving a vacuum. It was impossible to absorb or calibrate. For several moments, I was simply the skin, hair, bones, blood, fat and muscles of Melvyn Pettifer, a body without personality or identity, apart from the paper proof in my wallet. Looking back, I see it would have been a very good time to die, a good time to be hit by a bus or have a fatal heart attack in the street. In those few minutes, after learning who those rolling and bumping faces were, I would have felt no fear or alarm at the idea of my own imminent death. Instead, I would have welcomed it as a sudden and timely relief from the tumult building like a sieging army at the edges of my thinking.

I continued walking until I reached Cornerfield Lane, perhaps two hundred yards from our house. The fog hung thick all around. I could see the front gardens of the first two or three houses, then nothing but still, grey fog. I needed some time to think. I could not go home and face Margret. I had to tell her about the accident. Not my involvement, of course. But I knew she would see Barbara in the shop over the next couple of days and Barbara would say she'd seen me and told me. She would see it as her duty to tell Margret she'd told me. I could see her and hear her telling Margret, *As I said to Mr Pettifer on Sunday morning…* It would seem strange to Margret if I'd not told her straight away, something local of that magnitude.

I looked at my watch. It was five to ten. Five to ten and already the bad news was in the paper shop. Barbara's and Lennard's across the village green were the two main sources of news and gossip in Lyttleton. Within the next two or three hours before they shut at Sunday lunchtime, how many people from how many households, I wondered, would call in for their Sunday papers, a packet of bacon or some cigarettes? The fog might hide me, of course, but almost everyone in the village would know about the accident before the end of the day. It was a hideous thought, like an animated diagram of some spreading epidemic. I tried not to focus on it. But I could not help thinking about all those locals with their little fragments of news – fathers, mothers, sisters, brothers, aunties, uncles, sons and daughters all racing home to tell the rest of their families. I could see them sitting around breakfasts, their Sunday lunches, their pints in the pubs, shaking their heads, judging the perpetrator, saying what should be done to him, what should be done to *me*.

I stood in the fog looking towards my house, only my fingers moving on the damp rags in my pocket. I had to get rid of them. The thought of dumping part of someone's body, even such a small part, made me sick with fear and shame. But I could see it had to be done. I decided to walk along the edge of the park and through the alleyway at the far corner by the old vicarage. From there I could walk to the other end of Cornerfield Lane and circle back home. I hoped to find somewhere quiet and suitable along the way.

There was a gap in the long brick wall that bordered the north edge of the park. As I walked by, I caught a glimpse of the frosted expanse of playing fields and football pitches. I stopped and went back. Just through the gap there was a short railing. I leant on it and felt the intense cold of the metal through my jacket. The fog was thinner now, and I could see almost half the park before it disappeared into a huge grey-white curtain shrouding the rest. On the nearest football pitch, two teams were arranging themselves in opposite arcs around the centre-circle. A weak winter sun was trying to break through the fog. Rooks and crows cawed from the tops of the trees lining the border of the park and the Lyttleton Junior School. I watched the players on the pitch and wondered why they were trying to stand still in the cold. Then the referee in black blew his whistle and all the men in their kits and the straggle of people along the sidelines bowed their heads in silence. I wanted to leave the railing, but I was stuck there, rigid, as if my hands had frozen onto the metal. I retched, catching the warm odours of whisky and bile on my breath. They reminded me of the night before, *the faces in the headlights.* I retched again, deeper. A pale orange froth splashed onto the hard turf and steamed and fizzed amongst the frosted blades of grass. I straightened up and wiped my mouth with the cold sleeve of my jacket. My eyes watered and my nose ran. The referee blew his whistle again, and the teams dispersed into their warm-ups. The supporters along the sidelines blew into their hands and stamped their feet against the cold and clapped and shouted encouragements.

I staggered back through the gap in the wall, wiping at my nose and eyes, praying that no one had seen me. Further on, where the lane met the path beside the vicarage, there was a heavy iron gate in the old ivied wall. It hung rustily ajar, leaving a narrow gap into the small brambly wood that bordered the vicarage. I looked around to make sure no one was watching, then squeezed through and edged along the inside of the wall until I was well-hidden from view on all sides. I knelt and scrabbled at the earth and dug a little hole with my hands. The soil was cold and hard on top but softer beneath the frozen surface. The frost had not penetrated deep under the thick layer of ivy that covered the ground. I put the bloodied rags in the hole and fought against the urge to look again at the earlobe and gold stud. Instead, I filled the hole over with the dark wet soil and flattened it and knelt there for a moment, the damp cold seeping through the knees of my trousers. I closed my eyes tight and mumbled some hybrid of prayer and apology. I have no idea what I said, just a whispered babble in a place I often visit in my nightmares.

LISA

When Neil arrived, he was angry and full of questions. He barged through the door and moved me aside as if looking for the culprit. I half-expected him to say, *Where is he?* I followed him into the kitchen and sat down while he paced the short distance between the sink and the door, back and forth like a leopard in a cage at a zoo. I'd seen him do this before, pace and curse through his anger until he was steady enough to sit down and talk. It was pointless saying or doing anything to stop him. Better just to sit and wait until he was ready. Eventually, he stopped in front of the kitchen sink and stared out of the window at the small square of back garden draped in fog.

"Jesus Christ!" he said with his back to me.

I watched his body slump from kill-mode to resignation. He turned and looked at me, then came and sat at the table. I poured him a cup of tea and added two spoonfuls of sugar. When he had his tea in both hands, I went and fetched the biscuit jar from the shelf and put it on the table. Neil looked at it but didn't take one. He was quiet for a while. He stared at the teacup in his hands or out of the window, which had iced up in the corners.

I studied his face in profile. The small scar over his right eye glared pink. It always did when he was stressed or angry. I noticed a minuscule web of burst blood vessels on the wing of his nose. The rest of his complexion was ruddy, like he'd been scrubbed with a scouring pad or he'd stayed out late drinking with his mates, as he was prone to doing when he was home.

"I don't know what to do," he said, finally.

"There's nothing you can do," I told him.

He looked up at me from the table. Tears were forming in his eyes.

I told him I was sorry.

"What?" he said. "Why are *you* sorry? It's not your fault."

I knew he was right but I couldn't escape the taking hold of guilt, the self-apportioning of blame.

"None of this is your fault," Neil continued. "None of it."

We were silent again, and I became aware of the noises of the kitchen. The fridge. The clock. The irregular tap-drip in the kitchen sink.

Neil wiped at his tears and sniffed angrily.

"What about this bastard driver?" he said. "What did Dreek say?"

"Not much," I said. "They haven't got anyone yet."

Neil shook his head and scoffed. "What a *fuckin'* surprise."

I told him it had happened in the early hours. No one about. No witnesses.

"They're asking questions," I said. "Local residents and that."

"That means they know nothing, Leece," he said. "Fuckin' old bill round 'ere! Useless!" He put his face in his hands and shook his head. "Someone must have seen something, for Christ's sake."

I told him not to get angry. I told him that I couldn't take that.

"Not today," I said. "Not today."

He looked up at me, red-eyed, incredulous.

"Don't get angry?" he said. "Are you fuckin' serious? Shaun's…" The word stuck in his throat. Then he spat through his gritted teeth, "*Dead…* because of some… some fuckin' drunk driver, and you're telling me not to be angry."

I knew he was right but I wanted him to calm down.

"We don't know if the driver was drunk," I said.

"Oh, come on, Lisa," said Neil. "Why else would you drive away?"

"I don't know," I said. "Panic?"

I told him I just wanted him to be calm. And it was true. I did. Everything felt so squeezed and pressurised. Images of Shaun laid in some mortuary drawer somewhere haunted the edge of my thoughts. The fog pressed against the kitchen window. And Neil's boiling anger threatened to blow and shatter my ability to function.

"I'm calm, Leece," Neil said. "I'm calm. Sorry. I just... If they don't find him, I swear to God I'll fuckin'—"

I interrupted him, losing my patience.

"What, Neil?" I said. "What? What will you do?"

He stared at me, surprised by the confrontation in my tone.

"I'll find him myself, Leece," he said, "and I'll fuckin' kill the cunt. That's what I'll do."

I'd known this was coming, but I was still shocked when he said it. People, men especially, say things like this all the time to make themselves feel strong and in control. But this wasn't the case with Neil. He meant it. He might not actually do it if someone were there to talk sense to him when the time came. But in the moment he said it, he meant it, and if the driver had walked through the door right then, I have no doubt that I would have had to stop Neil from killing him.

Back when I was eight months pregnant with Shaun, and Neil was just fifteen, he was given a year in the Portland Borstal for grievous bodily harm. He'd been sat on the wall outside the White Lion with his mates, waiting for a drunk who'd take their money plus the price of a pint to buy them a bottle of cider from the off-sales counter. They'd all started laughing at some bloke snogging and fingering some girl up against a car when Neil had realised it was Terry, my boyfriend. From the accounts I heard, Neil had confronted Terry, and Terry had told him to *mind his own fuckin' business.* Bad move. Neil's anger had exploded like a gas can left in a fire, and he had knocked out three of Terry's teeth, split his eye socket and broken two of his ribs, kicking him while he lay on the tarmac in his own spreading pool of piss and blood. Those last two kicks, witnessed by that little tart still straightening her knickers, had been the deciding factor. The judge had seen enough intent to maim to warrant a custodial sentence. When the police had arrived at the house later that night to arrest Neil, he'd been pacing the kitchen, explaining to me what had happened, muttering to himself that the next time he saw Terry he'd finish the job. Thankfully, Neil never saw Terry again. I saw him one more time when he arrived bruised and brooding to pick up his things, wincing and moaning as he hauled his old holdall down the stairs. Shaun had been born five weeks after, two weeks late, nine pounds and four ounces, greedy as hell, no dad, no grandparents and his uncle in the nick.

"Perfect!" was all I could think of saying. "Fucking perfect!" My own anger momentarily got the better of me. "Then I would lose you as well, wouldn't I?" I said, staring at him in older sister mode, baiting him to dare argue. "Is that what you want, Neil, for me to be completely alone? Again?"

He looked at me through his tears and anger, his lips contracted inwards so that his mouth was little more than a stubbled crease in the skin of his face.

"No," he said, "course not."

We were both quiet for a while after that. To say *again* had been cruel of me really, to remind him of that time. It was the period of his life he regretted most acutely. Not beating the shit out of Terry. He was fine with that. I'm pretty sure that if Terry had ever walked through the door again, Neil would have done the same. It wasn't even the prison time. It was the fact that he'd missed the first year of Shaun's life.

"Anyway," I said, "Dreek'll be here soon, so don't go saying that kind of shit with him around. Okay?"

I waited for his response while he stared out of the window, his expression like a mad dog. I swear I could almost see the violence burning in his eyes, the beating he'd give whoever turned up as the culprit.

"Okay?" I repeated.

I needed to hear him agree.

"Okay," he said. But he didn't look at me when he said it, and his expression had barely changed.

I left him staring out of the window with his thoughts and went upstairs to get ready. I hadn't told Neil but Dreek was coming to take us to the hospital, to formally identify Shaun's body. Dreek had said he'd do it for me if he could, but the law required the next of kin or at least family. There was no need for me to put on make-up or be presentable. But this would be the last time I would see Shaun. At the top of the stairs I stopped and looked at the closed door of his room. I knew exactly how it looked behind the door. I didn't need to go inside. I had the perfect mental picture of its appearance, apart from the image of Shaun lying peacefully in his bed, like I'd seen a thousand times before. I spread my palm on his bedroom door and closed my eyes and told myself that I would make it through the day. I didn't fully believe it but it helped.

When I came back downstairs, Neil was smoking a cigarette and pacing again.

"What is it with you and him, Leece?" he said.

"Me and who?" I asked.

"Who d'you think?" Neil scoffed. "Dreek."

"Nothing," I said. "He's always been alright to me, that's all. You know that."

"It doesn't bother you that it was *him* that nicked me that night? It was *him* that knocked the fuckin' door."

"He was doing you a favour, Neil," I said. "Making sure you knew what was gonna happen."

"He still fuckin' nicked me, though, didn't he?"

"He didn't have a choice, did he?" I said. "You were screwed either way, Neil. You nearly killed Terry. Dreek wanted to make sure it was someone you knew. He was worried you might make things worse for yourself."

Neil continued pacing, stopping only to stub his fag and light another.

"You still haven't answered my question," he said, "about you and him."

I felt no obligation to answer. I knew he was hurting and looking for a fight. But I also knew saying nothing would only make things worse. I was tired. I wanted to think about Shaun. So I told him that Dreek had been there when there was no one else around to help.

"Yeah, I wonder why," he said.

"It wasn't like that," I told him. "He just called round now and again, that's all. See if I needed anything. And I did. I had a new baby, for Christ's sake! I was eighteen years old. Mum and Dad gone. You in the bloody nick."

"Juvenile detention," he said.

"Whatever," I answered. "You weren't here, were you?"

I didn't mean to. I promised myself I wouldn't. But I began to cry.

"And now Shaun's gone," I said, the words dragging the fact out of the dark and into the kitchen right there in front of us. "Shaun. Gone."

Neil came around the table and knelt down in front of me and took hold of my shoulders. All I could do was shake my head and look at him through my tears.

"Anyway," I said. "Dreek said he'd take me to see Shaun, so that's what I'm gonna do."

Neil stared at me, digesting what I'd said.

Eventually, he said, "You're gonna see him?"

His question surprised me.

"Of course I'm gonna see him," I said. "He's my son. I'm his mum."

Neil caved in then. He put his head in my lap and sobbed for several minutes. I should have stroked his hair and said some soothing words but I couldn't. Instead, I looked out of the window. The sun was breaking weakly through the fog and the kitchen brightened a little, as if to say *keep going*.

Neil mumbled, "Fuck's sake, Leece. Fuck!"

"You don't need to come," I said. I hoped he wouldn't. I didn't need his anger.

Neil raised his head and looked at me. All tears and snot and red eyes, like a child after a tantrum.

"What?" he managed.

"You don't need to come," I said, "if it's too difficult."

"Difficult?" Neil said, and he put his head back into my lap.

I told him I understood.

"I'll come," he whispered. "I'll come."

MELVYN

Back home, Margret said nothing about the time I'd taken. She was sat at the kitchen table reading a magazine with the radio on. A Christmas song was playing. I recognised it but couldn't remember the title or who was singing. My mind was withholding things from me. Things I knew.

I put the shopping bag on the table. Margret began to flick through the TV listings, suggesting films or programmes we might watch. I stood in front of the kitchen sink and looked out into the front garden and the lane. The kettle hissed and clicked. Another Christmas song came on the radio. A heartbroken American high school girl pined for her lost love over the sound of sleigh bells. The fog had thinned but not gone. *Stay*, I thought. *Hide me*. I couldn't bear the idea of the lane being fully visible from the window again, of our house being in plain view. *Their faces rolled and smashed over the bonnet in the darkness*. This time I could identify them, Shaun Terridge and his girlfriend, smiling like they had in the gift shop. My teeth were grinding.

Margret came up behind me and began to take my jacket off.

"God, you're freezing," she said, rubbing the tops of my arms. "How long were you out?"

"Not long," I said.

The damp, dirty rag in the muddy hole. My hands patting down the cold dark soil.

She put her arms around me and her head on the back of my shoulder. I could feel her hair against my neck and ear. I clenched my teeth to stop them grinding. My heart knocked in my chest like the fist of a child locked in a dark cupboard. Margret's body pressed against my back. My own body was incapable of reacting. There was no pleasure or comfort or discomfort in her touch. No feeling of any kind. The bushes in the front garden were thawing in the thin sun, *the park in the thinning fog, the footballers bowing their heads, the sound of the crows, my vomit fizzing and steaming like acid on the clean, hard ground.* Margret went back to making tea while I continued to stare into the garden. I was waiting for one thought to follow another. But all I could see were their white faces rolling and bumping over the bonnet, their bodies like refuse sacks dropped in the road, the bilious contents of my stomach, a steaming stain in the clean, white, frosted grass.

Margret placed a mug of tea on the draining board.

"That'll make you feel better," she said.

"Thanks," I managed.

"D'you want some breakfast?" she said.

"Yes," I said.

I could hear her behind me, opening the fridge and humming, placing and picking things up. Again, I wanted to tell her. Here. In the safety of our kitchen. But sunlight found its way onto the chrome of the sink and reflected off the tap onto the ceiling. Margret sighed behind me, cheered, it seemed, by the slight and sudden brightening of the room. I lost my nerve and the moment had gone. I told her I was going to get some things from the car.

"Okay," she said brightly. "I'll call you for breakfast."

The garage was cold and damp after the warmth of the kitchen. I walked around the car again, looking at it, inspecting it without thinking. I got into the driver's seat and sat in silence. I reclined the seat as far back as it would go and closed my eyes. It was dark and quiet. For several minutes, I stayed like that, drifting in denial, the real meaning of what I had done building at the boundary of my consciousness like a swarm of angry wasps on a window.

I felt safer inside the car, inside the garage. Doubly protected from the outside world, and the impression of its turning against me. But I could not bear the thought that the car might be my downfall, perhaps already was. I had agreed to collect Margret's mother on Christmas morning. Margret would want last-minute shopping before then. We would need the car over the next few days. It would be on show. The Jaguar garage in Bishopstowe was far enough away to be out of reach from Lyttleton's local news. I'd used it once or twice before for specialist parts. I could blame vandals for the damage. Lyttleton had its fair share of drunken yobs and mindless vandalism. Maybe I could snap off the chrome Jaguar mascot. A dreadful thought. Sacrilege. But I saw it might make my story more credible. A trophy taken by some envious lowlife. The Jaguar garage might take the car and keep it over Christmas. It was almost due a service. They would give me a courtesy car. I decided to call them first thing Monday morning. Leave the car where it was until then. In the dark. Hidden.

With the beginnings of a plan, I felt less panicked and partially in control of the situation. I got out of the car and stood at the top of the steps by the door into the house. The Jaguar sat squat and sleek and the light from the bare bulb bounced off its haunches and curves. I barely noticed its dents and scars before I turned off the garage light and locked the door behind me.

LISA

Dreek called the house to say he'd be twenty minutes. That was Dreek. Considerate to the last. Giving me time to make sure we were ready when he arrived. The idea of Neil and Dreek together in the small space of the kitchen made me nervous. So after he called, I waited in the lounge by the window, watching for the Panda car. When it came, I noticed a curtain twitching across the street in the Lockes' upstairs window. And old Mrs Dean at number twelve opened her door and brazenly came to the end of her garden path in her slippers, tights, dressing gown and rollers to watch. She beat herself against the cold with her wrestler's arms, but she did not go back indoors. No need to tell the neighbours the news. Lyttleton was a small place. Bad news was passed around, unwrapped and gobbled up like a big tin of Quality Street at Christmas.

Dreek got out of the car and came round to the pavement to open the front passenger door. Neil got in instead of me. I stood for a moment in the freezing cold, expecting him to realise his mistake and get out again. But he didn't. He just sat in the front seat and stared dead ahead. If Dreek was unimpressed, he didn't show it. He gave me a resigned smile and held open the back door of the car for me as I got in, closing it with a soft thud. As he walked around the back of the car, I leant forward to ask Neil what he thought he was up to. He shushed me, then started on at Dreek as soon as he got back in the car.

"So where did it happen then," Neil asked.

Dreek glanced at me in the rearview and then at Neil. He sighed and started the engine.

"Edge of the village," he said. "Old Church Road. Near Colemans'."

"And no one saw nothin'?" said Neil. "What about the houses opposite?"

Dreek checked his rearview again. Our eyes met but he didn't react.

"Well," he said, "there is one witness who might have seen a car drive away."

"Who?" Neil interrupted.

Dreek shook his head, probably realising he should have lied. But that wasn't his way. It was hard to imagine Dreek lying.

"Sorry, Neil," he said. "I cannae tell yae that."

"Why not?" Neil asked.

"It's confidential," said Dreek. "Could jeopardise the case brought against the driver."

"What case?" Neil scoffed. "What driver? You haven't caught anyone!"

They were both quiet then. Their discomfort at being sat next to each other was as palpable as a bad smell in the car. Even though I could only see his shoulders and the back of his head, I could sense the coiled-up tension in Neil's face and body. He was a rigid presence in the passenger seat, self-gripped and wound too tightly.

As Lyttleton passed the windows like a filmed backdrop, its familiarity horrified me, as did its same old boring winter Sundayness. Families walked home from church. Dog walkers stood on the heath and threw balls for their dogs, who chased and barked and sniffed at each other. I don't know what I'd expected, the whole place to be a smouldering ruin or something. But nothing had changed, nor would it. The indifference was enough to make me scream in the back of the police car. I didn't, of course. I just stared at the landmarks I'd known all my life – the church, the bus stop, the roundabout, the shops, the pub, the war memorial. I wondered how they could at once look so familiar and so monstrous.

"So he stopped then?" Neil said.

"What's that?" Dreek seemed surprised by the sudden question, as if he'd been in the same trance as me.

Neil turned from the window and looked at him.

"The driver," Neil said. "He stopped."

Dreek glanced in the rearview again, caught my eye and looked away.

"We're not a hundred per cent sure," he said.

"But if someone said they saw the car driving away," said Neil, "then it must have stopped first, right?"

"Again, we're not entirely sure. It's possible."

"He stopped then drove on," Neil said, more to himself than to Dreek or me.

"We don't know that," Dreek said. "We have to wait for the evidence."

"Oh, for fuck's sake," Neil shouted, and he banged his fist against the door.

I grabbed him by the shoulder and told him to calm down.

"But, Leece," he said, "if he knows he's done it, then it's fuckin' murder!"

"Now, hold on, Neil," Dreek said.

He pulled the car into the side of the road.

I began to plead with Neil to stop, but he ignored me and kept on at Dreek.

"Well, what is it then," he said, "if it's not murder?"

Dreek sighed and began to answer. "Well, technically, unless you can prove…"

"Stop!" I screamed. "Stop! Please! Both of you!"

It was the only way to get their attention. I didn't want to hear any more.

They stopped. Dreek turned and looked at me.

"Sorry," he said.

Neil just sat fuming, staring at Dreek, then turning his attention to the road ahead. Dreek pulled the car away from the kerb, and everyone was quiet for the rest of the short journey.

When we got to the hospital, Dreek spoke quietly to a woman on reception. She glanced at me and Neil with a practised sympathetic expression. Dreek then led us along several long corridors while we followed in a daze. It felt as if we were being led into the centre of a maze or labyrinth, and we might never find our way out. But Dreek seemed to know exactly where he was going, as if for him it was a well-trodden path. Outside a large set of double swing doors, he asked us to sit and wait. There were two rows of orange seats, and we sat in the front. Every time the double doors swung open, we turned our heads towards them, expectant and terrified. I caught a glimpse of our reflections in the glass each time the door became momentarily opposite, and we looked like transparent ghosts, visible for just a second, our expressions locked in the agony of limbo.

After what seemed like a long time and no time at all, Dreek reappeared through the double doors, followed by a hospital worker whose thick black body hair sprouted from the V-neck of his blue surgical scrubs.

"Mrs Terridge?" he said

"Miss," I said. "It's Miss Terridge."

"I'm sorry," he said. "Miss Terridge."

He paused and looked at Neil.

"Brother," Neil said, nodding towards me. "Uncle."

The man in scrubs nodded politely. He wore an expression much like the receptionist who'd caught my eye as we entered, sympathetic, cold and professional, all at the same time. The kind of expression achieved through practice and repetition.

"You can both see him now," he said. "He's ready."

Neil got up but I stayed sat for a moment and closed my eyes, looking for some kind of strength in my own darkness.

Then I opened them again and said, "Okay," but the word was just the word with no attached meaning, a cracked and whispered utterance and nothing else.

We followed the scrubs man into a brightly lit room. A body was under a sheet on a table. Scrubs pulled back the sheet gently, just enough to reveal Shaun's neck and face. I took a deep breath, then looked at Shaun to make sure it was him. Then I nodded to the man in scrubs, who passed me a clipboard and pen attached with a piece of string and Sellotape. I signed the form where it was crossed. I could have been signing anything, and I wouldn't have known or cared.

Then scrubs whispered, "I'll give you some time. I'll be just outside."

He left then and I focused all my attention on Shaun. There was a large gash running from the left side of his forehead to his left ear. No blood though. The wound had been thoroughly cleansed so that it was just a thick, red line that could have been drawn on with lipstick. The ear was taped and appeared to be missing its bottom half.

I leant down and whispered to him, something like, "Bye-bye, darlin'. Sleep tight." I can't remember my exact words, just mummy nonsense that didn't really make any sense. I'd forgotten Neil was even there until he left the room, swearing and muttering as he burst out of the big swing doors. When he'd gone and taken all traces and sounds of his anger with him, I pulled back the sheet a little more and laid my head on Shaun's bare chest and listened to the silence inside his cold body. It was like hugging a prone mannequin, but it was better than nothing, so I stayed like that until Dreek came in and gently fetched me away.

MELVYN

At around five, when it was dark and the freezing fog had thickened again, we heard carol singers outside in the lane. I had no reason to fear them, but I willed them to pass our door without stopping. Margret, on the other hand, seemed overjoyed.

"Oh, how lovely," she said. "Come on, Melvyn, let's go and listen."

"You go," I said.

"What?" she said. "Don't be a Scrooge. You get your wallet. I'll get the door."

I feigned good-humoured irritability as best I could and went to find my wallet in the kitchen.

Margret opened the door, and I heard the singers louder, their voices rushing in with the cold air. They were singing "Once in Royal David's City". I'd always liked that one, but hearing it then, standing in our kitchen, with the weak glow of Christmas lights creeping in with the cold, the song threatened to undo me. If it went on too long, it seemed I might liquefy into a puddle on the floor, a disgusting mess of my own blood, waste, bones and innards. The singers stopped, and I heard Margret talking to them.

She called me.

"Come on, Melvyn."

I took a deep breath, steadied myself then made my way to the door. There were six or seven of them, adults and children, the youngest about twelve. I recognised one or two of them as customers. I gave a couple of pound notes to the youngest child. She smiled at me and took them. All the carol singers smiled and thanked us. I tried to smile at them without making eye contact. Then they began singing "Silent Night". Margret smiled at me and put her arm around my waist. We stood at the door with the singers singing in front of us. The faces of Shaun Terridge and his girlfriend rolled and bumped and screamed over and over the bonnet and windscreen as the song poured into my ears like a poison. With every line sang I saw them, Shaun and his girlfriend, standing still yet zooming towards me in the dark. *Bump, scream, smash, crack, gone.* The song went on and on. The silhouettes of neighbours appeared at some of the windows across the street. They were watching and listening to the carollers, of course, but it seemed they were watching me, my face a bright and shining Christmas star of guilt.

The carol singers stopped. We thanked them and said goodnight. When we shut the door, Margret let out a happy sigh.

"What a lovely day."

"I'm going to have a drink," I said.

"Really?" she said. "Not like you on a Sunday."

"No," I said. "Still, nearly Christmas."

I went through to the dining room drinks cabinet and poured two large whiskies and brought them back through to the lounge. We sat on the sofa and watched television. An advert about drinking and driving came on. A young man took his girlfriend out after a few drinks. The car crashed into a post box, and she smashed through the windscreen. Then he visited her in hospital and recoiled as she turned her stitched-up face towards him. I watched it with the faces tumbling through my head, wondering if I would ever be rid of that image, those faces, rolling and bumping and smashing. I doubted it. Margret said we needed to be more careful. I nodded and said nothing, convinced my voice would crack if I spoke.

I drank two or three more large whiskies before bed. Margret declined after her first, saying one would help her sleep but any more would mean another hangover.

When I struggled into bed, I was drunk again. A warm swoon fuzzed the edges of my thoughts. Margret climbed in next to me in her silk pyjamas.

"Are you going to read?" she said.

"No," I said. "You?"

"No," she said, "too tired."

She leant away and turned off her bedside lamp. I smelt her soap and cream. Roses and shortcake. Usually pleasant but now somehow stifling and nauseating. She cuddled into me and sighed in the dark. I could see myself sitting in the car, staring into the rearview mirror at the lifeless dark patches on the road behind. One raised its head with sickening clicks and scrapes of broken bones. I shuddered. Margret asked what was wrong.

"Nothing," I told her. "Just a bit exhausted."

Her voice grew croaky with the onset of sleep.

"We're lucky, aren't we," she said, "in our lovely big bed with each other."

"Yes," I said.

A cold tear ran from the corner of my eye and dripped into the outer whorl of my ear. I focused on the smell and taste of whisky at the back of my nostrils and tried to lose myself in its golden warmth. Margret began to snore quietly, like a cat purring. Their faces rolled through the dark of the bedroom, bumping, bleeding and cracking, and again through the blackness behind my eyelids when I closed them.

The back of my car, moving fast, no one driving. Margret climbing out in a huff, even though we're doing sixty. Slams the door. Gone. Caroline in her cheap, clingy, green party dress, drunk, dirty, vicious, swearing and scratching. The reek of vomit. The car driving over bodies as we writhe and fight on the back seat. More bodies bump and crash over the bonnet and roof, landing splayed and twisted on the road behind. Then the dead girl. Shaun Terridge's girlfriend. Cheryl Ladd lookalike. Shattered body underneath me, bones protruding through her skin into mine. But I don't stop. Shaun is driving now, his bloody face watching me in the rearview while the car smashes into bodies and their bones crack and snap against the windscreen. Vomit swilling and stinking in the footwells. An ear comes off in my hand, its gold stud glinting in blood. The car skids faster and faster on the ice, screaming past the old Lyttleton Church towards some looming impact that waits ahead in the freezing fog.

LISA

I couldn't really function. I'd held it together in the car, at the hospital and even on the way back after seeing Shaun. But when I got back inside the house after Dreek dropped us off, I was all over the place. I just went in and out of rooms, opening cupboards, doing odd bits of housework, staring out of windows. Neil announced he would stay over for a few days, but he needed a few things first. I told him he didn't have to. I told him I was alright. I didn't really want him there, but I didn't have the strength to argue. Stacy would understand, he said. Of course, she would. You'd have to be a heartless cow not to. But she'd be on her own with their two kids just before Christmas. It wasn't what she'd planned. I pointed all of this out but there was no reasoning with Neil once he'd decided on a course of action. He disappeared in the afternoon, just as it was getting dark. He shouted from the bottom of the stairs that he was going and would be back later. Then the door slammed shut and he was gone. Just me left in the house. I crept into Shaun's room and lay on his bed. I could smell him on the pillow and the sheets. He'd always had a lovely smell. Even as a teenager. Like moist biscuits or something, flapjack just out of the oven. I lost myself in that smell and drifted off to sleep.

I woke up with Neil sitting on the side of the bed, looking at me and playing with my hair. He said I should get up and eat something. He had a Chinese takeaway from the Golden Turtle, some cans of beer and a bottle of Courvoisier. We sat in the kitchen and devoured the food. Christ, it was good. Chicken chow mein, pork chop suey, prawn crackers and big fat Chinky chips, as we called them. Nowhere made chips like the Golden Turtle. Fried in animal fat. There had been rumours of dogs' heads in their dustbins once, but I didn't believe that. Typical Lyttleton vicious gossip. Anyway, the chips were to die for, and neither of us had eaten properly all day. We were quiet as we gorged, apart from the odd appreciative grunt and comment about how good the food tasted.

"Shaun loved a Chinky," Neil said. "D'you remember how excited he used to get? Even when he was bigger."

I nodded but couldn't answer, so we just carried on with our food.

Afterwards we started on the beer and brandy and just talked and talked. About Mum and Dad. About growing up in this house, in this street, in this bloody village. I regretted drinking the next day, of course, but at the time it was exactly what I needed. I was thankful to Neil for understanding that without needing to be asked. The brother and sister thing, I suppose. It was strong. Sometimes. Not all the time. Sometimes we knew what the other was thinking. We knew when we needed each other and when we didn't. Like when Neil would come and stay in my room after one of his fights with Dad. This was definitely one of those times. It wasn't just Neil looking after me or vice versa. It was a mutual brother and sister thing. This time.

I was pretty sure that Neil had always viewed his seeing-off of Terry as a noble act, a defence of my honour, saving me from a life of misery with a randy dog for a husband. And I suppose, in a way, he'd been right. Terry would've made a dreadful husband and an even worse dad. Let's face it, the writing was on the wall. If you're getting into random birds' knickers in pub car parks when your girlfriend's in her third trimester, then you're probably not great husband material. But to be honest, and I've never said this to Neil, or anyone for that matter, there were many times in the months and years following, when I was boiling nappies and clearing up Shaun's sick in the middle of the night, taking him to school and having all the other mums whispering and gossiping, going to see his teachers about his behaviour, there were plenty of times when I'd've taken Terry back in a heartbeat. I knew he was far from perfect. I knew he had an eye for the girls. I'd been one of them, for Christ's sake. I'd been the other woman. At seventeen. I'd even been warned about him. But God I could've done with someone around. A husband for me and a dad for Shaun. Like I said, Neil had made up for his crime with a level of devotion to Shaun that was more like a dad than an uncle. But he never quite understood that I was lonely, that I would've liked someone to go to bed with at night, not for a bit of the other (although that wouldn't've hurt), but someone to sit in bed with on a Sunday morning, drinking tea and making plans, discussing a future, someone I knew was going to be there in five, ten years, whatever. Neil saw his own help and presence as enough. And of course, he had the right to be there. It was his house as much as it was mine. Mum and Dad had left it to *us*. Well, through the council. But for all Neil's help and being a good uncle, he wasn't a dad or a husband, was he? Sometimes, it seemed as if he wanted to be. But there's a big difference between the real thing and a stand-in. Plus, I knew he'd be gone one day, wife and kids of his own. And not many blokes are interested in taking on someone else's kid, especially with a hard-nut brother around with serious form when it comes to protecting his sister.

When Shaun was about six, and Neil was still living here, before the army, before Stacy, I got a call from the school asking if I could come and see his teacher, Mrs Lawrence. I remember sitting in the classroom with all the kids' paintings up on the walls, and all their little desks lined up, and their little rug where they had story time. And this woman, not much older than me but much better educated, and married, engaged first, judging from her nice rings, asking me how everything was at home, telling me how she understood how hard it must be. But how could she understand, with her rings and her perfectly manicured nails? I told her I appreciated her concern, but Neil was there and was like a father to Shaun, and we were all doing fine. It was when I mentioned Neil that she began to look uncomfortable and glanced at Shaun, who was outside kicking a ball against a wall. She told me that there'd been an incident. Two bigger boys had been picking on Shaun, and he'd attacked one of them. He'd had to be restrained by one of the dinner ladies. He'd split the boy's lip. "Quite a vicious assault for a little boy," she said. "Fights at this age rarely draw blood."

I told her *that* wasn't Shaun. That he wasn't usually like that. That those bigger boys must've done something nasty to have him react that way. But in my head, all I could hear were the details of what Neil had done to Terry, and what I'd seen Dad do to Neil. The black eyes and bruised ribs and fat lips. *Was it in the family to hurt and maim?*

Mrs Lawrence looked all uncomfortable again, squirming in her blouse and woollen skirt, twisting the ring on her wedding finger.

"It wasn't what they did, Mrs Terridge," she said.

"Miss," I corrected her.

"Apologies, Miss," she said, blushing around her neck where she wore a little gold cross. "I don't really know how to say this," she continued. "But when I asked Shaun why he'd attacked the bigger boy Mark, he said something quite shocking, Miss Terridge." She paused and sighed and then continued. "If I'm honest, I'm finding it very difficult to tell you."

I sat there, across from her, feeling like a second- or third- or fourth-class citizen while she complained about how uncomfortable *she* felt.

I told her I'd like to know exactly what was said. Mrs Lawrence looked at me and rubbed her lips together and rotated her shoulders back, as if she were preparing herself for some impossible task or trial.

"Very well," she said, with a big dramatic swallow. "When I questioned Shaun about what had happened, he was, I have to say, in rather a dreadful state, crying, etcetera and very upset indeed. So, one has to take that into account. But still, I find what he said a little disturbing."

I began to wish I hadn't asked her for the exact words. And to this day I would rather have never known what they'd said to him. Sometimes it's better not to know. I've often wondered if a very small part of Mrs Lawrence, with her lovely rings and her little gold cross, wasn't just a little bit excited by what she'd heard, titillated, as well as disgusted or "disturbed" as she'd put it, but I'll never know, will I? That's the nature of village gossip. You never know the source. You never know who believes it and who doesn't. You never know who's excited, disgusted or disturbed by it. But you know it's out there, and you know there's nothing at all you can do about it. And if you make a song and dance, it'll only make things worse.

Mrs Lawrence said that when she'd asked Shaun why he had hit Mark, it was because Mark had sung a song. I looked at her and waited for her to continue. Her blush had now spread from her neck to her cheeks, and she squirmed again in her thick woollen skirt. The song, she said, as Shaun had told it to her, had been of a "crude and sexual nature" about his uncle and me.

I looked at Neil across the kitchen table. He'd gone quiet and was pouring himself and me another large measure of brandy. I wondered, as I often had before, if he'd known of the rumours about us. If he had, he'd never said anything to me. I'd never told him what Mrs Lawrence had said to me that day at the school, and after hearing the exact words from Shaun, I'd made him promise not to tell anybody, ever. Christ only knows what Neil might've done if he'd found out. I'm pretty sure he never got wind of it. He'd've killed whoever he thought had said it. I thought about telling him there and then, while we were drinking and talking about the old days. He could hardly have gone looking for the culprits of decade-old gossip. But what would have been the point, other than to hurt him more than he was hurting already? I felt mean and cruel for even thinking it. I put it down to the brandy and what had happened that day. But there was bitterness buried deep inside me. Right there, at the table, when we were drinking and remembering in honour of Shaun, I felt aggrieved that I alone had had to carry that nasty stuff around with me, like a specimen of my own waste. When people had glanced at me in the village and at the post office and at Bishop's while I was doing the shopping, the looks I'd got, it was always me that had to wonder what they were thinking, if they were trying to decide if it was true or not, if I really was shacked up with my younger brother like some backwater hillbilly.

I didn't tell Neil. Of course I didn't. I'm not a monster. But I did remind him of the time that he and Dad had had a full-blown fight in the kitchen. It had been around the time that things had really started to deteriorate at home. Mum was sick and getting pretty immobile with her hips, and when she wasn't sat in the front room smoking and drinking her Harvey's Bristol Cream, doing the very things that were killing her, she was shuffling about in agony. Dad was drinking more and more. Not just at the pub but at home as well. He knew what was coming and couldn't face it, so instead he attempted to drown it in bitter and whisky. Neil was thirteen or fourteen and becoming a right little handful. He'd taken to staying out late, even on school nights, coming home in all kinds of states, drunk or stoned or torn and bloody from fighting.

Anyway, this one particular Friday night Neil rolls in about twelve, drunk as a lord, and all blue round his mouth where he'd been sucking on lighter gas. Lyttleton's latest teenage craze. Usually, he always managed to avoid turning up at the same time as Dad, but on this night he comes in to find me and Mum looking all worried in the kitchen, and Dad opening the door behind him, home from the Working Men's Club, three sheets to the wind, looking for someone to fight. Dad takes one look at Neil with his glazed eyes and blue lips and another look at Mum and me with our worried faces in the dim light of the kitchen and slaps Neil a peach right across the cheek, catching him flush with a sound like raw meat slapped on a butcher's slab, and Neil careens into the kettle and mugs then opens a drawer and he's pulling out the bloody bread knife and waving it around like some lunatic in a slasher movie, at which point Dad's colour explodes plum red and he launches himself at Neil and they roll around the floor all swear and spittle, a noise to wake the whole bloody street, smashing their fists into each other's ribs and ears until Dad rolls onto his back and starts wheezing and coughing and Mum's screaming because she thinks he's having a seizure or heart attack and Neil's crying and effing and blinding and stomping up the stairs and slamming his door.

Neil sat across from me, listening, shaking his head, laughing and crying at the same time. He poured more brandy and opened another can, and we drank and talked, and every time there was a silence, one of us would throw another old memory out there. We barely spoke about Shaun or what had happened to him. It was too soon. He was still present in the air of the house. His dirty clothes were still in the Ali Baba in the bathroom, waiting to be washed. He was more present in the house than he'd been in that cold room where I'd rested the side of my face on his cold body. The more I drank, the more the visit from Dreek and the trip to the hospital seemed like something I'd dreamt. I knew it wasn't. I knew there were demons lying in wait. But for the time being, as we sat there talking about the old days, I was content to live in the temporary lie, so much so that when the house creaked in the evening cold, I couldn't escape the notion that Shaun was upstairs doing what he used to do on Sunday evenings, listening to the radio, having a bath, and getting his things ready for school.

As Neil and I sat and drank, I felt like we were in a capsule, separate from the rest of the world. The ice began to climb the dark windows, so I turned up the heating and fired up the oven. I brought in the standard lamp from the living room because the overhead light in the kitchen was too bright. We needed to talk, but we definitely didn't need to see each other's faces in detail. With the dark and the cold outside, and the cosy glow of the lamp, and the heat from the radiators and the oven, the kitchen became our own little grotto that night, our cave, our den, hidden away like the ones Shaun and his mates had made in Lyttleton Copse in the summer holidays. We knew that sooner rather than later we would have to go outside and face the world, but for that short evening, at the end of the day that Shaun had been taken from us, we were content to stick two fingers up at the world and lose ourselves in beer, brandy and memories.

MELVYN

In the morning, before Margret awoke, I contacted the Jaguar garage in Bishopstowe. After her initial concern about me yelling in my sleep, she'd been irritated at being woken so early, especially as she had shopping and cooking to do. The garage said they'd take the car but it would have to stay with them over Christmas, and I'd have to take a courtesy car. I feigned disappointment and told them I'd be there in an hour.

I made Margret and myself tea. She stirred a little when I took hers to her and asked why I was up already. We had decided together that I should close the shop for the two weeks of Christmas and New Year. Margret had hinted at this for months beforehand, and I'd given in back in late November. Our plan had been to shop for presents, put up the tree and decorations, for Margret to cook and prepare for her mother coming. When I told her of my new plan to take the car in for a service, she seemed confused and annoyed.

"Why?" she said. "This is supposed to be our Christmas break."

This rankled as Margret no longer worked. Under normal circumstances, I may have reminded her of this, but instead I spoke to her gently and rubbed her shoulder through the silk of her pyjamas.

"It's making a knocking noise," I said. "I don't want it breaking down for Christmas when everywhere's shut. Who would get your mother?"

Margret made a short nasal humming noise as if she were considering this possibility.

"What's wrong with it?" she said.

"I don't know, darling," I said. "Probably nothing, but I don't want to risk it."

I cannot remember if I registered alarm at how smoothly my lies came, but they were out before I could even consider their plausibility.

"When will you be back?" she said.

I looked at my watch.

"Before lunch, easily," I said.

I could hear a fake cheerfulness around the edges of my voice, a sickly sugar coating, something I'd perhaps developed with my patients but not really noticed before.

Margret still didn't know there had even been an accident, but again it was not the time to tell her. She had just woken up, and I was desperate to be rid of the car. I could sense it, squat and cold in the garage with its guilty dents and scratches, waiting to be discovered.

I kissed Margret goodbye as she sat blinking sleepily, propped up on some pillows with her tea in both hands.

"Do you want anything?" I said.

"I don't think so," she said.

She looked peeved. This was not what she had planned for our first day off together.

"I'll be back before you know it," I said.

"Why don't you wait till I'm ready? We could go together."

"They want the car as soon as possible," I said. "I expect they're busy before Christmas." I didn't give her time to answer or argue. "I won't be long," I said. "You rest and take your time. Pamper yourself. We'll go shopping when I get back."

As I walked down the stairs, I could not shake my vexation at Margret's disgruntlement. Her morning was being spoilt by my actions, but I was doing everything in my power to protect *her* as much as myself.

Outside, the fog was still thick. The drive to Bishopstowe would be slow. I didn't care. I wanted to be in the car, driving, in control of something. When I got into the garage, I remembered the chrome jaguar. The idea of breaking it off, of vandalising my own car, seemed like some dreadful confirmation of my guilt, but I was convinced it was the kind of detail that might just be necessary. I went to one of the drawers in the work bench and took out a large adjustable spanner. I tightened the clamps around the head and body of the bent chrome jaguar and listened for any sounds of Margret in the house. Then I forced the wrench towards the windscreen, snapping the cat just above its hind haunches, leaving an ugly, broken lump with two poised feet. I put the wrench back in the drawer and hid the chrome mascot behind the chest freezer.

The village centre was busy, almost opening time for most of the shops and small businesses. Bishop's supermarket was already open. There was a trolley boy in a Father Christmas hat with a cigarette in his mouth pushing five or six trolleys and puffing clouds of smoke like an old train. I watched him as I waited at the junction by the bus stop. Several people stood waiting for buses. They jigged in the cold and rubbed their hands and blew steamy breath as they talked and smoked. Two women stopped talking and looked at the car. I could see them in the peripheral vision of my right eye. It was likely they knew me, but I could not bear to look at them. Instead, I stared ahead and watched the trolley boy. He took one last deep draw on his cigarette, stubbed it out under his boot, and left a cloud of blue-grey smoke dissipating as he plodded through the automatic doors. At the war memorial in the village green there was some kind of gathering. Only people's heads and shoulders were visible above the tall perimeter hedge.

The big brass bell of a tuba. Carol singers and a band for the pleasure of the Christmas shoppers.

I pulled out and headed for the roundabout by the White Lion. My palms were sweating on the wheel, and I became aware of my breath, heavy and ragged. My hangover pulsed within me, pinching the back of my eyes and secreting dirty sweat on my neck and my legs. I felt nauseous and flicked the button to let the window down. The blast of icy air made me catch my breath. I drove slowly around the small village bypass that ran behind the supermarket, the bookmaker's, the chip shop, the post office, the dental surgery, the estate agent and the pet shop to the roundabout at the start of the Old Church Road. The car idled silently while I waited at the junction. I thought about the bodies on the road, considered their injuries – smashed bones, limbs bent unnaturally, feet twisted in impossible directions. That morning's dream appeared to me again, and I leant my head towards the cold air outside the car. Someone beeped behind me, and I grunted in surprise and moved forward. I wanted to drive along the Old Church Road to see if there were any remnants of the accident. But I resisted the temptation and turned the car towards Farm Lane to pick up the main road to Cole's Hill and then the dual carriageway that would take me most of the way to Bishopstowe.

As I left Lyttleton I felt a small sense of relief, just to be free of the place, however briefly. Underneath this, though, was the foreboding certainty I'd started something that could not be controlled or altered, only followed and reacted to as each necessity required. The Jaguar glided slowly through the fog. I watched the red lights of the car in front, feeling empty of everything but the purpose of reaching the garage and ridding myself of the evidence.

After that, I had no idea what I would do, other than go home and pretend nothing had happened, and continue pretending until it was no longer necessary. I tried to consider when that might be, but it was impossible to calculate. I passed a temporary roadworks, its warning lights pulsing dimly orange in the fog while a neon word flashed on and off in my brain: *NEVER… NEVER… NEVER.*

*

When I arrived home, a weak, white winter sun had burnt away some of the fog, and most of the road was visible. The verges and gardens of Cornerfield Lane glistened with frost. I steered the courtesy Jaguar up onto the driveway in front of the house. It was the basic model of my own, plain white instead of dark metallic green. It smelt of other drivers, of cigarettes, damp clothes and shoes, a trace of wet dog. I'd bought a Feu Orange air freshener at a petrol station and hung it from the rearview mirror like a mini set of dangling traffic lights. But its cloying, sweet fruit-vanilla scent only seemed to emphasise the staler odours beneath.

I left the car on the driveway and went in through the garage. I took off my coat and shoes in the utility room. Margret had put on some washing and it was now drying in the tumble dryer. She'd not opened the window like I had often told her to, and the room was stifling and humid. The dryer's drum groaned. Margret had overloaded it. She always did. I opened the small window above the machines and stood for a moment by the kitchen door, listening for sounds from within. There were none. The room cooled quickly as the hot air raced for the window and the cold air from outside took its place.

The kitchen was empty but there were two mugs on the drainer. I heard Margret's soft footfalls above in our bedroom, then on the stairs. I grabbed one of the mugs and began to fill it from the tap. I drank the water and looked at the Jaguar on the driveway. It paled in comparison to my own. But I was pleased mine had gone for now. Within a few days it would be fixed, dents and scratches beaten out and spray-painted. Returned to its former glory. Cleansed of its guilty scars. Margret entered the room behind me from the hallway.

"Oh, you're back," she said. "How did it go?"

"Fine," I said. "They'll call when it's done."

"Right," she said. "How much is it going to cost?"

"I'm not sure," I said. "They'll let me know when they've had a look."

"I don't suppose they'll do it before Christmas."

"No," I said. "It'll be after."

Her smell filled the room. She was over-perfumed from her morning ablutions. I glanced at her. She was ready to go out. She had on a sleek black cashmere polo neck she'd bought second-hand from Angie's store, and she'd blow-dried her hair. *Shaun Terridge's and his girlfriend's faces rolled and bumped over the Jaguar's long bonnet and cracked and screamed as they disappeared over the roof.* I winced as if I'd just drunk sour milk.

"Is that the courtesy car?" Margret said.

"Yes," I said.

"It's not as nice as ours, is it?"

"No," I said. "But it'll do."

It jarred a little when Margret called the car *ours*. Like everything we owned, it had been bought with money earned from the business I had started and developed. Her casual assumption of half-ownership riled me sometimes, especially with the car.

"Have you heard about this awful accident?" Margret said.

Here it is, then, I thought, and steadied myself.

She was at my side, and we were looking at the white Jaguar on the driveway.

"Oh God, yes," I said. "Barbara told me yesterday at the shop."

"Why didn't you say anything?"

"I forgot. Sorry. Hangover, I guess."

"It's terrible, isn't it," she said. "Jenny told me this morning. Those poor families. Right before Christmas. What kind of person doesn't stop?"

I gripped the stainless-steel edge of the sink and continued to stare at the car on the driveway, convinced that Margret would suddenly see its significance.

"I know," I said. "Unbelievable."

"Did we know them, at all?" she said.

The question seemed stupid and snobbish, as if we didn't know who we knew and who we didn't, like royalty or TV celebrities. I wanted to remind her that they were people, that Shaun Terridge and his girlfriend had names and families. I resisted but the urge to protect them and stand up for them was tempting and confusing in equal measure.

"I think the boy has been in for a test or two over the years," I said, trying to sound relaxed and only mildly interested.

But I could see him in the chair, fit and strong, pale blue irises, diamond grey flecks. Perfect vision. Eyes like a hawk. *His face rolled in the dark over the bonnet, smash, crack and gone.* I remembered him in the dream from early that morning, driving while his pretty girlfriend squirmed beneath me, bones broken. The earlobe buried in the vicarage. His or hers? I'd probably never know.

"I wonder if the police have got him yet," said Margret.

"Let's hope so," I managed.

My teeth shut tight.

"Let's go and get the tree," Margret said. "I need some Christmas cheer. Speaking of which, Jenny and Michael are having a party on Thursday, Christmas Eve. I said we'd go."

I wanted again to tell her everything, every horrible detail, shock her out of her trivial ignorance. Instead, we went shopping, and I bought the biggest tree they had at the garden centre, the most expensive decorations, a Christmas wreath with little fake wrapped gifts and fake golden apples for the front door. Everything Margret wanted I bought, pointless, ephemeral things, anything which gave her pleasure and kept her from thinking or talking about the accident.

At the butcher's, she checked on her turkey order for Christmas Eve and bought meats and sausages for the rest of the holiday. I gave her the money she needed and stood at the back wall of the shop. It was busy. People were edgy and fierce in their ordering of meat. The butchers looked serious in their white hats and bloodstained coats, like battlefield surgeons in charge of amputations. *Shaun and his girlfriend laid out dead, cold meat on mortuary tables.* Customers rubbed their brows and brandished their lists. They frowned and sighed when what they wanted had run out. There was no pleasure, no *Christmas cheer*, as Margret had called it.

Again at the supermarket, I let Margret take control. We walked up and down the aisles and she filled our trolley. She stopped and happily held up items in front of me, comparing merits and prices. I may or may not have answered, I don't remember. I suppose I must have, or else Margret would have found it strange. *Bodies under sheets with dead open eyes. Shaun's boyish white muscles and strong frame. His girlfriend's softer form and smaller shape.* I hoped they were together somewhere, cold hands touching. I wondered about their physical relationship, whether or not they'd yet made love, innocent and precious. For the whole previous day, I had done everything I could to not think about them. But now in the refrigerated aisles of the supermarket, I let their deadness wash over me, allowing images of them to take hold. I did not once entertain the idea of going to the police. I couldn't see what good it would do, for them or us.

*

Later, after Margret had put our dinner on and we were drinking wine and decorating the tree, Geoff called. Margret answered the phone in the hall while I stood on the step-stool in the lounge, adjusting a fat fluffy boa of shiny green tinsel that reminded me of Caroline's dress. I listened as Margret thanked Geoff for the party and apologised for leaving without saying goodbye.

"Oh, that would have been lovely," she said. "But you know what Melvyn's like."

She laughed. "Yes, yes." Then laughed again.

She always gushed and laughed at anything Geoff said, especially jokes at my expense. In private, she often mocked him, his clothes or hair, his desire to look young.

She laughed again and called me.

"Melvyn, it's Geoff."

She came into the room flushed and grinning.

I picked up the phone in the hall and gave myself a moment to settle before speaking.

"Hi, Geoff," I said, sounding too happy.

"Melvyn, you old dog," he said. "I was just telling Margret, you two should have stayed yesterday. We had breakfast and Bloody Marys. Ended up a bit pissed again, to be honest. Nice Sunday, though."

I told him I'd been too hungover, exhausted from work.

"Ah, well," Geoff said, sounding bored. "Listen, you guys are still good for New Year's Eve, though, right?"

There was a party at a nightclub where Geoff and Angie sometimes went.

"Should be," I said, planning to make an excuse nearer the time.

"Great," he said. "Should be a proper bash."

Geoff was prone to this kind of youthful expression, picked up, no doubt, from his younger staff.

Then his tone changed.

"I take it you've heard about this hit-and-run, then, mate?"

I moved the phone away from my mouth and steadied myself.

"Yes, I have," I said. "Terrible."

"God, I know. You know Sharon in the Hareham shop?" said Geoff. *The smell of vomit in the back of the car.* "Her sister knew the girl, apparently. Pauline, I think..."

"Paula," Angie's voice interjected from the background.

So, the late-night wanderer returns.

"Paula, Paula," said Geoff. "Anyway, Sharon's sister's devastated, poor thing."

My mind raced with the news of these connections. Shaun's girlfriend now had a name. Paula. Her face rolled and bumped and smashed through the darkness just behind my eyes. She wasn't smiling anymore, as she had that day in the gift shop. She was seething and snarling, bloody and vengeful.

"Awful business," said Geoff. "Anyway, mate, the reason I'm calling is to let you know that Michael and Jenny were in Angie's shop today. They've invited us over on Christmas Eve. Just thought I'd let you know. Wouldn't want you to think we're crashing your scene or anything."

He laughed as he said this, as if the idea of Margret and I having a scene was preposterous. I was still thinking about Caroline's friend. Was *that* Sharon? I couldn't remember if she'd told me her name or if Caroline had used it.

"Oh," I said. "Great. See you there."

The idea of Geoff and Angie at Michael and Jenny's irritated me. Michael and Jenny were neighbours, nothing more. Michael liked to think of us as friends, but that was not the way I saw it. Geoff and Angie were our friends. Michael and Jenny's invitation to them was an unwelcome intrusion. The timing also worried me. Geoff and Michael together, now, in my proximity. Their initial connection was me, so it followed that *I* would be a topic of conversation, at least briefly. *So, how is the old bugger as a neighbour then?* I could hear Geoff joking. *Rather you than me.*

After the call, I went to the dining room for a drink. Margret heard me going and shouted a reminder that I had wine in the lounge. I ignored her. I needed something stronger and a few seconds on my own to recover. I poured a large whisky and drained the glass. Then I joined Margret in the lounge. She was standing on the step-stool with a basket of tree decorations in the crook of her elbow. I pictured her falling and the whole mass of tree, decorations and Margret catching fire, her running around the room with flames enveloping her, me throwing my glass of whisky over her in a panic, and her igniting even further, then falling and rolling and screaming in flames, blackened, bald and smouldering on a burnt patch of carpet.

"What's wrong," she said.

"Nothing," I answered.

"Then why are you making that awful face?"

"I'm not," I said.

"Are you worried about work?"

"Yes," I said. "A little."

Margret climbed down from the step-stool and came close to me, oozing sympathy. She kissed me and rubbed the back of my head. She spoke softly into my ear.

"You're probably just tense because you're not at work, darling. You've got to remember you've earned this holiday. You've not been off since the summer, and you work very hard."

This was a common theme of Margret's. She would reassure me we were entitled to everything because of hard work. Time off, new bed, utility room, Jaguar. She would soften me with whispers and touches, sensuously convincing me of our God-given right to all these things. Usually, I revelled in the reassurance, believing, feeling proud and even righteous. But now I could see that it was empty and self-serving on both our behalves. I could see Margret's part in it, her leaping to assuage even the merest hint of doubt. She clung to me and seemed to disappear, like a lizard camouflaging itself on a tree trunk. Our life together, and all its trappings, came to me in those long seconds: the business with its racks of spectacles and clean white expensive machines, the house with its luxury fittings and sumptuous soft furnishings, Margret with her expensive clothes, make-up and perfume, Geoff and Angie and their faux bohemianism, the Jaguar with its smooth silent speed; all of it rolled through my head with the broken young bodies of Shaun and Paula; all the things we owned seemed to tumble along with their faces, splashed and smeared with their blood, smashed and splintered with their fractured bones.

The sound of the letterbox flapping in the front door and the soft slap of the local evening paper on the hall carpet broke my trance.

"I'll get it," Margret said.

I sat on the couch and pretended to look out of the window. The whisky had gone to my head. I took deep breaths and tried to dismiss the previous moments as panicky nonsense, delayed shock.

I became aware of Margret's silence in the hall. I listened. Just a light shift of paper.

"Margret," I said. "Everything alright?"

There was no answer.

I sat and listened harder.

"Margret?" I said.

"Hang on," she said.

Then she came in with the paper and sat down next to me.

"It's just terrible," she said. "Listen."

I sighed.

"What's wrong?" she said.

"Is it the accident?" I asked.

"Yes," she said.

"Well, can't it wait?" I said. "We're doing the decorations."

She looked at me with a puzzled expression.

"Don't be silly, darling. I'm just telling you, that's all. You're having a drink anyway. We'll finish the tree after."

"Okay," I said.

"Young couple left to die," she said, reading the headline and shaking her head.

I sipped my whisky and looked out of the window as Margret proceeded to read me the rest of the story. As she spoke and I stared at the Christmas-coloured fog in the lane, Shaun and Paula tumbled endlessly over the car. When she'd finished, Margret put the paper on her knees and looked at me. I kept looking out of the window.

"Isn't that awful?" she said. "He stopped and then just drove on." She shook her head. "He must have known what had happened."

She looked at the paper again and began scanning the rest of the article.

"'The police want to speak to anyone who was in the area of Old Church Road between three and three thirty on Sunday morning'."

Margret put the paper down again.

"God, it's all a bit vague, isn't it?"

"Yes," I said.

I'd finished my drink and felt its warm softening of my limbs.

"Those poor families," Margret said. "One can only imagine what they're going through right now. Right before Christmas as well. You'd want to kill him, wouldn't you?"

"What?" I said.

"Can you imagine?" she said. "The anger!" She raised her voice a little. "It makes me angry, and I don't even know them. I mean, you imagine what those parents will be feeling. You'd want to kill whoever'd done it, wouldn't you? I would."

Their faces rolled again, angry, smashed and bloody.

Margret had stood up and was shaking the rolled-up paper to express herself.

"Doesn't it make you angry, Melvyn?"

I looked across the street at Mrs Thompson's Christmas decorations. They were lighting the fog around the house, green, white and red in alternate flashes. "I mean, if *we* had children and someone did that to one of them."

"It's just very sad," was all I could think of saying.

Margret looked at her watch.

"I wonder if there's anything on the local news," she said.

She put the paper down and switched on the television. She found the local news, but the weather report had begun.

"Damn," she said.

I became aware of my apathy and worried it might seem conspicuous.

I picked up the paper and began to leave the room.

"Where are you going?" Margret said, concentrating now on the television.

"Just to the bathroom," I said.

*

I sat in the bathroom and read the article. There was nothing in it that pointed to me. But the story was on the front cover. I closed my eyes and thought about the people of Lyttleton, sitting in their front rooms and kitchens, their Christmas tree lights on, damning me yet secretly wondering if they would have done the same thing. I concentrated and tried to close in on the reality of the situation. It was impossible. I was the one. *Me.* I was the one everyone, even Margret, hated at that very moment, the driver who went around slamming into innocent teenagers then speeding away. I kept scanning the article for anything that might implicate me. There was nothing. A day and a half had passed and the police had not called. The story was in the local paper but nothing pointed to me.

I heard singing from downstairs. Margret had put on a record. *White Christmas*, an album we'd had for years. Bing Crosby's sad and sonorous voice drifted up, muffled by carpet and floorboards. I began to tremble. I could just make out Margret singing in that way she had after a glass of wine or two. She never knew the lyrics to songs. She would sing a word or two, then hum along in a way that wasn't particularly musical, yet also not unpleasant. I cried into my hands and wiped at the wetness with my thumbs and forefingers, trying to focus on what to do. I told myself I was crying for them, for Shaun and Paula and their families. But if I'm honest, I wasn't. I wasn't even crying for Margret and her festive oblivion. I was crying for me. Shock, wine, whisky, the details of the article, and Bing Crosby of all things were combining to undo me, just as the carol singers had undone me the day before. I cursed my weakness. I sat and cried and looked through my tears at the blurred headline: *YOUNG COUPLE LEFT TO DIE.*

"It was an accident," I blubbed. "I panicked."

I thought about the bone-handled razor Margret had bought for my birthday. It had sat in the bathroom cabinet ever since, snug and shiny in its leather box. A pretentious present I had never used. *Maybe this was its moment? How long would it take? Two minutes? One minute? Less? Would it be painful? A hell of a mess.* I hated the idea of Margret finding me prone, white, empty of blood on the ruined bathmat. So, instead of slashing my throat or wrists, I washed my face and splashed cold water on the back of my neck. I rubbed my face hard with a towel and stared at my florid reflection in the mirror.

"Just keep going," I whispered, my hands gripping the sides of my face and head. "It will pass. Everything does."

When I was steady again, I opened the bathroom door and walked step by deliberate step back down the stairs. Margret was standing, admiring the tree. I put my arms around her waist and rocked her gently in time with the slow festive music.

"What do you think?" she said.

"Beautiful," I said. "Just beautiful."

Coloured fairy lights flashed and reflected off gold and silver baubles, while *Shaun's and Paula's sad, broken faces rolled and tumbled in the dark behind my eyes.*

*

I passed the build-up to Christmas in a low state of fear, kept at bay with whisky and mild sedatives from my doctor. I told him I was having trouble sleeping due to terrible dreams. He seemed to understand. I'd been ready to convince him with tales of stress and running the business, but he began writing my prescription and listing possible side effects (dizziness, water retention, diarrhoea and shortness of breath) before I had even started. When he said that it may have something to do with the accident, I panicked and my voice caught in my windpipe. But he went on, in his uninterested doctorly way, that half the village seemed traumatised, and several mothers had been in complaining of sleepless nights.

"Maybe you've a maternal streak," he said, smiling as he tore the prescription slip from the thick pad and handed it to me.

*

In the village centre, there was a discernible sombreness compared with previous Christmases. People talked earnestly and gave each other resigned smiles and grips of the shoulder rather than cheerful greetings. They moved from shop to shop with grim determination and thin smiles, in the hope, perhaps, that their Christmas routines might exorcise Lyttleton's newest ghosts from their thoughts.

LISA

Neil and I must have argued for a solid hour on the phone about what I would do for Christmas. I told him I wanted to stay home on my own. At first, he wouldn't accept it. He couldn't bear the idea. Me on my own in the house on Christmas Day. With everything that had happened. "It ain't right, Leece," he kept saying. "It just ain't right." Over and over, he told me that he would come and get me in the morning, bring me over to their house. Stacy would cook dinner. We could have a few drinks in front of the telly. The kids could open their presents. We'd all get through it together. He made it sound like a normal Christmas Day. The kind of thing we'd done since we were little, when Uncle Stan and Auntie Doreen would come in the afternoon, just in time for the Queen's speech, and Stan would fall asleep with his can of warm beer on his belly and his paper hat all skew-whiff.

I didn't react, but I was angry. I knew he was only trying to help, but he was doing that classic Neil thing, thinking he could right the situation through the sheer force of his will. I'd seen him do it again and again as a boy. When he was about eight, he'd taken Mum's bike without asking. All the kids in the close were racing their bikes up and down the street, but Neil didn't have his own bike. So he snuck around the little narrow path at the side of the house to the back shed, undid the big squeaky bolt as quietly as he could, and wheeled the bike right past the window while Mum and Dad dozed in front of the telly. I was sitting on the opposite kerb with Becky from across the road, playing pick-up-jacks with her dolls as spectators. I stopped and watched as Neil ducked his little head down below the level of the windowsill. He needn't have worried. It was after tea, and Mum and Dad were always too knackered to bother about what was going on outside. We could've been kidnapped from the street by helicopter and they wouldn't've had the foggiest. Neil looked tiny next to the bike. It must have been nearly a foot too high for him. He couldn't reach the pedals sitting on the saddle, so he had to stand on them and ride like that. But within seconds, he was down the path and onto the road, racing up the street to the other boys, who all laughed and made fun of him for riding his mum's bike. Then about two minutes later, they all came haring past like the clappers with Neil out in front, his fringe flying back and the biggest kid-grin you've ever seen smeared across his sweaty little face. Then *bang*! He'd been so desperate to win, so desperate to shove it in the faces of those other little shits (the ones who always took the piss out of his jumble sale clothes, second-hand football boots, and butchered mum-cut hair) he didn't brake until he was a hundred per cent sure he'd left his tormentors in the dust. But by then it was too late. Mum's brakes were virtually non-existent. She rode so slow because of her hip, she barely needed brakes. She usually just wobbled to a stop. The front wheel smacked the kerb at the top of the street and up and over the handlebars went Neil, charity shop shoes and all, onto the hard pavement, right below the big KEEP OUT! sign, while all the other boys skidded to a halt and laughed until they nearly wet themselves, as Neil picked himself up, sniffling and holding back the tears, dirty great graze full of grit on his chin, surveying the damage to Mum's front wheel, buckled so badly she'd have to get the bus to work until Neil scavenged another from the dump.

Instead of crying to his mummy like any of those other little boys would have done, he limped the bike round to the back of the house and proceeded to use just about every rusty tool from the old tumbledown shed to try to straighten the wheel. A full half hour he strained through his tears, snot and shame with hammer, spanner and crowbar, standing on that wheel, wiping his nose on his sleeve and dabbing at his grazed chin with his fingers, doing everything in his power to force that wheel back into shape.

I sat on the weedy back path with my jacks and bouncy ball and watched him and told him it was no good. He'd have to just go indoors and face the music. Easy for me to say, as that music would be a walloping from Dad. I guess that's why Neil kept yanking and banging and forcing that wheel until the noise finally brought Dad outside anyway. He'd struggled up out of his chair and made the short journey to the kitchen for a sneaky tot of cheap rum and heard the banging and looked out and seen Neil on the path with Mum's bike. Sure enough, Neil got the leathering he'd known was coming from the moment he'd hit that kerb and sailed through the air and seen the front wheel bent like it'd been left in the street and crushed by the coal lorry.

When I asked him to see my point of view about Christmas, when I explained over and over that I simply couldn't sit there and pretend to smile when everyone was opening their presents and Shaun was not even buried in the ground, when I told Neil that Shaun had been my sole reason for bothering with Christmas since Mum and Dad had gone and Terry had left, when I finally cried in exasperation down the phone that being at home alone I would feel closer to Shaun, Neil finally gave in. He settled for the deal that I could be on my own for Christmas Day if he could come and get me on Boxing Day and take me to the Working Men's Club, the family tradition, along with umpteen other Lyttleton families since Christ knows when. I didn't want to do that either but by then I was all argued out.

I tried to convince myself I was spending Christmas at home with Shaun. I know this sounds weird, even morbid, but it was all so recent that I could still feel him in the house, smell him, even hear him on the stairs. On Christmas Eve, just as it was getting dark, I caught the bus into the village centre to buy a tree. I hid myself at the back among the teenage smokers and snoggers so I wouldn't be spotted by someone who knew me. I couldn't bear the idea of talking to anyone, of someone touching my arm and telling me they were thinking of me, or even worse, praying for me, or any of that other rubbish people say when someone's died.

Thankfully, it was dark, freezing and foggy when I got off the bus. People were speeding about, finishing off their last-minute bits and bobs before everything shut down for the Christmas weekend. The shops would be closed for three days but looking at the piled-up trolleys leaving Bishop's, you'd've thought they were shutting for good. I put my hood up so as not to be recognised and headed for the common where some gypsies were selling trees. I found the smallest one I could carry and did my best to smile at the toothless old codger who wished me a Merry Christmas with his boozy breath and his roll-up stuck to his scabby lips.

After that, I crossed the road to the Parade and went into Sharp's Chemist. The bell on the door alerted Vicky Sharp behind the counter, who looked up from serving another customer and froze as she recognised me. We'd known each other since school but we'd never been friends. She'd had a crush on Neil on and off since second-year seniors and for some reason had always seen me as an enemy or competition. She'd worked in her parents' chemist shop and pharmacy since school and then taken it over and gotten plump from sitting behind the counter munching Penguins, Clubs and Caramacs and gossiping while the latest new girl did all the running around and shelf-stocking. My first instinct when I saw her was to turn around and leave, pretend I'd forgotten something important. But instead, I left my little tree by the door and looked for men's toiletries. In the last year or two, Shaun had become obsessed with his personal hygiene and seemed to take as much pleasure in his collection of talcs and deodorants as he once had in his Subbuteo teams and football cards. I chose him an upmarket talc called Mandate and approached the counter while Vicky did her best impression of looking busy.

"That's a nice one," she said as I placed the talc on the counter and took out my purse. "You know it's for men, though, right?"

I told her it was for Neil. "Last minute, as usual."

Her cheeks reddened beneath her thick foundation at the mention of my brother. She fussed with the till and peeled off one of the little bags that carried the family name and the teardrop logo they'd nicked from Palmolive. She seemed to be going unnaturally slow, thinking of something she should say, struggling with the gigantic elephant that had walked into the room and ruined the last hour of her Christmas Eve shift. She gave me my change and pushed the bag with the talc inside across the counter like it contained a bomb or a dead animal. I waited for the briefest of moments, steeling myself for *I'm so sorry about Shaun*, which I was so sure was coming I almost answered. When it didn't come, I snatched the bag and left without another word, aware of Vicky watching me as I picked up my scrawny little tree from beside the door where it had already started dropping pine needles like small mercies. *Something to get her up off her fat arse.* I shut the door and the bell announced my leaving.

From Sharp's, I walked back across the green and along past Bishop's to the White Lion off-licence and bought a bottle of sherry to go with some mince pies I had in the cupboard. I hadn't planned on the sherry but after seeing Vicky I needed a drink and sherry had always been Mum's tipple. As I waited at the counter for one of the bar staff to come through to the off-sales and serve me, I stared ahead so as not to catch the eye of any of the drinkers visible through the door into the lounge bar. I thought about Vicky Sharp and her inability to say something about Shaun. She would no doubt be gossiping by now with her next last-minute

Christmas customer, talking about how I looked and whether I was buying presents for my dead son. *She said it was for Neil but I think it was for Shaun, you know, the one who died.* Like all gossips, *yak-yak-yak* but nothing to say when it comes to saying something that matters.

I walked the mile or so home with the tree under my arm, praying I would not see anyone else I knew. Vicky had been enough. The thought of another uncomfortable meeting made me feel sick and dizzy. Back home, I took off my coat, poured a large shot of sherry into one of Mum's old gold-striped schooners and stuck two mince pies in the oven. The smell made me salivate and I realised I hadn't eaten since morning.

The silence in the house seemed to press in from the walls and down from the ceilings. I put on the radio. Back-to-back Christmas music and disc jockey drivel, but it was better than the big dark nothing that had greeted me when I'd first arrived home.

In our little front room, I stood the tree in its bucket on the small wooden table that filled the space between the two armchairs facing the telly. Then from the cupboard under the stairs, the one that Shaun had loved to hide in as a little boy, I dug out the Christmas decoration box, with its paltry selection of ancient baubles and threadbare red and green tinsel, and proceeded to decorate the tree, finishing it off with coloured flashing fairy lights and the gold-paper-covered cardboard star that had topped our Christmas trees since Shaun had proudly brought it home from primary school.

Living at the end of the street bar one, we had very few passers-by. But I felt better knowing that if anyone did happen to look in our front window, they would see the Christmas lights and assume there was life inside the house, even if I was beginning to doubt it myself.

When the tree was up, I went into the kitchen to check on the pies. Their warm spicy-sweet aroma had filled the room and the little hallway. Shaun's favourite at Christmas. It was overwhelming.

I had to sit down. I could feel him all around me, in that smell emanating from the oven, as a little boy, as a teenager, and as he'd been the week before, tearing around the house, always busy, always looking for something, poking his face into the steam from pans and sniffing food as it cooked. Food mad. Always hovering around the kitchen when a meal was just about ready. Never needing to be called to the table. Always there ten, twenty minutes early. *What's for dinner, Mum? Mmm, smells good. Shall I lay the table?* Tomato soup with toast, sausage, egg and chips, spaghetti bolognese, which he always repeated in a stereotypical Italian accent, kissing the ends of his fingertips, never turning his nose up at anything I cooked him, gobbling it down like his life depended on it, making me feel like a chef at the Savoy for giving him cheese and ham Toast Toppers, grilled the way he liked them until just about burnt.

I took the pies out of the oven and let them cool on the ancient brown baking tray. After a minute or two, I turned them out of their little foil dishes, upside down onto Shaun's Yogi Bear plate he'd had since he was a toddler. We'd bought it at a church jumble sale for two shillings, back before pounds and pence. Shaun had squealed with delight every time he'd finished his food and revealed Yogi and Boo-Boo's smiling faces. *Yodi Boo-Boo*, he'd say, his *g* sound not coming properly until he was five, *Yodi Boo-Boo*. I took the pies through to the front room, where the little tree now glowed and reflected in the window. I poured myself another large glass of sherry and opened the TV cabinet and turned on the television. I sat down in the left-hand chair where Dad used to sit, watching then getting up to change channels, as I'd done a thousand times with Shaun, him sitting in the dilapidated armchair next to me, Mum's old seat, the one she'd died in, hot and faint from her bike ride home from work, sherry untouched, Rothman's lungbleeder still burning in the ashtray. The programmes were just colour and noise, so I switched it off and it made that electric power-cut sound. But the quiet offered no relief. In fact, the opposite was true. Silence seemed to inhabit the darkness beyond the glow of the Christmas tree lights, as if silence and shadow were working together as a team. The house seemed to squeeze in on me. The sweet smells of sherry and mince pies threatened to block my airways, like I was being suffocated by Christmas, as if its red fur-lined gloves were holding my nostrils closed and forcing their fingers down my throat.

I stood up to take the plate and glass back through to the kitchen and something gave way inside of me, as if I'd slipped a disc or pulled a muscle. My hands suddenly weakened and I dropped the plate and glass. The plate bounced and sent the untouched pies and their crumbs tumbling onto the rug. The schooner caught the edge of the table and lost its stem and spilt its sickly sweet contents over the old, cracked veneer of the table and the carpet. I sat down again and fought against the feeling that I might disintegrate then and there on the old armchair, in the ancient imprint of Dad's backside. I imagined being searched for by Neil or a neighbour, my body having disappeared into the fabric of my clothes like the Wicked Witch of the West every year on the telly.

For several very long minutes, I sat in the multicoloured glow of the Christmas tree and waited for the sensation to pass. Tears flowed freely down my face and images of the previous week presented themselves to me as clearly as if they'd come on the telly after *Top of the Pops*: the luminous hands of the alarm clock at quarter to five, the police car at the kerb outside, the big blur of Dreek through the frosted front door glass, the weight and discomfort of Neil's head as he cried into my lap, Shaun's dead face with its bright red scar running temple to missing earlobe, and Vicky Sharp's manicured pink nails as she pushed the plastic bag towards me across the counter, as if I were contagious, as if I might infect her and turn her bright little Christmas into my dark empty one. Along with all these images came a tiredness so great it seemed to soften my bones and destroy even the idea of standing up. The need to sleep was instantaneous. Like a strong anaesthetic given before an operation, count back from ten, creeping from my fingers and toes up my legs and arms, winding itself around my torso and neck like fast-growing weeds made of shadow. All I could do was shut my eyes and become consumed by the darkness.

MELVYN

The stilted mood of the village found its way into Mike and Jenny's Christmas Eve gathering. At least, it did until people were drunk. Then they danced and laughed and flirted and made rude jokes, as they would have at any party. A few people mentioned the accident in that formulaic, headshaking way, *I know, isn't it awful... those poor families... and right before Christmas... can you even imagine...* then quickly changing the subject, remembering that if anything could kill a party, it was too much talk of dead teenagers.

I moved from huddle to huddle, feigning friendliness and Christmas cheer, stopping frequently at the punchbowl until I realised too late that I was drunk. It kicked in mid-conversation, distorting my face and slurring my words like a stroke or palsy. My thoughts became a lurid montage of incomplete images and maudlin self-pity, like a melodramatic painting in which the colours had begun to run. Twice I fell asleep on Michael and Jenny's huge sofa, and both times awoke and commented on its merits of size and comfort. When I was awake, I spent much of the evening with my arms around people. The alcohol had unlocked an underlying reservoir of fear I must have been suppressing since the accident, and now it was manifesting itself in uncharacteristic tactility. I was desperate for any available shred of affection. Several times I noticed Margret watching me, gauging if and when I should be taken on the short walk home. Eventually, she caught me alone in the kitchen, looking in the cupboards for whisky. She scolded me in a raspy whisper.

"Melvyn," she said. "What on earth's the matter?"

"I'm looking for a decent malt," I said. "What kind of people don't have a bottle of whisky at a party?"

"I think we should go home," she said.

"What time is it?" I asked her.

"Almost midnight."

"Yes," I said. "We should. There's no whisky here anyway."

Margret said she'd get our coats. I stood for a moment, leaning to stop myself swaying, taking large, drunken breaths of air through my nose.

I felt sick. Not yet, but it was coming.

Geoff and Angie stumbled into the kitchen, laughing, him behind her with his hand on her hip, her with her braless nipples showing proudly through the soft wool of her festive red sweater.

"Oh," she giggled. "Hello, Mel."

"Melvyn, you old sod," Geoff said, laughing.

He left a stroking hand on Angie's back. She nuzzled into him with her shoulder and hip.

"I think we're leaving," I said.

"Oh, really?" Geoff said. "What a shame."

"Margret wants to go," I said. "She's got to be up early for the cooking."

Jenny came into the kitchen.

"Lovely evening, thanks, Jenny," Geoff said.

She laughed.

"Oh, thanks, Geoff," she said. "It's great to have *new* people round."

The emphasis felt barbed and directed at me. Geoff and Angie just smiled and acted like people gushed at them all the time.

Jenny looked at me uncomfortably. My drunkenness was making me jerk and blink.

"Well," she said, "we thought about cancelling, what with the accident and everything. But then we thought, well, life goes on, doesn't it?"

"Not for them it doesn't," I said.

Jenny looked at me but said nothing.

Margret walked into the kitchen with our coats.

"I meant to ask you, actually, Mel," said Angie, looking at me. "Did you see anything that night?"

I glanced at Margret. She was looking from me to Angie with a puzzled expression.

"No," I said.

"Oh, you're not going, are you?" said Jenny, clearly hoping we were.

"'Fraid so," Margret said. "Mummy's coming in the morning."

Angie looked at me, waiting for an answer.

I thanked Jenny for the party and apologised for having drunk too much punch. She said it was fine but flinched when I tried to kiss her cheek.

Outside was a Christmas card Christmas Eve. The fog glowed multicoloured around the streetlamps and Christmas lights on people's houses, and frost glinted like quartz on the road and pavement.

But Margret's silence was ominous. She said nothing and she would not make eye contact with me. I fumbled with the keys for the front door and she snatched them from me. Once inside, she trotted briskly up the stairs and into the bathroom, locking the door behind her. I stood for a few seconds in the hall, swaying and listening, trying to think through my inebriation. I could not hold on to any consecutive logic, so I gave up and bumbled my way to the dining room drinks cabinet. I poured some whisky and staggered to the kitchen for ice, then bumped my way into the lounge and sat heavily on the sofa. The Christmas tree was a large shadowy presence in the corner of the room but getting back up to switch on the fairy lights felt like far too much effort. I could not find the remote control for the television, so instead I just sat in the dark and sipped at the whisky until my eyes closed.

LISA

I awoke in the paralysing thickness of a dream, *the house filled with the light of morning in early autumn, first week of the new school year, Shaun starting at the big school, the seniors, as he called it, racing around the house, packing his school bag, chomping down his toast and cereal, yabbling about this, that and the other, clean pale blue shirt, skew-whiff school tie, excited face* dematerialising into the reflection of my own face in the blank screen of the television, and the light and sound of that morning, six or seven years before, swallowed up by the fairy-lit darkness and silence of the front room and the sugary smells of sherry and mince pie wafting up from the carpet.

I struggled out of the chair and scuffed to the kitchen for the dustpan and brush and a cloth, turning on all the lights as I went. I cleaned up the worst of the mess and left a tea towel pressed into the carpet to soak up the sherry overnight. In the kitchen I noticed the bag from Sharp's Chemist and thought about wrapping Shaun's present and leaving it under the tree. My thinking was that if he were still here in some way, shape or form, he'd be happy to see that he was included in what was left of our Christmas. I sat down at the table and took the talc out of the bag and felt again that same all-consuming tiredness and weakness. I climbed the stairs and curled up in Shaun's single bed and fell asleep with the smell of his hair and skin in my every intake of breath.

KEVIN

On Christmas morning, Dad turned up early with presents. Mum enthused over her gifts, but it was forced, and she kept slipping out of the room to check on the turkey and stare out of the window into the back garden, where the apple tree and shed were draped in cold fog, like they had been all week. I'd been looking forward to Christmas since my birthday in October, and now it had been ruined by some drunk driver. My mood was lifted by the prospect of going to pick up Nan. But after making a fuss of me when we arrived, she sat in the front of the car on the way back and talked to Dad about the latest rumours surrounding the accident. Nan seemed to have all sorts of new information beyond what had been in the local papers. The gossip had come from her paperboy and mobile hairdresser, local shopkeepers and neighbours, and Dad listened and nodded and shook his head and made the odd comment about what so-and-so had said and how they knew the Terridges. I managed to get my story in about Sunday morning and PC Dreek, but neither Dad or Nan seemed that interested any more, now there were fresh details about the devastation of the two families, speculation and moral judgement about the driver. Dad was convinced it was someone local. He believed there was no real reason to travel through Lyttleton in the early hours of the morning unless you lived there, especially since the bypass had been finished. The village centre wasn't en route to anywhere, he said, and you had to come off the main roads to get there. Nan agreed. By the time we got back to the house, I was convinced the killer-driver was hiding in Lyttleton. At least that was exciting again, more exciting than Mum talking about how Lisa Terridge would never recover, and more exciting than hearing about how losing a child was the worst thing that could happen to a mother.

Mum pretended to be happy on seeing Nan. They hugged and Mum made a fuss of her. Nan had a big Spar carrier bag of wrapped presents.

"Eyes off, nipper!" she said.

I was ordered to pour Dad and Nan a sherry and make tea for Mum. Dad looked peeved that Mum didn't want her traditional Christmas morning drink. He, like me, seemed frustrated by the infringement on our usual cheer. He'd seen Christmas as a chance to patch things up with Mum, take advantage of the extra warmth and love around at that time of year.

Christmas Day passed as Christmas Days did. Dad and Nan fell asleep after lunch. I helped Mum with the washing up. This was a selfish gesture. I couldn't stand the idea of her alone with her thoughts, yet I was convinced that's what she wanted most. The photos from that Christmas prove me right. Mum is hardly in them because she kept opting to take them. Or if she is there, her smile is resigned, acknowledging the fleeting pleasure of the moment but weighed down with the true agonies of life, agonies of the kind visited upon the Terridges that year. I was simply too young to understand the depth of Mum's sadness at these deaths. They were, after all, outside of the family. But now I see they had ripped at her faith in the lives we led. Mum had always been the positive driving force of the family, always looking for the good in people and events. "It's an ill wind that blows no good" was one of her most repeated proverbs. But her separation from Dad and the flimsy deaths of these two *children*, as she kept calling them, smashed to pieces on the cold road just before Christmas while the rest of Lyttleton slept snugly in their beds, had shaken her resolve to the core and made her fearful rather than expectant of life.

LISA

I woke in Shaun's bed, having slept well for the first time in almost a week. My mind wandered over the previous day and I saw quite clearly that the worst part, the part I'd found hard to bear, was meeting someone I knew and having to pretend I was coping. Practically speaking, I suppose I was. Coping. I wasn't wearing the same underwear every day or neglecting to wash. I wasn't eating well but I *was* eating. Yes, I was coping, alone. It was when someone else came close that there was a problem. Not Neil. That was different. He was family. But Vicky Sharp, for instance. Someone I knew and who knew me. Having her close to me, speaking to me, handling Shaun's gift with her manicured hands had felt like someone rummaging around in my most private places. So the first feeling I felt on Christmas morning when I woke in Shaun's single bed was relief. Relief that the day stretched before me without the prospect of seeing anyone, relief that I could lie in my dead son's bed, in his room, watched only by footballers and pop stars who smiled and sulked from their posters in the early morning gloom.

After putting on my dressing gown to keep warm and making myself tea, I went back up to Shaun's room. It seemed as good a time as any to look through his things and decide if anything could go. I felt a tinge of reproach from some unknown source as I did this, as if a court of bereaved mothers sat watching and judging against an accepted code of behaviour. I wanted to be with Shaun but I couldn't, so what better way, I thought, than go through some of his things and try to feel just a fraction of what he may have felt by owning and handling them.

I started in his little cupboard under the eaves. It was so low inside that I had to sit on the floor cross-legged. I pulled the cord and switched on the bare-bulb light. Beneath a small rail of coats and jackets, there was a battered cardboard crisp box with Shaun's name on it and the word *private* neatly drawn in capitals. I pulled it towards me, smelling the shift of loosening dust and pausing to stifle a sneeze. I noticed that my breathing had become shallow, my heart knocking in my ribs. I stopped for a moment, worried that I might find something incriminating, something that would corrupt my maternal memory of Shaun. I should have taken note of this inkling but I was curious. I'd never known Shaun as a private boy, so the box was a surprise. He was always so open and talkative that I'd naively presumed he'd had no real secrets from me.

The contents were quite innocent at first, *Smash Hits* and *Shoot* and further down *Tiger and Scorcher*, and lower still, *The Dandy* and *The Beano*, the ones I'd bought him to read on the rare occasions he'd been sick and absent from school, propped up in bed with a comic and a glass of Lucozade. But at the bottom of the pile the titles and pictures changed from Dennis the Menace and Desperate Dan to front covers of pouting women and naked skin. At first I laughed, incredulous at the idea of my son looking at magazines like these, even while the offending objects were in my hands. But as I flicked through the glossy pictures of bras and breasts and pubic hair, I felt hollow and sick and cross with Shaun for having such filth in his cupboard, locked sneakily away under piles of innocent comics. I wanted him there so I could reprimand him for being crude and disrespectful, so I could punish him by having him take them outside and burn them. How dare he bring these into our house.

I took them out of the box one by one and stacked them just outside the cupboard, the women's ludicrous pouts piled one on top of the other. On the last one I noticed that the letters of the title, *Fiesta*, had been coloured in with purple felt-tip, a childish doodle out of place above a buxom young woman sulking in her knickers. I flicked through the magazine, wondering if there was something special inside, if the coloured-in title were some kind of clue. But there seemed to be nothing. Just endless shots of lace and flesh and adverts for cigarettes and cars and watches and whisky. It began to feel like a nasty trick, like I'd been drawn into looking at these pictures, searching for my son in the pages of a pornographic magazine.

Then several Polaroids dropped into my lap in a dusty flutter. I froze and closed my eyes. I reached above myself and pulled on the cord that turned off the light. When it was dark inside the cupboard, I opened my eyes again. Tears streamed down over my cheeks and I rubbed at them with the backs of my hands. In the dark I saw Shaun's smiling face as he unwrapped the Polaroid camera, a gift from Neil the previous Christmas. I knew I shouldn't look at the photos, but I also knew that I would. How could I not? I dreaded what I might see, so I waited a while in the dark. When the crying stopped, I gathered the photographs by groping around in my lap. Then I held the small pile for just a few seconds, steadying my breathing and bringing myself under control. When I was calmer, I turned on the light.

The pictures were of Paula, Shaun's girlfriend. In each one her skin was blasted white by the unforgiving flash of the camera, and her body, while young and trim, had the lifeless look of a corpse. In every pose she'd turned her face demurely away, as if she couldn't bring her full identity to the pictures, as if she'd been forced to pose naked, cajoled and convinced with soft words about her beauty, that it was just a bit of fun, private between them, that no one except the photographer and the model would ever see the pictures. Their little secret. I put the pictures back in the bottom of the box and covered them with the comics that had been there before. I took the other magazines downstairs and plonked them in a heavy pile on the kitchen table. Then I went out in the freezing fog to the coal bunker and filled a bucket of coal for a special Christmas Day fire, one that might make the house more cosy for Christmas and burn away my anger at Shaun and my own stupid curiosity.

MELVYN

I awoke to the smells of roasting turkey and pine needles. The Christmas tree lights were on and there were presents underneath. Outside was still foggy. The houses on the other side of the lane were only just visible. I sat for a while, going through the motions of waking up, widening my eyes and stretching my hands out in front of me. Another hangover, just a variation of the one I'd had all week. I told myself I must stop drinking but even as I said the words I knew I wouldn't.

I slipped upstairs quietly in my socks, undressed, showered and shaved, put on a shirt and the pale blue Pringle jumper Margret had bought for me during my brief dalliance with golf. Michael had taken me to his club in Sail-on-Lee, but I'd been unable to stomach his patronising coaching, and the new clubs had been in the garden shed ever since. I crept downstairs with a simple mantra in my head, *act normal, just act normal.*

As I entered the kitchen, Margret was knelt in front of the oven as if contemplating suicide rather than just checking on the turkey. When she stood up and turned around, she seemed surprised and annoyed by my presence. She recognised the sweater.

"Merry Christmas," I said.

She looked at me and blinked before replying, "Merry Christmas."

I moved around the table, hoping to embrace and perhaps even kiss her, but she picked up some plates and clutched them to her chest.

"When are you getting Mummy?" she said.

I looked at my watch. It was quarter to ten.

"When do you want me to go?" I asked.

It hadn't meant to sound subservient. I was sure that Margret would see through my compliance as an act. But it was impossible to behave naturally. Her anger was as palpable as the smell of meat in the kitchen.

I sat down and poured myself some tea.

"You should probably go quite soon," she said.

I told her I would finish my tea then leave.

"I'm sorry about last night," I said. "Just a bit drunk and tired."

She paused her rinsing of wine glasses. Her head twitched and her shoulders gave an almost imperceptible jolt as if she'd stifled a hiccup. When she spoke again, her voice was measured and calm.

"You won't be able to drink today," she said. "You'll have to take Mummy home later."

By the time I left, a weak sun was melting the frost on the front lawn. I felt its warmth on my neck as I lifted the garage door. It was soothing, like loving fingers rubbing a stiff muscle. I backed the courtesy Jag out of the driveway and onto the road. Margret was watching from the kitchen sink. At least, it looked like she was. A shaft of sunlight was reflecting off the window, rendering her head and face indistinct behind a dazzle of light. I waved anyway, just in case she was looking.

I drove into Lyttleton village centre, past Barbara's shop, which had opened for last-minute groceries. Frost was glinting on the pavements and roofs and several families were out enjoying a Christmas morning walk. They smiled and ambled while small children wobbled on brand-new bicycles.

I took the bypass around the back of the shops and drove without thinking across the roundabout onto the Old Church

Road. The route we always took to Margret's mother's house. We'd driven it hundreds of times, maybe a thousand. There were flowers near the site of the accident. People had placed them around the base of a sapling. Someone had tied a blue-and-white football scarf around one of the branches. I wondered if I should add my own tribute or whether that would be too conspicuous. I made a mental note to come back the other way. Margret's mother would complain it was longer, but I could use the excuse of wanting to drive along the seafront in the winter sunlight.

When I arrived, Alice was irritable. Since her husband had died, she had undergone a transformation. They'd been an active couple all their lives. Eric had played football and cricket well into his forties, and he and Alice had been keen dancers right up to his death. He'd complained about feeling *out of sorts* for a week or so and had intended to visit the doctor. Then he'd driven home one afternoon from one of his regular trips to the local garden centre, parked the car on the driveway, and died right there in the driver's seat. Massive stroke. Alice had been baking rock cakes with the radio on in the kitchen at the back of the house, so she had not heard the car pull up. She was on the phone to Margret, asking if Eric had called by, when she noticed the familiar blurred red blob of car through the frosted glass of the front door. "Oh, that's him now," she'd said and made her goodbyes. Then she'd phoned about two minutes later in a panic. She'd not even called an ambulance. He'd been sitting there dead for over an hour and his body had begun to cool by the time Alice found him slumped on the steering wheel. Margret had screamed at her to put the phone down and call an ambulance. I had stood uselessly with Margret in our own hallway while she'd cried and screamed down the phone at her mother. Eventually, Margret had simply hung up and called an ambulance herself. Then we'd turned off the oven and the lights and driven to her parents' house. By the time we'd arrived, Eric was being lifted into the ambulance, his head and body covered with a sheet strapped across the chest and waist.

At first, Alice had deepened her connection with the local church, attending more services, arranging flowers, singing in the choir, and baking cakes for functions and evening meetings. It had seemed her faith might get her through her loss without any lasting wound to her personality. But after a few months she had grown bitter and angry at what she called *the injustice* of Eric's death. She was still meticulous about the house and her appearance, but she'd begun to gossip about her neighbours, their shoddy gardens and overweight children. "How is it," she would hiss, "people like that get to walk around and breathe the air, when people who take care of themselves die too long before their time?"

On one of Margret's solo visits, she'd asked her mother why she'd stopped going to church. "Because if there is a God," Alice had replied, a little drunk on sherry, "then he's a nasty fucking hypocrite, and I'm having nothing more to do with him." Margret had been visibly shaken when she'd arrived home and said she'd never heard her mother talk that way, had never even heard her use the F-word. I had tried to console Margret by saying that it was her mother's way of dealing with her grief and that she had every right to be bitter and angry. But for Margret it had been too much. She had lost one parent suddenly, and she was now losing the other by degrees as Alice's bereavement took hold and slowly squeezed her remaining benevolence from her drop by drop and tear by bitter tear.

She had a bag with wrapped gifts inside. When I offered to take it from her, she held onto it.

"I was expecting you half an hour ago," she said. "I was starting to get worried."

I apologised and tried to smile it off, but she glared at me and narrowed her eyes, challenging me to dare mock her for worrying over someone being late.

I apologised again with more sincerity.

She stopped on the driveway and looked at the car.

"Courtesy car," I said. "Ours is being fixed."

"Oh," she said. "Not as nice, is it?"

"No," I said. "Better than nothing though."

She got in and sniffed and screwed up her face.

"Someone's been smoking in here."

When I turned off the normal route towards the seafront, she asked what I was doing.

"I thought we'd go along the beach road," I said.

She looked at me questioningly.

"We shouldn't be late for Margret if she's cooking," she said.

"It'll give her some space," I said. "It's only ten minutes longer."

I was aware of the weak register of my voice. I glanced at Alice. She looked puzzled and vexed.

Along the shorefront, the light from the weak sun and its reflection off the sea warmed the light in the car.

"I used to come along here all the time with Eric," Alice said. "He loved the sea. He was a fine swimmer. Taught Margret to swim here."

She drifted off into her memories. By the time we reached the end of the shore road, her mood had improved. She talked freely about the seaside, how it had always been the major feature of Lyttleton's charm.

Her spirits lifted further when we got to the house. I let her in the front door. There was a great warm waft of cooking from the kitchen. Margret appeared in the hall. Alice's face brightened at the sight of her daughter. Then her eyes narrowed.

"You look tired," she said. "Not sleeping well?"

"Too late to bed, that's all," Margret replied, hugging her mother and guiding her into the kitchen.

I left them and eased the car into the garage and pulled down the door behind me. Then I got back into the car and sat and thought. I only had minutes before I would be missed.

A normal, happy Christmas Day. All the components were there. I just needed to forget the accident and say as little as possible.

In the utility room, I listened at the door as Margret and her mother talked in the kitchen. I went back outside and closed the garage door, then in through the front door and straight to the dining room. Margret called before I'd finished pouring a small whisky.

"Melvyn, what are you doing? We're waiting for you."

"I'm getting drinks," I called back.

I stopped and waited for a reply. Nothing. I finished pouring the whisky, drank it down straight and looked at my hands. Steady. No shakes. A good sign. *Shaun's and Paula's white and bloody faces rolled over the bonnet and up the windscreen.* I shut my eyes and concentrated until they'd gone. I poured three schooners of sherry and took them into the kitchen. I gave one to Margret, who frowned and put it down on the table, and one to Alice, who began to drink immediately.

"Well," I said. "Merry Christmas, then," and took a sip of the sherry.

Alice drained the rest of her schooner and managed a smile as I kissed her on the cheek. Margret froze as I came close to her.

"Merry Christmas," I said softly into her ear.

She gave a small humourless laugh.

"Melvyn," she said, "why don't you put Mummy's gifts under the tree and put some music on."

"But you've got the radio on in here," I said.

She turned it off and looked at me.

"I'd rather it was on in the lounge, now, so Mummy and I can hear ourselves think."

Alice handed me her empty glass. I took it and smiled at her. She smiled back, but only with her mouth. Her eyes showed no happiness whatsoever. They were beautiful once, slate grey with the faintest radial spokes of aqua blue. But they were rheumy now, tired and sad, whites yellowed by grief, sedatives, alcohol and age.

I started to go into the lounge, but Margret stopped me.

"Could you get Mummy another drink first, please?"

Her voice was curt and superior, as if she were ordering wine from a waiter.

I poured Alice and myself another sherry and took them back into the kitchen.

"Is that for you?" Margret said, looking at the glass in my other hand.

"Yes," I said.

"But you're driving Mummy home later."

"I'll make this my last one then," I said.

"Oh, for God's sake, I'll get a taxi," said Alice. "There, problem solved."

"That's decent of you, Alice," I said.

She shrugged.

I looked at Margret for approval, but she'd already turned back to her cooking.

I couldn't find anything suitable for the record player. It all seemed too sentimental and likely to unravel me again. So I put on the radio in the lounge instead. I crept to the door and listened to the sounds coming from the kitchen. Margret and Alice were talking. I could tell from their tones it was nothing important. Just cooking talk and platitudes.

I took Alice's shopping bag over to the tree. Her gifts were loosely wrapped and the paper was cheap. They had the look and feel of last-minute, half-hearted presents. Needs must. I felt mine and looked at the card stuck on crudely with wrinkled Sellotape. *Melvyn, from Alice x.* I squeezed it. Gloves or socks. *Shaun's and Paula's faces tumbled in the darkness. Awful cracking sound. Elbow, ribs, skull. No Christmas for them.* The glow of green, orange, red and white fairy lights reflecting off the baubles and tinsel, the smell of pine needles, satsumas, chocolate and cooking from the kitchen, and the sound of the DJ's syrupy voice, all curdled together with Shaun's and Paula's faces tumbling and cracking over the bonnet, up the windscreen, *crack and gone.*

"Melvyn," said Margret. "What are you doing?"

She was standing in the doorway, looking impatient.

I started to answer, but she cut me off, saying the turkey needed carving before it got cold. The mention of meat made me nauseous. Margret had sat the turkey on a large chopping board and wrapped it in foil. I took the carving knife and fork from the drawer and stood in front of the turkey, collecting myself. The heat from the oven was stifling. I asked if I could turn it off, but Margret said she was keeping it hot for the Christmas pudding. I removed the tinfoil and was about to carve when Margret snapped at me.

"For God's sake, Melvyn, put an apron on. You'll ruin that jumper!"

I took Margret's floral apron from the back of the kitchen door and put it on. As I carved, boozy sweat oozed from pores in my armpits and behind my knees. The tender meat came away easily under the knife. I couldn't stop myself from thinking about their bodies again, splayed on the frozen road, broken, dying, dead, their bones and their flesh, legs and arms, chests and necks, faces and feet. I became lightheaded almost to the point of fainting and stopped several times for water. When I was finished, the pinkish-brown slices of meat lay steaming on the serving plate, and the carcass sat bare and exposed, a battered bone basket hanging grimly onto its last strips of cooked flesh and gristle. I took the serving plate into the dining room where Margret and Alice sat waiting. I poured glasses of sparkling white wine and was about to make a toast when Margret announced she wanted to say grace, something she'd not done for years. I was fearful of what she might say. Alice drew in her breath and took a gulp of wine.

"Dear God," Margret started, unsure of herself, as if writing a letter to him. Alice sighed, but Margret ignored her and continued. "We are extremely grateful for this lovely food we have today. But mostly we thank you for just allowing us to be here." I closed my eyes and bowed my head. "We ask you to support those who don't have their loved ones with them this Christmas, and particularly those who may have lost them recently." I sat still and concentrated on not looking up. "Please look after those that have been taken from us and help those still living to cope with their loss. Amen."

"Amen," I said, and looked up.

Margret's lips were tight together.

Alice's eyes were wet and angry.

"That was very nice, dear," I said.

Margret stared at me until I had to look away.

We began to pass around the dishes. The clinking of plates and knives and forks went some way towards filling the silence. But no one seemed able to speak after Margret's prayer.

Eventually, Alice filled the void.

"Eric loved Christmas."

Margret closed her eyes, inhaled, and opened them again.

I noticed Alice had finished her wine, so I poured her another. It was plain that she was becoming drunk, but I didn't see what harm it would do. I thought it might even make her happy for a while, divert Margret's attention away from me.

Alice took another gulp of wine and looked at both of us.

"I was never that fussed about it."

"Mummy, that's not true," Margret said. "You loved Christmas, too. I remember."

"No, not really, dear. I enjoyed you and your father at Christmas. Not Christmas itself."

Margret looked hurt.

Alice continued.

"He was like a little boy, though, Eric. The lengths he'd go to to please Margret." She almost laughed but seemed to hold herself back.

"One time he got up at four to put her stocking on her bed, then went downstairs to make tea. Then, when he came back up, he said he had an idea."

Margret had stopped eating. She was looking at her mother and holding her mouth firmly shut.

"He went downstairs again, in his pyjamas, silly fool, and took a string of little bells we'd put on the tree. Then he went outside in the freezing cold." She shivered as she remembered. "He hid behind the shed and started ringing the bells. I heard them. I think the whole bloody street heard them. So I went in to peek on Margret, and she was up on her bed looking out of the window, shouting 'Father Christmas. Father Christmas. I can hear him'." She took another mouthful of wine and nodded to herself, staring into her memory as if it were on a TV screen in front of her. "I found out later that several other children in our street had done the same." She stopped and stared again, lost in the images she'd created for herself. Then she took another gulp of wine. "That's why I liked Christmas," she said, "because of Eric."

Margret looked at her mother for a few moments. Alice continued to stare into the past. I wanted to say something, something nice about Eric, but could only think of banalities like *He was a good man* and *We all miss him very much.* No one could miss him as much as Alice. That was obvious. To offer such clichés while images of her dead husband replayed themselves in her mind seemed trivial and dismissive at best. So I said nothing.

We began to eat again in silence, just the thin clinking sounds of cutlery and crockery and Christmas radio filtering in from the lounge.

Alice spoke again.

"Of course, that was when you were little." She looked at Margret. "Eric always said that children made Christmas, that Christmas was all about children."

Margret stopped eating again and looked at her mother. I tried to offer a smile of support, but she would not make eye contact with me.

Alice looked from Margret to me and back again.

"It was always one of Eric's greatest disappointments," she said. "No grandchildren."

Margret put down her cutlery and picked up her glass of wine, her face a silent sculpture of blank deflation. But Alice hadn't finished.

"I explained to him, I don't know how many times, that everyone is different and has different priorities. But he never really understood. He pretended he did but he never really did."

Alice was drunk now. It hadn't taken much. I wondered if she was on medication for her moods and insomnia.

"Mummy," said Margret gently. I admired her patience. "Do you think we might talk about something else?"

Alice looked at her. It was a pronounced look, drunk and concentrated, vaguely confrontational.

"Can't I talk about your father at Christmas, dear? Don't we at least owe him that much?"

Margret took a small, deliberate sip of wine and swallowed and moved her tongue around her lips. Again, I found myself admiring her. But her calm also unnerved me. She excused herself and headed for the kitchen.

Alice watched Margret leave the room, then looked at me as if expecting me to speak.

"I'll get some more wine," I said.

Alice watched me as I got up. She seemed offended to be left alone at the table. I told her I'd just be a second.

Margret did not turn to face me in the kitchen. Instead, she busied herself with the pudding, taking it from its box, then wrapping it in foil.

"Are you alright?" I said.

She stopped but did not turn around. Her shoulders were rigid and hunched over her task.

"Don't, Melvyn," she said. "Don't say anything."

After lunch, Margret insisted on washing up alone. At three o'clock, we sat, as we did every year, watching the Queen and listening to Alice's commentary about the royal family. Princess Margaret's alcoholism and lovers, the power of the Queen Mother, their estate in Balmoral, and how Diana was too young for marriage and would be ruined by them. She spoke about them as if they were neighbours or a family down the street. Then she fell asleep.

Margret and I watched the television for almost two hours and said nothing. I continued to drink the wine I'd opened, but Margret barely touched hers. When I finished the bottle, I opened a red and drank a quick two fingers of whisky. Alice awoke irritable and said she wanted to leave. I called her a taxi, and she gathered her things and sat impatiently back in the armchair in front of the television. We heard the taxi pull up outside, and Alice got up quickly and strode into the hall. She went through the motions of suitable Christmas goodbyes, with kisses and hugs, but seemed uncomfortable and desperate to be gone.

Margret and I stood on the front step in the light from the hall and waved goodbye as the taxi pulled away. Through the condensation of the car's windows, Alice looked like a ghost in the back seat, barely turning her head to look at us and wave as she left.

The fog had settled again, and I was glad I wasn't driving.

"I think I'm going to have a bath," Margret said.

"Really," I said, "on Christmas Day?"

She looked at me for a moment, her frown registering the stupidity of my question.

"Yes," she said, "on Christmas Day. I feel disgusting." She paused as her breath dissipated into the fog. "All that meat and pudding," she added and went inside.

I watched the lights of the taxi disappear into the fog, then went back indoors and straight to the drinks cabinet. I poured a large whisky and took it back through to the lounge. I stopped in the doorway and looked at the tree with its fairy lights and tinsel. Not one of us had opened a gift.

I sat in front of the television and flicked through the channels. I couldn't concentrate. Nothing was funny or entertaining. It was just there, a brightly coloured, confusing babble of jokes, laughter and clapping. I turned it off and sat and drank and listened for noises from upstairs. The house gave the odd creak but otherwise there was silence.

Perhaps it was the amount I'd drunk, but it was hard to battle against the rising notion that I wasn't guilty. It was like a salve or a balm, or some protective chemical released by the brain, like adrenaline to the area of a broken bone, numbing pain too great for the body to stand. I was confused. It had now been nearly a week, and the experience had never been sharp or clear. I remembered my reactions, the things I did immediately after, better than I remembered the incident itself, apart from their tumbling faces.

I heard the bathroom door open upstairs and the soft padding of Margret's feet on the landing. She was light-footed. She always had been. She had a dancer's gait, accentuated when she was unadorned with clothes or shoes, her feet at five to twelve, crossing one in front of each other as she walked.

I sat on the couch, staring at the Christmas tree lights, thinking about Margret in the bedroom applying cream and maybe a little night-time make-up.

I climbed the stairs, not really knowing why or what I would do at the top. The light was already off in the bedroom, so I thought she might have got into bed. I stopped in the doorway and held onto the frame, swaying a little from the wine and whisky. I could not see Margret. When her voice came from off to my left, it startled me.

"Oh," I said. "I thought you'd gone to bed."

She was sitting at her dresser in the dark. I peered round the door so I could see her. She was lit only by the weak light of the streetlamp outside straining through the fog.

"No," she said. "I'm just going to change. It's still early."

"Yes," I said.

I went into the room and sat down on the bed.

She stayed in the same position, facing the mirror. It was too dark to tell if she was looking at herself or me or at nothing at all. The darkness made me nauseous and swoony. I lay back on the bed and breathed deeply through my mouth, but my head swam and the room spun. I could smell the central heating, and the food and alcohol in my stomach and on my breath.

"Was it you, Melvyn?" Margret said. "Is that why the car is at the garage?"

I tried to think about the question and the right way to answer, the right thing to do for her sake as well as mine. But in pausing I *had* answered, as clearly as if I'd shouted, *Yes, it was me!*

Margret sighed and whimpered.

There was a bang as she dropped something onto the wood of her dresser, her hairbrush perhaps. I rolled off the bed and staggered to the bathroom with my stomach and chest rising and my teeth forced shut as my mouth filled with hot, sour liquid and small pieces of undigested food. I burst through the door, not looking for the light switch, and threw myself at the toilet bowl, like a serf begging for mercy at the knees of a vicious master about to flog him. *Shaun's and Paula's faces rolled and tumbled*, along with Margret's, Alice's and even poor Eric's, smiling as he so often did. I heaved and retched until nothing but ropes of snot and saliva hung from my nostrils and mouth, and tears clogged my eyes and soaked my cheeks. I moaned into the echoing toilet bowl that stank with the remnants of my boozy Christmas lunch. The bathroom darkened further. Margret stood in the doorway behind me. I turned and saw her silhouetted against the faint light filtering through from the street. For one moment, I thought she might attack me with whatever she had at hand – hairbrush or eyebrow pencil. But instead, she just stood there, a blank, judgemental shadow in the bathroom doorway, watching as I cowered and half-hugged the toilet.

"I'm sorry!" I cried. "I'm sorry!"

KEVIN

On Boxing Day, we went to the Lyttleton Working Men's Club. It was a family tradition, my favourite part of Christmas. Dad and I had to collect Nan again in the morning. She didn't like to stay the night, so Dad always had to drive her home then do it all over again the next day. When we arrived back home, Mum was cooking for later, homemade pizzas and a big pot of turkey curry. The kitchen window was all steamed over so you couldn't see out. She made a show of kissing everyone, then announced she was running late and we should go ahead without her. Dad looked peeved and worried that Mum would not come at all.

"I'll walk," Mum said.

"It's freezing," said Dad.

"I'll wrap up," Mum replied, surprising us with her curtness.

"You'll catch your death," Nan pitched in. "Why don't you get ready, and I can finish off here."

Nan began to take her coat off.

"No, Mum, please," Mum said. "I just want to take my time. Then I'll walk. I feel like a walk."

Something about the way she said it made Nan back down.

Nan and I waited in the hallway. I heard Dad talking to Mum in the kitchen. Not the words. Just earnest tones and murmurs beneath the babble from the radio and the clangs and bangs of pots and pans.

"It's still our Christmas," I heard Dad say as the door opened. Nan and I pretended not to be listening.

Mum got her way. Dad, Nan and I drove the short distance in the car, and Mum stayed behind to finish up and join us later. The club (as we called it) was about half full in the front bar. I went straight through to the dancehall at the back to see if any kids I knew were there. Two boys of about five or six were running the length of the dance floor and skidding on their knees. There were hundreds of balloons around the edges where the tables were, and the stage was set up for the house band. Back in the front bar, Nan had sat down, and Dad was waiting to be served. I sat with Nan, and she smiled, winked, and popped the clasp on her handbag and offered me an Extra-Strong Mint.

"I prefer Mint Imperials but the shop had run out," she said. "You alright, cocker?"

I told her I was fine.

"These things just happen sometimes," she said. "It's awful. But everyone's just got to get on with it. Otherwise, everything would just stop, wouldn't it? When I was in the WAF, there was always someone not comin' home. You got used to it. Just carried on."

I told her Mum was upset because she knew Shaun Terridge's mum.

"I know that, lover," she said. "I know." She paused and looked around the bar to where Dad was standing. Then she spoke again. "You make sure you look after your mum just now. Give her a bit of support. Yer dad works hard enough for two men if you ask me. Up at Christ knows when in that bloody lorry and not back two days at a time." She shook her head and looked at him. "Yer granddad was the same. Would've worked himself to death if I'd let him." She turned back to me and looked serious. Her face was close to mine, make-up powder dusting the webs of red and blue veins in her cheeks, tiny clumps of pink lipstick in the corners of her mouth. She smelt of Yardley Lily of the Valley, the talcum powder and perfume she kept on a doilied wooden table next to the sink in her spotless bathroom. "And what with them bein' apart an all." She tutted and shook her head again and looked at Dad at the bar. He was talking to a small bald man who only came up to his chest. They were also shaking their heads, their expressions acknowledging the tragedy. "You're fifteen now," Nan said.

"Fourteen," I corrected her.

"Fourteen," she said and tutted again. "That doesn't mean you don't have responsibilities. Both my brothers were working at fourteen, laying bricks. Earning a good living. Things've changed now, I know, for the better if you ask me, but you're a young man now and you can help."

Dad put a bottle of stout on the table for Nan and a Coke and some nuts for me. He seemed to register that Nan and I had been talking. I must have looked concerned. I was worried by the idea of Mum needing support. I had no clue how to support her. I thought that was Dad's job, not mine.

Some of Dad's football friends arrived, and I was ordered to give up my seat. There was a lot of handshaking and fussing over Nan, more drinks bought, and questions for Dad as to Mum's whereabouts. He said she was finishing the cooking and coming later. When she finally arrived, Dad looked relieved, then relaxed, then happy. Again, there was lots of hugging and fussing and people finding seats. The main bar got busier, the jukebox louder, the hanging ceiling of blue smoke thicker. Dad stood at the bar with a large circle of men, while the women, including Nan and Mum, sat round a low table with their drinks, smoking and talking constantly. I wondered what they were talking about. It seemed every single one of them was talking at once. They would touch each other on the arm or the shoulder and lean in close as if to say something important. I couldn't imagine what they might be saying, or that there might be so many important things to say.

LISA

If Christmas Day had been a mostly empty affair, tears, television and not much else, Boxing Day made up for it with trauma. Neil arrived with Stacy and the kids at eleven, and I wasn't ready. I'd been up for hours but I'd dawdled at every opportunity, staring at photographs for ten minutes whilst drifting through whole periods of the past, sitting in my dressing gown at the kitchen table, watching the grey light brighten outside the window as the morning wore mercilessly on. I felt like a living cliché of grief, slow and pondering, talking to myself and Shaun, prone to sudden floods of tears and anger, dreading the prospect of going outside and being on show to the people of Lyttleton.

Neil was frustrated by my slowness, my lateness. The soldier in him had kicked in, the paratrooper. The tearful drunk from earlier in the week had gone. He had a new crew cut and was freshly shaved. He had on his green army sweater with the epaulettes on the shoulders. His eyes were bright and his cheeks were flushed pink from a cold run along the beach that morning. He went around the house, tidying and looking at his watch. As I finished getting ready upstairs, I could hear him pottering around, grumbling about how the bar would be shut by the time we got there.

When I came down ready, he scrutinised my clothes like some sergeant major checking for creases or stains. He frowned at the black fake fur coat I wore. I'd inherited it from Mum. It was ancient but I hadn't been able to bring myself to get rid of it. It smelt slightly fusty from its years in the cupboard, but it was black and it was warm, and with the collar up it hid me to the tip of my nose.

Neil asked about the ash in the fireplace. We hadn't used it since Neil had paid for the central heating to be installed. No need, he always said, *Why have dirty and dangerous when you can have clean and safe*. I told him I'd had a sudden fancy for a fire, for old times' sake. Only the whitest of lies. He answered that I was lucky I hadn't suffocated or burnt down the house. I didn't tell him about the magazines. What good would it have done? And anyway, Neil was a man and a soldier. He'd probably given them to Shaun in the first place.

We filed out of the house to the car. The kids were giddy and oblivious, dressed in their Christmas best, sugared up and armed with brand-new Christmas toys. I asked Neil if they knew, and he mumbled that he was working on it. Stacy got in the back with them, which I appreciated. I wasn't feeling much like being Auntie Lisa. I wasn't feeling much like being anything at all. As we drove away, I felt the safety of home stretch and snap like a thin rubber band inside me. I longed to be back inside the house, alone with the ghost of my son.

The nearer we got to the club, the more anxious I became. We arrived in the car park and I saw that it was almost full. I was hot inside Mum's fake fur and desperate for air. The freezing cold outside the car was a brief respite of freedom, and I took great lungfuls of foggy air and blew out clouds of steam as we approached the doors. I could hear music and voices from inside but I daren't snatch a glance at the window for fear of catching someone's eye. Inside the foyer, Neil offered to take my coat and hand it in to the cloakroom. I declined even though I was too warm. I kept the collar high in a vain attempt to remain hidden. We approached the double doors into the main lounge bar and as they opened ahead of me, the rush of noise, heat, voices, laughter, smoke and stink of warming beer and spirits took my breath away and hit me with a wave of nausea that filled me from my feet to the top of my head. We entered the bar and the din faded out to silence, apart from some Christmas song on the jukebox. All I could do was hold on to myself and stop myself from being sick right there in front of the staring eyes of just about everyone who knew me, glasses half raised towards their mouths, faces registering a whole gamut of emotions from sympathy to downright disappointment that the holy grail of Boxing Day had been ruined by the arrival of the Lyttleton's most recently bereaved.

KEVIN

At around two, the Terridges came through the big swing doors. A stunned, uncomfortable silence crept around the bar like a fast-working infection. People stopped talking or were tapped sharply on the shoulder if they hadn't noticed. It started in the corner by the fruit machines. Dad and his crowd fell silent all at once. That caused the bar staff to note the sudden change in mood. Then the people along the bar all fell silent too and watched the Terridges. The silence crawled over us to the next table and the next, all the way to the darts players near the front window, until everyone in the main bar of the Lyttleton Working Men's Club was silent. It hung there for a full minute, the silence, trapped beneath the blue hanging ceiling of cigarette smoke. Lisa Terridge looked hollowed out, as if she'd not eaten for days. Maybe she hadn't. She stared out over the high collar of a black fur coat, confused and black-eyed, like someone woken from a long coma.

It was Mum who broke the trance. She stood up as I watched, mortified, as if she were making some dreadful mistake. She went to Lisa and hugged her and began to talk to her in a low voice. Then someone else, another woman from the group next to Dad's did the same, and then several more people followed, and the noise of conversation returned and again became the inarticulate din of a large, busy lounge bar.

Lisa was overwhelmed. She wept and was comforted by what must have seemed like the whole of Lyttleton. Tables were rearranged so she and her brother's family could be seated. A stiffened normality continued until the bell was rung for last orders and the bar closed. There was much less of the usual riotous laughter. Rather, a sombre level of conversation and pleasure, quite unsuited to the season.

I kept looking over to the Terridges' table. There were two or three extra people there constantly, women mostly, coming to pay their respects by kneeling down alongside Lisa's chair, holding onto her arm, and nodding and shaking their heads. When Lisa's brother went to the bar, he had to fight his way through well-wishers and offers to buy his drinks. He was patted on the back by sighing, headshaking men and seemed close to tears by the time he got served.

Neil Terridge had a serious face, tight white skin and cropped hair. He sat next to his sister Lisa. Every now and then he would place his hand firmly in the crook of her elbow. He made several trips to the bar but seemed to get no pleasure from his drinks. He nodded to whoever spoke to his sister and took long, careful gulps from his pints of lager, saying nothing. He caught my eye once or twice but did not acknowledge me in any way. When I asked Mum later about Neil, she said that Shaun had been like a son to him, and he had taken his death very badly.

LISA

Neil stopped dead in his tracks. Even the kids, whose babble had been incessant since their arrival earlier that morning, momentarily froze in wonder at the sudden silence and attention that now confronted them. Of all the dreadful moments I remember from that week, this is the one that haunts me in my nightmares, like a dream of being naked in public or paralysis at the need to escape. And just as it became too much, and I felt myself about to turn and run for the safety of a bathroom cubicle, the sharp sound of a chair being moved broke the spell, and a whole table of people began to stand up and start clearing a space for us to sit. Then they came forward, one at first and then more, with soft voices and softer grasps, ushering us to our seats like victims chosen for sacrifice. I had no idea who they were. I recognised their faces but their names escaped me. They spoke to me gently, sat me down, and proceeded to bring us drink after drink. But I heard only sympathetic murmurs and the echoes of platitudes and my own voice, for some reason, thanking them. Because that's what we have to do when we lose someone; we have to thank everyone who is forced to show their concern and offer their condolences.

To this day, I have no idea how long we stayed there, maybe an hour, maybe two. We passed the time in stunned silence, apart from thanking people for drinks and well-wishes. Neil, at whose insistence we'd all been forced to come, sat close to me throughout the ordeal, oftentimes holding onto my arm so tight that I could feel his grip through the thick fake fur of Mum's old coat. From the outside looking in, it must have appeared as brotherly support for the weaker sister and mother. But I could tell from the tension in that grip, how it tightened from time to time as various patrons of the Lyttleton Working Men's Club came to pay their respects, that this was the grip of the little boy, hanging on to his sister's arm for dear life, the same grip as on the ghost train at Barmush Fair, the same grip as the one in my bed in the dark when Dad had thundered up the stairs bellowing like a monster.

We must have stayed until closing time because I remember the barman ringing the bell and shouting at everyone to drink up and go home. We'd stayed, I guess, not because we wanted to but because leaving may have drawn the same silence as arriving had, and none of us wanted that again. We must have been drunk, considering how many drinks we'd been bought. Just a big blur of faces and voices, then the cold air of the car park again, the grey fog of the short drive home, more drinks and snacks in the kitchen as the children played and bickered, and then Neil helping me up the stairs to bed, offering only the weakest resistance to my demand that it be in Shaun's room.

*

The funeral was held in the old Lyttleton Church, just a few hundred yards from the site of the accident. Paula's was on the same day. There'd been brief talk of a joint service but Paula's parents had put paid to this idea almost immediately. They had, by all accounts, tolerated Paula's relationship with Shaun, but they had not been fans. Paula's father, Ken, owned a car sales firm in Hareham. He was a member of the local Rotary Club. He golfed and hobnobbed with well-to-do publicans, high-ranking policemen and other local businessmen. According to Neil, Ken was a *rich wanker* who'd suffered his daughter's liaison with a Lyttleton council house boy to keep her and his wife happy. But there was a line, and the association, as far as Ken was concerned, would not continue after his little princess's death. He had stopped short of holding Shaun responsible. How could he blame a popular local dead boy when police were still looking for a hit-and-run drunk driver? But Neil had said he'd heard it in Ken's voice when they'd spoken on the phone, the insinuation that had Paula not fallen in with village riffraff, she might still be alive today. The call had ended with Neil calling Ken a "snobby cunt" and telling him he was "not fit to walk the ground that Shaun'll be buried in." And so it was that a family who may have become our in-laws, had things worked out differently, became our unseen enemies before we'd even had the time or opportunity to meet them, our potential ties having been nipped in the bud, much like the lives of our Shaun and their Paula.

The day of the funeral passed in a foggy shroud, much the same as the one draped over that whole midwinter. The "Southern Freeze", as the local paper called it, had not lifted since its arrival in early December. It sat like a misty death pall over the whole of Lyttleton, giving the village a ghostly, quiet atmosphere, as if its voice was solemnly lowered in respect for the recently deceased. I, for one, was thankful. The fog helped hide my mourning. But I did wonder, here and there, if it had aided the driver by hiding him as well. I raised this point to Neil as we sat in the back of the car on the way to the church. He looked at me sideways, as if I'd said something ridiculous. Then he assured me that it would make no difference. When I asked a question about whether the gravediggers would be able to dig Shaun's grave out of the frozen ground, he put his hand on my arm and said, "Leece, please, let's not worry about stuff that's not our concern." I wanted to tell him that Shaun's final resting place was very much my concern, but I let the subject drop all the same.

In the church, the vicar droned on about youth and about how we are all God's children and how Shaun would be welcomed into the Lord's arms in Heaven. I hated this idea and wanted to scream, *If he loved him that much, he should have let him stay with his mum!* When the service was over, Neil and three of his para friends, all in their uniforms, carried Shaun's coffin down through the freezing graveyard. I followed behind, alongside the vicar, at the head of a large train of sombre Lyttleton locals. When we arrived at the open grave, Shaun's coffin was laid on a strip of fake turf alongside. The crowd formed a thick human horseshoe around the frosted hole. And from my place in the centre, directly opposite the foot of the grave, I could now scan the faces of some of the mourners. I recognised most of them as friends of Shaun, football club members, and several teachers from Lyttleton Secondary. But there were also faces I didn't recognise, and they prompted the dreadful idea that *he* might be there, the driver, drawn by his own guilt to pay his final respects, apologise, and repent at the graveside. When I mentioned this to Neil later, he bristled visibly inside his uniform, as if someone had walked over *his* grave.

The wake was back at the Working Men's Club. This, again, had all been arranged by Neil. The club put out soup, sandwiches and sausage rolls and free glasses of sherry and cans of lager and bitter. We didn't have to pay for a thing because of our family's long-standing membership. I didn't want to go there ever again after Boxing Day, but Neil felt we had to offer something to those who'd come out on a freezing cold morning to pay their respects to us and to Shaun. *Couldn't we just come home and be done with it?* I'd argued. *Is it not enough to be on show while I bury my son? Do I have to then thank everyone and watch them get drunk and stuff their faces?* He hadn't said as much but I knew Neil had thought I was being selfish. I could see it in his eyes. Instead, he had told me that Shaun had been a big part of the community and that the community had the right to give him a proper send-off. He'd emphasised the word *community* as contrast to my selfishness. And in a way, he'd been right. As far as I was concerned at the time, the whole community could have gone and taken a running jump off one of the sewage groynes that stuck out into the sea.

As it turned out, the wake was not as traumatic as Boxing Day. This time I was ready and I knew what to expect. An endless stream of people talking to me like I was a child or a sick dog, touching the crook of my elbow and looking like they might cry. Some of them did. And I had to comfort *them*. The low point was Vicky Sharp, tipsy after one too many Babyshams, leaning all over Neil and telling him how her family were thinking of our family every day, and how the whole of Lyttleton would help us through. I wanted to remind her that my brother was married and ask her out loud, so *the whole of Lyttleton* could hear, *How, exactly, would the whole of Lyttleton help us through?*

The only person I was happy to see there was Dreek. He only made a brief appearance, ignoring the glances and hush that always followed him around a room. I felt for him. A desperately private man cursed with an imposing uniform and the height of a giant. He stood in front of me with tears in his eyes, his large frame and gigantic shoulders blocking out the rest of the room. Then he hugged me and his enormous bear arms gathered me into the folds of his police jacket. I would have willingly stayed there but for the realisation of the eyes of Lyttleton Working Men's Club lounge bar watching, recording and judging. When he released me from his embrace, he held me at arms' length in a concrete grip and said, "If you ever need anything, anything at all."

I told him I needed a lift home, and he waited patiently as I gathered up my coat and bag, as the whole wake watched with questions on their lips, and Neil glared as if tied up while, in slow motion, someone stole all his possessions.

Outside, I barely made it to the Panda car without falling. I staggered in my heels, and Dreek steadied me with a grip of my shoulder and an arm about my waist.

"Come on," he said. "Let's get yae home."

We drove in silence along the foggy and ghostly streets and lanes of Lyttleton, and Dreek's quiet presence next to me was just enough to temper the sense of the end of things. With Shaun buried, I realised that the limbo of the previous two weeks had only been a preamble to what was ahead, the rest of the winter, the new year, and all the years to come without him. When we arrived at the kerb outside the house, I looked up at my bedroom window and remembered standing there, looking down at Dreek's Panda car, parked exactly where we sat now. I invited him in for tea but he declined the offer, looking uncomfortable, saying he had work to do. The earlier spell cast by his affection had been broken, as if the drive from the club through the village he knew so well had given him time to shrink back inside his uniform and remember his role as community policeman, not knight in shining armour. I put my hand on his giant hand as it gripped the steering wheel, and I thanked him for the lift home and for everything else he'd done. He nodded and stared at my hand on his and then ahead at the MOD KEEP OUT sign at the end of the road.

"Don't forget what I said," he whispered without looking at me. "Anything you need…"

We both knew he couldn't give me what I needed. What I needed was my son back and a husband to take care of me.

I got out of the car, and he started the ignition immediately. I stood on the pavement in the freezing fog and watched him turn in the circle at the end of the close. I waved as he drove past me and lifted one big hand off the steering wheel as goodbye. Then I watched as the car disappeared into the fog. Only its lights were visible as it reached the main road and turned back towards the village centre.

PART II

The Dead of Spring

KEVIN

Some idiot came up with the idea that our next game of catch and kill should take place at night in the old Lyttleton churchyard. I knew this was a bad idea. But I went along with it anyway. The game was discussed at school all week. There would need to be new rules for this special version. It was agreed that digs (beatings for those captured) would be too noisy for the graveyard. Jase protested, arguing that catch and kill without digs was not catch and kill.

"We might ath well play fuckin' kith chathe," he hissed through his lisp.

There were meant to be ten of us, five per side. But when Saturday night came at the arranged time and place, seven o'clock outside the Spar, there were only five: Jase, Geddy, Parker, Walks and me, sat in the cold, waiting for the others.

"Where the fuck are they?" Geddy moaned.

"Bottled it," said Jase.

I scanned every passing car for Mum or Dad, every pedestrian, jogger, dog walker and cyclist for anyone who might know my parents. I'd told Mum I was going round to Walks's to watch a video. He'd told his mum he was coming to mine.

"I think we should go," I said.

"Worried about Mummy or Daddy theeing you?" said Jase.

"No," I lied. "I'm freezing sittin' 'ere."

We waited a little longer while Jase went into the shop to buy cigarettes. He never got asked for ID and would often boast that he could even buy booze. I'd never seen him do it, but other kids had verified this. I couldn't understand where his money came from. He didn't have a paper round like some of us, but he always seemed to have money. Parker had told me he stole it from his mum. Jase came out of the shop and spat through the gap where one of his front teeth was broken.

"Cuntth wouldn't even let me buy four canth of fuckin' Thkona," he said and spat again.

So we all had to wait with Jase in the cold for anyone who might take his money and buy him beer.

Alan Mitchell appeared from around the corner of the shop and came and stood nearby, pale, snivelly and shivery as usual. He sniffed and wiped his nose on his sleeve, spat a couple of times and kicked at a ridge between two uneven slabs of pavement.

"What the fuck do you want?" Jase said.

A smattering of laughter.

"What you doin'?" Alan said.

Parker began to answer, but Jase butted in, "None of your fuckin' bithnith, Mitchell."

Alan pretended to laugh.

"Leave him alone, Jase," Walks said.

Jase rolled his eyes and mimicked Walks in a high-pitched voice, "Leave him alone, Jathe!"

"Old church for catch and kill," Walks said. "You wanna come? Six'll make it even-steven."

"Well done, Einthtein," Jase sneered.

Alan came and stood nearer with his hands in his pockets, still shivering.

"Where's your coat?" Walks said to him.

"Left it at home," he said. "I thought it was warmer."

"Yeah, right," Jase said. "More like you can't afford one."

Two older boys approached and Jase went to ask them if they'd buy his cans.

Jase was strong for his age with a vicious temper. A play-fight with Jase could end in serious bruising, fat lips, or an arm twisted so far back it was useless for a day or two. I'd seen him demolish boys of eighteen and nineteen who'd mocked the way he talked. His thick lisp gave his speech a camp turn of phrase. He even played on it now and again to amuse his friends. Once, however, outside the community centre, an older boy, Mark Davis, sat on his scooter with his girlfriend on the back, had told Jase that if he "kept talking like a poof," he'd "end up being bummed like one." Davis had had about half a second to laugh at his own joke before Jase had split his nose and sent him and his girlfriend reeling off his bike. Jase had then stood over him, kicking his ribs while his girlfriend screamed at Jase until he backhanded her off her feet too.

I was scared of him. We all were. He was unpredictable. But at fourteen you can't tell someone like Jase you don't want them around. You just humour them and hope that one day they'll move on.

He came out of the shop smiling with a bulging carrier bag.

"How many d'you get?" said Geddy.

"Got a few ecthtrath, didn't I, tho you cuntth wouldn't whinge about it."

This was classic Jase. He'd surprise you with generosity, and you'd think, *maybe he's not so bad after all.* Then he'd throw your school bag over the fence of a lekkie substation, gob a greenie in your Panda Pop, or give you the worst Chinese burn of your life.

"Nice one, mate," said Geddy.

Geddy was bigger than Jase, and almost certainly stronger, but he didn't have Jase's temper or propensity for violence. They were similar in some ways, but Geddy liked being fourteen and doing stupid fourteen-year-old stuff. Jase, on the other hand, seemed to be just killing time until he could get into the local pubs with his older brothers. You could leap on Geddy's back and he would play-fight without maiming you, like a tamed bear. You wouldn't dare do that with Jase. He would pin you down and throttle you or kneel on your stomach till you pissed yourself or give you the screwdrivers into your temples or petrol pump your arms until you screamed for him to stop. He liked inflicting pain and humiliation.

We walked along Apple Tree Lane in the dark to the Old Church Road. There was a small flimsy-looking sapling near to where Shaun Terridge and Paula Werth had been killed back before Christmas. Walks shone his torch on the tree. Some flowers had been placed around the thin trunk. Most were brown, drooping and dead, and the ink on the cards had run, as if the messages had cried themselves illegible.

"Ahh, that'th thad, init?" said Jase.

We looked at the small patch of torch-light and the collection of dead flowers and wet cards. Somebody had tied a football scarf around a branch, but the white stripe down its middle had become dirty and grey. It looked miserable and sodden in the beam of the torch, like it belonged to a tramp or a dug-up corpse.

"Shaun coulda been a pro," Geddy said. "Best in the vill, easy."

Jase sniffed and spat through the gap in his chipped tooth.

At the church, I drank my can of lager and tried to imagine myself dead. I could see myself white and dark-eyed like a zombie, but it was still me and not my empty body. There was a consciousness I couldn't escape. I couldn't imagine myself simply not existing, not being able to think or feel. Death was inexplicable, unreal, especially when it happened to someone you knew, someone you'd seen score four goals on a Saturday afternoon just a few weeks before. Someone so alive.

We picked teams for catch and kill, and I was with Jase and Alan. After winning spuds and choosing to run first, we trotted off down the wall to the locked gate near the stream and climbed over.

The churchyard was split into two halves with a path that crossed a small, ancient stone bridge. The side where we came in was newer and had a road leading to a large gate onto a lane at the back. We crossed the stream at the bridge and went into the old part of the churchyard, more crowded with graves, some broken at crooked angles, black in the dark, silhouettes of crosses, angels and cherubs.

Most kids in Lyttleton had been to the graveyard at some point, either to play or to look at the graves. I'd come several times with Emma Hanes, my first girlfriend. We'd looked at the graves then gone round the back of the church to smoke and kiss until it had grown dark and we had to go home for tea. I thought about Emma as we ran low between the graves following Jase. I'd heard a rumour she wanted to go out with me again. The idea made me nervous. She'd been going out with Roy Chivers, who was sixteen and had a motorbike. He'd told me to "fuck off" once when I'd been speaking to Emma after school.

"Where we going?" Alan whispered.

"Shut up and follow me!" Jase said.

We moved between the graves and made our way up to the path near the old church itself. There was a large war memorial there, three square marble slabs, decreasing in size up to a tall stone needle with names of the dead on all sides. In the dark it looked even bigger than usual. We went round behind it and crouched on the steps so we could look back down the hill towards the stream, where Geddy, Parker and Walks would come from. We couldn't see them. Either they were in the other part of the churchyard, or they were coming around the perimeter to fool us. It was unlikely they'd split up. None of them would want to be hunting on their own in the graveyard.

It didn't matter how hard you were. Old Lyttleton churchyard was spooky. There had been a spate of ghost sightings there since some of the church-owned land had been sold off for housing. The old dear who owned the Manor House Hotel next door had seen phantom monks there in the middle of the night. Most locals had put the sighting down to her loneliness, her penchant for barley wine, and her need to attract guests by any means possible.

"Come on," said Jase.

We followed him up to the main door of the church. There was a large fir tree off to the left by the wall that bordered the hotel. Between the wall and the church, there was a gap of about five or six feet that ran down the side to a small private graveyard for parish vicars.

Jase ran over to the gap.

"Yeth!" he said. "Come on!"

About halfway along the gap, a small tower of scaffolding reached up to the roof. Within the outer poles, ladders zigzagged up to the top through wooden planks. Jase climbed up to the first level.

"Come on," he whispered. "Hurry up!"

We ran along the gap between the church and the wall, keeping our heads down out of the light from the Manor House. Jase carried on up the zig-zag ladders to the top, and we followed him, slowly, trying to be quiet. When we were all crouched on the top deck, about twenty feet up, Jase told us to wait. He climbed onto the roof's gable, with a leg on either side as if riding a gigantic black horse, then slid himself along towards the middle. Alan began to do the same.

"Fuckin' wait there!" Jase whispered.

Alan stopped and crouched next to me.

Jase got to the middle of the roof and laid himself low along the gable so he could peer over into the churchyard and down the hill. He turned his head back towards us.

"They're comin'," he whispered, and he began to push himself backwards along the gable to the scaffolding. "Let'th get back down and hide round the back."

But then we heard Geddy's voice from the front of the church.

"Fuck!" Jase said, and he put his finger in front of his lips. "Thhhhh."

We all crouched low on the planks.

We could hear them at the entrance to the gap.

"Shit," said Walks. "I thought they'd be here."

Jase stifled a laugh. So did Alan.

We waited.

They came along the gap to the bottom of the scaffolding and stopped.

We stared at each other in the dark, hardly breathing.

"Fuck it," said Geddy. "They're probably down by the stream."

We listened to them walk back along the gap. Their voices got quieter until we couldn't hear them.

"Fuckin' twatth!" Jase whispered and started back down one of the ladders. We followed him down. On the second floor of the scaffolding, about fifteen feet up from the ground, he stopped and waited for us. We could see into the garden of the manor, the ivied walls of the house dark around the lit windows.

Jase pointed at a narrow slit in the church wall.

"You know what that ith?" he said.

"What?" I said.

"Leper thquint," he whispered.

I told him it was just an old window.

"What's a leper squint?" Alan asked in the dark.

"It'th where the leperth yooth to beg for food, you idiot!" Jase lisped.

"It's too high up," I said. "The lepers'd 'ave to be massive."

Alan laughed.

"What you laughin' at?" Jase said. "There yooth to be thtepth 'ere. The leperth came up and begged for food through that window. I dare you to look into it."

"Why?" said Alan.

"Thee if you've got any bottle, that'th why."

"I'll look in it," I said.

"I didn't fuckin' dare *you*, did I?" said Jase.

"Come on, let's get down," I said, and I started towards the ladder.

"Fuckin' wait," Jase said. "I mean it."

I waited by the ladder.

"Come on, Mitchell," said Jase. "We've all done it."

I wanted to protest that this was bullshit but Jase read my mind and glared at me in the dark, eyes all psycho, *don't even think about it!*

Alan sighed and crept up to the slit in the wall. He paused then went on tiptoe and peered into the gap.

"Clother!" Jase said.

Alan moved his face closer to the gap.

Jase grabbed the back of his neck and pushed his face hard into the gap so that it disappeared up to his ears.

Alan made a high-pitched sound, and Jase pushed his face harder into the hole.

"That hurts," Alan squealed, sounding as if he was about to cry.

Jase bent close to his ear.

"Leper thquint," Jase whispered. "Leper thquint!"

Alan's cries echoed in the hole.

"Leper thquint," Jase whispered. "Leper thquint!"

Alan started hyperventilating as if he was panicking. He pushed backwards against Jase's grip. Then he screamed, and it echoed inside the church.

Jase held him there while he struggled, then suddenly let him go.

Alan staggered back fast and fell backwards over a low scaffold bar. There was a crack, a tumbling and crashing sound and the scaffolding wobbled and something fell off one of the planks above and hit several bars on the way down as Jase and I ducked and covered our heads with our hands. I held my breath, fearing the whole structure would collapse or topple over the wall. But then it steadied and was silent again.

"Alan!" I whispered down into the dark. "Alan!"

No answer.

"Mitchell," Jase said. "Mitchell, for fuck'thake!"

Nothing.

We waited.

Jase said nothing.

We climbed back down the ladder to the first floor.

"Alan," I whispered again.

He still didn't answer.

Panic started to flow through me. A sudden damp warmth in the front of my pants. I stopped and tensed and held it in.

We stood on the first floor of the scaffolding, our feet level with the top of the wall. We leant out as far as we could without falling but neither of us could see down the opposite side of the wall. It was too dark. The lights from the Manor House windows did not reach to the perimeter of the garden and we were obstructed by the wall itself.

We climbed down and ran back along the gap to the front of the church, then took the path to the front gate. I heard Walks spot us.

"There they are!"

We stopped and waited for them to get to us.

"He jutht fell off, right!" Jase whispered close to my ear, his fingers digging into the soft crook of my elbow.

I said nothing but watched the three shadowy figures making their way through the graves, Geddy at the back, big square head like Oddbod Junior from *Carry on Screaming.*

Parker got to us first, grinning and puffing. Then he stopped twenty feet away by a gravestone.

"What's up?" he said. "Why aren't you running?

"We need to go and find Alan," I said.

"Why?" said Parker. "Where is he?"

Geddy and Walks were alongside him now, puffing in the dark.

"Little twat fell off the thcaffolding," said Jase.

"You were on the scaffolding?" Geddy said, smiling.

"We need to see if he's alright," I said.

I started walking towards the gate. I could hear the others talking behind me.

"What happened?" Walks asked Jase.

"He jutht fell!" Jase said. "It'th your fuckin' fault for inviting 'im."

We went out through the front gate of the church, along the iron fence and the old brick wall of the Manor House. At the driveway we stopped and peered into the garden. We could hear kitcheny noises from the back, a snippet of voice, the faint banging of plates and cutlery and pans, but nothing else. There were lights on in the house itself, but no noise of people or activity. The light from the porch reached only a few feet into the front garden, leaving a dark expanse of ground before the hedges that bordered the perimeter wall.

"Come on," I said.

"Wait!" said Parker.

"What?" I said.

"Someone should be lookout," he said.

"You stay here, then," I said.

"Okay," he said.

"Fuckin' chicken!" Jase whispered.

The rest of us ran into the large shadow that stretched along the front of the garden all the way to the corner by the churchyard.

I stopped there and waited for the other three.

Walks reached me first.

He knelt beside me.

"This is stupid," he said. "Alan probably just went home."

I thought about it. It was possible he'd got up and sneaked off. I hoped he had. I pictured him walking back along Apple Tree Lane in the dark, shivering and crying, holding onto some injured part of himself.

When the other two got to us at the corner of the garden, I ran low along the edge of the thick bushes next to the side wall that bordered the churchyard. I got to where I could see the scaffolding on the other side of the wall and stopped. I looked at the house and waited for any sound or a light to come on. The others arrived and stopped. Geddy was puffing like a big bear in the dark.

"This is where he fell," I whispered.

I could feel the wetness in my crotch now beginning to cool.

"He'th not here!" said Jase. "Let'th fuckin' go!"

"Wait!" I said. "Walks, gimme your torch."

Walks gave it to me.

I switched it on and shone the beam at the bushes.

"Turn it off, you idiot!" Jase said. "Thumwun'll thee!"

"Wait!" I said.

I managed to step into a thinner part, where the branches of two hedges met, then worked my way in towards the wall. I could feel the cold wetness through my clothes. The leaves gave off a sodden, sweet-rotten smell, like gutters and drains after heavy rain. When I reached the wall, I had to crane my neck and stand on tiptoe to see the others.

"Fuckin' hurry up!" Jase said.

I shone the torch towards the scaffolding, up to the second level from where Alan had fallen, then down onto the wall. I knelt and shone the torch along the foot of the wall at the back of the bushes.

Nothing.

I sighed and turned off the torch and closed my eyes for just a few seconds. I had half-expected to see Alan Mitchell's white face, eyes open, head twisted round the wrong way. But there was nothing there, just mud and the dark roots of hedges, shrubs, bushes and small trees.

"He's not here," I whispered.

"Derr!" said Jase. "Let'th fuckin' go!"

*

On Monday after school, Mum told me Alan Mitchell was dead. The details were patchy. People had their own take on what had happened. Some were putting it down to his father, known locally as a gypsy and a heavy drinker. Rumour had it that Alan's mother, Susan, had found him unconscious in bed at two o'clock on Sunday afternoon. The men of the house, Alan's dad and uncle, had been at a car auction in Hambledon. In her panic at not being able to wake Alan, Susan Mitchell had phoned the Lyttleton surgery and had been automatically transferred to Dr Dawe, who had scolded her for not calling an ambulance. He did so, and one arrived promptly. But Alan had never regained consciousness.

By Monday evening many people in Lyttleton knew of Alan's death. His absence from school had not bothered any of us particularly. We had simply assumed that if he'd got up and gone home after his fall, then surely he was fine. And anyway, Alan was regularly absent from school, doing gypsy stuff with his dad or just skiving off to avoid his bullies. When he was there, he was often unwashed and without most or all of his uniform. He smelt fusty and cheesy, his nose always ran, and he was regularly teased and abused. And when he wasn't there, nobody noticed. So when I came home from school that day and Mum sat me down and warned me she had some very sad news, I did not expect it to be about Alan.

As she told me, I found myself hoping against my better knowledge that the gossip was true, that Alan had been beaten by his father or one of his uncles, and this was the cause of his death.

"What happened to him?" I asked, picturing his head jammed in the church wall, Jase lisping into his ear.

"I don't know," Mum said, and she got up to fetch the teapot over to the table.

I could see her thinking through what to say.

"Not all families," she said, choosing her words carefully, then pausing, reconsidering, then starting again. "Some families," she said, "have got a lot of problems."

I wanted to say, "What, like us?" but resisted.

She stopped again and poured the tea.

"I think Alan's family has a lot of problems," she said.

"Did Alan's Dad kill him?" I said, hoping she'd say yes.

Instead, she looked at me and furrowed her brow and curled her lips inward until they disappeared.

"I don't know," she said. "Possibly." She paused, thinking. "But you mustn't say that to anyone. Do you understand me?" Her look darkened. "I mean it, Kevin. This is very serious. People can't just go around spouting gossip, not about something like this."

She paused again and made another troubled face. Then she sighed and looked defeated.

"It's just too awful for words," she said. "That poor little boy. Thirteen."

She began to cry but then stopped herself.

Panic rose in me again and my bladder ached. Mum rubbed her eyes and apologised. I should have cried as well, for the same reasons as Mum, for Alan Mitchell's short, unhappy life, for all the times I'd heard him called *stinky, smelly, fleabag and gyppo*, for all the times he'd been left out or not picked for teams, for the days he'd spent alone, bunking off to avoid the horrors of school, for the time he was dragged into the toilets by his hood and had his head shoved in a flushing bowl, for being wedgied and having the other kids mock his dirty, threadbare underpants. I'd been to school with him for nearly ten years, from infants through juniors to seniors, but I didn't even know him. No one did. I'd never been to his house, nor had he to mine. He didn't have any friends. Kids spoke to him here and there and let him tag along now and again like we had. But I couldn't think of one boy or girl who would have named him among their friends. He wasn't in any teams or clubs, he didn't get invited to birthdays or sleepovers or video nights, and no one phoned him on the weekend to see what he was doing. I would bet that no one even knew his number. But even as I felt sorry and guilty for Alan's miserable life and my small part in it, I prayed that he had been killed by his father and not by his fall from the scaffolding in the churchyard. Such was my desire for that to be true, I even imagined the scenario: Alan arriving home and his dad confronting him in the hallway, knocking him into the bannisters with a swipe of his big hand, Alan staggering up the stairs with his drunken father bellowing behind him, Alan crawling into bed, bleeding, never to wake up again.

*

By Friday of that week, I was exhausted and fearful. The night before at dinner, Mum had told me Alan's father had been released without charge. She had seemed relieved. She preferred to see the good in people and enjoyed seeing the Lyttleton gossips proven wrong.

"But even if he is innocent," she said, "he'll always be under suspicion around here."

Twice on the way to school I had to stop and find somewhere to piss. Once behind the big metal bins on the forecourt of the old Lyttleton Hall, and once by the ancient fir tree next to the cricket hut in the Rec. Every small boy with brown hair looked like Alan, every larger boy with black hair, Jase. I'd not seen him since the weekend. He'd not been at school on Monday or Tuesday. Not unusual for Jase. His mum went to work early most mornings. If he wanted to skive, he simply stayed home, watched videos, smoked fags and made sure he was in his uniform by five with a story or two about school if asked. On Wednesday and Thursday, I'd managed to avoid him. So by Friday I was dreading him.

At morning register we were told there was a special school assembly. Almost unheard of. The only time I'd known of it happening before was when Mr Toller, the previous headmaster, had died suddenly in his sleep. Many students and teachers had cried openly as we'd sung "All Things Bright and Beautiful," his favourite hymn. It had been my first experience of public grief, apart from when Elvis and John Lennon had died, but those had been mostly on the telly.

As the class began the short trip across the school square to the assembly hall, my bladder again felt full and sore. I began to sweat and smelt a trace of urine emanating from my body, an unwashed patch of skin, perhaps, after another night of nightmares and bed-stripping. I glanced around at my classmates, but they were all whispering about the assembly and taking no notice of me.

We filed into the main hall. Mrs Harrison was telling students to get seated quickly and quietly. She was deputy head, a tiny woman with an enormous voice that could stop schoolkid nonsense from a hundred yards away. The front-row seats were taken by first and second years. Several teachers were in hushed conference on the stage.

I shuffled along a row with the rest of my class until the line came to a halt and we sat down. Then I scanned the backs of the heads in front of me, looking for Jase or Geddy or Parker or Walks. I spotted Parker, and he nodded, then looked away. I looked behind me. Jase was looking at me from the back row, diagonally along a line of heads facing front. He pointed at me and mouthed the words, *lunchtime, copth.*

I turned back to face the front. PC Dreek, holding his police cap in both hands, was now talking with teachers on the stage. I felt sick and my bladder throbbed. My hands were slick with sweat, my collar tight around my throat. I bent my head forward so that my chin was on my chest. Then I undid my top button and loosened my school tie.

The hall quietened and Mrs Harrison stepped forward.

"Good morning," she said, her voice serious and sombre.

"Good morning," the students responded in unison.

"Before we hear from the headmaster and Mr Dreek, I want us all to pray for the family of Alan Mitchell, who are this week mourning the death of *their* son and *our* student and classmate."

Everyone bowed their heads.

Mrs Harrison gave a short prayer for Alan, followed by the Lord's Prayer.

I glanced up and watched Dreek. He seemed gigantic behind Mrs Harrison, a great ogre that might pick her up, tear her limbs off and eat her. I remembered him on the Old Church Road back before Christmas, lumbering through the fog to speak to me, his sad face and the way he called me *son*.

I murmured along with the prayers and closed my eyes and thought about Alan, as I had every night that week, getting home with his clothes torn and his neck twisted, lying down in his bed to die.

"Forever and ever, Amen," said Mrs Harrison.

"Amen," sighed the whole school.

She stepped back from the microphone, and Mr Goulden, the headmaster, stepped forward and gave a short speech about honesty being the best policy. I listened to Goulden and the sound of my own breathing, trying to ignore the growing pressure in my bladder. Then it was Dreek's turn. He thanked Mrs Harrison and reiterated the message of Goulden's speech. I bowed my head so he wouldn't recognise me or read the guilt stamped on my face. I felt Jase watching me from the back row.

Dreek gave a summary of the day and time the police were interested in and said that anyone who'd seen Alan during that time or who had information at all should tell their teachers. I barely listened, desperate to get out of the hall to the nearest toilet.

The din of chairs scraping and students talking exploded before Mrs Harrison roared for everyone to leave quietly. I hurried along my row. Parker passed me at the end of the line of chairs but ignored me, staring at the floor. Outside, Jase grabbed me with a horse bite on the back of my arm.

"Lunchtime in the copth," he spat into my ear. I felt and smelt his warm faggy breath and the bubbly saliva of his lisp. "Make thure you're there. Don't fuckin' thay anything to anyone."

Science after morning break was in the laboratories on the top floor of H Block. From my seat in the back corner of the classroom, I could see the copse at the far end of the school playing field, and the houses of the close where Shaun Terridge had lived. I thought about his mum alone in her house with the ghost of her son, mangled and bloody after being hit by the car. I daydreamed and stared out of the window while Miss Griffith wrote chemical compounds on the board and the rest of the class copied them into their notebooks. When the lunch bell rang, she was still explaining the homework. I pretended to write it down like everyone else, then ran for the door and the toilets on the floor below.

Students weren't allowed into the copse at lunchtime. There had been complaints from parents and residents. Our lunchtime games of catch and kill had been stopped with threats of suspension. Too many boys caught hiding in people's gardens, too many returning to school with split lips, bleeding noses, torn and dirty uniforms.

I crossed the field near the long jump and high jump pits to the perimeter fence and then walked in the cover of the overhanging trees, all the time checking back towards the school buildings for any sign of a teacher. There wasn't one. I reached the place where the meshed wire fence had been pulled down and stepped over into the daytime darkness of the wood. I went back along the path that ran inside the fence behind a line of trees to the large ditch where we often sat and smoked and organised games. It was dark and cool and hidden from the school and the houses whose back gardens opened onto the woods. I'd always envied the kids who lived in those houses. They could escape into the mazy freedom of the wood in seconds, whenever they wanted. It was a natural adventure playground, big enough for hunt, hide and chase games, but small enough that you could be out with a five-minute run in any direction.

I sat on the old tree trunk and picked at the loose bark while I waited. It came off easily, like dark scabs from week-old cuts and grazes. Soon I heard voices coming along the path. Then Jase, Parker, Walks and Geddy came into view, Indian file, like explorers and slaves in an episode of *Tarzan*.

Jase scowled at me.

"We waited for you by the fuckin' thportth hall!"

"You said the copse."

"Yeah, but we alwayth meet by the thportth hall!"

"Yeah, but I thought today was different because of assembly."

"Well, you're fuckin' lucky you're here."

He took angry breaths while everyone got seated. Then he started.

"Right," he said. "If fuckin' Dreek wantth to thpeak to uth, we need to make thure we all thay ecthactly the thame thing, okay?" Jase's lisp got worse the more agitated or excited he became. "It'th pretty fuckin' thimple. On Thaturday night we met at the Thpar. We have to thay that coth people fuckin' thaw uth there. But after that we went to the Rec and thtayed till about eleven, then went home, okay?"

I raised my hand. Schoolboy habit.

"Fuck thake, what ith it?"

"I got home about half nine. My mum saw me."

"Fuckin' 'ell," Jase said. "Right, you came with uth to the park but left about nine, okay? But the retht of uth were at the park till eleven."

We all murmured and nodded. I glanced at Walks and Parker. They were both chewing their lips.

Then Walks said, "Why do we have to lie?"

Jase stepped towards him and spat, "Coth if the fuckin' poleeth know we were at the church with Alan, they'll think we did thumthing. That'th why!"

Walks sat rigid on the log.

Jase glanced at me. I looked at the ground.

Everyone was silent. Geddy handed out L 'n' Bs from a silver pack.

The bell sounded for twelve forty-five. We had fifteen minutes to finish our meeting, sneak back across the school field and get to class.

"I don't see why the police would ask us anyway," Parker said, "unless someone saw us with Alan."

"Then we don't have to fuckin' thay anything, do we?" Jase said. "But if they do thpeak to uth, it'll be eathier if we all jutht thay exactly the thame thing."

More silence.

"Whatever," Parker finally said.

Walks nodded but looked miserable.

"Okay," I said.

The twelve fifty-five bell sounded.

"Right," said Jase. "Let'th go. And remember what we thed. Anyone theth different, they're dead."

LISA

When you work in a post office in a place like Lyttleton, you see everyone who lives there, some of them on a daily or weekly basis. It's like that policewoman said, Dreek's colleague, Pam or Pat or whatever her name was, "Lyttleton by name…" But what's worse is that they get to see you. That's why I couldn't go back to work straight away. If I'd been a seamstress or worked in a kitchen like Mum or a factory like Dad, some job where you're mostly shut away in your own little world doing the same small task over and over again, then maybe I could have thrown myself back into work and found it healing or cathartic or whatever the correct term might be. But sat behind the glass in the post office in the back of Lennard's, with the whole bloody village lining up and gawping at me and praying it wouldn't be me to serve them, the bereaved mum, cashing their pensions, dole checks or postal orders, *that* I could not hurry back to. I couldn't bear the idea of all those people, from kids to grannies, quietly judging me or sympathising while thanking God it wasn't them in my shoes.

To his credit, Mr Lennard said I could take as much time as I needed. I took him at his word and took two months, the whole of January and February. I guess it must have done me some good, purely from the point of view of time passing, if nothing else. But

I remember it as a bleak time, a blank time, locked away from a world that seemed to have disappeared under a cloak of freezing fog. I barely left the house. Neil would turn up with the shopping once or twice a week, depending on his shifts at the base, and we would usually have Chinese takeaway or fish 'n' chips and a few drinks. Sometimes we'd talk at the kitchen table till late, about the old days when Mum and Dad were still around, about Shaun when he was little. Sometimes Neil would stay over, and sometimes he'd risk the drive home to Stacy and the kids.

Since the funeral, Neil had locked away his grief and anger, like you might a rabid dog or a deformed relative. His regimental training had kicked in. He'd hurled himself back into his role at the camp, keeping the younger recruits in line and going about his duties with even more diligence and efficiency than before, if that were possible. I could sense his distaste whenever he turned up here to find me on the couch in the afternoon, with the dishes from breakfast and lunch still floating in the kitchen sink. I'm not slovenly by nature, never have been. But during that time, especially in late December and early January when the pain was still raw, I would run out of energy halfway through a task or chore. I'd climb the stairs to make my bed, then find myself half an hour later sat in Shaun's room doing nothing, staring at one of the posters on his wall, lost in the toxic fug of exhaustion and memory.

There were physical changes in Neil too. I noticed he was lither than before, gaunter in the face. He'd upped his regime as if back in basic training. His eyes were often pink, either from tiredness or from drinking or maybe even tears. He had small nicks on his cheeks and a barber's rash around his throat from shaving once or twice a day. He'd developed a tick, as if someone were pulling on a piece of string that yanked up his right cheek and closed his right eye when something riled him. But while he may have retreated into his soldier shell for defence, he had kept me and the house intact while I'd been at my lowest ebb, missing Shaun with an ache so acute it curled me up in a ball on his bed like a teenage girl with period cramps, an old T-shirt with Shaun's scent clutched to my chest.

When March came, the garden reappeared, and the sudden thaw brought bursts of colour in the form of daffodils and bluebells. I was still not ready to go back to work, not ready for being on show, for smiling and speaking to everyone from Lyttleton as they posted their letters and updated their savings books and planned for their and their children's or their grandchildren's futures. But I had no choice. I couldn't expect Mr Lennard to keep my job open forever, and Neil could not keep covering the rent, no matter how subsidised it was. As gladly as I would have remained hidden like a miserable, lonely spinster, I was not yet thirty-five, and as Neil kept reminding me, I had to get back out there at some point before I shrivelled up and died myself.

The first week back was hellish. I rode into the village centre on Mum's old bike, my headscarf so low I could barely see where I was going. I spent the days avoiding eye contact with customers, dreading the simpering looks of old dears who desperately wanted to talk to me about Shaun and tell me he was in a better place or whitter on about a husband or brother or son they'd lost. I hated the way most people adopted a sad expression as they looked at me, then literally snatched their chequebooks or stamps or change and were gone before they had to suffer any more discomfort from being in my presence.

When I heard about the Mitchell boy, I had very mixed feelings. I was sad for him and his family, of course, but only through the thick veil of my own grief. I was angry and relieved. Shaun was no longer the last boy to die in the village. I didn't know how to feel about that. I hated being the local figure of pity, but I wasn't yet ready for someone else to take over the role. I wasn't ready to pity someone else. I read about the boy's death in the local paper. No one would dare talk to me about it. I'd come into our little staffroom at work and voices would hush into an excruciating silence. Then I'd hear the chatter start up again before the door was even fully shut behind me. Everyone was desperate to discuss Lyttleton's latest tragedy, just not with the mother of the previous one. Not only did it seem to me in my bitter state that Shaun had been forgotten, but also that I was excluded from the latest round of ghoulish excitement. I suppose everyone thought the last thing I'd want to hear about would be another dead child. They were right. But I felt angry that it was not my choice, that it belonged to the village, not me. It was the proverbial kick in the teeth when I was already bleeding in the gutter.

Careful what you wish for, as Mum had been prone to saying. She would sit in her chair on a Friday and Saturday night and wish my dad would come home from the pub. Then she'd run up the stairs when she heard his footsteps on the path, scramble into bed and pretend to be asleep by the time he entered their room, just in case he was angry or randy or both. When someone did finally talk to me about Alan Mitchell, I thought I was going to be sick. It was old Mrs Jaraway, who was losing her marbles, had been for years. She did not know me from Adam even though she saw me every week. She came to the counter in her usual state of dribbly confusion, all wonky false teeth, Extra-Strong Mints, wig skew-whiff and wrinkles as deep as drainage ditches.

"Terrible about this Mitchell boy," she started. I was stunned and stopped what I was doing. "Poor little mite," she continued, "born into that brood."

I looked around to check if anyone was listening in, half-expecting to see a Mitchell next in the queue.

"Yes, it's awful," I whispered, hoping she would take the hint and talk more quietly, or better still, not talk at all.

Instead, she leant in closer to the glass without reducing the volume of her voice.

"I heard his neck was broken," she said, looking about as if divulging government secrets.

Without meaning to, I thought of Shaun in the hospital morgue, the thick wound from his forehead to his ear. A wave of nausea rose in my throat and I swallowed.

"Imagine doing that to your own flesh and blood," Mrs Jaraway spat through the glass, her eyes wide and her teeth so far forward it seemed they would drop onto the counter in a pool of minty spittle. "Your own child!"

By now, people were staring.

I stamped Mrs Jaraway's pension book and gave her her money and said, "Yes, terrible, have a good day," or something equally dismissive, anything to get her away from my counter.

She stared at me, with what might have been offence. Then she gathered her book and her purse and her tissues and her mints and was gone, her filthy old bungee-strapped shopping trolley rattling and squeaking behind her. The other women behind the counter, Mary and Sue, and the other customers in the queue, all stared at me, waiting it seemed for some reaction. I wanted to run from my desk, kick my way into the bathroom and smash the mirror, but instead I said, very carefully and slowly, "Next, please." Not really seeing their face or hearing what they said in reply.

That evening, I spoke to Neil on the phone. He hated being called at work but I was desperate to talk to someone, just to muddle through some of the things I was thinking. I was jumbled. Sad and angry all at the same time. Confused. I told him about Alan Mitchell, how Lyttleton was all abuzz with gossip and rumour about how this little boy had died. Whether he'd been beaten by his father or had had some kind of accident, no one really seemed to know. As I spoke, Neil was quiet. All I could hear was his breathing quickening on the other end of the line. Eventually, he responded.

"That'll be that then," he said matter-of-factly.

"What do you mean?" I asked him.

"Oh, come on, Leece," he said, "use your brain."

I still didn't understand.

"Fuckin' Dreek and co, the police," he said. "Perfect excuse for them to give up on the driver. All their attention'll shift onto the *fuckin' Mitchells* of all people."

Since the funeral, I'd thought less and less about the driver of the car. I still hated him, of course, for what he'd done. But it was a dull hate, vague, with no face or name to take aim at. Hearing Neil mention the driver again gave me a small shock, like being pinched awake or touching the electric fence at the pig farm. Again, I saw Shaun in the morgue, white as the sheet that covered his body, the red scar livid like lipstick from forehead to ear. I almost said *I couldn't care less if they catch him or not. Either way, it won't bring Shaun back.* But I held my tongue. I knew that beneath Neil's brusque efficiency, his return to being a soldier, there still burnt a deep desire to put a name and a face to the driver. I knew better than anyone. I knew he fantasised about the two of them together alone, just him and the driver, enough time and space to exact his own concoction of justice. He'd internalised this since the funeral but it was still there, simmering away like a chip pan left on the hob, just waiting to burn down the house. The thought occurred to me right there and then, on the phone while Neil was talking, that maybe, or even certainly, it would be better for all concerned if the driver were never caught. After all, what difference would it make? None that I could see. But what further damage might it cause? Plenty.

MELVYN

We still slept in the same bed, but since Christmas, Margret had retracted herself from me, like a snail into its shell. She bristled whenever I entered the room. Her features soured when I spoke. She couldn't very well banish me from our own house. The mortgage was paid with money from the business, and she would be forced to answer questions if I left. For her to vacate our marital bed, even though we had spares, would have figured as some kind of defeat. But she was a rigid presence there. On the odd occasion I'd nuzzled into her back in a bid to rekindle some semblance of our romantic life together, she'd stiffened as if grabbed from behind by an assailant rather than cuddled by her husband.

Again, I read the headline in the local paper.

MYSTERY SURROUNDS LYTTLETON BOY'S DEATH

I read the first few short paragraphs. Police were treating the death as suspicious. The boy's father had been taken in twice for questioning. It was clear from the story that nobody really knew what had happened. It seemed the boy had been found unconscious by his mother. I scanned further. The last paragraph caught my attention. *Lyttleton has been rocked to its foundations recently by unsolved deaths*, it said, *the horrific hit-and-run just before*

Christmas, which killed two local teenagers, and this new tragedy, which has shocked locals and raised strong suspicions of foul play.

That word – *horrific* – stood out on the page as if in bolder print.

The earlobe in the rag. The tumbling white faces in the dark. I saw these things less now, but they still returned at the merest prompt, vivid and palpable as ever.

The phone rang in the hall and startled me. Margret. She was leaving her mother's and wondered if we needed anything. On my way to check the fridge, I considered how, in spite of everything, Margret had remained an impeccable housewife. It was a perfection with which she punished me. The duties and details of keeping house, important to her before, were now something of an obsession. I told her we were fine for milk but needed bread for toast in the morning. I began to ask after her mother but she cut me short.

"I have to talk to you when I get home. You have to do some things for me."

"Okay," I said, about to ask her what they were, but she hung up before I could question her.

I listened to the silence and then the single continuous blank tone before putting the phone back in its cradle. Her voice had worried me. Belligerent, robotic even. Not angry but singular in purpose, *have to*, *have to*, no arguments, no messing around. She meant business.

I wondered if this was the moment I'd hoped would never come. Was Margret going to tell me she couldn't cope, that she was leaving to live with her mother? My mind began to put all of it in place: increased visits, obsessive housekeeping, her growing distance from me. I suspected they'd all been part of an act, a cover-up of her intention to leave. But then something Margret had said returned to me. *You need to do some things for me.* Surely, she wouldn't say that if *she* was the one leaving. Unless one of the things I had to do was accept it and not make it any harder for her than it already was. It didn't sound like Margret though. She was many things but cryptic with her words was not one of them. In fact, her curtness could offend if one wasn't used to it. I'd seen friends and neighbours wilt at Margret's dismissive shutdowns of small talk. Indeed, at times, she possessed an almost autistic honesty, a blade in the blubber of the trivia and piffle most people preferred to uncomfortable silence.

She wants me to confess, I thought. *She's thought it through, discussed it with her mother and come to the conclusion that I must confess and face the consequences.* Again, though, it didn't seem like Margret. I'd told her what would happen if I turned myself in, what we stood to lose. *Everything.* Not just the material things, but our friends, our community, our home. We'd be outcasts, both of us.

I needed a drink. One of Margret's caveats after Christmas had been that we stop drinking. Both of us. "If we're going to get through this," she'd said, "we need to be clear-headed." I would have agreed to anything just to have her support. But I'd known the opposite to be true. If I were to have any hope of continuing in some way close to normal, I would need alcohol's blurring of guilt's sharp edges.

I looked at my watch and thought about how long it would take Margret to drive home with a stop at the shop. Then I went quickly to the garage and to the drawer in the workbench where I kept repair bills for the car. At the back of the drawer I'd hidden a quarter bottle of whisky. I'd been keeping one there since Christmas. I knew if Margret found out she would see it as yet another betrayal. But it was worth the risk. I stood by the bench and drank two capfuls and waited for the harsh taste to turn into a warm glow in my throat and chest. Then I drank another capful and went back into the house. I checked the clock in the kitchen, then climbed the stairs to the bathroom to brush my teeth to hide the smell.

When I heard the car pull onto the driveway, I went downstairs to the front door. I opened it and stood waiting for Margret. She did not get out of the car right away. She sat with the engine running, her hands on the steering wheel in a fixed tableau of driving. For one horrible moment, I thought she might accelerate through the garage door. She did not look at me. She must have known I was watching. She would have seen the porch light come on. But she sat and gripped the steering wheel and stared ahead. I grew uncomfortable watching her. I looked across the street to see if anyone else was watching.

Eventually, she turned off the ignition and got out of the car and clicked along the path past the kitchen window.

"What are you doing?" she asked impatiently.

"Waiting for you."

"I'm perfectly capable of opening the front door," she said.

She made eye contact with me for just a second, then lowered her head as she passed me on the front step. I smelt her perfume and the bread she was carrying. I followed her into the kitchen and stood just inside the doorway as she busied herself and avoided looking at me.

"How's your mother?" I said.

She sighed. "The same."

She put the bread in the bread bin and began looking in cupboards, considering their contents.

"Are you hungry?" she said.

"Not really," I answered.

I was, but I wanted her to tell me what she had to say.

"Margret," I said.

"What?" she replied.

"You said on the phone you had something to say to me, something I need to do?"

I thought about the whisky in the drawer in the garage. I wanted another capful, one more to face what was coming.

"Just let me get in," she said, as if I was harassing her. "I need five minutes."

"Right," I said. "I'll get the car in."

She looked at me in a resigned way, the way someone might look at an old photograph they passed every day on the stairs.

"There are some things in the boot," she said. "Mummy gave me some things."

"What things?" I said.

"Just an old blanket and some things from her fridge."

"Right," I said. "I'll bring them in."

I was glad to get out of the kitchen. She was not ready to tell me. And being in the same room as her was like watching the paint slide slowly from the walls.

I went first to the car boot and brought in an old crocheted blanket and two Tupperware containers. It had got colder in the few minutes since I'd stood at the doorway. I pulled up the garage door, then eased the car inside. I sat there for a few moments and looked at myself in the rearview mirror.

"Just keep going," I said. "You'll be fine."

I got out of the car and went to the step by the door into the utility room and listened. I could not hear Margret. I guessed she had gone upstairs to change. I went back to the drawer in the workbench and took out the whisky. It was almost gone. I'd have to get another. It was a nuisance. I couldn't use the off-licence in the village centre. Too risky. It would only take someone to say they'd seen me there, and Margret would know. I finished the bottle in two more capfuls and placed it at the back of the drawer, making a mental note to get rid of it later.

Back in the kitchen I put the kettle on for tea and turned on the radio. I heard Margret upstairs. Her footfalls were soft, muffled bumps on the ceiling. I listened and watched her in my mind, undressing and throwing her clothes on the bed, opening the wardrobe and scanning it, her arms out wide on the handles of the open doors, her right stockinged heel balanced on her left knee like the beginning of a dance. I'd told her many times how uncomfortable it looked, but she'd always insisted she wasn't even aware. The image was broken by the sound of her louder steps on the stairs.

I took out the cups and the tea, feigning nonchalance and Saturday relaxation. Margret entered the room behind me, all agitation and hackled unhappiness.

"I don't want tea," she said. "It's too late. I won't sleep if I have tea too late."

She moved quickly around the other side of the table to the utility room door. She opened it and cold air drafted in from the garage. I wanted to shut it to stop the heat escaping from the kitchen, but I continued making tea for myself instead.

She came back into the room and shut the door behind her. She stood for a moment and pursed her lips from side to side. I sat down in my usual chair with my tea. She looked at me. Then she looked at the radio and turned it off. The abrupt end to the song was followed by a creeping silence.

"Why don't you sit down?" I said.

"Perhaps I *will* have some tea," she answered, and she turned round and flicked the kettle on again and looked for her cup.

"It's on the drainer," I said.

She took it and went back to making her tea. The kettle began to bubble and spit and steam rolled flat along the underside of the cupboard above. She poured the water and then stood moving the teabag around in the cup. She squeezed the teabag, opened the cupboard under the sink and threw the wet teabag into the pedal bin. Then she came behind me to the fridge and took out the milk and finished off her tea before putting the milk back, all on angry autopilot.

She went back to her spot by the kettle and stood with her back to it, her cup held in both hands.

"I suppose you've heard about this little boy," she said.

"Yes," I said. "I read it in the paper."

I'd not brought it up before for fear of reactivating Margret's thinking about the accident.

I was afraid of what she was going to say, but the whisky had done its work, my fear dampened enough for me to sit there and listen.

"I feel like *you* killed him," she said.

I was shocked but said nothing.

"I know you didn't," she continued, "but I feel like you did."

I was angry at this, outraged, in fact, but still I said nothing and listened.

"I think it's because you've not apologised properly," she said. "You've not repented."

She looked at me. It was a black look, no trace of love or respect. Closer to disgust. The way you might look at a patch of mould or at a neighbour's dog squatting to shit on your lawn.

"You've said sorry to me, but that was just for *fucking* up our lives."

I flinched at the obscenity. Margret rarely swore.

"I haven't forgiven you for that," she continued. "I doubt I ever will."

"I understand," I said.

"You don't understand anything," she countered. "You killed two children and you've not even apologised!"

Her voice grew louder.

"Margret, please don't shout. Someone might overhear you," I said.

I imagined our neighbours eavesdropping under the window.

"You see," she hissed, "your only concern is not being caught."

"That's not true," I said. "There's not a day goes by—"

"Don't!" she whispered harshly. "Don't you dare say that. Don't you dare!" She was angry now, snarling like a vicious dog, top lip curled, revealing a cream-coloured incisor. "You go to work. You drive that *fucking* car. You act like it never happened. In a way, you are guilty of killing that little Mitchell boy."

"What do you mean?" I said.

"You've not paid," she said. "Your life is the same. I'm here all day, Melvyn. All I've got is Mummy and her misery. And these dead children. *None* of my own! Just *your* dead ones. And you, you just carry on, getting away with it day after day."

She paused and began to cry.

I waited to see if she would continue.

She took a tissue from inside the sleeve of her sweater and wiped at her nose.

"I'm not sure I understand," I said. "What else can I do?"

I waited for her to reply, but she seemed to be thinking.

"How can I apologise now?"

She wasn't listening.

"While Mummy was making lunch today, I came across my old Sunday School Bible."

An automatic protest rose in me, but I thought it best to say nothing.

"She's been clearing out the loft. I couldn't believe how many notes and underlinings there were, how much faith I had back then. Real belief in something."

She stared out of the window.

"But you were just a girl," I said.

She ignored me and continued.

"I read a few passages again." She took a long pause, then sighed. "Do you know it was the first time I'd felt some kind of peace in months. Do you understand?"

I was confused. I had not expected this. The sudden presence of religion. I didn't like it. It felt like an unwelcome, invisible stranger in the room, whispering holy catechisms in Margret's ear. Her sudden calm at the thought of her old Bible had a glaze of madness to it, the instant tranquillity of a drugged lunatic.

"Margret," I said. "I know what we're going through is bad."

She cut me off again.

"There was this one passage," she said, still crying but soothed, it seemed, by the forming of her own words. "Let the wicked forsake his way." She paused and stared at me. "Let him return to the Lord, for He will abundantly pardon."

"Margret, please," I said.

She seemed suddenly deranged. I imagined standing up and slapping her.

"You're not listening," she said. She repeated with emphasis, "*For He will abundantly pardon*."

She stared at me, waiting for a response. I did not have one. My mind veered in all directions, looking for something sensible to say but hamstrung by the fear of saying the wrong thing and only making matters worse.

"I'm going to church tomorrow," she said, "and I want *you* to come."

I sat and sipped at my tea, watching her.

"It's not something I feel comfortable with," I said, finally.

"*Comfortable*?" she said. She shook her head and blinked, incredulous, wiping at her eyes with her tissue. "It's not about feeling *comfortable*, Melvyn, for Christ's sake!" Her voice rose again. "It's about begging God to forgive you for what you've done!"

She glared at me, wide-eyed, exasperated by my reluctance to see the sense in this new scheme of hers.

"How can I do that?" I said. "It would be a lie. I've apologised to *you* because you're my wife."

She was shaking her head at me as I spoke, crying and laughing all at once.

"Yes, I'm your wife," she said, "and I'm not *fucking* asking you, Melvyn, I'm telling you. I'm telling you. If you don't come with me and apologise for what you've done, repent, like you mean it, not just tomorrow but every Sunday, I swear I'll call the police myself, so help me God, I will."

She trailed off and gave in to her crying, her shoulders juddering up and down. I felt the urge to go to her and comfort her, but I knew she would not want me near her, let alone touching her.

Once she'd caught hold of herself, she continued.

"I don't care what you think about going to church, Melvyn. I don't care. I feel damned. Dirty and depraved. I'm having dreams,

Melvyn. Awful dreams like I've never had before, like my soul has been blackened or something."

I thought about my own night terrors, broken bodies rising from the frozen tarmac and searching for me in the streets and lanes of Lyttleton.

Margret trailed off again and looked out of the window into the dark. Then she shut the blinds, as if suddenly frightened of someone watching or listening.

"I felt better today," she said. "Even with Mummy and this... this... dreadful thing. I felt better when I read those words. I just want to feel better."

She sat down and held onto her mug with two hands. She looked spent and ten years older. Her eye sockets were black with wet mascara.

"What else do you want me to do?" I asked.

"What?"

"On the phone you said there were some things you want me to do. Things, plural. What else is there?"

"Oh," she said, almost in a whispered afterthought. "You have to sell the car."

"Why?" I said.

"Are you really asking me that question, Melvyn?"

She glared at me.

"I just don't see that it will make any difference," I said. "It might even still look suspicious."

"Again, Melvyn," she said. "I'm not asking. Take it back to the garage, advertise it in the paper, dump it in the blasted sea if you have to. I can't believe we're still driving it anyway. It's disgusting."

*

The next morning, Sunday, we went to church. Margret was already up when I woke, padding busily around in her dressing gown, a pink towel tied tall upon her head.

"Come on, Melvyn, get up," she said. "We can't be late."

I showered and shaved like a man readying himself for execution. I had awoken several times in the night, each time to an image of myself in church, guilty and conspicuous. I was dreading it. The short walk through the village. Filing in and finding a place. Nodding pleasantries to other members of the congregation. The inevitable looks and whispers from the regulars of the flock. *What's brought them here all of a sudden?* I could already hear the gossip.

At work, since the accident, I'd seen and talked to many of Lyttleton's residents. But that was different. The practice was my place, where people expected me to be. Turning up at church was another matter altogether, like being on show. I was convinced people would question why we were there. The whole endeavour signified a change in my public behaviour. We had avoided interest up to that point by doing nothing to attract attention, nothing out of the ordinary, living the same lives we had before. Now we were about to put ourselves on display. I wasn't sure which was worse, the stupidity of the exercise or the hypocrisy. The lie without the language to spell it out. The show of righteousness. The idea that all we had to do was go to church, stand there, sing a song or two, bow our heads, supplicate, and not only would all be forgiven, but a sham of goodness and innocence would also be projected. To me, it was a greater sin than hiding. Hiding, living our lives like insects under rocks, was precisely the penance we should have been paying, with the bonus of reducing our chances of being caught.

We left the house at twenty to ten, even though the walk would not take more than five minutes. It was cold and bright in the road and the pavement was wet from rain the night before. Margret said she would go back for an umbrella, just in case. She came back out with a red one that clashed with her mauve suit and felt like a bad omen.

Once we entered the village centre, there were other families and couples dressed far too formally for a Sunday. They moved slowly and respectfully in the same direction, as if drawn by some silent beacon that pulsed out a hypnotic tone. The worshippers smiled benignly at each other. Smiles devoid of humour or reason, smiles which embalmers might work onto the faces of corpses to be laid in state. Their children looked bored, understanding only too well the hour that lay ahead, droning sermons, dirgy hymns, and repeated scoldings for talking, fidgeting or anything other than sitting and standing still in the most unchildlike zombification. I remembered my own trips to church as a boy, squirming in my formal clothes while my mother sang in a strange and strangled soprano that only ever aired on Sundays.

Margret hooked her arm into mine and gave me the umbrella to carry. It was her first affectionate gesture towards me in months, but I knew it was only for show. I could feel her bolstering herself next to me, convincing herself, muscle by muscle, that this was the right and righteous thing to do. I was hot inside my suit, even though the weather was cold and squally. I needed the bathroom. I'd drunk tea, then coffee while getting ready. A bad mistake. Diuretics. My daily hangover was festering, *in the post*, as they say. I could feel sweat on my legs and in my chest hair. I caught a faint whiff of body odour from my armpits and couldn't remember if I'd rolled on any deodorant.

The two entrances to Lyttleton New Church were busy with cars creeping respectfully in and out, avoiding pedestrian worshippers. There was a colourful confusion of people, some going straight in and some stopping to talk to friends. It almost had the appearance of a wedding but was too sombre and serious in atmosphere. There was no cackling excitement and most just nodded to other members of the congregation with resigned smiles or no smiles at all.

We worked our way inside without stopping to talk. A few people noticed us, but most were concerned with their own families and children. We found a place at the end of a pew about halfway back from the altar and dais, below a great stained-glass window that spilt a rainbow of different coloured light shafts into the main hall of the church. I looked at the glass, mildly interested but mostly to avoid eye contact with other members of the congregation. A Christ on the cross, his creamy white glass face and golden halo shining brighter than its surroundings. Three women, two with their heads bent low and one with her arms up, her hands forming a bowl, trying to catch the victim's blood as he was speared through his side. I looked at Jesus again, his pale glass face and brown innocent eyes, and began to wonder about the real Jesus's sight, whether he'd had perfect vision, being the son of God, or if, being human like the rest of us and a carpenter in a time before electric light, he'd been shortsighted or afflicted with an astigmatism from all that concentration by candlelight. Margret tugged at my sleeve and made a face at me, thinking perhaps my distraction conspicuous.

Most of the congregation had found a place, and the vicar walked slowly up the central aisle, smiling benignly at little children who pointed at him, this strange man in a long white dress. As he climbed the steps into the ornate dais, I became nervous again. He stood and scanned the congregation from his place above us. As his gaze fell upon me, I was convinced he registered some kind of surprise. This seemed confirmed when he said, "I'm so glad to see all your faces again, and happy that we have some new ones here today also." A few heads turned this way and that to see if they could spot who he meant. "Those of you who are new among us today," he said, "we welcome you with the love of the community, as does the Lord God and all of his vast community on Earth."

Again, the vicar's eyes caught mine. I was sure of it.

I glanced at Margret. Her head was bowed and her lips were moving, almost imperceptibly. She seemed to be praying already. I wondered if she was praying for our forgiveness, or simply for us to get through the next hour or so.

The vicar continued, "... times like these when community comes into its own, takes on a new life and works in the sight of God to do His work in healing those who need His love."

I looked around at the congregation. A woman on the opposite side of the church caught my eye and looked away.

"It's all too easy to focus on our prejudice at present," the vicar said, "and eye those around us with suspicion. It's understandable even, given our community's relative glut of tragedy and horror." He paused. "But now is a time when we need to focus on our love; when we need to" – he paused again as if thinking – "draw in the energy from prejudice and suspicion..."

I glanced left and right to see if anyone was looking at me. The vicar seemed to notice the movement of my head and looked at me like a teacher staring at a daydreaming pupil. I looked down again.

"... and channel those feelings into love for those in our community who need it most."

I began to feel nauseous. The heat from the large iron radiators on the side walls fuelled the musk of damp sweaters and coats.

A child said something inaudible, and a mother shushed it.

I became aware again of the sweat in the small of my back and on my legs. From nowhere, I pictured a snake coiled in my gut, nudged through my intestine by the vicar's syllables.

"I ask you now to bow your heads in prayer..."

The snake in my gut slipped an inch or two lower.

"... those families in our community who've lost sons and daughters. And I ask that while we pray, each of us might focus the energy of our love towards those families."

I breathed deeply and glanced at Margret. Her eyes were tight shut and she was wincing as if in pain. Then she nudged me and nodded, keeping her eyes shut.

I bowed my head and closed my eyes and tried to block out the drone of the vicar's voice.

"Our Father," he said, "who art in Heaven, hallowed be thy name..."

The snake moved, and I clenched, sensing that the contents of my bowels were liquefying.

Oh God, I thought, without reverence, *not here, surely*.

I began to apologise, clenching more tightly and repenting with a matching zeal. I was sweating harder now as the shit-snake moved and the effort of clenching and repenting simultaneously generated heat throughout my body.

"Amen," the vicar said.

"Amen," said the flock.

As the congregation audibly loosened and fidgeted after the focus of prayer, as though released from handcuffs or a tight corset, I wound my muscles tighter, squeezing my back passage shut as if it were a portal to hell.

I could now feel beads of sweat at the roots of my hair, forming like drops of blood from pinpricks. I glanced up at the glass Jesus with his crown of thorns. Light shone through his face onto mine, and for just a moment, I thought I felt his pain.

The organ fired up so loudly it startled me. I jumped in my clothes, then held myself still, hoping no one had noticed. The terrible sensation of imminent diarrhoea had passed, but my sweating had increased in the heat of the church and my clothes clung to me on the inside, fastened to the slick damp of my skin.

"God of mercy and compassion / Look with pity on me," the vicar sang, in a surprisingly smooth baritone, followed by the congregation, some of whom had turned their heads upwards and closed their eyes and raised their hands.

"Father let me call thee Father, / Tis thy child returns to thee."

I wiped my forefinger knuckle across my eyebrows, damp with sweat, and tried to focus on the blurry words of the hymn book Margret held in front of us. I felt her glance at me. I didn't look at her. Instead, I closed my eyes and hummed. *Shaun and Paula tumbled over the car; lay ghostly and white under white mortuary sheets.* I hummed and thought my apology and penance. The snake moved inside my gut again, and again I clenched. I saw the word *sorry* in large burning letters inside my head. I tried in other languages but couldn't produce the same effect. I hummed and listened to the voice of the vicar, audible above all the members of the congregation. I envisioned myself in the stained-glass window, flat and two-dimensional, in medieval clothes, kneeling beneath the smooth-faced Christ, who registered no emotion or pain from his torture, soothed, it seemed, by his Father's light that shone through him. I whispered a quiet prayer for forgiveness, drowned out, I hoped, beneath the congregation's singing of the hymn. I hummed and prayed as the snake slithered and I clenched and sweated into my clothes.

Could this be it? I wondered. This serpent of filth in my bowels. This heat in my skin. Could this be the fever of God's compassion and mercy? I could not stop asking these questions. Was I experiencing some flame of contrition? Here with the stained-glass Jesus shining just above me, and the sound of the organ and hymn in my ears? Was my sweat some flood of purification? The impending sense of losing my bowels, also, was that part of the cleansing ritual, an evacuation of the darkest reaches of my soul, where the truth lay twisted and broken on the road? My prayer shifted to a simple hope that all of these things were true, that I'd come to church, unbelieving, and been purified anyway by a compassionate God and his eternally suffering Son, both of whom understood my sin as an accident followed by panic. Even as I welcomed these thoughts, I knew them to be nonsense. But just for a moment or two, I let myself drift in the aesthetic wash of the church, with its blowing organ, its crooning vicar, its angelic Jesus, and its congregation, some of whom, judging by their entranced postures, clearly did believe. Just for a few more seconds, I allowed myself to bathe in the hokum and feel the great lie within me, offering to clean my soul and forgive me murder if I could just give myself over to it, unquestioningly. And while the salve was tempting, especially with the false promise of its bigger sister, salvation, I knew I could not be proselytised and conditioned into believing that the forgiveness I felt was anything more than the product of a transient hypnotherapy and an oozing, lucid hangover. Instead, quite unmiraculously, I saw into the future. I saw myself coming to church every Sunday, silently apologising to Shaun and Paula and their respective families, repenting to a God I had no belief in, doing whatever it would take to remain free, whatever it would take to appease Margret and keep her loyalty, whatever it would take to set right our little apple cart.

KEVIN

Emma's friend Catherine said Emma wanted to meet me after school. I knew I shouldn't go. I didn't want to go. It was another of those instances of feeling one way and acting the opposite, like smoking on the way to school every day even though it made me feel sick, like catch and kill in the old churchyard. I knew these things were stupid, even then, but I did them anyway, as if my role in life were idiotic, self-destructive teenager, and I was playing the part to perfection.

We met at the school gate. She was blushy and giggly in her red duffel coat. We didn't look at each other as we spoke. We'd been friends since I was ten and she was eleven, and boyfriend and girlfriend on and off over the last couple of years. Innocent though, the odd kiss here and there, lots of hand-holding. Now she was fifteen, her extra year felt more like three.

There had been rumours at school about her and Roy Chivers. I'd tried unsuccessfully to avoid and ignore them. But some kids take pleasure in shattering your world. One particularly lurid story, Jase had gleefully told at morning break as he dished out B & H in the drizzle behind the tennis courts. "Fuckin' dirty little thlag or what," had been Jase's grinning epigraph to the tale. Everyone, including me, had laughed, while some unnamed inner part of me had shrivelled and died, and a hot blush of anger and embarrassment had warmed my cheeks and stuck its sharp nails into my bladder, so much so that I had slipped away to find solace and relief at the urinals. As Emma and I walked away from the school gates, I tried not to think about her and Roy together, her touching him or him touching her, the dreadful details of Jase's story. I tried not to make eye contact with the other kids leaving school. I prayed that I would not see any of my friends. I feared being mocked by Jase, or worse, beaten up by Roy.

When we arrived at Lyttleton Hall, the woods behind it were dripping and dark from the rain. The ground was soft and crunchy with rotted twigs. We took the wide path that led in from the rope swing, then turned left into the small wood itself. There was a large fir tree, which blocked out much of the fading light. Beneath it, Emma turned around and put her bag down and pulled me towards her. She closed her eyes. I glimpsed her eyelashes in the dark beneath her eyebrows and dark fringe. Her nostrils flared a little. Two black circles above her lips, like the twin barrels of a toy shotgun.

"What's wrong?" she said.

"Nothing."

She grinned. "Are you scared?"

"No," I lied.

I kissed her and she tasted like bubble gum and menthol from the cigarette we'd shared on the way. The tip of her tongue probed wetly around the underside of my top lip. I felt an ache somewhere behind my pelvis, like the daily bladder strain I was used to but different, yet still with that same fear of imminent emission.

There were twig cracks on the periphery of my hearing, *Alan Mitchell circling us with his head twisted back to front, Roy Chivers belly-crawling Viet Cong guerilla-style through the woods towards us, knife to slit my throat between his teeth.*

My breathing became shallow. Emma guided my hand inside her coat to her breast. Again, that pelvic ache. New. The same. I couldn't tell. The light rain on the leaves around us sounded like the fizz of a freshly opened Pepsi when you put your ear to the mouth-hole. The warmth of Emma's breast under my fingers, *Alan's head shoved in the church wall, Jase's lisping whispers, "leper thquint", "dirty little thlag", Roy Chivers beating the living shit out of me, the dark damp stains on my mattress airing by the window, the enuresis alarm rising in my ears like an air raid siren.* My thighs bubbled like boiling water. Emma's fingertips were at my belt, then inside my trousers. I grabbed her wrist as she took hold of me with her cold hand. My eyes shut tight while the hot spasm faded into a damp and cold sensation, and I wilted like a sapling in a downpour.

Her tongue stopped moving just inside my lips. I held her there for a moment, half-excited by the clinch and closeness of her body, half so as not to move and stand on my own. The cooling damp prompted more thoughts of the bedside alarm and nightly bed-stripping.

I pulled away and fastened my belt and told her I had to go.

"Really," she said, cocking her head to the side. "We only just got here."

In the dim shadow of the tree, I saw Alan Mitchell instead of Emma as she spoke, blue-lipped, pale, poor and forlorn, brick-dusted hair and broken-necked, head bent unnaturally to his shoulder.

I picked up Emma's bag and handed it to her. She took it and hung it on her shoulder, then asked me if I was okay.

"I won't tell anyone," she said.

"What," I answered, "like you didn't tell anyone about Roy Chivers's dick?"

She looked at me through the gloom with her mouth slightly open. She went to say something, but it caught in her throat.

"I'm sorry," I said, wishing the giant fir behind me would fall and crush me into the wet earth.

"I suppose Jase told you that," she hissed. "And who do you think told him, you fucking idiot?"

She marched out of the wood while I gathered up my bag and

ran after her. I caught her up and we walked back to the road in silence. I was suddenly hungry and exhausted. I had no idea what to say. I wanted to take it back, VHS rewind the whole scenario and go back to the school gate and see her all blushy and giggly again, see her wet eyelashes as she closed her eyes to kiss me. I wanted to tell her it was my first time. I wanted to tell her about Alan, about Mum and Dad, about my fears and nightmares, the machine by my bed. But instead, I just kicked at some gravel in a puddle and felt the water soak through my shoes and into the toes of my socks.

"I thought we were friends," she said.

"We are," I whined.

"Not anymore," she said. "I'm not speaking to you from now on."

She turned and walked away while I stood and watched her, the drizzle turning into rain and whispering then hissing in the trees around the Rec, the puddles reflecting streetlamps as they winked on along Lyttleton Lane.

LISA

I arrived home to the smell of Chinese food keeping warm in the oven and Neil pottering around in the kitchen, wiping plates dry and sticking them away in the cupboard, like he lived here and did the same thing every day at the same time on autopilot. The table was laid for two, wine glasses and all, and there were two bottles of half-decent-looking French red wine on the table. I took all this in from the kitchen doorway while Neil wiped a cup without acknowledging I was there.

"What's going on?" I asked, half-pleased at the prospect of company for the evening, half-worried by the strangeness of it all.

"Leece," he said. "Sit down, I'll get you a drink."

I did what he said. I was exhausted from smiling and being pleasant all day to half the village, so I just sat and watched him as he uncorked a bottle of wine and poured two large glasses.

"Cheers," he said, tapping my glass with his. "Here's to us."

"To us," I repeated, still confused but enjoying the change from my normal routine of getting home, cooking something cheap for tea like cheese on toast, staring at the television and changing channels, forcing myself to wash and clean my teeth, then crying myself to sleep in Shaun's bed.

While Neil took the food from the oven and apportioned it

onto two plates, I sipped at the wine and breathed in the smells and started telling him about my day and my week and the whole scenario of being back at work, who I'd seen from the village, the gossip I'd heard, about the Mitchell boy and other less dramatic village affairs, who had ignored me and who had been sweet, who had behaved like a stuck-up cow, who had a surprising amount of money in their savings and who was just as surprisingly broke. For five minutes or so while he laid out the food, hardly saying a word, Neil let me talk, just smiling and nodding and laughing along, and it dawned on me, in the kitchen as I sipped from my wine, that the feeling I felt was something akin to contentedness, not real and permanent because all around was the empty space that Shaun had left never to be filled. But between the wine and Neil and the warmth from the oven and the smells rising up from the food on the table and the kitchen window open onto a spring evening that was lighter now the clocks had gone forward, I felt a smidgen of pleasure for the first time since Dreek had appeared at my front door that morning about four months before.

We sat and started to eat, and Neil poured our second glasses, my head already afuzz from drinking the first too quickly. I continued to talk, but I noticed that Neil had begun to lose interest and fidget. His tick started. His right eye blinked as I spoke. So I stopped and watched him. The sudden silence made him concentrate on his food, his head not more than five inches from his plate of chow mein. He paused with a forkful of brown saucy noodles hung just beneath his chin while he chewed and stared at a spot of grease on the table just in front of his plate.

"What's up?" I asked him.

At first he said nothing but gave an enormous sigh into his food. Then he stopped and raised his head and placed his fork carefully onto his plate, as if he were fighting the urge to throw it across the room.

"For Christ's sake, Neil, what is it?"

He sighed again and looked everywhere in the room apart from at me. Then he picked up his fork again and pushed his food around his plate before he spoke.

"Gotta go away," he said, finally.

Away had meant different things with Neil in the past. The borstal after he'd beaten Terry half to death. Then his training up in Aldershot after he'd joined up. Then two times to Northern Ireland. So when Neil said "away" he usually meant away, far away, abroad somewhere for his job. I stopped eating and took a gulp of wine and allowed myself to savour its warm flush in my throat and chest while I waited for him to continue. I almost laughed to myself, or rather *at* myself for the glint of pleasure I'd felt just minutes before. I'd known it was temporary, but not this temporary. Stupidly, I'd found the temerity from somewhere, the wine most probably, to think that little flourish of something near happiness might last longer than twenty minutes.

"Falklands," he said.

"What?" I answered, confused. "What do you mean?"

"It'll be on the news later. Maybe has been already. Government's sending a task force to take 'em back. Us first… with the fuckin' marines."

I was speechless. I'd seen the odd report on the news but had paid it no attention whatsoever. It had seemed like nothing important, some minor dispute a million miles away, near the South bloody Pole, for God's sake.

"Gotta get my kit and be ready to sail on Monday. We're going from Pompey, on a fuckin' cruise ship, of all things."

I was still a few steps behind as I struggled to take it in.

"You mean Argentina, right? Those Falklands?" I said, feeling immediately stupid.

"Mmm," Neil said, going back to his food.

"You mean you're going to war?" I said, my voice becoming shriller.

"Please, Leece," Neil said, putting his fork down again and

raising his hands in a calming gesture. "It'll be nothing. They'll have sorted it all out by the time we get there. The whole thing'll be a wasted fuckin' journey. You wait and see."

He almost seemed disappointed, which only made me angrier.

"Well let's fucking hope so!" I said.

"Leece, calm down, please," Neil said. "I know the timing's not great."

"Not great?" I shouted, incredulous at his understatement. "Not fucking great?"

He threw his fork down and it bounced off his plate and onto the floor, and I felt rage whip up inside me like a fire receiving a sudden bellow of air from an open door. All the anger of my grief, not the love or maternity but the self-pity, the *why's it always me*, the toxic stuff I'd felt towards Mum and Dad and Terry and Neil and the whole village, and that nameless, faceless bastard driver who'd broken my son to pieces and left me with nothing but an empty bedroom where even the smell of Shaun was disappearing day-by-day along with the memory of how he felt in my arms; all of that rose up at once like a bilious retch in my throat and before I could help myself I let out a torrent of words that, even as I said them, through the skin-burning sensation of my anger, I knew them to be wrong and unfair and hurled at only one of the many who deserved to hear them.

But I couldn't help myself. It was as if I'd caught fire, as if I were a Molotov cocktail thrown at an armoured car. I cannot to this day remember my exact words, but I told Neil that this was typical of him, that he'd only ever chosen when to care for me and want me and be with me and Shaun when it suited him and that when I needed him most he'd gone to prison, into the army, to Ireland and God knows where, to Stacy and the kids and now to some war on the other side of the planet. And when I'd finished and I stood there still trembling with rage but without any further words to do it justice, I swiped what was left of my meal off the table and barely heard the plate smash against the cupboard doors, leaving a dirty great smear that looked as if someone had offed themselves and sprayed the contents of their skull across the kitchen, which was apt, I thought, because I'm sure I would have done so if someone had only handed me the gun.

Then, fully spent, I sat down and cried like I'd never cried before, not when Mum had died, not when Dad had died, not when Terry had left, not when Neil had been put away, not even in the morgue with Shaun, not even when he'd been lowered into the ground. It was like after the fire came the flood, a tidal wave of tears that just kept coming and coming until all the flames had been drenched and my anger was nothing more than a sopping pile of ashes. For a long while, I've no idea how long, there was virtual silence, punctuated only by my juddery, snotty sobs and the odd shout from a child somewhere in the street that filtered its way through the open kitchen window.

After many minutes had passed, I managed to straighten myself and pour myself another glass of wine. Neil took this as his cue to clean up the mess I'd made. When he was done, and he'd wiped the cupboard doors clean, and located as many of the broken shards of dirty plate as possible, and wrapped them in a newspaper and shoved them into the bin beneath the sink, and when he'd washed the remaining plates and bowls from the table and had left them drying in the drainer, and the kitchen could have been any little council house kitchen after an evening meal, he sat back down and poured himself another glass of wine, the whole time without saying a single word.

Eventually, when I was calmer, I asked him if he'd told Stacy and the kids. He said he'd told Stacy but they were waiting for the right moment when they could both sit down with the kids and explain the situation. I asked him how long he thought he might be away, and he said that he had no idea, a few weeks, a few months, he really didn't know. I asked him if he thought it would be dangerous, if there was a possibility he might not come back at all. This he answered by saying that his unit was one of the best in the country and that the Argies, as he called them, were mostly a bunch of conscripts and teenage boys who would probably shit themselves and run when they saw the ships turn up and the British paras and marines landing on the beach. The soldier in him materialised as he pictured these things, and he finished by saying, confidently, "I'd run or surrender straight away if I was them, otherwise they won't know what's fuckin' hit 'em."

It was probably foolish of me, but the macho soldier talk reassured me. I'd never liked Neil's job but I'd always been just a little in awe of it. When the wine was finished, I said that it would be nice to have some more, especially as I wasn't going to see him for a while. I asked him if it was alright, if it would be okay with Stacy and the kids for him to stay a while longer, and he said he'd already told them he'd probably stay over and see them in the morning, when he planned to take them all for some proper family time. He said that Stacy understood, that she was good like that, especially where *I* was concerned.

While he was gone, I freshened myself up and washed my face and changed out of my work clothes so that when he came back I would feel more relaxed and determined to make it more like the goodbye he'd obviously had planned with his older sister – a decent meal, a few drinks, and a chit-chat about the old days. Just in case. But when he returned and we settled back into our drinking, it was impossible to paper over the earlier incident, and our conversation was stilted and even a little embittered, the more drunk we became.

Neil reminded me of another of his run-ins with Dad. It was after Mum had gone, when Dad had given up and would drink himself to sleep every night in his chair in front of the telly. Neil had crept in late again and had tried to tiptoe along the hall while Dad snored in the front room. But he'd been drunk and stoned and noisy while he looked in the fridge and ran the tap for a glass of water before bed. He told me that when he had looked around from the sink, Dad had been watching him from the kitchen doorway. Neil paused as he remembered this.

"I'll never forget the look on his face, Leece. Never. It was hatred. Pure hatred."

"He'd just woken up, Neil," I said.

"No," said Neil, "that wasn't it. He was scowling at me, like I was some intruder in the house, like I'd broken in. I asked him what was wrong and d'you know what he said?"

"What?" I asked.

"He pointed at me and said, '*You*, Neil, that's what's wrong.' He said I was everything that was wrong with this house. He said I'd put Mum in an early grave. I argued and said it was the fags, not me. But he said that was rubbish, that it was me, the worry I caused her, her disappointment in me."

He paused again and poured himself more wine as the memory burnt somewhere behind his eyes. Then he continued.

"I tried to get past him and up the stairs 'cos I could see where it was going. He wanted a fight, a proper one. I could tell. I was genuinely scared that we'd hurt each other, maybe even kill each other. He grabbed me by the arm as I went past. His face was right up close to mine, like this." Neil put his palm just in front of his face. "He stank, Leece. I remember 'cos it upset me. That smell. I couldn't believe it was coming from him, like he was rotting inside. It was fuckin' awful. That was the moment" – Neil nodded to himself – "right then."

"What do you mean?" I asked.

"He wasn't our dad anymore. He was someone else. I managed to pull away from him and get up the stairs. I noticed under the door your light was on. I wanted just to be with you so badly. It was the only thing I thought would help. But you'd locked your door somehow. You must have had a chair behind it or something. I tried it but it wouldn't budge. I was panicking 'cos I thought Dad would follow me up the stairs, still looking for a fight. Before, I might have given him one, like that time in the kitchen. But the way he looked at me, the way he smelt, I just had to get away from him. I went into my own room. I jammed the door shut by shoving the handle of my flick-knife under it. Then I laid on the bed in all me clothes, listening to him while he stumbled about downstairs. I just lay there listening as he climbed the stairs. He stopped outside your room for about five minutes. Then I heard him come across the landing to mine. I'm pretty sure he put his hand on the door handle. Christ knows what he thought he was gonna do. In the end he just went into his and Mum's room. And that was that."

When we'd drunk ourselves into weary silence, and there was nothing more to say to each other, I told Neil I was going to bed and that I would sleep in Shaun's room and he could have my bed. I told him also to make sure he didn't leave without saying goodbye in the morning. Then I struggled up the stairs and just about found the energy to brush my teeth. When I came out of the bathroom and I was fumbling with the light cord behind me, Neil was there in the dark of the landing, his hand firmly on my hip and his lips against mine in what I thought was a kiss goodnight until I felt his tongue inside my mouth and his hand sliding up to my breast. I pushed him back, and his head broke the thin glass of a black-and-white picture of Mum and Dad on their wedding day. He took hold of my wrist and pushed my hand down until I felt the hard lump in the crotch of his jeans.

"No," I said, as if scolding a randy dog.

"Whatever," he mumbled, his breath all wine and fags, and let go of my hand and staggered along the hallway into my bedroom, knocking pictures skew-whiff as he went, and slamming shut the door behind him.

When I woke in the morning, he'd cleaned up the glass and straightened the pictures and gone. He'd left a note saying he would write as soon as he could, as if the end of the evening had been forgotten. I was suddenly frightened I might never see him again but relieved he wasn't still here in the house, and we wouldn't have to pretend the night before had never happened.

MELVYN

The first buyer bought the car. I knew he would as soon as I saw him. He pulled up outside, and I watched from the dining room window as he stepped out of his brown Rover. He marched straight up to the Jag on the driveway and touched the left fender before even coming to the door. I'd taken it to a carwash the night before and had rolled it out into the spring sunshine first thing and buffed here and there, like any other proud car owner might. Now it sat gleaming, sleek and metallic green on the driveway. The stranger strode up to the door while his wife made her way up the driveway, carrying a toddler who pointed at the car, then stuck the same finger in its mouth.

When I opened the door, he introduced himself as James and shook my hand. He said we'd spoken on the phone the day before. He was boyish and thirty-something and looked so pleased I had to swallow down the guilt and shame and work at acting normal. *Shaun's and Paula's faces rolled behind my eyes.*

We walked out onto the driveway, and I greeted his wife and child. I wanted to stop the transaction, the selling of this death machine to this young, innocent family. I didn't agree with Margret. *We* should have remained the owners and drivers. After all, the car's secret was our secret.

James began opening and shutting the doors and listening appreciatively.

"Nothing quite like the sound of a Jaguar's door shutting, is there?"

His wife smiled and so did the child in her arms.

"It's that deep thud of quality, isn't it?" he continued. "Shut a Cortina door like that and you'll wake up the whole bloody street. 'Scuse my French."

His wife raised her eyebrows at me.

He began kicking the tyres, each of them, then nodding. We looked at the engine with the bonnet up, and he kept rubbing his hands and saying things like, "Just look at that, darling, look at it."

His wife kept smiling. "Very nice. Yes, it's very nice."

Then she showed the little girl.

"Look at the big engine."

The little girl laughed. "Jin jin."

"Yes, engine," the mother said.

"Jin jin."

The happier they became, the worse I felt.

"Can we take her for a spin then?" James said.

"Of course," I managed. "I'll just be a minute."

I went inside and upstairs to the bathroom. I stood in front of the mirror and breathed in through my nose and out through my mouth. My skin prickled and there was sweat on my top lip.

"Come on, Melvyn, for God's sake," I said. "Come on."

I opened the bathroom cabinet and gulped down one of Margret's Valium with a handful of water from the tap. When I closed the cabinet door, I saw Shaun's and Paula's faces behind me in the reflection, staring bloodily over my shoulders, straight into the rotten heart of my guilt. I splashed water over my face and looked again in the mirror. They had gone, but their expressions remained as I dried my face.

In the bedroom, Margret was sitting on the bed reading her Bible, her lips moving but making no sound.

"They want to test drive the car," I said.

I could hear their happy chatter below on the driveway.

"Of course they do," she said without looking up. "They're not going to give you four thousand pounds without driving it, are they?"

"No," I said. "I suppose not."

I took a jacket from the wardrobe. Margret looked at me and frowned, sensing my reluctance to proceed with the deal.

"It's the right thing to do, Melvyn. We should have done it ages ago."

"Yes," I said. "Nice family, though."

She considered this for a moment, then went back to her reading.

"I'll be half an hour or so," I said.

"Mmm," she murmured. "Okay."

I went back down the stairs and out into the sunlight, as I imagined myself running down the lane and screaming.

On the driveway, I began to open the driver's side door, then stopped as James looked at me, puzzled.

"Sorry," I said. "Habit."

I sat in the passenger side and adjusted the seat. It felt odd and unfitting, like someone else's bed.

James made himself comfortable in the driving seat. He ran his hand along the walnut dashboard.

"Beautiful," he said. "Beautiful. You've kept her in great condition."

He checked the rearview mirror until his wife had seat-belted herself with her daughter on her lap.

"Clunk-click," he said, and laughed.

He turned left out of the driveway and headed up Cornerfield Lane. He seemed to know where he was going, so I said nothing. I sat and looked out of the window, wistfully remembering buying the car and driving it home, how pleased I'd been, how privately proud of myself, how desperate to show Margret. A

Jag. A Jaguar. I saw the same pride and pleasure in James now, the feeling that he'd arrived, that this car was proof that he was a man of means and substance. He passed the steering wheel through his hands and grinned as if he were undoing the ribbon of an expensive gift.

"I can't even hear the engine," he said, laughing. "Can you, darling?"

"No," she said.

"Jin jin," the daughter said, and they all laughed again.

We'd come to the end of Apple Tree Lane, at the junction with the Old Church Road. Ahead to the left I saw the tributes to Shaun and Paula around the Lyttleton road sign, dead flowers, and the greying football scarf still hanging in the sapling close by. There were a few fresh flowers. I wondered again if I should add some floral tribute of my own, if enough time had passed for me to do so without arousing suspicion.

James tutted and shook his head.

"Sad that," he said. "Why are you selling her?"

We passed the old Lyttleton Church on the right. I remembered the steeple in the rearview mirror. *Shaun's and Paula's faces again, lit and shocked as I burst out of the fog towards them.* I pictured myself swerving and missing them, crashing through gardens and dying smashed and bloody at the wheel, dying heroically, knowing I'd avoided hitting them, sacrificing myself for their young lives and futures. The daydream was strangely comforting until I realised I'd not answered James's question.

"Sorry," I said. "Miles away."

"No second thoughts, I hope," said James, laughing nervously.

"No," I said, still considering my answer. I had a sudden, overwhelming urge to tell them the truth. To offload and be done with it, face the consequences. *Oh, by the way, this is the car, the car that killed those two teenagers. My wife has rediscovered God. He told her we have to get rid of it. That's why I'm selling it. Just so you know.* "Time for a change, I guess."

James glanced at me, frowning, apparently unimpressed with my answer.

"A change is as good as a rest," his wife said.

"Yes," I said, but I saw how that cliché no longer applied to me. Neither a change nor a rest would do me any good at all. I could think of nothing that would, other than travelling back in time, seeing Shaun and Paula a moment earlier and swerving to miss them. *Their white faces tumbled again in the darkness.*

We drove out along the new dual carriageway, past the spot where I'd dropped Caroline and her friend after the party. I remembered Caroline in the back of the car, thumping my shoulder and snarling while the stink of her friend's vomit rose from behind the passenger seat.

James took the car up to seventy and smiled.

"She wants to go a lot faster, doesn't she?"

"Yes," I said, wincing every time he called the car "*she*", every mention of *her* torque, *her* comfort, the feel of *her* seats, the way *she* sat on the road.

He drove back the same way, past the old church again, the floral tributes and the hanging scarf. I thought about suggesting another route but couldn't think of a plausible reason. I simply sat in the passenger seat and went through it all again for the second time in the space of half an hour. The party, the garden, the girls in the back of the car, the church, the fog, the faces as they tumbled up the bonnet. It was part of me now. Real. Physical. Like a twitch, a tic, a limp, a lump, a scar, a cyst, a tumour. Yes, a tumour. The events of that evening were malignant and cancerous. They were not content with my guilt and shame. They wanted everything, every aspect of my life.

When we arrived back at the house, I invited them in for tea. Margret was downstairs now. For a moment I panicked, wondering how she might behave, boss me about or worse still, quote from the Bible, as she had done more and more since attending church again every Sunday. Instead, she greeted James and his wife and child as if they were old friends. An act that took me by surprise with its authenticity. She ushered us all into the lounge, accepting compliments about the house. Then she disappeared to make tea in the kitchen and could be heard humming along to the radio. When she came back in with the teapot on a tray and chocolate biscuits, she asked if James's wife and daughter would like to see the back garden.

"Let the men thrash out a deal?" she said, smiling.

I stared at her, agog at her act of normality. She caught my eye. A brief ripple of displeasure passed through her smile, revealing for the slightest of moments a hard, prematurely aged expression, the picture of her venal soul she kept covered in the attic.

James asked if I'd take three and a half thousand for cash, and I accepted. I'd meant to hold out for at least three thousand eight hundred, but the whole experience had flattened me, and I just wanted James and his family gone, regardless of their genuine happiness, or rather, because of it. Selling the car was a further crime. If cleaning up the evidence and fixing the car had been my own personal nadir, then making money from the sale was scraping the shit from beneath the bottom of the barrel. If I were ever caught, I considered, as James counted out the notes, surely the deal would compound my guilt and add to the severity of sentence passed down on me.

He finished counting the money and shook my hand, assuring me he'd *treat her like a queen*.

I smiled and made some stupid comment about *that making him the king*.

"I'll feel like one, driving her," he said.

Margret came back in from the garden, spouting pleasantries about the weather and spring, and how *Lyttleton came into its own at this time of year*.

Then we stood together on the lawn and watched them drive away, him in the Jaguar and her in their Rover, the little girl safely buckled and seated in the back. Margret and I waved and smiled as if saying goodbye to relatives or old friends. To further the act, I tentatively touched her fingers with the intention of holding her hand. She swatted my hand away as she might have a bothersome fly. When both cars had turned out of sight, Margret stopped waving, looked at me and seemed to read my thoughts.

"I am only doing what you asked of me, Melvyn. I am doing what needs to be done. This began with you, not me. Don't ever forget that."

Then she turned away and marched back into the house and disappeared up the stairs, leaving me staring at the open front door and the empty hallway.

That same afternoon we took a taxi to the Ford garage in Hareham and bought a second-hand bronze Granada with a black vinyl roof for two thousand pounds. The salesman showed us the car's most attractive features, its low mileage and brand-new tyres, its pristine interior. Margret acted impressed and made appreciative noises while I sulked like a schoolboy being bought sensible shoes instead of fashionable ones. On the way home, Margret put the remaining cash in her handbag and said she'd bank it for us on Monday morning at the post office.

"Save it for a rainy day," she said, without irony, and she breathed in then sighed with palpable relief and satisfaction. She took her small, battered childhood Bible from her handbag, opened it where the frayed purple ribbon sat crushed in the centre and read with her lips moving silently all the way home, as I drove, unfavourably comparing every aspect of the car's performance with the one we'd just sold.

KEVIN

I waited outside Coopers' for Walks. Jase was there but he ignored me. He'd hardly spoken to any of us since the meeting in the copse. He seemed more interested now in hanging out with fifth- and sixth-formers and some of the Lyttleton mods. They congregated most days outside Coopers' to show off their scooters and parkers, or just to chat, smoke, swear, spit and impress schoolgirls. I watched Jase and wondered if he was troubled by what he'd done to Alan. He didn't seem to be. I hoped he had nightmares like I had. I hoped that twisted spectres with Alan's face hovered around him in the dark while he slept. But somehow, I doubted it.

Walks came out of the shop and handed me a Sherbet Dip Dab from the waistband of his trousers.

"Courtesy of Mr and Mrs Cooper." He grinned.

Walks loved to shoplift. He was good at it too. He never got caught. He said his secret was just sticking to small stuff. Whenever someone was suspended or even expelled for stealing, Walks would always shake his head and say, "Well, serves 'em right for being greedy."

Since Alan had died, Walks and I had become closer. We met most mornings on the way to school to cut through the copse and smoke if we had any cigarettes. After school we met to walk home via the Lyttleton Hall, climb our favourite trees and smoke and talk until we had to be home for tea.

As we left the shop forecourt, we both acknowledged Jase with nods. He looked at us and shouted something about being gay. A few of the older crowd laughed, but most paid no attention.

Walks looked at me and said nothing. When we were further away, he said, "I fuckin' hate Jase!"

I said nothing.

"And you know what?" said Walks.

"What?" I asked.

"I'm pretty sure everyone does. They're just too scared to admit it."

"S'pose so," I said, reluctant to commit to the obvious truth, for fear of it getting back to Jase himself.

Walks was right, of course. Most people did hate Jase, and with good reason too. He was nasty and violent. He sometimes smelt bad. There was often food debris between his teeth. He spat when he talked. And he always seemed just moments away from attacking someone.

I had an image of Jase in my head, forcing Alan's face into the gap in the church wall. I could hear his cruel, lisping whisper, *leper thquint, leper thquint.* Alan's whiny squeals, like pigs in the abattoir on Farmhouse Lane.

I wanted to tell Walks what had really happened in the churchyard. I'd wanted to tell Mum, but I had been too fearful of the consequences. Walks was braver than me by a long way. He was in none of the top classes at school, but to me he seemed as smart as anyone I knew. He said things that sounded grown-up. He read all the time. He told stories as scary or as funny as anything I'd read or seen on the telly. And he seemed to have the ability, even at fourteen, to see through everyone and land on the essence of their character. Incredibly, he didn't seem that frightened of Jase. He knew that Jase could kill him in a fight. There would be no fight. Rather a one-sided grim affair, like a wild dog killing a rabbit or a kitten. The fact they'd once been so-called friends would count for nothing if Jase lost his temper. Walks knew all this but still wasn't scared of him. I didn't understand. I was terrified of Jase and would have done just about anything to avoid a confrontation with him.

Our route home took us along Lyttleton Lane towards the village centre, which we'd taken to calling "the vill". Then left onto Denrick Road, which headed towards the Rec and Lyttleton Hall. We took the narrow footpath to the back of the hall. Its old red bricks, dirty windows and rusty fire escape all blazed in the afternoon sun. A ghostly sounding piano echoed inside. I imagined it playing itself, keys depressed by invisible fingers. There must have been a children's ballet class or an old people's dance group. The high tangle of bushes prevented us from seeing through the filthy windows.

Near the end of the footpath, we turned into the small wood and walked the thirty or forty yards to the large, leaning fir tree where I'd been with Emma just a month before. Now summer was coming, the hollow was littered with empty cans and cigarette packets and fag butts from more and more kids who used it to smoke and drink and bring their girlfriends and boyfriends. There were a couple of old milk crates and two stool-tops to sit on. Once, we'd found a whole bag of porno mags there and had sat for a long time, just smoking, spitting, passing round the damp and mouldy pictures of women, marvelling at the size of their breasts, laughing and recoiling at the close-ups.

I thought about being there with Emma, when it had been darker and colder. I remembered her face, the blackness of her nostrils, the taste of her tongue. I wanted to tell Walks but decided against it, thinking he might laugh or ask for details of what we'd done. Emma had been true to her word on both counts: she hadn't told anyone about what had happened in the woods, and she hadn't spoken to me since. We sat down, and Walks took out a new ten-pack of John Player Specials. We liked the design. The black background with interlocking embossed gold letters, JPS, the same as on Mario Andretti's Formula One Lotus, featured in miniature in our Scalextric sets. We lit our cigarettes and smoked and said nothing. It was peaceful in the hollow behind the tree. Just our blue-grey smoke rising and dissipating into the air. Dappled sunlight warmed our faces and played on the dark littery earth around the base of the tree.

"What d'ya think'll happen about Alan?" Walks said.

I thought about the question, clicking my jaw and trying to blow smoke rings.

"I dunno," I said, and spat through the gap in my front teeth.

I wanted to tell him about Alan in my dreams, but I was worried he'd think they were stupid.

"My mum says the police won't do anything," he said, "now that Alan's dad's off the hook. She said that's all they were really interested in, nailing him."

"Why?"

"'Cos Alan's family are gyppos, Mum said. And the police hate gyppos. If they can't nick Alan's dad, that'll be it. They won't do a fuckin' thing."

"Alan's dad's not a gypsy," I said. "They've got a big house."

"Yeah, but have you seen it?" said Walks. "Looks like a fuckin' scrapyard."

"Dad says they've got more money than most people in the whole vill," I said.

"Yeah, so what?" Walks said. "All the more reason for the fuzz to hate 'em. Doesn't matter how much money they've got. *Once a gyppo, always a gyppo*. That's what the old bill think. Least, that's what my mum says."

I stubbed out my cigarette between the roots of the tree. If I closed my eyes, I could see Alan with his face in the church wall, hear Jase whispering into his ear. Alan was dead and no one would do anything. I imagined myself going to the police, telling them everything I knew. After what Walks had said though, it seemed unlikely the police would care. If they did interview Jase, he'd know it was me who'd told them. After all, I'd been the only one there. Already, at school, hardly anyone mentioned Alan. He'd been as good as forgotten by students and teachers, as if he'd never really existed.

Walks took a can of gas from his bag and began to fill his lighter.

"D'you wanna do some?" he said.

"I dunno," I said.

I was nervous. There had been talk at school, kids saying it was the best buzz in the world. But there had also been stories of instant death and lungs full of blue froth.

"We'll both just do a little bit," Walks said. "I did some the other day with Geddy. It was fine. Just pissed ourselves."

"Pissed yourselves?" I said, my bladder twitching.

"Just laughed a bit," he said. "That's all."

"I dunno," I said.

"I'm gonna do a bit," Walks said. "S'up to you."

He held the bright yellow can to his mouth and pushed the red nozzle against his teeth. A small white cloud appeared at his lips and then disappeared as the can hissed and he widened his eyes at the sensation of the cold gas in his mouth. After five or six seconds he handed the can to me and sat back against the tree and laughed.

"Oooh," he said, and stared at me. "Go on, do some, quick."

He rolled onto his side and giggled.

I watched him for a while. Then he sat up.

"Woah," he said. "You look weird."

He giggled and rolled again, moaning a little.

I held the nozzle against my teeth and pushed the canister. The cold gas froze the inside of my mouth and nostrils. I kept the can pushed in until a *vup vup vup* helicopter sound filled my head and the light in the trees around me turned chequered then danced in impossible pulsing patterns. Walks said something that sounded like "fuckin' legs are lent out," played at a slow speed on a warped record. I lay on my back and stared at the canopy of branches and leaves and the patterns that the sunlight made in the trees. I was vaguely aware of Walks taking the can from my hand and a warm feeling of relief in my stomach and bladder.

I sat up and rubbed at my head. Walks was on his side again giggling. I rubbed hard at my brow but couldn't relieve the sense of someone shouting inside my skull. I put my hand between my legs and felt wetness in the crotch of my trousers. I looked down. It only just showed on the black of my school trousers, but my skin felt drenched and soaked and dirty.

"I'm going," I said, and I got up and picked up my school bag. It felt heavier than when we'd arrived. The shouting in my head was now mean laughter and my feet were cold, sweaty and weak.

"Eh?" Walks said. "Don't you wanna stay for a fag?"

I mumbled something about an early tea and walked out of the wood and into the field between the hall and Lyttleton Lane. There was a circle of kids, sitting smoking beneath the large oak with the rope swing. One of them shouted my name, and I waved but kept walking. I heard Walks behind me. I felt the dampness at my crotch and held my school bag in front of me. Walks was running to catch up, still high and giggly.

"Hang on," he kept saying, laughing as he spoke and ran at the same time. "Wait! I'll walk back with you."

He caught up and walked alongside me.

"What's up with you?" he said.

"Nothing," I said. "Just gotta get home."

"It's only half four. Four-twenty-eight-to-be-precise," he said in his best Metal Mickey voice, laughing and flashing me the red numbers on his digital watch.

I pretended to laugh and kept walking.

"What did you think of the gas?" he said. "Pretty good, eh?"

"Yeah," I said. "Great!"

We walked along Lyttleton Lane. At the corner of my street, we stopped.

I held my school bag back in front of my pelvis and tried to act relaxed.

"Meet you here tomorrow then," said Walks. "'Bout eight. I'll save two of them fags."

"Okay," I said.

He turned and walked away. I started towards home, relieved he'd not seen or suspected. But the piss was there again, the wetness, night or day, always ready to dampen any instance of fun or pleasure with a dark patch of shame and the familiar terror of ridicule.

MELVYN

With two Lyttleton men dead and several injured on bombed and burning ships in the Falklands, a reporter from a national tabloid had concocted the story of a "Cursed Village," leaving out the fact Lyttleton was next to an enormous naval base and home to a disproportionate number of sailors and ships' crew. He had littered his report with adjectives about the "courageous", "stoic", "Blitz-time" character of Lyttleton's residents, who were only just recovering from the "tragic unsolved deaths of several local youngsters." Through my horror at being involved and culpable, I could imagine people around the country gobbling up the details with their toast and tea, imagining life in this dreadful place, where children weren't safe and untimely death stalked the streets on the lookout for its next young victim.

I heard Margret on the landing, padding to the bathroom in her slippers. She was humming to herself. The tune had a churchy feel to it, a hymn or something. I stopped reading the paper and listened. The bathroom door shut, abruptly cutting off the melody, leaving just the soft morning silence of upstairs again. I tried to go back to the story, but the sound had bothered me. Margret would be downstairs soon. I was fearful that the story in the paper might undo the benign spell recently fallen upon her. She hummed a lot now.

Whenever she moved or did anything, she hummed some nameless hymn, as if her own voice offered her divine support between our Sunday visits to church and her times with her Bible. I thought about putting the paper in the bin or in the garage, saying it had not arrived that morning. But part of me wanted to see how she'd react, to see if this new breezy ether was truly within her or just some religious fairy dust she'd managed to sprinkle upon herself.

The bathroom door opened to the receding sound of the toilet's flush and the same hymnal humming as before, now growing louder as Margret's soft footfalls descended the thick-carpeted stairs. The humming neared the open kitchen door, more formless now it was louder, then broke off again.

"Morning!" she said, almost with a shout. "It's so bright and cheerful in here."

I still had hold of the paper.

I put it down and said I'd make some tea. Margret glanced at the paper.

"No, no," she said. "You'll be late for work."

I looked at my watch, knowing it was not yet eight-thirty. The walk to work was about four and a half minutes, maybe five or six if I stopped at Barbara's shop.

I folded the paper and Margret turned to making tea, humming to herself again. I watched her for a few moments, trying to discern her body beneath her thick lemon-yellow dressing gown. We had not really touched each other since the accident. I had tried once or twice in bed. But her frigid reaction, her inner female self rolling into a spiky ball, had dispelled even the faintest hopes of physical affection, let alone sex. I had to resign myself to that part of my life being over, to no longer having even the trace of a sex life. It was difficult. I am a man, after all. But if I was honest with myself, it seemed like a fair punishment. Church-going and celibacy, I considered, were a small price to pay for the lives of Shaun Terridge and Paula Werth, who had been gone almost half a year by then.

Margret was an older woman now. Her body was still shapely beneath whatever she wore. She was buxom and her hips had always been wider than her waist. But her humming and detached, airy deportment had somehow added a decade or so to her overall appearance.

She turned and caught me staring at her. She paused as a brief look of distaste blanched her features, as if she'd swallowed bitter medicine. Then she began to hum again, a little louder.

"Didn't you ought to go to work, Melvyn?" she said.

She'd taken to using my name more often. It had a formalising effect, a cleansing of anything relaxed or intimate between us. The *honeys* and *darlings* were long gone and now met with a cold scowl if one slipped out through force of old habit.

"Yes," I said, standing up.

"Good," she said. "Have a nice day."

She tottered over to me with a teaspoon in her hand and leant towards my right shoulder in an imitation of a hug. A little hum escaped from her as she did so, like a snippet of discordant choir practice heard through an open church door.

I took the paper with me into the hall and listened to Margret's humming as I readied myself to leave. She put on the radio but continued to hum at odds with the music. I stood for a moment, hot and cheerless in the sunlight that poured through the front door glass and filled the hallway.

Outside was one of those Lyttleton mornings, neither spring nor summer, yet both. The sun gilded the houses, trees and hedges along Cornerfield Lane, and birdsong loudly filled the warm air. My mood should have been lifted. I tried to drink it all in, as I would have done the previous May or the one before that. But the pleasantness of the morning met with a new immoveable part of my personality, the killer who'd got away with it, the skulking pariah dwelling just below the surface of my visible self, the Hyde to my Jekyll, the hidden picture of my mouldering soul. I strode quickly for fear of meeting a neighbour or customer and having to stop and talk.

At Barbara's shop, the newspaper rack had been placed outside with a sandwich board: *LYTTLETON MAKES NATIONAL FRONT PAGES.* Inside, Barbara was talking with a group of women. They were all nodding and shaking their heads. I picked up some chocolate and made my way to the counter. Barbara spotted me and excused herself from the group. They immediately stopped talking to turn and smile sadly at me. At the counter, I chose some chewing gum and smiled at Barbara, passing her a pound note.

"I take it you've read the paper this morning, Mr Pettifer," she said.

"Yes, Barbara," I said, remembering that cold Sunday morning six months earlier. "Awful news."

"It is," she said, looking at the floor and shaking her head. "It's hard to put it into words, isn't it?"

"Yes," I answered, "it is."

As I opened the door to my shop, I heard the low electronic beep from upstairs in reception. We'd had the system fitted the previous autumn. Laura, my receptionist, assistant and trainee, had thought it would be a good idea. She was constantly having to move between reception and the display and testing areas. Walk-ins were often left dithering alone at the front desk. "Bad for business," she'd said, "and a security risk." When I'd run it by Margret, she'd said it sounded like Laura was "getting too big for her boots" and "since when did you start taking advice from a junior receptionist?" Eventually, I'd had the system installed and just not mentioned it again to Margret. I had also thought it a good idea, but mostly I'd agreed to please Laura. She was good at her job, and I feared losing her and not finding a reliable replacement. I'd be lying if I said I'd never had fantasies about her. They were much less romantic than those about Angie, cheaper, more lurid boss–worker scenarios about half-dressed, breathless trysts after the door had been locked on the final customer.

When I got to the top of the stairs and into reception, Laura had several cabinets open and was cleaning glass shelves and polishing frames. I watched her for a moment, marvelling at her efficiency and taking in her delicate, youthful body. She turned with a duster in her hand and smiled at me. She was a perfect, walking advertisement for the business, suggesting it was almost impossible to look pretty *without* wearing glasses.

"Morning, boss," she said.

This was her gentle joke with me. I would have liked it to be flirtatious but it wasn't. I'd asked her not to call me Mr Pettifer. But she found Melvyn too informal, blushing the couple of times she'd tried it.

"Morning, Laura," I said. "How's the book looking?"

I knew as I'd already checked it the night before.

"Nice quiet start," she said, "but busy-busy after ten."

"Good," I said.

The door alarm beeped in reception.

"Maybe not such a quiet start after all," Laura said.

I told her I'd be back through in a moment and let myself into my office and put my case on the desk. Then I hung my cardigan on a hook and selected one of the white coats hung on the others. Whenever Margret came into the shop, she would scoff at my white coats, saying they were unnecessary and too formal. But they helped me to feel professional. And since the accident, putting them on had reassured me of my worth. A medical practitioner of the community. Someone who had his paying public's interests at heart. Someone who cared about the health of their eyes and sight. The irony of their not seeing my guilt was not lost on me. But sometimes, at night while Margret slept, I would calculate the approximate number of patients I'd helped over the years and weigh that work against my crime, picturing the scales of justice in my head and wondering if I'd done enough, piecemeal, to counterbalance those tumbling faces and bodies on the road.

I readied myself, checking my breast pocket for pens and turning on the equipment in the testing area. I could hear Laura's pleasantries in reception.

"Just have a seat and help yourself to a magazine," she said. "Mr Pettifer won't be long."

When I was ready, I walked out into the waiting area, my hands in the pockets of my white coat. My attempt to appear casual and doctorly, a reassuring, authoritative, professional presence.

"This is Mrs Terridge," Laura said, smiling from me to a pale woman sat on the couch with a magazine in her lap.

She smiled in a resigned way, lowering her eyes.

"It's Miss, actually, Miss Terridge."

Laura blushed and apologised. "Sorry, Miss Terridge."

I knew instantly she was Shaun's mother. *Her son's face in the headlights exploded in my brain.* I shrivelled inside my clothes. Beads of cold sweat dribbled out of pores in the small of my back and ran into the gorge of my backside. Her name caught in my throat and upon the sudden dryness of my lips as I tried to repeat it. Her smile altered into a brief register of offence or confusion. I couldn't tell which. I looked at Laura, who stared at me, then frowned.

"Miss Terridge," I finally managed. "Come right this way."

I concentrated on breathing and walking but could not escape the impression that she had looked right through my eyes to where the accident played over and over on repeat, to where her son and his girlfriend tumbled up the bonnet and windscreen, over the roof of my car and onto the freezing road. I managed a glance at her as she placed her bag on the floor beside the chair. She looked tired and flustered. *Just a regular eye test*, I told myself, thinking the routine would cover the initial blip. After all, I'd done thousands over the years.

"So," I said, my back to her, washing my hands at the small basin, "how long since your last eye test?"

A pause and silence in which I heard myself swallow. I was convinced she was staring at my back, but I daren't look round.

"I don't know," she said finally. "Five years? Maybe six or seven."

Her voice was quiet and breathy, as if speaking was an effort.

"Have you experienced any problems or deterioration in your sight in that time?"

Each routine question helped me to relax a little. I absorbed my surroundings. White cupboards. Large plastic cross-section eye model. Sterile robotic optometry machines. This was *my* environment. *I* was in charge here. Safe.

"A little," she said. "I've started back at work at the post office. I'm struggling with letters and numbers up close. Envelopes and cheques. That sort of thing."

I was pleased she had returned to work, that she was coming to terms with her loss. A surge of hope rose in me, that I may not have ruined her life forever. At the same time, I thought of Margret banking the money we'd made from selling the car. Whether she'd been served by Miss Terridge. The thought made me wince with discomfort. I pushed it aside and continued with the examination. The routine helped calm the sensation of wanting to run and keep running.

"I've been under a bit of strain lately," she said. Sweat broke out on my back again. "I'm not sure if the problem is just tiredness or something."

"Are you getting enough sleep?" I asked.

The question itself and my tone jarred me. It was a doctor's question. Or a friend's. Not an optician's. She seemed a little surprised.

"No, not really," she said, finally.

She looked ashamed of her admission, and she closed her eyes and took a breath.

"I'm worried about my brother," she said. "And..." She paused. "Other things."

I should have cut the conversation short. It was pointless and risky. But I was curious. I wanted to help her. And talking to her, I thought, might offer some important information, some further way of avoiding detection. Maybe even relief of some kind.

"Why are you worried about him?" I asked.

"He's gone to the Falklands," she said, monotone, as if saying he'd gone to the pub or the shops.

I was stumped. I wanted to offer reassurance, *Oh, I'm sure he'll be fine*, but that seemed dismissive and even offensive, especially as Lyttleton men had already been burnt and killed.

Miss Terridge broke the uncomfortable silence.

"He's in the paras," she said, "so he might see some action."

"Oh," I said, struggling for something comforting to say, "that is worrying."

I began some simple eye coordination tests. I held my two forefingers erect about eighteen inches in front of Miss Terridge's face, then asked her to follow each finger with her eyes. I drew my right finger out to the right and then the left out to the left. The tests were pointless. I knew from what she had told me she most likely had astigmatism in one or both of her eyes. But I needed time to think. I asked her to read the letters on the Snellen chart and adjusted the testing lenses in front of her eyes. I decided that following procedure was probably the safest option. So that's what I did. When the test was over, I explained her condition with the help of the cross-sectioned plastic eye model. Then I asked if she'd like to choose some frames.

She looked worried and asked how much it would cost. I told her it depended on the type of lenses and frames she chose. Then before thinking it through I said we could offer a discount for a first-time customer. In the display area, she spun a couple of racks distractedly, then checked her watch. I went to reception to tell Laura about the discount. Miss Terridge appeared at the counter with the cheapest set of tortoise-shell frames. I told her she could take more time to choose if she wished. She said she had to be at work by ten and that these were fine. I thanked her, and Laura told her to come back in three days to collect the glasses. Then Miss Terridge turned and was gone, flustered again, it seemed, agitated and desperate to leave the shop.

Laura made a concerned face.

"She seemed a bit upset."

Then she looked at me, expecting an answer. I pretended to look at the appointment book, running my finger over the list of names.

"Did she," I said, as nonchalantly as I could.

"D'you know her?" said Laura.

"No," I said. "Do you?"

"No," she said. "You seemed shocked when you saw her."

"Did I?" I said, still looking at the book.

"Yes," she said. "A bit. I think she's that boy's mum."

"Which boy?" I said. *Shaun's face tumbled up the windscreen.*

"The one killed at Christmas," she said.

"Really?" I said, walking away so she could not see my face.

"Yes," Laura said. "Terridge. Lisa Terridge. I'm pretty sure that's her."

The door alarm sounded again and the small red light behind reception flashed.

"Tell them I'll be five minutes," I said.

I hurried into my office and took a small bottle of whisky from under some papers in the bottom drawer of the filing cabinet. I gulped two quick swigs and grabbed my cigarettes from the desk and went through the back door onto the small iron balcony behind the parade of shops.

"Christ," I breathed, once outside in the air and sunlight.

I lit my cigarette and inhaled, feeling the warmth of the smoke and whisky in my stomach and chest. I tried to calculate the risk of what had just happened. I thought it all back through in quick time, from my reaction in reception to Lisa Terridge's abrupt departure. I assured myself there was no harm done, that she'd have to be some kind of mind-reader to suspect me. But doubt stirred somewhere, and I winced as if I'd swallowed a tiny shard of glass. I finished my cigarette and tried to focus. Throughout the day, I kept seeing her pale face, worn and tired, flushed with agitation as she had left. I hoped I would never see her again, and I hoped she would come back in three days for her glasses, as this would surely mean she suspected nothing.

ASCENSION ISLAND, MAY 8TH, 1982

Dear Leece,

We've just arrived at Ascension Island. A few days R 'n' R and last-minute prep before we head south again. The lads are in high spirits. Too high if I'm honest. Sometimes it's like being on a bloody school trip. Some of these boys are not long out of basic. They think they're invincible. I remember that feeling. I have to keep reminding them they're not, specially if they fuck about. You should have seen them when we arrived in the harbour here. Some of them had to be restrained from diving off the ferry for a swim. Bloody idiots'll get themselves killed before they even see an Argie. Hard to blame them, though, after being cooped up on this thing for twelve days solid. Some of them were sick as dogs.

I suppose there'll be a real battle now. The Sheffield was a harsh wake-up call. I guess you must have seen it on the news. A lot of the lads, myself included, were under the impression the Argies would sod off when they saw Her Majesty's finest on the horizon. Well, we got that wrong, didn't we? I'm trying not to dwell on it, but I can't help thinking about those poor bastards below decks. The ones who didn't make it off, and even some of the ones who did. Jesus! Thank Christ I'm not in the Navy.

I reminded some of the boys on the way down here, "This is not a fuckin' holiday!" But for some of the younger lads, specially the ones from Glasgow and Birmingham and that, perhaps it is. You'd think they'd never seen the sea before. Maybe they hadn't. They're good lads though. I just hope to Christ they all come back in one piece.

I have to admit, Leece, it's tough for me being around the younger lads. I've tried not to become too attached but it's hard, you know? Some of them are not much older than Shaun. One or two of them even remind me of him. Not in looks or anything, just in their ways. Being young and that. Fuckin' teenagers, some of them! Maybe it's being so far away from home, but I've been thinking about Shaun a lot. It's hard to accept that he won't be there when I get back. But you will, and Stacy and the kids, of course, and that's what I have to keep in mind.

Love,

Neil x

PART III

The Dead of Summer

KEVIN

One Saturday night, early in the summer, we decided to sleep out. I had to tell my mum I was staying at Walks's house, and Walks said he was staying at mine. It was the classic kid con, the oldest trick in the teenage playbook, and incredibly, it worked. Walks's dad was in a burns unit in Salisbury after his ship had been struck by an Exocet. He wasn't as badly burnt as some of the men who'd survived, the ones whose faces had become blisters with eyes, but his legs and arms had been scorched, and Walks said it would be a while before he could come home again. His mum was making the hundred-mile round trip three or four times a week in their Austin Allegro. My mum was working more and more, saying that we needed the money, what with Dad still being away. She spoke about him like he was on holiday somewhere, rather than living in a bedsit a couple of miles away in Sail-on-Lee.

Jase was back. The older kids he'd been hanging around with had tired of him. Of course, he never admitted this. They'd all got shitfaced one night, and after Jase had passed out, they'd stripped him, scrawled obscenities all over his chest and stomach with red lipstick, singed off one of his eyebrows, shaved his pubic hair, pissed on him and tied a ribbon round his cock. To make matters much worse, they'd taken some Instamatic photos, which had done the rounds at school.

Things change quickly in adolescence. Jase's star had fallen overnight. He'd gone from being feared to being ridiculed. Everyone was laughing behind his back and even *Jase* couldn't beat up everyone. He was used to being the tormentor, not the tormented. He was not used to being a figure of fun, having girls giggle as they passed him in the school corridors, seeing *Jathe ith a wanker, Jathe hath got no pyoobth, Jathe likthe a golden shower* written on cubicle walls in the boys' toilet. So he was back with us, where I suppose he felt safer. Back with Geddy, who seemed happy at his return, and with Walks and me, who had no choice but to put up with him.

We met at the rope swing and hung around until it began to get dark. Then we set off for Haven Head via the Beach Road off-licence. We clubbed together enough notes and coins for eight cans of lager, eight bottles of barley wine and forty cigarettes. We did spuds for the brand as Geddy smoked Lambert and Butler, Jase Marlboro Reds, and Walks and I smoked JPS. The last man in got to choose the brand. It was Walks. He pumped his fist at me and grinned. Jase cursed us both, "Fuckin' JPEth thmoking poofth."

We headed out along the cliff path, past the collection of old weatherbeaten beach huts and shacks we called the Shanty Town and set up camp on the beach itself between Haven Head and Barmush. We dumped our sleeping bags and beer in a natural cove at the foot of the sandstone cliffs. Then with Walks's torch lighting a jittery circle on the shingle, we formed a skirmish line across the narrow beach from cliff-foot to shoreline and picked up all the dry wood and litter we thought would burn. When we'd walked the best part of a mile to the Dog Snout, and we could see the lights of Barmush Harbour in the distance and the Chorley Oil Refinery lit like some futuristic city beyond, we headed back, picking up anything useful we'd missed on the way.

When our fire was burning well, Geddy added one of the large washed-up logs he'd found. He'd trudged half a mile of beach with it on his shoulder like some ancient slave from the time of the Pyramids.

"This fucker'll burn all night," he said.

We sat up to our waists in our sleeping bags with the fire lighting our hot faces, smoking, drinking, belching, spitting, talking, swearing, laughing and feeling like men of the outdoors, with the rush and roll of shingle in our ears, the crabby smell of the dirty sea in our nostrils, and the fresh buzz of drunkenness in our young, stupid brains. When we'd finished the beer and barley wine, we passed round the remains of a bottle of whisky Jase had stolen from his mum's drinks cabinet, each of us coughing and laughing as we drank. Walks was sick by the foot of the cliff while everyone cheered, and Geddy tried to fart into the fire to make a flamethrower. It didn't work but it made us laugh until we cried.

Then when the fire was low and the others had passed out, I went down to the water's edge in the dark, took off my shoes and socks and jeans, waded in up to my knees, and pissed into the sea, swaying and enjoying the relief, the cold grip of water on my thighs, the feeling of tiny stones rolling over my toes, and the undertow sucking out hollows of shingle under my heels. Amid the fug of drunkenness, I prayed for a night off from my enuresis and pulled myself back and forth, imagining Emma's hand instead of my own, faster and faster until I came with the sound of the waves in my ears and the blurry lights of the oil refinery and the stars blinking in my half-shut eyes. When I woke warm and blissfully dry in my sleeping bag at dawn, with the sea a mercurial mirror of silver, pink, blue and gold, I felt for a few perfect moments like the happiest boy alive. Luxuriating in bed in the morning was a rarity for me, as I was often on the floor while my mattress aired at the window. I found the cigarettes, lay back in my sleeping bag, and smoked and stared at the shifting sky until the others began to stir.

Once everyone was awake, we added small branches to the white-hot log that had burnt all night, as Geddy had said it would. They crackled into a new fire. Walks produced a yellow box of Wall's sausages, which had thawed in his bag overnight, and he stood and bowed at the applause and Geddy shouting, "You sneaky little fucker!" We cooked the sausages on the end of sticks over the fire and ate them too hot with the fatty juices running down our chins. After breakfast, we splashed our faces with cold seawater and smoked our last cigarettes, squinting in the morning sun like restful cats. We skimmed a few stones, set up the cans and bottles as target practice, took turns at pissing on the fire, then decided to head back to the swing.

We took a shorter route along Haven Avenue, the plushest street of houses in Lyttleton; huge, squat, Edwardian, Georgian and Deco affairs with giant firs on the front lawns and long gravel drives that swept past glossy, porticoed and pillared entranceways. We stood at the front gate of one called Beachwood, massive and red brick with a wide red front door that seemed half a mile away. On the lawn either side of the driveway were giant pampas and short thick tropical palms.

"Thatth a nithe fuckin' houthe," Jase said. "How much d'you think a houthe like that cothts?"

"Fuck knows," said Geddy. "More than you'll ever earn though, that's for sure."

"We'll thee," said Jase.

We laughed a little, then all went back to staring at the house, mesmerised by its size and pristine appearance. I wanted to stroll down its driveway with my shoes crunching on the gravel and wander in the back door to the smell of cooking.

Walks broke my daydream.

"Look how much milk they've got. There must be about twenty of 'em in there."

"Either that or they're away and forgot to cancel the milkman," said Geddy.

We all stood and looked at the six or seven bottles of milk on the bottom step.

Everyone was thinking the same thing, but Geddy said it.

"That's just askin' to be nicked."

"Fuckin' right, mush," Jase added.

I looked at Walks.

He smiled and shrugged. "Why not? They won't miss one or two."

We trotted in fast and hunched, single file like raiding soldiers, and gathered puffing and giggling behind the first large pampas beside the driveway. We sat there for a while, facing back towards the tall hedge and front gate.

Jase lay on his stomach, his left ear touching the grass, his eyes on the front of the house.

"Fuck it," he said. "I got a better idea. Walkth, gimme yer catapult."

"No way," said Walks. "I'm thirsty. Let's nick it."

"Gimme yer fuckin' catapult or I'll jutht take it and keep it," Jase said.

Geddy laughed. "Just give 'im it."

Walks sighed and dug inside his bag. He handed the Black Widow to Jase. Jase snatched it and went back to watching the front door.

"Gimme a thtone," Jase said in a harsh whisper.

"I 'aven't got any," Walks said.

"Gimme a fuckin' thtone!" Jase said. "I thaw you put thum in yer bag at the beach."

"This is stupid," Walks said.

He rooted inside his bag again and pulled out a smooth black pebble.

Jase smiled.

"Perfect," he said.

Jase and Geddy laid one way out from the pampas so they could see the front door. Walks and I laid the other. I had to lie in close behind Walks and look over his shoulder to see the door. I could smell the meat fat of the sausages we'd eaten that morning. I looked over my shoulder and saw Geddy and Jase arranged symmetrically to Walks and me, the upturned soles of our shoes almost touching.

Just then, a large tabby cat walked tigerishly slow around the corner of the house. It sniffed at the tops of one or two of the milk bottles, then sat facing the red door. It mewed once, licked its shoulder and looked both ways as if checking for something. Then it just sat there, staring at the door like a visitor who'd just rung the bell.

"Jeethuth," Jase whispered, and we all heard the anticipation dripping from those lisped S's, the hush of pleasure at the very thought of killing.

Walks said, "Jase, don't."

But Jase already had. The twang of the thick rubber straps of the Black Widow was followed instantly by the dark shape of the cat smashing into the white milk bottles on the doorstep, the sound of breaking glass crackling through the quiet garden, a sonic announcement of yobboes and wrongdoing.

Jase and Geddy were both up, laughing and running for the front gate.

"Fuckin' bastard," Walks was saying as he got up to run after them.

They disappeared around the front hedge of the garden and were gone.

"What about the cat?" I whined, but the question died limply into the silent sunshine of the garden. I remembered Mum crying in the kitchen with our tabby Milly in a binbag on the table, Dad doing his best to keep it together as the man of the house.

I stayed rooted in the grass, watching the front gate in the hope that Walks might come back for me. Then I watched the front door, waiting for a reaction from inside the house. I wanted to run but instead I tucked myself closer into the base of the pampas and watched the red door and listened.

There was nothing. The silence of the perfect June morning had returned as quickly as it had shattered.

I had to get the cat. I couldn't bear the thought of some kid, no matter how rich or spoilt, finding the cat with its skull smashed in on the doorstep.

I checked the gate and watched the door, expecting a mother or child to come crying onto the front step at any second. But nothing. It seemed strange, like no one in this beautiful, affluent neighbourhood cared. Or no one was even there, in Beachwood, next door, in the street, or anywhere in Lyttleton. I'm sure in those moments, in that garden, under the pampas, with the soft dewy grass beneath me, and the low sun hitting the large square windows of the huge house, some unwanted understanding slipped virus-like into me and stayed there. It mocked my belief in the general benevolence of things and seemed to cackle at my assumption up to that point in a lifelong protective goodness in the world. Maybe it had started at Christmas with Shaun Terridge and Paula Werth mown down without anybody brought to justice. Maybe it was my imagination, but while I watched the front door, half-hoping the tabby might spring up, chase its tail and trot off, my insignificance and the inevitability of the death of myself and everyone I knew seemed to permeate my whole being, as if the Grim Reaper had glided into the garden and hovered now behind me with his scythe gripped in his skeletal fingers. I couldn't fight it. It was like the tide coming in or the sun going down. It came out of the ground beneath me like the hungry hands of the dead, and it crushed me from above like being bottom of a pile-on. It was ugly, sour, cold and thick, like gone-off milk or a hot gravied dinner left out to turn gelid for the flies. And when it had passed, I realised I had pissed into my pants, jeans and the soil beneath me, my warm urine turning quickly cold and damp against my skin.

When I stood up, I was snivelling like a tired child. I brushed at the pampas fronds on my clothes and in my hair and walked towards the house, expecting at any moment some furious dad to come roaring out of the front door and down the driveway to shake me until my ribcage fell to pieces and my neck broke. Part of me even wanted that. But the huge house and garden remained exactly as we had found it, silent, expensive and indifferent, unchanged apart from the smashed milk bottles and the dead cat on the doorstep. My night on the beach now hung heavy upon me, trampish and crumpled. Unwashed and dirty, I was like a beggar approaching a scullery door to ask for food, a starving leper of yore looking for the dark squint in the wall behind the old Lyttleton Church.

At the doorstep, I stopped and stared at the cat. Its skull at the back had been crushed inward by the stone. Blood from its mouth and eye socket was marbling the milk pink as it dripped from the bottom step into the gravel. I touched the cat with the toe of my shoe on its soft, stripy flank. I bent down and stroked its warm, tan underbelly, as I used to do with our cat when she stretched herself out in the sun. Then I picked the cat up and held it under my arm while I shoed the broken glass and bloody milk around until it was barely noticeable amongst the gravel. I grabbed one of the unbroken bottles of milk and trotted back to the gate where my sleeping bag had been left by the others as they'd fled. I thought about taking the cat to the beach to bury it in the shingle or throw it into the sea from the end of one of the long sewage groynes that ran perpendicular to the shore. But I was certain there would be people there by now, walking their dogs or arriving early for a day at the seaside. So I decided on the swing, where I thought the others might be, where we might bury the cat in the woods. The stain in my jeans was barely noticeable, and I figured it would dry while I walked. I sniffed hard but thankfully couldn't smell anything beyond my own grubbiness from a night on the beach. I forced the milk bottle into the waistband of my jeans and rolled the cat in the sleeping bag to carry under my arm. Then I ran and walked and ran and walked the length of Haven Avenue, feeling out of place and criminal in the clean, quiet and leafy road. The cat slipped once from the front of the rolled-up sleeping bag and hit the pavement awkwardly with a crack, leaving a bloody smear on the stone. I looked around to see if anyone was watching me, then put the cat inside the sleeping bag itself, all the way into the bottom, where its blood browned the orange nylon lining. It was ruined now, and I decided I would bury the cat inside it, a soft makeshift coffin as payment for its life. It seemed like the right thing to do, and I was sure the sleeping bag would not be missed, at least not for a while anyway.

When I got back to the swing there was no one there, so I went into the woods to the large fir. Walks was sat smoking on one of the beer crates.

"Fuck, there you are!" he said. "I'm sorry. I went after Jase about the cat. I thought you were behind me. Those fuckers went home. Jase took my catapult."

"What did he say about the cat?" I asked.

"He said he was aiming at the milk," Walks said. "Lying cunt!"

I told him what had happened after they'd run, just the part about getting the cat and coming back to the swing. Then I unrolled the sleeping bag, unzipped it, and showed the cat to Walks.

"Fuckin' Jase," he said.

We stared at the cat. It was curled up in the foot of the sleeping bag as if asleep, except for brown bloody smears around its head, its mouth open, exposing its tiny fangs and protruding pink tongue.

"Poor thing," said Walks.

He looked like he might cry.

I told Walks we should bury the cat. I thought he might laugh at me, but he agreed and said his dad had shovels in the shed. Then he was quiet for a while, and I said nothing. He hadn't really said anything about his dad, other than he was back, injured and in hospital. But everyone knew it was burns. It had been mentioned in the local paper, along with other men from Lyttleton and nearby towns and villages who'd been injured or killed.

We rolled up the cat in the sleeping bag and hid it under some bushes. It was still only just after nine. We figured we had at least until half ten before any kids would arrive at the swing.

On the way to Walks's house he was quiet. I was sure he was thinking about his dad. I wanted to ask him how he was but thought it would sound stupid in the circumstances. I expected Walks's reply to go something like, *He was dragged from a burning ship, for Christ's sake, how do you think he is?* I'd wondered about him, though, how he might look now. I'd only ever seen one burns victim before at the Working Men's Club, and he looked like his face had been made too quickly with cheap plastic, then poked through the bars of a gas fire.

When we got to Walks's house he told me to wait by the front gate. I'd been in his house several times before, so it was strange to not be invited in. He appeared again a few minutes later with shovels. He gave me one and said, "If we see Dreek or anyone, I'll just say we're going to my dad's allotment." I nodded and took the shovel, and we walked in silence back to the swing, and then to where we'd left the cat. All the way I wondered about Walks's dad's allotment, about who was looking after it while he was away, whether Walks was going up there, weeding and planting and digging up vegetables on his own, or if the place was just abandoned and overgrowing. Both scenarios seemed sad – a boy digging alone on his father's allotment, a vegetable patch overgrown with weeds and rotting potatoes and carrots, all maggoty in the mud.

We thought it would be unwise to dig the hole where we usually hung out and smoked in case other kids might be curious about the freshly turned mud. So we carried the cat and the shovels further along the path to a small clearing within some thick bushes and tangly trees. Once in the clearing, we were completely invisible to anyone on the path and well-hidden from the swing and the hall.

Walks had a small orange transistor radio that he hung by its cord from a branch. Its thin, tinny music seemed to cheer him instantly. It was warm and sheltered in the clearing, and the sun was now filtering through the canopy of the wood. We took off our shirts and hung them on branches. Then we cleared a spot of leaves and twigs with the tips of our shovels and began to dig.

At first it was hard work, and I kept stopping and taking deep breaths while Walks took my turn and said nothing. I wasn't used to that kind of work but Walks seemed fine. Maybe he *had* been keeping up his dad's allotment. It would have been just like him to have some secret sideline activity. He was, as they say, *a dark horse*. I watched him slicing clods of mud and lifting them carefully out onto the growing mound at the side. After a while I caught my second wind and we got a rhythm going together. We even sang along to songs we knew on the radio. In about half an hour we had the hole deep enough for the rolled-up sleeping bag, but we kept on digging anyway. We took a cigarette break and leant on our shovels like workmen, smoking and talking and wiping our sweaty brows with dirty hands before beginning again. In digging, we forgot about the cat, about Jase, about Walks's dad in hospital and mine not living with us anymore. We sang along to songs, dug, smoked, sang, dug, and laughed at each other's impressions of pop stars, our shovels as guitars or microphones, until we were stood in a hole that came up to our waists.

When we were satisfied, we stopped for another cigarette break. We were filthy. Our jeans were dark with mud, and our trainers were caked and unrecognisable as shoes. Our faces and torsos were covered in brown smears, as if we'd gone feral or savage like the kids in *Lord of the Flies*. We sat with our legs dangling into the hole, our heels kicking off mud-dust as they banged against the inside wall and the stringy, exposed roots that poked out like twiggy witches' fingers. For a while, we said nothing. We just sat and smoked, proud of what we'd achieved in one short morning, convinced, as so often not, that we were doing the right thing.

Walks got into the hole, and I passed him the rolled-up sleeping bag with the dead cat inside.

"Ain't your mum gonna flip when she finds this missing?"

"Nah," I said, trying to act confident. "I doubt she'll even notice."

Then we heard Jase's and Geddy's voices approaching through the woods. Walks put the sleeping bag in the bottom of the hole by his feet.

"That's all we need," he said.

Jase pushed his way through the tall bushes into the clearing.

"What the fuck are you two gaylordth up to now?" he said, laughing.

Geddy sniggered behind him, Mutley-style.

"What's it look like?" Walks said back.

I was stunned. Jase stared at him for a few moments, a perplexed frown creasing his brow.

"Alright," he said, pretending to laugh, "keep yer fuckin' hair on."

Jase and Geddy were drinking Tab. Jase pulled two more cans from a Spar bag and threw one to me and one to Walks. I opened mine immediately and started gulping it back, thirsty from the digging. Walks just held his can tight in two hands as he'd caught it and stared at Jase.

"Don't thay thankth or nothing," Jase said.

"Thanks," I said, and belched.

Jase continued to glare at Walks, waiting for a response.

"Well," he said.

"Thanks," Walks murmured, and climbed out of the hole.

He got a shovel and began to heave dirt from the pile back into the cat's grave.

"Woah, woah, woah," Jase said, and stepped between Walks and the hole. "I jutht wanna 'ave a quick look."

He jumped down into the hole and pulled out the rolled-up sleeping bag and placed it on the ground.

Walks had the shovel clenched in both hands and was staring at Jase's head below him. My bladder throbbed as my imagination played the scene out. *Walks striking down on Jase's head, splitting it open on the mud like a watermelon, Geddy dropping his can in shock, then all of us having to bury Jase along with the cat.* But Walks just stood there, tight-mouthed and lock-jawed, eyeing Jase, not moving or saying a word.

Jase climbed out of the hole and unrolled the sleeping bag and unzipped it, revealing the blood-smeared orange nylon inside. The cat was now laid out flat with its crushed eye socket facing up towards the sky in a gory wink.

"Bulltheye!" He laughed, and Geddy sniggered behind him.

"I thought you were aiming at the milk," Walks said.

"Well, it duthn't really matter now, duth it?"

Walks looked at Jase for a second or two. Jase turned and smiled at him.

"I can't believe you two queerth are gonna bury thith fuckin' cat," he said, adding in a little girly voice, "were you gonna thay a little prayer ath well and lay down thum flowerth."

Walks and I said nothing.

Geddy giggled and wheezed like an obedient bulldog sidekick.

Jase stood up.

He was now holding the cat by its tail, its front paws limp in the dirt, thick, dark blood dripping from its missing eye.

"Fuckin' put it down, Jase," Walks said.

He clenched the shovel harder and stared at Jase.

"Why?" Jase said. "I fuckin' killed it. I should be the one who decidthe what to do with it."

"Put it down," said Walks, "or I'll knock your thtupid lithpy fuckin' head off with thith thpade!"

The silence that followed seemed total. There must have been bird noises, wind in the leaves, the odd car passing on Lyttleton Lane, maybe even church bells from the village, but all I remember is total silence, as if even the trees held their leafy breath while everyone waited for Jase to explode.

My bladder throbbed like a water-filled balloon. I tightened my muscles and grimaced.

Geddy's pink can of Tab was raised halfway to his mouth, sniggers paused, eyes wide with shock.

Jase stared at Walks like a snake at a rat, the dead cat bumping softly against his leg, dripping blood down his jeans and onto his shoe.

Walks, shovel in hands, stood so rigid it seemed he might never move again, a petrified monument to adolescent defiance against the odds.

Around our tense tableau, the trees shifted and creaked and were shushed by the leaves.

"Alright," Jase said. "I will," and he swung the cat in two wide circles above his head like a cowboy on *The High Chaparral*, the long grey-black striped body and legs stretching outward, tail-bones cracking audibly, as Jase launched the cat-corpse into the air, where it sailed upwards in its final spinning cat-leap, snagging on the knobby hook of a thin branch then dropping, even deader, it seemed, just beyond the clearing with a sharp snapping of twigs and a brief hissing of disturbed dead leaves.

"There," said Jase, theatrically putting his hand to his ear. "Thatithfied?"

"You're a wanker," Walks said, shaking his head.

"Yeah, well," said Jase, "leatht my old man wothn't melted by the Argeeth."

Walks continued to stare at him but said nothing.

Jase continued. "Maybe you thould make the hole bigger for your dad now that the cat won't need it."

He backed away, watching Walks the whole time, ready, expecting, hoping, perhaps, to be attacked at any moment. But Walks stayed still, his mouth shut so tight his lips had disappeared, two deep vertical creases in his forehead, just above the bridge of his nose, making him look ten years older than a boy of fourteen.

"C'mon, Geddy," Jase said. "Let'th leave theeth little girlth to their playtime."

When they were gone, I turned and unzipped my jeans and pissed into the bushes. The relief was intense. I sighed as my stream of urine spattered on the leaves, smelling all yeasty and beery in the clean warm air.

When I'd finished and zipped-up, I looked at Walks. He was still standing in the same spot, holding onto the shovel, knuckles white with the force of his grip, watching the bushes where Jase and Geddy had left.

"Are you alright?" I asked.

"Fuck off!" he shouted.

"What?" I said.

"Managed not to piss yerself this time, I see."

"What?" I repeated.

"You heard," he said. "That's about all you're fuckin' good for, isn'it? Sayin' nothin' and pissin' yer pants."

He started to cry as he spat his words out and began to gather his shovel, the radio, and his T-shirt.

"What about the cat?" I whined. I wanted to go back half an hour, back to Walks and I digging the hole, working together as a team, as friends.

"Fuck the cat!" Walks said. "Fuck the cat, fuck Jase, fuck this whole fuckin' village and fuck you!"

He smashed his way out through the branches of the clearing and disappeared. I listened to him stomping off through the woods, shovels clanging, then sat down on the edge of the hole. A cloud moved across the sun, and the woods darkened and cooled as a breeze lifted dead leaves into a swirly dance around the clearing. I put my dirty T-shirt on and considered looking for the cat and finishing the burial. But I was exhausted and aware of my filth and smell from sleeping rough and a morning's digging and yet another piss incident to add to the collection.

I kicked some of the dirt back into the hole but gave up after a few minutes. I had neither the will nor the energy. So the hole remained, about three feet wide and four feet deep, in the small wood at the back of the old Lyttleton Hall, with the dead tabby somewhere nearby, no doubt attracting its first battalions of ants and flies.

LISA

There was a party for Lyttleton's service men at the Working Men's Club a few days after Neil arrived home. The Heroes Homecoming they called it. We all went but Neil hated every minute. I could tell. It was boozy, loud and raucous, a lot of singing and dancing and backslapping and drunken, teary hugging. Every time he caught my eye, Neil's smile disappeared into a look of something much more serious and questioning. He wanted to talk to me. It was all over his face, as if tattooed in the simplest of words. Typical Neil.

After he had done the rounds and been bought a drink and hugged and patted on the back by just about everyone in the place, he plonked himself down in the chair next to me and let out an enormous sigh. He scanned the drinkers at the bar and the dancers on the dance floor, then spoke into my ear.

"I take it you weren't involved in organising this fuckin' nonsense."

"No," I said.

He half-smiled without humour and looked at me for a long time.

"They mean well, Neil," I added. "They're pleased you're home in one piece."

"One piece," he repeated, laughing. "One piece."

His head was bobbing, face pale and sheened with a thin sweat. His expression was off, wonky, as the muscles in his face tried to smile but betrayed a leering sneer instead.

"And what about you? Are you *pleased* I'm home in *one piece*?"

His emphasis was mean and sarcastic.

"What kind of question is that?" I said. "Of course, I'm pleased. Especially for Stacy and the kids."

"For Stacy and the kids, eh?" He laughed. "I was askin' about you, Leece. How do you feel about me bein' 'ome. You know, in one piece?"

"You're drunk," I said without looking at him.

"Yep," he said. "Fuckin' hammered!"

We sipped our drinks and smiled and nodded and waved at anyone who looked our way. When I glanced at Neil again, he was moving his lips round and round as if ruminating on what he wanted to say. I waited until I couldn't bear it any longer, then asked him, "What is it, Neil?"

"What?" he said. "Nothing."

I told him I wasn't stupid. I reminded him I'd known him since he was born, and I knew when he had something to say.

He sighed again and took a long gulp of his pint.

"You haven't even asked me what it was like… out there."

"I figured you'd tell me if you wanted to," I said.

He went quiet again and stared into his pint as if it contained more than just liquid and bubbles, a vision of some kind, an answer to something.

"Do you want to?" I asked him.

"I dunno," he said. "I need to talk to someone about something. But I don't know what it is. It's confusing."

"What is?" I asked him.

"The war… out there… Shaun… You. It's all in there together, all a bit tangled up."

He put his fore and middle fingers to his temple and pretended to shoot himself. For a moment or two he was my little brother again, twelve or thirteen, having been caught smoking or fighting, looking for some reassurance from his big sister before the letter or phone call from school. I wanted to put my hand on his shoulder and comfort him, give him a hug and tell him everything would be alright. But the last time I'd seen him came back to me, his grip on my wrist forcing my hand downward, his drunken breath all over my face. I gripped my drink instead and steadied my expression. It wasn't easy. I was suddenly angry with him. Furious.

"Something happened," he said.

Here it comes, I thought.

"Something happened there. It got to me. Got inside me. I can't stop thinking about it. I can't sleep for thinking about it. And when I do sleep, I dream about it. I see *him*."

"Who? Shaun?" I asked.

"No. Well, yeah. This kid. Sometimes it's Shaun. Kind of."

"What kid?"

"This kid out there."

"What kid? Tell me."

So he told me. And to be honest, I wish he hadn't.

NEIL'S STORY

(as told to Lisa the night of the Heroes Homecoming Party at the Lyttleton Working Men's Club)

We were trying to take this fuckin' mountain. Last line of defence before Stanley. Some of the lads thought the Argies'd fuckin' scarper once we got close. They soon put us straight on that score. They'd been there about ten weeks, for Christ's sake. Dug right in. Fifty cals, grenade launchers, snipers, night sights and orders to hold out as long as they could. Did a pretty good fuckin' job as it turned out.

Three fuckin' days it went on. Christ knows how many dead. A fair few of ours and a shitload of theirs. Some of them blown to fuckin' pieces, Leece. I mean literally. Picked 'em up like litter and put 'em in fuckin' bags. Buried 'em in the morning. Different parts together, maybe, I dunno. Hard to know who's who when there's no face to go on.

Our company had to get up the western side of the mountain to a place called Fly Half. Top brass had given all the targets rugby names. Fuckin' says it all, really. Anyway, the Argies were using it as one of their key positions, so this place was defended to the fuckin' hilt. Bunkers, trenches and snipers all over the fuckin' place. Like pickin' your way through your worst fuckin' nightmare. Argies behind every rock, just waitin' to blow your fuckin' head off. Least that's how it seemed to me.

Anyway, we shake out from our start lines, and the fuckin' moon appears, big and full, over the top of the mountain. As if it weren't bad enough already, there we are, lit up like a fuckin' Christmas tree from the word go, by the full fuckin' moon of all things. You'd think someone might've considered that. Or maybe they did. Maybe they thought the Argies wouldn't expect us on a full moon when they could see us comin' half a mile away. Either way, I saw it as a bad omen, like in that werewolf film, you know. "Beware the moon, lads. Stick to the road. Oops!"

I was right. It was a bad omen. Within minutes there's a bang and fuckin' screamin', and we realise we're in a fuckin' minefield. Our first fuckin' instinct is to hit the deck and stay there but the explosion's given up our position and all of a sudden it's started, just like that. *Bang*! Then fuckin' fireworks night. Flares lightin' up the whole fuckin' sky, green tracers flying down the mountainside and fuckin' rounds sparkin' off the rocks. And in the middle of all this we get the word to move forward and find cover. I fuckin' tell you, Leece, tryin' to move when every single part of your body and mind is sayin' *stay fuckin' still* is one of the hardest fuckin' things I've ever done. I swear I was frozen against the ground. Then someone screams right in my ear, *Terridge, move your fuckin' arse!* That did it. Got me movin'. Saved my fuckin' life, in fact. Argies blew that spot to fuckin' pieces about twenty seconds later.

Anyway, we make it to cover. Well, most of us do. A couple don't. Wounded without even gettin' a fuckin' round off. See you later. Left there moanin' and groanin' till a medic arrives. We can 'ear 'em but we can't go back for 'em. Gotta keep pushin' forward. Slow fuckin' slog uphill. Shot at left, right and centre. Fuckin' literally. Belly crawlin' through grass, rocks, shit and blood with tracers and rounds flyin' just over our 'eads in both directions. Blokes bein' hit and shoutin' for medics, bein' told to shut up and wait it out, stop screamin', givin' away their positions. Christ knows how long some of 'em were laid out there in the cold. Five, six hours? I dunno. Too fuckin' long, that's for sure. Some were singin' to try and stop 'emselves from driftin' off. Imagine that, 'avin to sing to stop yourself kickin' the bucket. There'd be a moment of quiet and you'd hear a bit of fuckin' Neil Diamond or Elton John comin' from somewhere out in the dark. You 'ad to laugh, you know? Fuck knows what the Argies must've thought. *Fuckin' nutters*, I'm guessin'.

About halfway up to the target, after about two fuckin' hours of inchin' forward, I find cover with five or six other lads from our company. We're behind some rocks but stuck there. There's an Argie trench with a machine gun. Snipers dotted about. They've got us totally pinned down. So we're all tucked in tight behind these rocks, 'avin a right old conflab about what the fuck we're gonna do. We've got Sergeant Perry with us, and he's callin' the shots. I'm thankful because next in line is me, and I don't wanna be the one makin' decisions and gettin' blokes killed. Not very heroic, I know, but that's what's goin' through my mind as he's briefin' us, *Don't die, Perry, don't fuckin' die and put me in charge!*

He tells us we're closest, so we're gonna have to take out the trench, the fifty cal, the snipers, the fuckin' lot. Jesus Christ! The plan's pretty simple. Two flankers are gonna head out either side of the rocks and crawl close enough to grenade the gun, while the rest are gonna hit the trench with a fuckin' barrage to engage the fifty and the snipers and distract 'em from the flankers, or better still, kill the fuckers outright before the grenades are even needed. It sounds pretty primitive but it works. At first. We get into position just below the ridge. Then Perry gives the word and we open up on their positions with everything we've got. Meanwhile, out go the boys with the grenades, workin' their way up the flanks. We nail one of their snipers pretty sharpish. We hear a scream and his muzzle flashes stop. Can't be more than forty fuckin' feet away. Mental. Then Peasey, you remember 'im, blond hair, good lookin' sod, you danced with 'im at mine and Stacy's wedding, he gets one right in the face, right next to me, just this awful fuckin' slappin' sound and he slides back down the rock and disappears like he's been buried at sea. For fuck's sake. I move to check 'im, but Jones screams at me to keep firin'. Then there's two fuckin' explosions. The first one's a grenade thrown into the machine gun hole. It explodes and lights up the guys on the gun as they're thrown back, and just for a second, I swear, they look like they're dancin' in a fuckin' disco. One of 'em catches fire, maybe from the ammo he's carryin', I dunno. He's got belts of fifty cal rounds crossed over his shoulders like he's in the *Magnificent Seven* or something. Anyway, he's screamin' and scramblin' over the all the sandbags at the front of the trench with his chest and head on fire, and Jones is shoutin', *Fry you Argie fuckin' bastard*, then someone shoots the poor cunt and puts 'im out of 'is misery but he's laid there about thirty feet away, still on fire. We can smell 'im burnin'. Then we hear the whine of a shell and somebody shouts *incoming* and I catch a glimpse of Dave Gells, Geller, one of the flankers, about eight feet from the Argie gun hole with 'is hands over 'is head and then *boom*, the fuckin' earth in front of their trench just lifts into the air like there's some giant fuckin' monster wakin' up underneath and we're all knocked back off of the ridge by flyin' fuckin' mud and rocks which almost fuckin' bury us alive and for a few seconds we all just lay there gettin' our 'eads back together, feelin' ourselves to see if we've still got all our fuckin' arms and legs. Then Perry's fuckin' spittin' mud and blood and shoutin' into the radio about the heavy stuff being too close, lisping 'cos 'is front teeth have gone, the rest of us just listenin' and waitin' and prayin' it's stopped. When there's nothin', we do a quick bonce count and see that Darky Bird's laid at the foot of the rocks next to Peasey. We knew it was Darky straight off 'cos all we can see is 'is fuckin' teeth and a big sharp stick of white bone where 'is arm should be. None of us can stop starin'. Perry checks 'em and shakes his 'ead. *Let's clear the fuckin' trench*, he says, *come back for these boys later.*

He gives the order, and we shake out either side of the rocks, stayin' low in case of snipers. I'm tryin' not to think of Peasey and Darky, but it's fuckin' hard, you know, seeing as they was alive about five fuckin' minutes before. The ground between the cover and the trench is all churned up and there's no sign of the burnt Argie or Geller, just mud and blood and bones and boots and whatnot. Fuckin' obliterated! When we get to the trench, it's a fuckin' mess. Bodies everywhere, some shot to fuckin' bits, some hit by heavy artillery from the ships. Just parts, Leece. Meat. I mean, literally. So we have to move through, you know, shittin' ourselves in case of booby-traps or sniper fire, shootin' rounds or stickin' bayonets into bodies to check if they're still alive. Some of 'em are. Playin' dead. Openin' their eyes and screamin' once they've got a six-inch blade between their ribs. One boy's under a blanket with a phosphorous grenade, just waiting to blow himself up and take us with 'im, daft cunt. When we pull the blanket off 'im, 'e's shiverin' so hard he can't work the grenade. Just laid there with 'is 'ands shakin' and the grenade knockin' against 'is chest. We're all shoutin' at 'im to put the fuckin' thing down but 'is 'ands are frozen to it. Then there's a quick burst of fire an' he stops shiverin'. Just lays there with that fuckin' grenade still tight against his chest like a fuckin' teddy bear or something.

Then out of nowhere, this cryin' starts. Not loud. More like a child snivellin', you know. Like a kid that's been bollocked and slapped. Same words in Spanish repeated over and over again. *Mama... agua... Mama... agua...* It's hard to hear because of the wind. Fuckin' wind like you've never felt in your life, Leece. Fuckin' freezin'. And this sad cryin' over and over. *Mama... agua... Mama*, like a fuckin' ghost or spirit in the wind or somethin'. Spooky as fuck. Course, we've just wasted the kid with the grenade, so most of us are freaked out and jumpy. It's pitch black and freezin' and we can't find who's cryin' anywhere. And it goes on and on until some of the boys are losin' it, you know, Jones especially, he's freakin' out, sayin' stuff like, *Find that Argie cunt and stick 'im.* Fuckin' nightmare, Leece.

Anyway, we finally find 'im, the cryin' guy, in a machine gun hole at the far end of the trench. He's underneath two bodies that have been ripped to shit by the big stuff. They've taken the brunt of the blast and shielded 'im, I reckon, and he's survived, if you can call it that. He's fucked, Leece, totally fucked. We give 'im a quick once-over and he looks like he's been attacked by fuckin' lions or something. Seriously. You can see 'is fuckin' ribcage and everything. I swear I have no idea how this boy's alive, specially as it's about twenty fuckin' degrees below freezin'. But he is. He fuckin' is and he's still cryin' in this weak snivel, *Mama… agua… Mama… agua,* bits of his mates all over 'im and shrapnel in his face and chest and us all stood there starin' at 'im. I didn't wanna feel sorry for 'im. He was the enemy. An Argie. But I couldn't help it. Him lyin' there dyin', freezin' 'is arse off and wantin' 'is mum, you know? Fuckin' awful! If you think about it. And I can't fuckin' stop thinkin' about it. Woke up last night an' 'e was there, in bed with me! I ain't fuckin' jokin', Leece. All shot-up and cryin' and whisperin', *Mama, agua, Mama, agua*, over and over, right fuckin' next to me in bed where Stacy should have been.

Anyway, we're all stood there shiverin' while this boy's cryin' for 'is mum and some water. Perry goes to give 'im some, and Jones smacks 'is canteen away and asks 'im what the fuck he's doin'. And Perry shouts back in 'is face, *He's a fuckin' prisoner, Private!* You know? Pullin' rank. *We have to take care of him. Somebody give him a shot of morphine.* And Jones fuckin' loses it and says, *This fuckin' Argie an' 'is fuckin' amigos have just fuckin' done Peasey and Darky and fuck knows who else and you wanna take 'is fuckin' pain away. I say we do the little cunt and be done with it!* But Perry stands 'is ground, and fair play to him 'cos Jonesy's a big scary cunt, and Perry says, *'E's just a fuckin' kid doing his job! And rules are fuckin' rules! You stick 'im now, while 'e's sat 'ere defenceless, and it's fuckin' murder, court martial, the fuckin' nick. Is that what you want, Private?* Jones has got this big Bowie knife from his sock, and I swear he looks like he's gonna do Perry *and* the fuckin' Argie boy as well. Everyone's freezin' and had enough and from nowhere I say, *I'll look after 'im.* I don't know why I say it but I do. I tell everyone to calm down, clear the trench, search the bodies and make a fuckin' brew. I'm expectin' some resistance. Jones looks at me like he wants to cut my bollocks off, but the mention of a brew seems to remind everyone how fuckin' cold they are. So they all wander off, mutterin' and swearin' like how's your father, but clearing the trench and securin' the area like they're s'pose to.

That leaves me with the kid. 'E's still cryin', but it's weaker now, quieter, like 'e knows 'e's a fuckin' goner and 'e's repeatin' himself just to keep himself from slippin' away, you know? So I drag his mates out the way, or what's left of 'em, and I sit myself in close next to this boy, right in next to 'im so I'm almost out of the wind, so 'e can get some of my warmth, you know, and me some of 'is, if I'm honest. I'm guessing 'e's got about half an hour, tops, so I think *fuck it,* we're goin' firm while we wait for orders from Company HQ, I might as well just sit 'ere and rest with this kid.

I light two fags and give one to him. He takes a puff and coughs like it's gonna kill 'im on the spot. Looks like there's smoke coming out of 'is wounds but it's probably just 'is innards steamin' in the cold. I realise then that the smell I'm smellin' is 'im and 'is mates, their insides and their shit all over the place. The cold's coverin' it a bit. But it's there, underneath, like fuckin' death itself. It's about then I really start thinkin', *What the fuck am I doin' 'ere? And what the fuck is 'e doin' 'ere, this kid? Should be at 'ome with 'is mum, not 'ere in this fuckin' shithole.*

I ask the boy 'is name an' 'e answers but I can't fuckin' make it out at first. Alessandro or Sandro, something Spanish with an O on the end. That's all I get at first.' 'Is voice is so weak now, like a fuckin' whisper, and there's wind and guns and explosions and shoutin' an' all sorts goin' on. That's one of the things that no one ever seems to mention about war, the fuckin' noise, Leece, the constant fuckin' noise. Honestly, since I left Portsmouth, the ship's engines, the other blokes snorin' and fartin' in their bunks, the voices in the canteen, helicopters, landin' craft, guns, grenades, mines, artillery, shell-bursts, and worse of fuckin' all, blokes screamin' and moanin' when they're hit, you know? It's hard to describe the noise a man makes when he's had his fuckin' legs blown off. Part of it's pain, of course, but part of it's also the realisation that they're fucked, maimed for life or maybe even about to fuckin' croak it. All these noises make you fuckin' crave just a second of peace and quiet so you can hear yourself fuckin' think so that you can just 'ave a fuckin' thought or just not think about anything at all, you know?

Anyway, I start to tell the boy about Shaun. I'm not sure why. Their age, I s'pose. 'Bout the same. They don't look alike. This boy's dark, you know, like all Spanish or South Americans, I guess. An' he's smaller than Shaun. 'E's lying down all crumpled up, but 'e's definitely smaller. Long eyelashes, almost like a girl's. I notice 'cos when I light 'is fag I can see 'em, all frosted up in the cold. I tell him about the accident, about how some drunken cunt ran down our Shaun an' left 'im in the road for dead. I tell 'im that it was freezin' the night Shaun died an' all, just before Christmas. The boy ain't said anythin' up till that point, just *Mama*, *agua*, and breathin' all ragged and slow. But at least 'is cryin's stopped, you know? I don't think he's listenin' or understandin'. I'm just talkin' while he's dyin'. But when I say *Christmas*, he whispers a word I don't understand, *Navidad*, which someone tells me later means Christmas in Spanish. *Navidad*. That's all he says the whole time I'm tellin' him about Shaun. *Navidad*. I tell him that when I get back home, I'm gonna find the bastard who killed 'im. I tell 'im I've decided to hunt the fucker down until he's either in jail or in the fuckin' ground. What else can I do? I say. What kind of uncle or father or brother wouldn't do the same?

Anyway, I stop talkin' an' he's dead, the Argie, gone. 'E's still got steam risin' from 'is wounds an' 'is eyes are still open but 'is breathin' and cryin' 'ave stopped completely and 'is fag has frozen to 'is lip. I 'ave a dig around in 'is pockets and find 'is ID. Alessandro Romero, born 10th of July, 1964. Seventeen, Leece, fuckin' seventeen, same as our Shaun. An' there's this little photograph as well, a woman, in 'er forties or so, thick black 'air and eyelashes just like 'is, an' on the back it just says, *Mama, Navidad, 1981.* I swear that fucks me up good an' proper, Leece, that fuckin' photo of 'is mum. An' I 'ave to sit there and get my shit together 'cos I'm shakin' all over, uncontrollably, cryin' like a little girl, and I don't know if it's the Argie or Shaun I'm sat next to 'cos all of a sudden my brain's like fuckin' soup, you know.

Eventually, I get one of the other lads, Smudge, I think, to 'elp me drag 'im to where the other dead Argies are all laid out in a line under their coats and ponchos. A sorry fuckin' sight if ever I saw one, I tell ya, just fuckin' kids mostly, you know. Prisoners 'ad to bury 'em in the morning. So I guess 'e's still there, Alessandro, on that fuckin' mountain. Probably not that far from where I left 'im. White flags over Stanley two days later. Top brass flown in by helicopter. Negotiate a surrender. Two days, Leece. Two fuckin' days.

LISA

Tuesday evening the following week, Neil called from a payphone, saying he was coming over and would probably stay a night or two. I began to tell him I wasn't sure if that was a good idea but he cut me off by saying he needed to be away from Stacy and the kids for a few days, for their sakes as much as his. Emotional blackmail, I know, but what could I do? My brother was home from the war and in a bit of a mess. What kind of sister would say no?

I tidied up the house, putting things back in their place, straightening ornaments and pictures, opening the windows to let the house breathe. I thought about suggesting he sleep in Shaun's room, wondering whether the material closeness of his nephew might soothe him in some way. Shaun's footballer and pop star posters were still on the walls, his books, medals and trophies still on the shelves. But the very idea of Neil in Shaun's bed was suddenly disgusting and polluting, like a rat nibbling on something in the larder or a spider crawling into your open mouth while you slept. So instead I hoovered and dusted in the room that used to be Neil's. The spare room. The room he usually slept in if he needed to stay over.

When he arrived, I watched him park his old chocolate brown Cortina all skew-whiff with one wheel on the kerb and the bonnet slanted down into the road. I stood back from the lounge window so he couldn't see me through the glass, and I watched him leaning on the car door while he took big gulps of air and steadied himself. He stumbled and nearly fell as he slammed the door and threw his army kit bag over his shoulder.

In the hallway, I stopped briefly and watched Neil's blurred outline through the frosted glass of the front door as he fumbled for his key and scratched ineffectively at the lock. I remembered Dreek's big shadow there on the morning he had come to tell me about Shaun. I pushed the memory aside and opened the door. Neil looked up at me from a stooped position, where he'd been trying to get the key into the lock. For a moment he seemed deformed or disabled in some way, as if his spine were bent and twisted and his face wore a cripple's grimace of discomfort and pain, as if the frustration of trying to open the door had revealed the true ugliness of his soul. As he straightened up to his full height, he must have noticed my expression because he frowned and slurred, "What's with you?"

I made light of it and told him it was nothing, just wondering what he was up to, *faffing about in the porchway like an old man.* He responded by grunting but not answering the question. I led him into the kitchen, very aware of his staggery fag and beer-smelling presence behind me.

"Do you want something to eat?" I asked him.

"Only if you're making it," he said.

"I'll do you some cheese on toast," I said. "Just have a sit down."

He plonked himself so hard into a chair I thought he might break it. Then he dumped his kit bag onto the floor. All his actions seemed emphasised and clumsy, as if his body had forgotten and was relearning its most basic motor functions. He took two four-packs of strong lager out of his kit bag and dumped them on the table. Swaying and bobbing, he cracked one open and took a large messy swig that left him with beer on his chin and froth in the bristles of his light moustache. He asked me if I wanted one, and I said no. I felt them and they were warm, so I put the remaining ones in the fridge and a couple into the freezer compartment.

As the bread toasted and the cheese bubbled and browned, Neil sipped his beer, stared out of the window and said nothing. Once or twice I glanced at him. He looked pale and tired and ten years older than when he'd last sat there. When it was ready, I put the toast in front of him and he ate it without words, expression or pleasure, just large, hungry bites and crunching and chewing and staring out of the window. When he was finished he had crumbs in his moustache and sticky trails of cheese grease in the long stubble on his cheeks and chin. I took a sheet of kitchen roll and moved around the table to wipe him, but he grabbed my wrist as my hand neared his face, then wiped his mouth himself.

"I'm not a fuckin' invalid, Leece," he snarled, and he threw the crumpled tissue onto his plate.

I didn't respond. Instead, I washed up his plate and got him a glass for his beer, which he ignored, continuing to drink from his can. I went about these tasks slowly and deliberately, as the silence in the kitchen melded with the dying smells of toast and melted cheese. When I could stand it no longer, I turned from the sink and stood with my back to the kitchen window and asked him, "So, what's up with you and Stacy?"

At first he didn't answer. He stared past me into the back garden as if he saw something there, something which held his attention.

"Neil," I said, "are you gonna talk to me?"

He adjusted his drunken gaze just enough to meet my eye and his look made me swallow and shift on my feet. It was desire and aggression, love and hate, pain and helplessness, purpose and loss. It was also none of these things but rather vacancy and void.

"You can't just come here drunk and say nothing," I said.

"Can't I?" he answered, responding to what he perceived as a challenge. "It's my house as much as it is yours. Mum and Dad left it to both of us. Half each, remember?"

"Of course, I remember."

"Well then," he said, as if that were enough.

"But I live here, Neil," I said. "I brought up my son here."

At this he snapped. "And whose fuckin' money has paid for most of the repairs and decoratin' and whatnot, eh? Mine, that's whose." This was true, so I thought it best to say nothing more on the subject. "And anyway," he said, his eyes boring into mine, "how do you know that Shaun was not *my* son as well?"

I laughed involuntarily.

"What's so funny?" he snapped.

My words were paralysed. I simply continued to stare at him, scoffing instead of speaking.

"Well?" he said, waiting for an answer to his question.

"Jesus Christ, Neil," I said. "Please tell me you're joking."

"Joking?" he said, his look darkening even further. "This has been on my mind for fifteen fuckin' years, Leece. So, *no, I'm not fuckin' jokin*!"

All I could do was turn around and face the view into the overgrown back garden, the weedy path to the shed, and the tall wooden fence topped with barbed wire, courtesy of the MOD. I shut the window with the sudden fear that someone might overhear what was being said inside the kitchen. The world outside had never seemed so close or far away. I just stood there, staring at that tall fence, aware of Neil behind, watching me, as the events that had led up to that one night ran through my mind like a silent movie, all jittery and too fast to grip onto their meaning.

Mum had gone, and Dad was drinking himself to death. He'd given up even trying to hide it from us. Special Brew or barley wine for breakfast and anything he could get his shaky hands on in the evenings. Neil and I began to plan our days to avoid meeting him on the stairs or in the kitchen. He seemed to hate the sight of us both, as if we were reasons for Mum's death and all his failings.

With me, it manifested as a brooding silence, a sickening look of desperate desire when he was very drunk. Several times I'd caught him leering at me, as if he'd forgotten I was his daughter, and all he saw was the shape of a young, unavailable woman. Once, he'd walked in on me in the bathroom as I'd just finished inserting a tampon. Instead of shock or embarrassment, as you might expect from most fathers, he stared at my crotch and dragged his knuckles hard across his lips as if removing unspeakable words from his mouth.

With Neil, however, Dad was different. He glared at him whenever he saw him and never missed an opportunity to ask him what he planned to do with his life, then mock his answer and goad him into a fight. In response to this baiting, Neil became a rarer and rarer presence in the house. He got a job with the local Unigate dairy, starting at four in the morning, loading up milk trucks and sitting in on the rounds of older drivers who wanted a younger pair of legs to run up and down the driveways. Then he would sleep his way through classes at school or just skive off and come home after Dad had gone to work. Then he'd be out of the house again before Dad came home, and he would not return until he was sure Dad was in bed. Most of the time this schedule worked, and they could go weeks without laying eyes on each other. Dad would grumble to me some mornings, "Not seen that useless brother of yours in a while. Up to no good, no doubt." To which I would always answer, "He's fine, Dad, just working hard." But then one night, Neil crept into the house, presuming the darkness to mean, as it usually did, that Dad had gone up to bed. But when he flicked on the kitchen light, with the intention of a swig of milk from the fridge and maybe a cheese sandwich before sleep, he found Dad waiting for him with his belt buckle around his knuckles and the leather, a yard-long whip coiled on the table like an adder in the sun. I woke up to the sudden bumps and crashes and curses of their fight, followed by the sound of Neil escaping up the stairs and into my room as the first safe haven on the landing. I propped myself up in bed as Neil's shadow shouldered the door against Dad's roaring and shoving presence outside. Neil seemed instinctively to know that Dad's efforts, with his pickled liver and fag-ash lungs, would only last a matter of seconds. And he was right. In less than a minute, Dad's shoving and banging on the door stopped and were followed by several half-arsed coughed and gasped insults and threats; then the sound of his drunken footsteps staggering into his room and the squeak and strain of his and Mum's old bed as he flopped upon it, fully clothed, for another bout of unconsciousness that, for him, passed as sleep.

Neil stayed by the door, breathing heavily and whispering about what he was going to do.

"I swear, Leece," his shadow said, "if he ain't dead soon, I'm gonna fuckin' kill 'im myself."

I told him he shouldn't say things like that. I told him that Dad was lonely and suffering because of Mum.

"It's what he wants, Leece; he wants me to kill 'im."

I think he began to cry then because he lay on the bedspread next to me and I hugged him and held him close and whispered things like, *There, there, it'll be okay*, like he was little again. In truth, I felt our world disintegrating in the darkness around us. We must have fallen asleep like that because the next thing I remember was waking up pinned to the bed with Neil on top of me, all tears and sweat and hair and breath and grunts and groans, then done and flat upon me, whispering over and over, *I love you, Leece,* as shock moved through my body like poison, and I became the replica of a young woman lying down in bed, a stone likeness carved on the heavy lid of a churchyard tomb.

I turned and faced Neil, sat at the kitchen table, staring at me, still waiting for an answer.

"I was already late," I said. "I was sick in the mornings on the way to work. I was already pregnant when you did what you did. That's how I know, Neil, that Shaun wasn't yours."

He stared at me, studying my face for signs of a lie.

Then he said, "Why didn't you tell me at the time?"

"You didn't ask," I said. "I presumed you were too ashamed. I know I was."

Neil drained his can and got up from his seat and went to the fridge for another. Then he returned to his seat and sat down, all crestfallen and defeated. I took a can from the fridge and sat down across from him at the table. Eventually, he spoke without looking at me.

"Thought I might come back and live here with you. Think me and Stacy might be done."

I told him that he had to go home and look after his wife and children. It was his duty. Surely he could see that. He nodded in agreement, but his expression was that of a man a million miles away, his body in one place but his mind in another.

When he spoke again, it was on a different subject altogether.

"Got some photos, if you're interested, from my trip."

He spoke about it as if he'd just returned from a holiday to Spain. He took a yellow Kodak envelope out of his kit bag and placed it on the table. I got up and went to the middle kitchen drawer for my glasses as Neil started looking through the photos.

When I sat down again, he looked at me and asked, "Since when do you wear glasses?"

I told him I'd been struggling with small print on cheques and bank books at the post office and that I'd been for an examination while he was away.

"These were the only ones that looked okay," I said, trying to lighten the mood that had settled in the room.

He grunted and said, "It would take a lot more than glasses to make *you* ugly, Leece."

Then he stared at me with a look I could not decipher. It might have been sadness, resignation, self-pity, mental fatigue or just blank bitterness. I really couldn't tell. But it troubled me, both at the time and later in memory, because it lacked his personality. It was uncanny. It was Neil and not Neil, himself and someone else all at once.

I broke the silence by asking to see the photos. He snapped out of his trance and began passing me pictures, one by one, telling me what I was looking at. Most were poses of Neil with his mates, in various army uniforms, on the decks of boats in the sun, and then in a bleak landscape that looked like the one on the news clips I'd seen on the telly, miles of nothing but windblown grass and craggy hills. Then he passed me a photograph that at first I could not make out. There were soldiers standing twenty feet or so away. Some smiling, some not. The ground was strewn with dirty old uniforms, which then revealed themselves as bodies, a boot on the end of a leg, a face not quite covered by a hood.

"That's Alessandro, closest to the camera," Neil said, "the one I told you about." He leant over the table and took the picture from me and held it between us and tapped it with his finger on a bundle of rags in the foreground. I looked at the picture long enough to make out a hand laid across a chest and the shadow of a mouth and chin barely showing beneath a jacket placed over the head.

As I squinted at the blurry image, Neil said, "You look quite different with glasses, like a teacher or something. Were they expensive?"

I told him that the optician had given me a discount but that I thought it was because he knew who I was.

"What do you mean?" Neil asked.

"I think he knew about the accident," I said, "that I was Shaun's mum."

"Was it the one in the village?" he asked. "Pettifer's?"

"Yes," I said, remembering the morning of the visit. "He was pretty weird, come to think of it."

"What do you mean, weird?" Neil asked.

I told him about the appointment, about how Pettifer had acted strangely on hearing my name, about how he barely looked at me, other than to inspect my eyes.

"Some people don't know how to act around other people's grief," I said.

But Neil was looking at the table, blinking and flicking his eyes from side to side.

"Pettifer," he said. "I know him. Drives a Jag. Big flash green one."

"I think he might have sold it," I said.

"Why do you say that?" Neil asked.

"His wife came in and banked a load of money," I told him.

"How much?" Neil asked.

"Dunno," I said. "Few grand, I think. I didn't serve her. Theresa did. She told me, but I can't remember. They're pretty well-off, I think, the Pettifers."

I picked up the photo and looked at the boy in the foreground again, the shadowed lines of his chin and mouth and the grainy blur of his crumpled uniform, undefined from the other crumpled uniforms around him, like a miserable army surplus sale. A sudden memory formed itself vividly behind my eyes – Shaun in the morgue, his chin with its light teenage shadow, not yet a grown man's stubble. I closed my eyes and swallowed.

Neil got up and went to the fridge for another can of beer. He opened it and then stood with his back to the room, taking long gulps and staring out of the window as the sun disappeared behind the barbwire top of the naval base fence, leaving the overgrown garden in a cold shadow that crept its way into the kitchen.

I watched him as he drank his beer by the sink, his silhouette framed against the window. When he'd finished, he crushed the can in his hand and whispered something that I could not quite hear. It was only later I realised what he'd said. Just one word. *Pettifer.*

MELVYN

Margret called me at work in the afternoon, distressed. I came home to find her crying at the kitchen table. Her eyes were black and smudged with wet mascara, and her tears had made tracks down her cheeks through her make-up. My first thought was that her mother had died. I moved forward to comfort her, but she backed into her chair and brought her arms up to her chest. I saw a scrunched-up sheet of paper in her fist. She held tightly onto it, then thrust it out to me, sobbing, looking towards the window where the late afternoon sun was shafting downwards through the slats of the half-drawn blind. I struggled to imagine a letter with this effect. Somebody's sudden death? A diagnosis of terminal disease? I held the paper and waited for Margret to speak.

"Look at it, for God's sake," she said. "Look at it!"

I opened the sheet of paper. The words were written in red felt-tip capital letters that had purpled against the pale blue of the cheap, thin writing paper. They said *WE KNOW AND WE ARE WATCHING...*

I sat down at the kitchen table. Margret continued sobbing. Eventually, I said I'd make some tea. Margret stood up so violently her chair shot backwards and clattered against the fridge door.

"Melvyn, for God's sake!" she spat.

She looked deranged, a picture of female hysteria from some antique journal of mental illness. Her hair had come loose from its grips on one side, and her eyes glowered from clownish black sockets.

"We can't just drink tea and act like nothing's fucking happening," she hissed, wanting to scream but trying to whisper. "What are we going to do?"

I stood by the kettle, rubbing at the bridge of my nose. It was neither soothing nor helpful, but I could do nothing else. I had no placatory words for her.

Margret made a noise behind me, desperate and frustrated. Then she slammed her chair back under the table, left the room and thudded up the stairs.

I continued to make tea. It was all I could do while I waited for my brain to calculate the situation. While the kettle boiled, I sat looking at the letter and glancing at the strips of sunlight on the chromium draining board and the kitchen table, inching towards me as the sun sank lower in the sky.

"Come on, Melvyn," I said, "think."

But my mind was jammed. The note didn't make sense. How could they know? No one could know for sure. Only Margret and I knew.

"And who is *WE*?" I said. "Why not *I*?"

If it had been *I* then maybe the note could have been more easily dismissed. But *WE* suggested a team of at least two or more people together, scheming and planning somewhere right at that moment. The possibilities of who sent the note slithered through my thoughts. Whoever it was knew where we lived. The letter had been delivered by hand. The open envelope, with our names – *MR AND MRS M. PETTIFER* – lay on the table. No address or postal marks. Poked through the letterbox in broad daylight. The audacity was unnerving.

I made my tea, then returned to the note. When I read it again, I noticed the three pronounced dots at the end of the message, **...**, their suggestion of more to follow.

"Bastards," I whispered.

My thoughts turned to Margret. I pictured her opening the letter, thinking perhaps it was an invite or a card from a neighbour. I couldn't help but ponder her shock and realisation that the worst had somehow happened, that all her re-found faith and contrition had not been able to save her from my crime and her complicity. I saw her there in our bright kitchen, paralysed by the sudden sense of her world about to collapse around her, just when she thought she'd found a way through. *Sod's law*, as her mother was fond of saying.

I made more tea and took two cups up to the bedroom, where Margret was sitting on the bed, her feet tucked beneath her, reading her Bible with her lips moving as if recanting some ancient mantra. I placed her cup on the coaster on her bedside table. Then I moved back round to my side and sat staring into the landing, thinking of something I could say that might soothe or make either of us feel better. There was, of course, nothing. But I spoke anyway.

"I think it's a lie."

Margret's faint whispering stopped. I could hear her breathing, quiet and rapid.

"What do you mean?" she said.

"Well," I said, "I don't see how anyone could know for sure."

I listened to Margret's silence. When she didn't speak, I turned to look at her.

"Well, think about it," I said. "How could anyone know? I haven't told anyone. You haven't, have you?"

"Of course I haven't," she whispered.

"Well, then," I said. "How could they know? I mean, for sure?"

"But, Melvyn, don't you see?" she said. "It doesn't matter. If they, whoever that is, even think it's you or us, surely that's enough."

"No," I said. "No, it isn't. Not by a long way."

At that point I saw the only course of action we could take.

"If we do nothing," I said. "If we show no signs of reaction, as if we've simply dismissed it as some stupid prank or kids' game, and we have no idea as to what it could possibly mean, then I really think it might go no further."

Margret frowned at me. Then she sighed and sat back on the bed.

"So, do nothing," she said. "Is that what you're saying?"

"Yes," I said. "Isn't that what's got us this far?" I felt empowered by my own words. Their truth seemed to form itself as I spoke. "I mean, it's been seven months, for Christ's sake.

"Melvyn, please," she said. "Don't blaspheme."

"Sorry," I said. "But we've got by for nearly seven months by not reacting or bringing attention to ourselves." I wanted to add, *apart from going to bloody church*, but instead said, "Surely that's the best way to continue."

Margret sat breathing deeply and pursing her lips. Her thumbnails had whitened with their grip on the cover of her Bible.

Eventually, she said, "Wouldn't it seem more natural to go to the police?"

"What?" I said.

"Well," she said. "If none of this had happened. If you hadn't... and we had got this letter out of the blue..." She paused, letting her thoughts hang in the air between us while I worked through them. "Would you just ignore it then?"

I thought about her question. I was sure I would indeed call the police if I received threatening letters for no reason. At least, I would have in my previous life.

"No," I said, looking down at the bedspread and shaking my head. "I mean, *yes*. Yes. That's exactly what I'd do. I'd ignore it."

"Really?" she said.

I sat back against the headboard and held my tea in both hands. Margret sat holding her Bible in her lap and staring at the window. I followed her gaze and noticed the evening outside. It was clear and warm, and there were voices, audible but wordless, just fractured calls of parents and answers from children punctuating the endless bird chatter, the intermittent languid purr of a passing car, the groan of a garage door being pulled shut.

We both sat like that for a long time, neither of us speaking. At some point we must have fallen asleep. When I awoke, it was dark. Margret had got under the duvet next to me and was snoring. For a few minutes, I drifted in the stupor of post-sleep. I passed like a ghost through our holiday in Spain the year before and felt the sun on my skin and heard children splashing in the hotel pool. I wafted like smoke through whole days at work in seconds, twenty, thirty pairs of eyes passing before me, their pupils expanding and contracting in the bright white light of the retinoscope. I floated through whole nights out with Geoff and Angie, all drunken smiles and not a hint of jealousy or suspicion. But finally, without meaning to, I settled on that shimmery green dress and the feel of Caroline's leg under my fingertips, the smell of vomit, warm and bilious in the carpeted plush of the Jaguar, the tumbling faces of Shaun and Paula, their prone bodies on the frozen road, dead in the distance of the rearview mirror, Lisa Terridge, sad and flustered in the waiting area of the shop, and the note downstairs in the darkening kitchen, its large, purpled, capitalised letters, words and dots, ominous and foreboding like a message from hell.

Once fully awake, I lay in the dark with the worst possible scenarios haunting my thoughts. I saw dark shadows inside our house, creeping murderously up the stairs while Margret and I lay in our bed. Strange, faceless figures outside in the road, standing at the end of the driveway, watching and waiting. Margret raped and beaten by men who laughed behind their masks while I was forced to watch. In the dark, the hard edges of reality, like the corners and cornices of the walls and ceilings, melted away into protean images of the most horrible and terrible possibilities my mind could conjure. Lampshades became grinning gargoyles. The black shape of the corner chair with clothes thrown over it became a hunched and monstrous demon. The ruched curtain bottoms slithered serpentine in the gloom of the thick carpet, and the soft hump of Margret next to me in bed became a huge, washed-up, crab-eaten carcass with a human face and cold dead fish eyes.

*

For the next few days we pretended nothing was amiss. I went to work for the remainder of the week. Margret stayed at home and did the housework, visited her mother and went shopping for our provisions. I assured her that if she felt scared or threatened alone in the house, I could be there in minutes if she called me at work. I advised her to go out as much as possible, so she would feel safe where there were people, and to give the impression she was not hiding.

When the weekend came, Margret arranged flowers at the church, and I played squash with Geoff on the Saturday afternoon. Margret and I took a walk in the park and sat on the patio in the back garden in the early evening. All of this was done, of course, with the knowledge that someone might be watching. During those few days it was almost impossible not to feel fear at the sound of footsteps behind, impossible not to linger a safe distance from an upstairs window, watching the street for anyone loitering or acting strangely. The nights were worst. Each tick and creak and shift of the house could rouse either of us from our sleep. Several times that week, I woke to find Margret sat upright in bed, staring into the darkness at some noise she may or may not have heard.

Sleep itself did not offer much comfort. In my dreams I was chased and cornered, slashed and beaten, hung in the village square while people laughed and threw rotten fruit, stones and even faeces. My customers were often dead, their eyes hanging out of their sockets on bloody tendons or replaced by corks or buttons or marbles. And always there was the sense of a threatening presence, an impenetrable solid shadow stalking the border of the dream, features elusive to configuration or recognition, yet exuding hate and vengeful violence.

At eleven thirty on the Sunday night, after Margret and I had gone to bed, the telephone rang in the downstairs hall. Its loud double peels drilled into the darkness like alarms. We both lay rigid in bed, both certain, I'm sure, that this was the continuation the note had forewarned of with those three purpled dots.

When I got to the phone, I looked back upstairs and saw Margret's dark shape in the bedroom doorway. As I lifted the receiver, my senses atomised into tingling panic that stuck pins into every pore of my skin.

"Hello?" I said, like a child speaking into the black space of an open cellar door. "Hello?"

At first there was nothing. Then someone's breathing. The background sound of an idling car.

"Hello?" I said.

Again, nothing, except, almost imperceptible, the faintest sonic trace of a mouth opening, the weak glue of saliva allowing the lips to part before the mechanical click and dead tone of the ended call.

"Who was it?"

Margret was still in the bedroom doorway.

"No one," I said.

"What do you mean, no one?" she whispered.

"I mean there was no one there," I said.

"What, nothing?"

"Nothing," I said. "Go back to bed."

I went into the kitchen and heard Margret cross the landing and creep down a few stairs and stop.

"What are you doing?" she whispered.

"I'm just getting some water," I said.

I turned on the tap so she could hear the running water drumming in the sink. Then I turned it down to a dribble and stood holding onto the tap, thinking. I heard Margret tiptoeing back to the bedroom. I pictured her getting back into bed, frightened, holding her Bible under the covers against her chest.

I turned the water off and waited until the silence of the house had settled around me. Then I went to the door of the utility room and opened it, all the time listening for the sound of Margret upstairs. In the garage I almost turned on the light, then stopped, remembering the note: *we are watching*. I crept down the three steps onto the garage floor and stood listening for any noises inside or outside of the house. Nothing. I walked along the side of the car, touching its cool metal for guidance in the dark. I thought about the Jaguar, sitting in its new home, all squat and shiny with its secret.

When I reached the other side of the car, I pawed the workbench, feeling for some familiar object. My fingers moved something cold and heavy and it scraped over the wooden surface of the bench. I paused to let the residue of sound disappear into the dark, then felt for the dimpled rubber handle. I tapped the hammer against my free hand to make sure of its identity. I stopped again and listened to the silence, then crept back inside the house, locking both doors as I went.

I didn't feel any safer with the hammer, but I imagined smashing it into the face of an assailant. The thought made my throat dry and my stomach tight.

I climbed the stairs, trying to quiet my breathing so as not to alarm Margret. When I reached the doorway, she whispered in the dark, "What are you doing?"

"Just checking all the doors," I said.

I held the hammer flat against my thigh, then slid it under the pillow as I climbed into bed.

"Why?" Margret said.

"What?" I said.

"Why were you checking the doors?"

I could hear fear in her voice, raspy and breathy as she whispered in the dark.

"Just checking," I said. "Don't worry."

I laid my head on its side and stared at the glowing red numbers of the alarm clock. *11:58*. Beneath the thick softness of the pillow, I felt the hard outline of the hammer, its long shaft and anvil head. I closed my eyes and tried to cancel the image of the mouth at the end of the phone line, with its stringy tendons of saliva stretching between its parting lips, about to whisper some heinous threat but then saving it, perhaps, delaying it for the right time, or knowing its silence was enough.

*

In the morning when I came downstairs, Margret was already up, in her dressing gown, making breakfast.

"Morning," she said without looking at me. "I was hungry. I thought I'd make scrambled eggs."

I looked at her back while she was busy with a saucepan on the hob.

"There's tea in the pot," she said. "I'll have another if you're pouring one."

Her stock morning phrases alarmed me. In the shower, I'd gone over what I'd say to Margret before I left for work, reassure her the call had been a coincidental wrong number. But maybe, if she were worried, she should go to her mother's, make an excuse and stay for a few days, that kind of thing. I'd expected to offer these comforts from the bedside like a visiting doctor, speaking softly with a hand on her arm if she'd allow it. But her pretence at normality, though admirable, made me fearful for her. She'd taken literally what I'd said about acting normal and was acting for me as well as anyone else who might notice. I shouldn't have, but I decided to go along with it.

"Great," I said. "What a nice surprise."

I walked near to where she was standing with the intent perhaps of holding her or touching her shoulders, giving her some physical sign of my support and appreciation. But when I came close, she stopped stirring the wooden spoon in the pan and noticeably stiffened inside her robe.

We ate our breakfast and drank our tea mostly in silence, punctuated here and there with patches of banal conversation – how my appointment book was looking, shopping to pick up, housework to do.

Margret said, "I think the weather's about to change. It felt a little cooler yesterday in the garden."

"Yes," I said. "It'll be autumn before we know it."

She asked me what time I expected to be home. I told her I wasn't sure, that one could never tell with Mondays.

When I left, she came and stood at the door. She offered her cheek with a wince as I bent to kiss her goodbye but then stood in the open doorway waving as I left, glancing from left to right. I looked back to wave and she was still there, waving and glancing both ways, up and down the street. To anyone watching this show of happy domesticity, she must have looked a little crazed.

Work was quiet, only seven or eight customers all day. I busied myself by tidying my office and avoiding conversation with Laura. Now and again, I sat down and tried to think things through. I was convinced that whoever had sent the letter and called the house was suspicious rather than certain, their claim of knowledge a ploy. At around three o'clock I checked the book in reception and saw that there were no customers booked in for the rest of the day. I told Laura we were closing early and jokingly added that I wouldn't dock her pay. She looked irritated.

"What if someone comes for an eye test?" she said.

"Then they'll have to come back," I answered, rankled by her questioning of my authority.

"But that's not very good for business, is it?" she said.

I pretended to laugh.

"I'm sure a couple of hours won't bring us to our knees," I said.

Laura looked unimpressed but began to tidy the reception

desk and collect her things. When she called "goodbye" and told me she'd see me in the morning, I didn't come out of my office but rather shouted back through the closed door. There was a pause. Then I heard her leave and the shop was quiet. When I was sure she'd gone, I drank two fingers of whisky from the bottle I kept in the filing cabinet and phoned Margret to see if she was alright and to tell her I was coming home early. She took a long time coming to the phone. As I listened to the long, blank double tones in the receiver, I couldn't help but picture a series of tableaux – Margret prone in different parts of the house, strangled in the hallway, hanging from a noose tied over one of the exposed beams in the garage, neck broken, tongue out, Bible on the floor in a pool of urine, flat on the bed with vomit around her mouth, vodka and pills strewn across the covers.

"Hello?" she said.

Her voice was sleepy and fearful.

"Margret?" I said.

"Oh, thank God it's you, Melvyn," she said. "I must have fallen asleep on the couch. I had the most terrible dream."

I told her I was coming home. She was surprised but relieved.

As I locked up the shop, I heard brass band music coming from the direction of the park. Lyttleton was gearing up for its Bank Holiday Fair, and there were already bunting and flags draped between the lamp-posts. The village centre felt festive and busy and more colourful than usual. The heavy heat of July had been carried away by August's breezier sunshine, and I felt an overwhelming desire to melt into the afternoon and disappear.

When I arrived home, Margret was panicky and frightened. I reassured her everything was fine, but she insisted on telling me her dream. She said that while we were sleeping, we were dragged from our homes and murdered in the front garden, in front of our neighbours who did nothing to help. Instead, they watched and some even cheered and applauded. I did not tell her I'd had similar dreams myself. As she spoke, she snivelled and sobbed and dabbed at her eyes and nose with a tissue. I tried to convince her that everything was alright, that she'd done nothing wrong, other than support me when I needed her most. She said that she was complicit and was sure she would go to hell.

"It's there in the Bible, Melvyn," she said. "Only this morning I saw it."

"What?" I asked. "What's there?"

"Proverbs twenty-four," she said, "'The accomplices of thieves are their own enemies; they are put under oath and they dare not testify'."

"But that's nothing to do with us," I said. "I'm not a thief and nor are you."

"Of course you are," she said. "You're the worst kind of thief. You've stolen lives, Melvyn, and I'm your accomplice."

*

Later, I convinced Margret we should go out for dinner. I told her it was too late for her to start cooking. At first she was reluctant, saying it seemed wrong in the circumstances, immoral even. I told her we still had to eat, that we'd only get through this thing if we behaved normally, and normal people like us went out to dinner now and again. She finally agreed and said she'd need a while to get ready. I phoned the Golden Turtle and reserved a table. We'd eaten there many times before, and I hoped the familiarity and cosy atmosphere might help relax us and calm Margret's nerves.

When she was ready, we drove to the restaurant. She was silent in the car and seemed uncomfortable being outside of the house. We arrived, and the owner, Mr Lee, said something in Chinese.

"What?" said Margret, a little too abruptly.

"Long time, no see, Mrs Pettifer," Mr Lee said.

"Oh," Margret said. "Yes. Sorry. Long time no see."

She seemed embarrassed but Mr Lee registered no offence.

He took our coats and showed us to our table. The interior of the restaurant was plush and dark, and red lanterns hung above every table, casting warm orangey glows over large paintings of sublime mountain scenes where grinning tigers paused on jutting rocks and snowy egrets flew high over improbable valleys. There were several other couples and one family already eating. Thankfully, none of them knew us or paid us the slightest attention.

At first, when we sat down, Margret was distracted. She started at every clang from the kitchen or noise from outside in the street. But after a while, she relaxed. The soft interior of the restaurant, its thick carpet, soothing oriental music, and warm smells worked on both of us. We ordered copious amounts of food and ate like we'd not eaten for days. There were moments during the meal, I'm sure, when we both almost forgot our situation. The intimacy and cosy grotto feel of the restaurant smothered the reality outside. We talked about how flavoursome the food was. We talked about times we'd been at the same restaurant in the past. I reminded Margret of a drunken night there with Geoff and Angie, when we'd arrived late, eaten, and then carried on drinking at home. When we'd finished our main courses, we ordered dessert, and Margret went to the bathroom. While she was gone, I sat staring at the candlelight that shimmered inside a red glass pineapple on the table. I hadn't forgotten what was happening. It was there at the edge of my consciousness. But I needed a break. And I was sure Margret did too. I felt justified in this small respite. I knew the pleasure of the meal couldn't last. Somewhere in my thoughts an alarm was sounding the ultimate nature of the evening's denial. But I was convinced for once, since this situation had begun, that I'd done the right thing for Margret. At the very least, I'd given her some hope that one day our lives might return to somewhere near normal, even if I didn't quite believe this myself.

Margret returned to the table as the desserts arrived. She seemed delighted at the fritters bathed in sticky syrup.

"Not had one of these for a while," she said.

"No," I said. "A real treat."

We ate our desserts in silence.

Margret spoke first.

"I'm sorry about earlier, Melvyn," she said.

"It's alright," I said. "You were right."

"What?" she said, a little confused.

"About what you said," I offered, "from the Bible."

"Oh, I know that," she said, as if that were obvious. "I meant for panicking. About the dream."

"Oh, I see," I answered.

Margret continued.

"It was just so real," she said. "But usually, you know, when you wake from a dream like that, you have a sense of relief, don't you? I mean, once you know it isn't real, and that everything's okay."

She paused and looked worried again, the lines in her forehead deepening in the shadows from the lantern above us. My full contented feeling passed and I grew uncomfortable. My belly pushed against the top of my belt.

"But it wasn't okay," she said. "It isn't okay, is it?"

She looked at her half-eaten pudding and sighed. Its heat had gone. It looked greasy, congealed and unappetising.

"It *will* be okay," I said. "I promise."

She gave me a resigned smile.

"We just need to keep being ourselves," I said.

Quite calmly, she said, "I disagree." She paused and looked at me as if giving me a chance to ask why. When I didn't, she continued. "It was the way we *were* that got us into this, Melvyn. It was you. And that car. And Geoff and Angie. Their stupid parties. Everyone acting like teenagers. Don't you see? The accident, those young people, dead, they were our punishment."

I told her to keep her voice down, which only seemed to spur her on, albeit in an intense whisper.

"That was God," she continued, "showing us that we were living our lives in useless and selfish ways."

For the short remainder of the meal, Margret continued in this vein, piecing together the ungodly aspects of our lives which had brought about this reckoning. Internally, I disagreed with everything she said, but I nodded and accepted it like holy communion wafer and wine. Anything to avoid conflict. Anything to avoid a scene or Margret raising her voice.

On the way home, a heavy gloom descended upon me. It would have been a relief to cry, but it was way beyond tears. It was dark and suffocating, amplified by the stuffy air inside the car. It crushed my emotional responses to nothing but the impossible want to cry, the impossible want to scream and shout. Desires like dead limbs, paralysed and unable even to twitch.

As we drove along the quiet and dark familiar lanes and roads of Lyttleton, I gripped the wheel and glanced now and again at Margret. She was a dark silhouette against the window. When we passed beneath a streetlamp, pale orange light would pass up her body and over her face. It may have been a trick of moving shadow, but she appeared to be smiling benignly, as if her diatribe in the restaurant against our sinful lives had filled her with her God's glow.

This was it now, I realised, this muffled and smothered life. Margret's presence next to me suggested that what had gone before had just been preliminary, a preamble to this new puritan reality which had been waiting in the wings all along. Her stillness was statuesque and Buddha-like, mocking my inner turmoil with a façade of Zen serenity. I imagined her smiling, or smirking rather, in the dark, congratulating herself on her stoic patience, feeling the Christian hubris of God's words inside her, applauding her return to his numb, lobotomised flock.

We stopped at traffic lights and waited to make the turn into Lyttleton village centre. I stared at the red light, and beyond, across the dark patch of waste ground waiting for its development of new houses, to the dark outline of the church we attended, feeling the lies of my life wash though me, like effluence in the drains beneath the road after heavy rain.

Margret had changed for *me*. I could see that now. I had a perfect image of her at twenty-four, shy, godly, unfashionable, a little plain with hints of prettiness around the eyes and mouth. And me, gawky, unathletic with thinning hair and smoky breath. I watched the red light and searched for a memory of loving her. I remembered wanting her, drunkenly undressing her, excited at the sense of violating her primness. But I couldn't remember loving her. I remembered looking for houses with her, her mother's obvious disgruntlement at our union, her father's uninterested friendliness, countless evenings out as one great drunken blur. But I couldn't remember loving Margret, not with that unconditional feeling Geoff and Angie seemed to have for each other, that sparkle when their eyes met, like something from an Osmonds song.

Since the accident I'd been waiting for reality to return, for things to get back to normal. But now I saw that *this* was reality. *This* was normal. It had been there the whole time, this normal life, beneath the business, beneath the house and its luxuries, beneath the Jaguar, beneath the alcohol and the parties, and beneath mine and Margret's pretence at love. This void. This abyss before, above, around and within us was normal. It *was* reality. It had been exposed, not created, by my crime. It had been there all along, passively waiting for the right moment to reveal itself in all its banal, self-righteous glory.

As we passed the bus stop and its usual gathering of teenagers smoking and pretending not to be bored, my thoughts returned to the note and the phone call. And somewhere, in the outer or inner reaches of my being, some tiny part of me wanted what was coming. A small jolt shot through me, as if I'd gripped an electric fence or the dentist's drill had hit a nerve. The idea of someone stalking us was terrifying. Like vertigo, it turned the tops of my thighs to jelly. And yet, the prospect was not bereft of relief. It held an aptness that increased with clarity and outline the more I considered it. There was justice in its horrible fantasy. There was punishment and an end rather than this dreadful search for contrition, forgiveness and normality.

I turned the car past Barbara's shop and the entrance to the park and drove slowly past the doctor's surgery into Cornerfield Lane. The familiar landmarks no longer gave me comfort. In the past, I'd always enjoyed returning to the house, leafily tucked away, as it was, just beyond the main centre of the village, far enough away to be quiet at night and in the morning, yet close enough to walk for a paper or an extra pint of milk. But now it all disgusted me. The peaceful lanes and corners smacked of death, and the darker darkness of the tall firs in the park was threatening rather than reassuring. And at the centre of our world, what disgusted me most was *us*, Margret and me, our stupid lives and pointless spending, her rustled-up religion and my breathtaking cowardice, her pernickety housekeeping and my fussy profession, her fleshy hips and my growing paunch, her thick make-up and my bald scalp, her luxurious bed wear and my large collection of ties. As Margret sighed some banal platitude about being home, I imagined the whole lot burning, our house, the street, the village, our charred bodies scorched naked and blackened on the bed, flame-flayed, discovered by great lumbering firemen in thick black coats, yellow helmets and gas masks who carted us out in black binbags like burnt junk.

I must have made a noise of some kind, as Margret asked me, "What's the matter?"

"Nothing," I said, as I turned onto the driveway and noticed something stuffed in the chrome mouth of the front door letterbox. I looked to see if Margret had seen it, but she was looking at me instead. "Nothing," I said again. "Just tired, I think."

I pulled the car up as close to the garage as possible and got out quickly to open the door. Margret was staring ahead. I flicked on the garage light and got back into the car then drove forward until the bumper was almost touching the chest freezer along the back wall, so Margret wouldn't be able to get past the front of the car and into the house before me. I climbed out of the car and pulled down the garage door from the inside, then opened the back door of the house and the kitchen door and raced through the kitchen into the hall to pull the note from the letterbox.

"Melvyn, what's the matter," Margret called after me.

"I need the toilet," I shouted, and ran up the stairs two at a time and into the bathroom, locking the door behind me.

I stared at the note in my hand, listening to Margret in the kitchen, placing her bag on the table then running the tap for cold water. It was the same kind of envelope, cheap, light blue airmail paper. It was thin and insubstantial, weighing nothing. Yet I held it at arms' length like the head of a spitting viper.

I closed my eyes and tried to think. No thoughts came, only blank fear and blood roaring in my ears and temples. My previous thoughts of wanting what was coming evaporated, leaving only panic and the sense of my dinner liquefying inside me.

I opened the envelope and pulled out the note. The same purple felt-tip capital letters: *HOPE YOU ENJOYED YOUR MEAL...*

I sat on the edge of the bath and stared at the note, thinking about the previous one and the clicking mouth at the end of the phone line.

I heard Margret on the stairs, then at the bathroom door.

"Melvyn, are you all right," she said.

"Yes," I answered. "Fine."

"Are you sure?"

"Yes," I called.

I heard her go through to the bedroom.

I noticed the *YOU* of the note and stared at it. It had the ominous feel of the *YOU* on old conscription posters. The mustachioed man who knew your cowardice and pointed directly at you.

I stuffed the note into the breast pocket of my jacket and went through to the bedroom. Margret's eyes followed me. She asked again if I was okay.

"Fine," I said. "Just tired."

I hung my jacket on a hanger and fingered the note through the silk lining, just to check it was there, that it hadn't fallen out for Margret to find on the floor. Then I waited for her to get up and go to the bathroom. I didn't want her to look at my face, as I was sure she'd see some giveaway sign and question me. When she left the room, I went and got quickly into bed and picked up my book and stared at it without reading. I tried to think about what I should do. But there was nothing. What could I do? I saw that if I told her about the second note, any sense of calm she'd regained since the first would be shattered. While I distrusted her growing reliance on her re-found religious faith, I saw that it would do no good to have it undermined and her panicked again. I saw that Margret's behaviour was just as important as my own. And I saw again that doing nothing and acting as if nothing were happening was, ironically, the only course of action. The idea that we would get through this unscathed was disappearing. The coward in me wanted to show Margret the note so I would not be alone with the latest threat from our tormentor. But through my fear I realised it was simply the wrong thing to do, that just a thin strand or two of ignorance might be Margret's best hope.

She came back through the bedroom in her dressing gown. She had taken off her make-up and her skin shone in the light with the cold cream she'd applied. I could smell her cleanness. It was stifling and made me think of her bathroom cabinet, its lotions, creams, powders and perfumes. As she fussed with the belt of her robe, I battled a stupid desire. It was ludicrous that I should suddenly want her through all that was happening, typical that at this peak of fear and uncertainty, I should be aroused at the thought of Margret's clean body. But I was. I watched her over the top of my book. She flicked on the small lamp by her dresser and turned off the main light at the switch by the wardrobe door.

I wondered if anyone outside had noticed. Margret removed her robe and sat in front of the mirror and began to brush her hair. The lamplight gave a peachy hue to the skin on her shoulders, and I could just make out the darker brown of her freckles contrasting with the white satin straps of her nightie. It was so long since I'd seen her naked, so long since I'd buried my face in her breasts and lost myself in the womanly softness of her body. I slid my hand into my underpants, trying to catch the merest glimpse of her cleavage in the shadows of the mirror. But then I saw her face, and my desire froze. Her lips were moving. She was praying. Her eyes were fixed upon her reflection. At first, she did not notice me watching. She put down her brush and closed her eyes. Her lips continued to move. Then she opened her eyes and her lips stopped. She noticed me watching and turned off the lamp by the mirror. In the semi-darkness she slipped into bed.

"Goodnight, Melvyn," she said.

I switched off the bedside lamp and turned away from her. The red glowing numbers of the alarm clock said *10:55*.

I thought about the note in my jacket and the opening and closing mouth on the other end of the phone line. I wondered whether Margret's lips were moving again in the dark, whether she was saying prayers for herself, or if I was included, or if she was just repeating psalms over and over.

I felt the hard shape of the hammer beneath the pillow then became aware of the house, large and dark around us. I closed my eyes and searched through the familiar darkness of each room, listening for sounds of intrusion, vicious whispers or malevolent footfalls. As I drifted towards sleep, I passed through all the darkest spaces of our home, looking into shadowy corners for the shape of an unfamiliar presence.

The glowing red numbers of the clock said *02:59*. I sat up, took the hammer from under the pillow and walked round to Margret's side of the bed. I stood looking down at her as she slept, her moving lips just noticeable in the dark, rasping out a meaningless whispered catechism. I focused on the dark moving patch of her mouth and raised the hammer above my head. Her whisper grew more intense and was suddenly punctuated by a deep metallic vibration as her eyes opened wide in horror and I brought the hammer down and awoke at the moment of impact, gasping and sweating, staring at the glowing red numbers of the clock that told me it was *02:28*.

I lay still, letting the dream subside, forcing out its dreadful pollution. But I could still hear Margret whispering, and I wondered if I had really woken up. I rolled over and brought my face close to the back of Margret's head. I could smell her shampoo and skin cream. I listened to her low, catarrhal snore. Hints of whisper still bristled around the edges of my hearing like radio interference. Then a quiet cough and a further faint metallic wobble, quieter than the one in the dream. I sat up and blinked in the dark, sure that my dream had gone, yet confused by its residual sounds. Margret stirred next to me as I sat still and listened. Nothing. A distant car. A nocturnal animal noise from the direction of the park, the coughed bark of a fox or stray dog. But nothing close by.

I climbed out of bed, stepped into my slippers and crept out onto the landing and stood looking down at the front door. The streetlamp one garden to the left made a dappled triangle of yellow on the stippled paint of the right-hand hallway wall. I squinted in the direction of the letterbox. It was empty. I stepped deliberately down the stairs, holding the bannister to prevent heavy footfalls, watching the front door and the doorway into the kitchen, all the time listening for whispers, coughs, and that odd vibrating sound again. In the kitchen, I took a dinner knife from the cutlery drawer and used it to separate two slats of the blinds. The lane was dark and empty and silent. I waited a few seconds, watching and listening for some hint of movement or intrusion. But there was nothing. I went through the lounge to the dining room at the back of the house and the back window and did the same there, holding the curtain open with the knife at arm's length and peering into the garden. The dark shapes of garden furniture, trees, shrubs and hedges were black and shadowy, but nothing moved among them. I went through to the kitchen again for water, took one more look into the front garden and then crept back up the stairs to bed. For a while, I lay on my back listening to the creaky silence of the house and Margret's breathing. Then I rolled onto my side and stared again at the glowing red numbers of the clock that said *02:43*.

"Three hours till light," I whispered to myself.

*

I woke groggy and thick with sleep, drool on my cheek and pillow. Morning light filtered through the gap in the curtains. My six-thirty alarm had not yet sounded. I switched it off in the hope Margret would sleep late. I got up, showered, shaved, and dressed quietly, feeling the thin hope of morning dissipate into the reality of the day ahead and the implications of the note in my jacket. I decided to head to work early, drawn by the prospect of two fingers of whisky and space to think. But when I came back into the bedroom from the bathroom, Margret sat blinking and yawning against the headboard. I wished her good morning and went to kiss her. She recoiled under my touch and barely offered her cheek.

"Why are you up so early?" she asked.

"I want to get a head-start at work," I said.

"Will you be making tea before you go?" she said.

"Yes, all right," I said. "Do you want it in bed or downstairs?"

"I'll come down," she said. "Just let me wake up a bit."

Downstairs, I opened the front door and took the cold pint of milk from the basket on the step. It was still early, and the lane was empty. The curtains of all the houses opposite were still drawn shut. I made tea and Margret came downstairs in her dressing gown. It was early for her. She looked tired and half-asleep as she sat down. We ate breakfast in silence.

As I was readying myself to leave, she said, "I think I'm going to Mummy's today. I might stay there for dinner."

"Okay," I said. "Send her my best."

She nodded, headed back into the kitchen, turned on the radio and began to hum a tune, different to the song that was playing. I waited to see if she'd return to say goodbye. When she didn't, I opened the door to leave.

Outside, the paperboy was standing astride the crossbar of his bike at the end of the driveway. I smiled and lifted my hand to greet him. He looked at me and glanced towards the garage. Then he took a paper from his bag, dropped it onto the driveway, and rode away, his eyes on me as he went, standing on his pedals to gain extra speed. Bemused, I watched him go, then walked to where he had dropped the paper. I picked it up and turned back towards the house and saw red paint daubed across the grey garage door, then Margret adjacent at the kitchen window, watching me with a puzzled expression on her face. For several moments, I was unable to move. I had no thoughts other than the sudden recognition of the metallic wobble I'd heard the night before, the vibration of our garage door. Across it, in dripping red, one word above the other, someone had painted *FUCKING MURDERERS.*

I stared at the words, not so much in disbelief, but shocked that what had woken me in the night had not been imagined; that the whispering and coughing I'd heard had been real rather than the remnants of a nightmare.

Before I had time to think of what I should do, before even pulling up the garage door to hide the words, Margret was striding across the grass towards me and tightening the belt on her dressing gown, repeating my name in a harsh whisper.

"Melvyn! Melvyn! What are you doing?"

She took the paper from my hand, then seemed to realise something was wrong. Following my dumb stare, she turned towards the garage and emitted a sickening sound, the kind of noise you make if you pour boiling water over yourself or discover a loved one dead. Panic, pain and catastrophe all in one inarticulate sound. I was convinced the whole lane had heard, and it shocked me into action.

With my hand at the small of her back, I walked Margret into the house. She was babbling something incoherent, something about how she'd warned me, about punishment. I told her to get ready and go to her mother's, but she stood in the kitchen gripping the collars of her robe to her neck, repeating, "I can't believe this is happening. I can't believe this is happening."

I shouted at her to get ready and go to her mother's then went to open the garage door from inside. As I gripped the handle, the door made that same metallic wobbling sound.

"Bastards!" I spat.

Margret had come from the kitchen to the doorway at the back of the garage.

"What are you doing?" she said.

"Putting up the garage door," I said. "So no one can see."

"Everyone's probably seen it by now," she said.

"No, they haven't," I said. "It's too early."

I thought of the people who may have been past that morning – the milkman, the paperboy, shopkeepers, early workers in the village centre.

"Christ," I said.

"What?" Margret said.

"Please, Margret," I said. "Go inside and get ready to go to your mother's."

"Why?" she rasped.

"Because that's what you said you were doing today."

"That was before someone wrote" – she stopped as her mouth contorted – "Fucking… on our garage door!"

She was unable to repeat the whole phrase. The second word was jammed inside her clamped lips like suppressed phlegm or vomit. I could see the tendons in her neck, taut and stretched, the skin of her throat a violet rash.

"Please go back inside, Margret," I said, more gently, in the hope of calming her down. I was afraid of her becoming hysterical.

"What are you going to do?" she said.

"I'm looking for paint," I said.

"We don't have any paint," she said in an angry whisper.

"I'm just looking," I said.

She was right.

I looked at my watch and saw that it was just after eight. The ironmongers would be open.

"I'm going to take the car into the village," I said. "When I come back, you can go to your mother's."

I pushed past Margret into the house, through the kitchen to the basket by the telephone where we kept keys. Margret followed me.

"Aren't you coming to Mummy's?" she said.

"I'll get a taxi later," I said. "Please just get ready, Margret."

"Why won't you come with me?" she said.

"Because I need to paint the garage door before the whole fucking world sees!" I shouted.

She stared at me and began to cry, wiping her eyes with the backs of her hands.

"Margret," I said. "Please just trust me. Go and get ready. When I come back, you can drive to your mother's."

I went through to the garage again and got into the car. Margret followed again and stood on the steps, watching me. I wound down the window and stuck my head out.

"Whatever you do," I said, "don't shut the garage door."

"What if someone steals something?" she asked.

The question was so stupid I stared at her before answering. "In the circumstances," I said, "I don't think it matters. Do you?"

As I backed out of the garage and down the driveway, the road was clear. I had the impression that, perhaps, not too much harm had been done, and if I could paint over the words before anyone else saw, then maybe, just maybe, we could carry on as if nothing had happened. But as I changed gear to pull away, I saw that Margret had come to the entrance of the garage. She looked at me then in both directions up and down the lane. Then she looked down at the floor and I noticed red paint on the driveway in bloody smears just in front of her. She stepped back as if from a rotting carcass or from the edge of a high cliff, then stood in the relative gloom of the garage, clutching her robe to herself, looking far older than her forty-six years.

At Fletcher's ironmongers in the village, I bought two tins of dark green outdoor paint, some white spirit, two large brushes, and some overalls from a rail near the counter. I figured they would save me the time of having to change. Mr Fletcher, a stiff man with limited neck movement in a long brown shop coat, tried to engage me in conversation, first about the paint and what I needed it for and then about the weather for the coming fair. I did my best to be polite, but he seemed a little offended by my brusque manner and obvious hurry to leave.

On the way out I saw Reg the road sweeper. He was manoeuvring a small pile of dust, leaves and cigarette ends onto a flat rusty shovel. The scrape of metal against tarmac set my teeth on edge. Reg stood up to empty the contents into a black binbag that was taped to his pushcart. He looked at the paint I was carrying, then acknowledged me with the smallest of gestures, an almost imperceptible nod and raise of one eyebrow.

I put my purchases on the back seat and got into the car. In the rearview mirror I saw Reg watching me in classic workman's repose, both hands on his shovel and head cocked as if trying to work something out. It dawned on me that Reg may well have been in Cornerfield Lane that morning. I'd seen him there many times over the years, and I'd heard him sometimes, before it was fully light, scraping his way along the gutter towards the village. I nodded at him in the mirror, but he just stared back, his eyes bright against his dirty, tanned skin and filthy shock of hair. He had the look of an old male lion after a fight with a younger rival.

I drove away around the war memorial with an image in my mind of Reg at dawn at the end of our driveway, his bright eyes staring at our garage door. I wondered how many people had seen it. At least one, I was sure. The paperboy. But I had to accept the possibility of at least a few more. It seemed likely then, as I drove past Barbara's shop and the doctor's surgery, that many more might know by the end of the day. I thought about people in shops discussing the meaning of the message on the optician's garage door, men in pubs over pints and cigarettes, drawing their conclusions and connections, espousing their theories and shaking their heads at the possibilities of my secrets. "You think you know someone," they might say, in that clichéd village way. Again, I felt that sickening desire to see it all burn, this village, Lyttleton, with its pubs and shops and shopkeepers and barmen and road sweepers and husbands and wives and children and dogs and parks and playgrounds and flags and fairs, all razed to the ground so that I might sleep a little easier again.

I turned the car onto the driveway and saw the bedroom curtains twitch open, and Margret's face, a ghostly pale and featureless disc in shadow. I took the paint, white spirit, brushes and overalls from the back seat of the car into the garage and put them on the workbench. I left the car on the driveway close to the entrance of the garage, in the hope it would partially block the view of anyone passing by. I pulled on the overalls then, with the flat end of a screwdriver, prized off the lid of one of the paint tins and gave the paint a stir with an old piece of glossed window frame I found amongst some junk under the workbench. I took the open tin to just in front of the entrance and placed it on the ground where the red smears were. I decided *they* could wait. I felt hot and conspicuous in the overalls and wished I'd simply changed into old clothes.

I pulled down the garage door and it groaned and wobbled that same sound I'd heard the night before. The words, as they came into view, shocked me all over again. The urge to conceal them was frantic and physical, like an imminent and desperate need to vomit or defecate. With the sense of being watched from every window in every house across the lane, I roughly painted over the words, starting with *MURDERERS*, feeling huge relief as the dripping bloody redness of each letter disappeared beneath the green. It was a dark, earthy colour, the colour of mulched leaves or silage, but it was better than the bright red letters that screamed my guilt to anyone who happened to be passing.

By the time Margret came out dressed, with her handbag in the crook of her elbow and her sunglasses on her head, the whole garage door was dark green. The slightest of outlines of the painted words beneath remained, but I felt sure that they would only be noticed if someone stopped and studied the door.

Margret looked at the door and then at me. Her face was a picture of fear, distaste and disgust.

"You'll need to do another coat," she said. "I can still see it."

"Go to the end of the driveway, will you," I said, "and see if you can see it from there."

"No, Melvyn," she said. "You can do that when I'm gone."

I stared at her, speechless at her reply.

"Are you going to tell Alice?" I said, finally.

"Don't be ridiculous," she said. "Mummy's got her own problems without being burdened with this..." She fumbled for a word that didn't come.

As she backed down the driveway in the car, I followed her. She glared at me once or twice whilst concentrating on her manoeuvre into the road. I waved as she pulled away, acting for anyone who might be watching from a window. She did not wave back as she drove away. I watched the car until it turned the corner and was gone.

I stood for a moment and looked at the garage door. The words beneath the paint were not visible from the road. The air was warm and I guessed the paint would dry quickly. I decided to go to work and cancel as many of the day's and week's appointments as possible and then come back to paint another coat. My fear had been replaced by the dead functionality of my daily life, and I began simply reacting as problems arose. The things I was doing seemed unreal and ludicrous, but that I would continue them was as certain as day passing from morning into afternoon.

What I thought would take an hour at work took closer to three. There were customers waiting when I arrived. Laura was agitated and clipped in her responses to my excuses. When I told her to set about cancelling the afternoon and the rest of the week's appointments, she flushed with anger. She barely listened as I explained that Margret was sick and needed looking after, and she began the work of calling customers in what seemed like a silent rage. I told her I would pay her in full, there and then in cash if she liked, but she continued to act offended and made no further eye contact with me until she said goodbye just before noon. When she was gone and the shop was empty, I finished the bottle of whisky in my office, then sat at the reception desk looking at the appointment book. There were five or six names that Laura had been unable to contact, but I'd told her I'd place a sign of explanation and apology on the door when I left. I found a piece of white card on the desk and wrote *Closed due to illness. See you after the bank holiday. Apologies for any inconvenience.*

I closed the shop and stuck the sign on the door with Blu Tack. Then I walked home, into the garage, and changed back into the overalls I'd left draped on the workbench. The second coat of paint obscured all traces of the letters and words. But when I'd finished, I thought I could still see them there, red under the dark green paint, waiting, perhaps, to be uncovered sometime in the future, an obscene palimpsest of my guilt. I cursed myself for not having scraped off the red paint first, but this would have taken time, and the scraping of paint off metal early on a Tuesday morning would have drawn unwanted attention. Plus, of course, the words had needed covering immediately.

I changed out of the overalls, washed my hands and face in the downstairs bathroom, and ate a sandwich with a cup of tea in the kitchen, listening without interest to the babble on the radio. When I was done, I washed my plate and cup and placed them on the drainer. I peered through the kitchen window, looking both ways and checking the street for any sign of someone watching the house or acting strangely. Then I phoned a taxi and waited by the large window in the front room. There was an inch of sweet sherry left in a bottle in the drinks cabinet. I drank it from a whisky tumbler whilst waiting.

The taxi rolled into view and stopped directly in front of the house. I left by the front door, locked it and then paused by the garage to inspect my paint job. It was shoddy and there were pieces of grit and dust in the paint, drips on the driveway, and dark green smears on the surrounding brickwork. But the words had gone, and the dark green colour was even enough to be inconspicuous to the casual passer-by.

I told the taxi driver Alice's address and asked him to go via the seafront. I wanted to avoid the Old Church Road and more thoughts of Shaun and Paula. He looked surprised and glanced at me in the rearview mirror. I smiled at him, and he set off with a shrug. When we reached Alice's house, he took my payment and nodded in polite appreciation of the tip. I stood on the pavement considering Alice's small, neat, pebbledashed semi from across the road, a sense of foreboding gnawing at the prospect of having to face Margret and her mother all at once.

I crossed the road and went around to the back of the house, where Alice usually left the door unlocked. I let myself in and called as cheerfully as I could from the small galley kitchen. When no one answered, I went back out into the garden and down the short path to the vegetable patch behind the shed where Margret sometimes helped her mother with weeding, planting and digging. They weren't there. Alice's next-door neighbour, Mr Rice, was in his greenhouse beyond the low privet hedge that separated the gardens. The red blur of his sweater was visible through the ancient filthy glass. He didn't see me, so I returned to the house, not wanting to catch his attention. In the kitchen I called again and then went through to the front room to look out of the window and check our car was there. It was. I figured they must have walked to the shops or to the park for some air. A pot of tea had been left to go cold. I made myself more tea with the teabag in the cup and took it into the lounge and switched on the television, only to turn it off again almost immediately. When the static of the screen had faded, the silence of the house seemed to close in.

I'm not sure what made me go upstairs. I rarely went upstairs in Alice's house. I had no need. I'd always used the small toilet near the backdoor. But the intense silence of the house, accompanied by the tick of the gold carriage clock on the mantelpiece, somehow drew me upstairs to check the rooms.

I found them in Alice's bedroom, side by side on her bed. I stood and stared, not quite able to process what I was seeing. The image stayed trapped in my eyes while its meaning struggled to reach my brain. Alice was laid in her bed like she'd not got up yet and was still sleeping. Except she was whitish blue with a fly twitching and turning unbothered on her bottom lip, venturing boldly in and out of her mouth. Her hands were outside the bedspread and folded across her chest like the tomb lid of some holy saint at rest in the crypt of a cathedral. Alice and Eric in Spain a decade earlier, sunburnt and holiday-clothed, were smiling out of a photograph just a foot to the right of her head on the bedside table beneath the reading lamp.

Next to her lay Margret. She was on the bed rather than in it, her head inside a white plastic bag so that only her chin and mouth were visible from where I stood. Her lips were apart in what looked like a gasping, silent scream, and the bag rustled in the breeze from an open window.

I stared at Margret and Alice while all the details of the scene made their way slowly into my consciousness. Margret's knees were raised, and the bedspread was messed around her feet where her heels had struggled and kicked against her own grip on the bag. The backs of her hands lay oddly either side of her chin as if she were performing some kind of mime. After a while standing and staring from the doorway, I sat down next to Margret on the bed and lowered her legs so they were straight. I had no idea what I was doing, but I smoothed out the creases in her skirt and fussed for a few moments, straightening her blouse, which was askew at the collar and cuffs, and untucked from the waistband of her skirt. Then I took the bag from her head and felt my stomach rise and heave at the sight of her eyes. They had bulged to the point of bleeding thin teary blood into her make-up. I'd seen many optical disfigurements over the years, from trauma, disease and congenital conditions, but I was still shocked at how Margret's eyes had risen from their sockets as if inflated from within. I managed to close the lids, and I used the corner of the bedspread to wipe away small traces of blood from the powdery foundation on her cheeks. After doing this I went to the bathroom and vomited until I could retch nothing but saliva. Then I went downstairs and made myself another cup of tea and drank it while I stood by the kitchen sink, staring out of the window. I then went back upstairs and sat on the bed next to Margret. I noticed a piece of folded paper on the round table in front of the window. I opened it and sat back down on the bed next to Margret and began to read. Some of the words were blotched like little bluish flowers from what must have been tears. *Melvyn,* it said,

I can't call you dear, and I can't apologise. When I arrived today, Mummy was in bed. I think she'd been there for two days, perhaps more. I'm not sure if she was trying to starve herself, but she had given up and kept saying that she wanted to die. She kept talking about Daddy and saying that she wanted to be with him. She kept saying that all she could feel was death. I almost told her our secret. That it was you who killed those children. But what would have been the point. She couldn't understand us, she said. She cried and asked why we'd never given her and Daddy any grandchildren. She even said that maybe Daddy wouldn't have died if he'd had a grandchild. More to live for. I was shocked. All this time. I never knew that Mummy partly blamed us. You cannot possibly imagine how that felt. To have your own mother blame you for your father's death. It was only then I saw the irony in all of this. The horrible irony. That you never gave me any children. And when you did, they were dead ones. Maybe Mummy was right. Children might have changed everything. If we'd had children we probably wouldn't have been at Geoff and Angie's party that night. Geoff asked me about it once, a few years ago. He couldn't understand it either. He even offered to help. Can you believe that? If the problem was medical, he said. Typical Geoff. Thought he could fix anything. We tried all the same. We both wanted to feel guilty, screwing in the afternoons like out-of-work teenagers. But the way you looked at Angie, how could we? We pretended it was under the premise of him being a surrogate father that you would never know about, but I don't think either of us believed in that really. For Geoff I think it was just a continuation of his superiority over you in all areas of life. And yes, if you're wondering, he was much better at that as well, much bigger and much better. No wonder Angie always looked so happy. For me, well, it was nice to have some excitement and a secret of my own for once. I don't think you've ever considered just how long and boring my days could be. If it's any consolation, it was only a few times when he could get away from the salon and you and Angie were both working. I stopped it quickly. We both knew it was very wrong. I was even disgusted with myself for a while. But not anymore. Especially not now. I've always tried to support you, Melvyn. I've tried to be a good wife. But in doing so, I've reached a place I can't come back from. It's not just what you did last Christmas, although that would have been enough for any wife, I think. It's what you've done to me. You've emptied me. I see that now. I see what Mummy and Daddy had. And then I look at us and this recent descent. It's too much, Melvyn. Too much. I feel so ashamed and angry that while Mummy was in her worst hours of need, we were dealing with the horror that you created.

She begged me with such force today that I finally gave in. And now it's done. Now I'm like you. All that's left is our life together with our dreadful secret. And you've already ruined that. So I've decided I'd rather be with them. With Mummy and Daddy. And with God. What you did, Melvyn, you did on your own, and therefore it seems only fair and right that you should face it on your own.

Margret.

I stared at the letter after reading, the paper trembling in my hands. Then I noticed Margret's old Bible on the table, close to where she'd left the note. I opened it where the page was marked, and a passage was underlined in the same ink as the letter. *And these will go away into eternal punishment, but the righteous into eternal life*. I sat in silence while the meaning of the words worked its way into me. Then I ripped out the page and screwed it into a ball and stood up, a rage like I'd never experienced before rising inside me and blanking out the possibility of thinking. I'd never been as angry. That she should blame me for her mother's demise was incredible. That her parting words were a religious judgement and that she'd seen fit to damn me were too much to take. And as for her revelation about Geoff, it was the flame for the touch-paper, the fuel poured on the fire. I ripped at her Bible in a growling fury, snarling things I can barely bring myself to remember, stuffing balled-up pages into Margret's sagging mouth, hurling pieces of torn paper at Margret's face where they fell like confetti on her eyes, lips and hair and on the pillow beneath her head, until all the pages were gone and I was ripping weakly at the cover. Finally, I tore it in two, holding both halves in front of her face, sobbing words that weren't even words but rather phlegmy noises in my throat. When I was done and my energy was spent, I collapsed on top of her and sobbed into the pillow next to her head, where I could still smell her shampoo from what must have been her final hair wash. I have no idea how long I stayed like that, but at some point I must have fallen asleep. When I woke, the light in the room had changed and it was cooler. My head had cleared of its earlier rage. I went back downstairs and washed my teacup. Then I locked the house and left them there, together on Alice's bed, with Margret's torn-up Bible strewn all over them.

KEVIN

When Lyttleton Fair began on the last Saturday in August, I had a job on the Chair-O-Plane ride. Eddie Rinch, a kid I'd known since I was about ten, was helping to set it up and run it. His dad knew the owner, who wanted another worker for the evenings when it was always busier.

"Easy-peasy," Eddie said. "Just make sure the riders pay, then hand the money over to Jerry at the window. When the ride's running, we just stand there and listen to the music, look up a few skirts if we're lucky. When the ride shuts down each night, we get a tenner. Maybe a bonus if it's good takins and that."

Tenner plus a bonus. A fortune compared to the pittance I was paid for my weekend paper round.

Mum wasn't keen on me working with *gypsies* or *fairground types*, as she called them. Or with Eddie Rinch for that matter. She'd always seen him as a bad sort. He had an earring and swore like a docker. But when she'd consulted Dad, he'd said, "Why not? Do him good. Nothing wrong with gypsies. We were all gypsies once."

"Speak for yourself," Mum had said, but she'd seen his point and allowed me to take the job.

I was nervous at first. It was difficult to remember who'd paid and who hadn't. I felt clumsy and stupid asking riders for their fifty-pence pieces. My money was short several times. Jerry would shout and gesticulate behind his perforated Perspex, "Fuckin'… fuckin'… fuckin'…" in thick Bristolian; it was the only word I caught over the din of the generator and the distorted music from the huge speakers. He was dark and hairy with bulky, tattooed shoulders. He wore a vest and an ancient, filthy trilby. Eddie tried to reassure me Jerry was alright, but I wasn't convinced.

We worked on a system using the seat numbers. Eddie seemed at home on the ride, like he'd worked on one for years, like he'd finally found his calling in life. He'd never been particularly confident at school. He wasn't clever or good at sports. He had an elfish face with creamy white hair and an upturned nose, features which gave him a pointed and cheeky look that got him into trouble with teachers and bullies alike. But on the Chair-O-Plane he oozed confidence, jinking between the chains and seats, grinning, winking, and wisecracking with girls as he collected their money.

I copied Eddie and soon our system became slick and efficient. We could fill and empty the ride in a matter of seconds. Jerry's mood improved as we brought in each hoard of coins and notes and asked for change. He swigged constantly from a bottle of fruit wine and tossed his empties onto the rotting wooden floor of his booth. A soggy brown rollie hung from his fat bottom lip, and his smile revealed a mouth of blackened and broken and missing teeth.

The late summer evening was warm and the air thick with the smells of hot dogs, burgers, candyfloss, toffee apples, beer, and the Portaloos behind the makeshift bar tent, where long queues forced men into the darkness under the trees.

As the evening wore on, ride after ride, Jerry started singing and jigging his big hairy shoulders inside his Perspex booth, empty bottles clanking around his feet. At around eight, with the fairground in full swing and every spinning seat taken, he came out and gave me and Eddie a can of strong scrumpy each. He rubbed our heads and play-boxed with Eddie before strutting back to the little door at the side of the tower and into his booth behind his Plexiglass, twisting open another bottle of fruit wine and tossing the lid onto the floor.

"See!" Eddie shouted in my ear. "Jerry's alright!"

"Yeah!" I shouted back, but in truth he scared me. His quick shift from fierce to happy seemed based on money and booze. There was something simian about him, hairy in his cage, jiggling his shoulders and scratching at the black abysses of his armpits like a performing primate. I'd never seen a man that hairy before. He made me feel smooth and sexless, like a plastic Action Man or a Barbie's Ken. As he danced and sweated inside his box, man-odour swelled like an invisible toxic cloud. Sweat and meat, sex and alcohol, fags and farts, all in one overwhelming funk. I began to dread each trip to his booth, the absorption into his cloud of smells, the black holes of his armpits and the stumpy graveyard of his teeth.

The lights and circling riders began to leave traces in my vision, and the roar of the generator blasted out all other sounds, apart from the distorted music from the ride's sound system. I looked out at the families and couples and groups of kids visiting other stalls, eating their hot dogs and their candyfloss, and I began to feel envious of their fun and free time. I imagined Emma out there somewhere, with Chivers or Catherine or another of her friends, enjoying the fair while I was stuck on this stupid ride, literally trapped by a spinning fence of chains and seats and people's feet, and by a man-ape who seemed to be just waiting for any excuse to lay his hairy big hands on me. *All for a fuckin' tenner,* I said to myself as the ride slowed and the seats lowered again, and Eddie shouted, "Wakey-wakey, Kev!" and we went to work again, helping and ushering people off the ride and making sure the new riders were fastened in before taking their money and giving them their change. I told myself I'd stick it out for one night, then make an excuse for Sunday and enjoy my wages as a punter rather than a carny.

This plan lifted my mood, and I went about the work with a renewed sense of purpose, buoyed by the idea of spending my hard-earned cash the following night. As I collected the money and handed it over to Jerry in his box, I had fanciful daydreams of running into Emma and winning her a cuddly toy and kissing her at the top of the Big Wheel. Then Jase and Roy Chivers got into two of the seats on my section of the ride and refused to pay, and my daydreams deflated like a circus big top with its central poles removed. They were drunk and their lips were blue from sucking on gas.

Jase said, "Jutht thay we paid for fuck thake. Fuckin' gyppothe can't count anyway."

Typical of Jase to read a situation one hundred per cent wrong. If there was one thing that fairground gypsies were masters at, it was counting money. And Jerry, for all that he looked like a drunken monkey, did not miss a trick when it came to totting up his takings.

Roy laughed and studied me sneeringly. I moved away to get the money from other riders. I knew if I pressed Jase in front of Roy he'd just laugh at me or tell me to *fuck off*. But I also knew Jerry would see I was a pound short, and I feared even the slightest deterioration of his mood, anything that might make him angry.

When the ride span again, and the seats lifted their riders up and out over the grass and they began to laugh and scream and whoop, I took the money to Jerry and stood breathing in his many odours, praying he was too drunk to notice, knowing all along he would not be.

And sure enough, he stopped jigging his shoulders to the music and said something that sounded like, "Wait a fuckin' minute!" Then he scowled at me and got out of his seat and disappeared before coming out of the little side door. He shouted at Eddie to come over then yelled something into his ear. I couldn't hear what he was saying, but Eddie kept shaking his head, looking at me, making out that it wasn't my fault. Then he pointed up at Jase and Roy as they flew past, shouting and laughing and spitting the beer they'd snuck on out into the night. Jerry went back into his box and slowed the ride, then came back out and stood with Eddie. I went to start unchaining people from their seats, but Jerry told me to stop. I dreaded what was coming.

When the ride had fully stopped, Jerry approached Jase and Roy and snatched their cans and tossed them onto the grass. It was impossible to hear what he was saying, but his fists hung in clenched balls beneath his hairy shoulders and arms. He cut a comic yet imposing figure from the back, a gorilla in a waistcoat and trilby, silhouetted against the coloured lights of the opposite stalls, where punters threw hoops over wine bottles and darts at playing cards, and fired airguns at balloons, oblivious to the stand-off behind them as they tried to win goldfish and bottles of cheap wine and sherry. I half-expected Jerry to bring a large fist down on top of each of Jase's and Roy's heads and concertina them into the ground, slapstick cartoon style. Within a few seconds, Jase and Roy had handed over their money. Being the hard kids at school was one thing, but confronted with this man-beast whose every gesture smacked of learnt and practised violence, Jase and Roy shrank visibly until they looked like scolded children. But Jase being Jase, he couldn't resist a cocky comment, and barely had he finished the word *gyppo* when, with a deft flick of his arm, Jerry cuffed him across the side of his head with an audible slap, which sent him stumbling down the metal stairs and sprawling onto the grass. He got to his knees and held his ear and stared back at Eddie and me with coiled hatred. I felt my bladder twinge then Jerry and his smells were beside me.

"Next time someone don't pay you come straight to me, right," he said, his wet boozy lips and spittle brushing against my ear.

"Right," I heard myself squeak. "Sorry."

Jerry went back into his booth and started the ride. The people still in their seats whooped and cheered. The lights began flashing again, and the music's bass distorted along with the generator's roar.

"Don't worry about it," Eddie shouted into my ear. "Jerry ain't scared o' nobody, 'ard as fuckin' nails, mate. Jase ain't got no chance."

His attempt to make me feel better had the opposite effect. I now had the immediate fear of Jerry and the longer-term terror of Jase, who I knew would not stand for being humiliated publicly in front of an older friend. The cider and tension had brought on a desperate need to urinate, so I stood in Jerry's man-stench in front of his booth and asked if I could take a toilet break. He stared at me, sizing me up with suspicion. Then he nodded and said something about not taking "all fuckin' night". I ran off into the fair, towards the beer tent where the Portaloos were, next to the gathering darkness of the park's bordering trees.

The tent was lit dimly inside and was full of shadowy clusters clutching plastic glasses of beer. The toilet cabins were full, with long queues snaking back into the fairground. I made my way round to the back of the beer tent, where just a few yards of dark grass bordered the trees, and there was enough darkness to piss without being seen. With the fair behind me, I emptied my aching bladder, rocking gently back and forth, enjoying the release before zipping up my jeans and heading back towards the Chair-O-Plane.

When I was almost there, Jase grabbed me from behind by my hair. I could smell lager, cigarettes, hot dog and ketchup on his breath as he lisped lisp into my ear.

"Which one o' you little cuntth grarthed uth to the gyppo?"

"Neither," I said. "He just saw you."

"Bollockth," Jase said. "We were round the uvver thide. There'th no way that cunt coulda theen uth."

He closed his fist on my hair, and my scalp moved backwards in a tight, excruciating yank that pulled up my eyebrows. I was sure he'd pull my hair out and my scalp with it. The pain was too much to bear, and I blurted out, "Eddie. It was Eddie!"

Jase let me go, and I ran back to the ride without looking behind me. Eddie told me to take the next spin on my own while he went to buy more cider. I nodded and said nothing. I took the money from the riders and waited for the seats to rise, then gave the takings to Jerry without making eye contact. Then I watched as the riders span and screamed and laughed, and I began to feel dizzy and sick with guilt, praying that Eddie would appear, smiling and unscathed. Less than five minutes later I saw him coming back through the crowds between the stalls, his nose bloody and his collar torn away from his shirt. He came closer, up the stairs of the ride, and I could see he was crying. I went to ask him what had happened, but he pushed me away.

"You grassin' cunt," he said. "I got you the fuckin' job an' all."

Eddie wiped his nose and stared at me, the flashing lights of the central tower illuminating his blood, tears, and snot, his blond cowlick smeared with mud where he'd fallen or been kicked or held against the ground. For a few seconds he just looked at me, a mixture of incredulous anger and hurt in his face. Then he said, "I'm fuckin' tellin' Jerry."

"No," I shouted. "Eddie, I'm sorry."

But he was already on his way, and the ride was beginning to slow down.

Fearing a mauling at the hands of Jerry, I panicked, ran and jumped off the raised platform, catching a kick in the side of the head from a rider as the seats lowered. It knocked me flailing into the grass. I stood up, staggered and vomited down my chin and shirt.

I thought I heard Jerry's Bristolian voice shouting from the ride, but when I looked back it was just formless, blurred, coloured lights and fairground noises. There was a loud roaring in my ears, a knifing pain in the side of my head, and a feeling of queasy misery in my stomach.

I turned and ran between two brightly lit stalls into the darkness of the trees and tracks behind, crashing over twice, then swooning in the dark, feeling like I might pass out. My head pulsed thickly at my temple. I made it across the lane to the black expanse of the school and playing fields, then half-climbed and half-fell over the wire mesh fence into the dirt and twigs and grass on the other side. From there, I ran hunkered down, falling several times, to the line of dark poplars that formed a boundary between the field and the concrete playground and school buildings. I sat down against one of the trees, and again I was sick, this time onto the ground directly between my feet. Just liquid that smelt strongly of bile and cider.

I moved to the next tree to get away from the smell and to make sure I didn't sit in my own puke. I looked back towards the fence where I'd climbed over and thought I saw figures there and heard voices, but it was dark and the noise of the fairground beyond made singular sounds impossible to identify. I thought about going home, but I didn't want Mum to interrogate me. I considered the possibility of slipping in and creeping upstairs to bed unnoticed, but this reminded me of Alan Mitchell, who had mostly likely done the same, crept in with his torn clothes and injuries, scared of his parents' anger, only to fall asleep and never wake up.

I decided to head to the swing and felt in my pockets for cigarettes. I had two in a crumpled packet of JPS. I wanted to light up but I was worried that Eddie or Jerry might still be looking for me and might see the spark and glow of my lighter, like snipers watching an enemy trench.

The pain from the blow to my head had dulled, but my right cheek was numb and my right ear seemed only to register booming sounds with no recognisable source. I walked and ran and walked across the playground to the corner of the caretaker's shed. From there, I ran and walked again across the school's back field. Every time I ran I had to slow down to a walk. My head ached and I felt a rising sickness in my stomach. When I reached the fence I was back closer to the park again, and the fair was now some distance off to my left. I could see the lights of the Chair-O-Plane ride through the trees, its distorted music punctuated with cries and screams from the riders and the mad mix of bells, whoops, cracks and bangs from the rest of the fair. This was all in my left ear. My right was just a repetitive boom that sounded like big naval guns out at sea or bombs dropping at a distance.

I climbed over the fence and ran across the path and through the trees to the border of the park on the other side. Then I skulked along the tree-line to where the park met the path which ran alongside Lyttleton Lane. I could see the shape of Lyttleton Hall across the road, huge and dark in the twilight. Just a few coloured distant lights from the fair reflected in its dirty old windows.

I crossed the road and went first into the adjacent field where the swing hung, deserted. Everyone was at the fair. It was strange to see the place so empty. Usually, on summer evenings, there would be several groups of kids, their small dark forms hunched around the lights of cigarettes or small fires. The darker darkness underneath the full summer canopy of the trees was emphasised by the distant noise and light from the fair.

Instead of the tree I'd intended to climb, I headed for the iron stairs at the back of the hall. It was close enough to feel its dark emptiness inside. But from the platform at the top by the fire escape door, I knew I'd be able to see the swing and woods and anyone who might come there looking for me.

I placed my foot on the bottom step and it gonged and wobbled. I froze and waited for the vibrations to stop. I moved away from the wall, where the bolts had become loose in the brick dust, and I climbed up the outside of the steps with my hand on the iron rail. Here, the sound and vibration were lessened by the support of the vertical iron pillars beneath, but the low metallic noise reverberated in discord with the booming in my right ear, and I was relieved to reach the top and sit down with my back against the rotten white wood of the fire exit.

For a while I just sat and stared over the top of the woods to the houses beyond, their roofs just visible in the increasing darkness. I lit a cigarette and blew a thick billow of smoke into the darkening air and the cloud of tiny flies that had collected in front of me.

I dabbed at my ear and my fingers came away bloody. My jaw had begun to swell and stiffen and was agony to open and close. I tried to remember being kicked off the ride, but I could only see Eddie's angry face and Jerry swearing inside his box. The events of the evening had already begun to seem unreal, as if just a short time passing had reduced their credibility. I closed my eyes and imagined a different evening, one in which I'd eaten dinner at home with Mum and watched telly with her on the couch before going to bed.

I stubbed out my fag and placed my head between my knees and closed my eyes. I stayed like that until my fear and nausea had passed. Then I lifted my head again and looked around me. It was almost completely dark now. The tops of the trees in front of me and to either side were silhouettes without the detail of branches or leaves. But from off to my right, something dull and grey protruded in a perfect partial arc. I stared at it absently. Then I looked harder. I squinted to make sure it was not a trick of darkness or concussion. After several blinks, it was still there, solid and grey in the dense shadow of the treetop. I crawled over to the bars of the platform to look through like some curious zoo animal in a cage. I still couldn't tell what it was, but I noticed that from beneath the canopy of the tree, a straight, runged, metal post ran vertically parallel to the trunk, so close to the wood that they seemed almost one thick pillar. I stared, wondering what it could be, amazed that in all the time I'd spent in this place, climbing trees, playing on the swing, hiding for hours in games of catch and kill, I'd never noticed this strange object in the tree. I snapped out of my daze and ran down the stairs, wincing at the pain in my jaw from the jarring clangs and jolts as my feet hit the steps. At the bottom of the staircase, I doubled back and ran the thirty or so yards past the iron supports to the trees where I'd seen the post. At first, I couldn't find it. I looked up to the platform where I'd sat and then up into the trees, trying to work out where I'd been looking, worrying it had been a trick of the darkness after all. Then I saw it. I ran my hand first over the bark of the tree and then over the post next to it, feeling the stark contrast between the cool, damp scales of the trunk and the cold, rough and rusted iron of the post, different to touch yet almost identical in appearance in the dark.

I looked up to where the post disappeared into the blackness of the tree canopy. The first rung was above my head, and I noticed that several lower ones had been removed, leaving just a ladder of holes. I stretched for the first one and hung onto it whilst scrambling my feet high enough to lunge for the next. On the first attempt, the soles of my shoes slipped and my knees scraped down the post, tearing the worn denim of my jeans and the top layer of skin beneath. My head and jaw throbbed painfully but I was desperate to see what was at the top. I hung onto the first rung again and edged my feet slower this time in little scraping shifts upwards until they were almost level with my eyes. This time I made the second rung with my left hand and managed to hold my feet in place while I grabbed with my right. I brought my feet up to the first rung and rested for a moment. I was sweating and trembling, and the pain in my head and jaw was thick and sickly. It pulsed around the roots of my top teeth and along my cheekbone to my ear, then up over my temple and back again. When I'd regained a little strength and the throbbing in my face had reduced, I forced my way into the thick canopy of the tree, using the rungs to pull myself through the branches until I came to the top, where a square metal base supported a cylinder about the size of a large dustbin laid on its side. It had vented turbines like jet engines at each end. I managed to position myself almost alongside it, just below, half-hanging and half-sitting in the topmost branches of the tree. I stared at the object, confused, my head aching hard from the climb. It was old, and there were dark patches of rust where it was welded onto support struts, which attached it crossways to the square base at the top of the post. There were three encased wires connected to it, one at each end and one that reached over the top of the central barrel. I followed them down, first with my eyes and then with my hands as they disappeared behind the post and connected to a metal box. Using the tree and post for support, I manoeuvred myself around to where I could see the outline of the box in the dark. It was fastened to a metal plate on the post with four big screws, one at each corner. At the bottom, a thick wingnut held the lid of the box in place. In the lid, now facing me, there were two holes with buttons inside, like robotic eyes, one dark and one light. Below the buttons was a black panel with words I could not read in the shadow of the canopy. Hanging onto the post with my left hand, I felt in my pockets for my lighter with my right. I lit it and read the capital letters by the glow of the small flame. *PRESS CONTINUOUSLY TO SOUND SIREN. RED FOR ALERT. WHITE FOR RAIDERS PASSED.*

As I read the words, I heard the sound, the rising wail held at an unnatural constant pitch before falling in a baleful moan. Images of people running and screaming, of searchlights crisscrossing the sky, terrified faces in shelters where dust fell from low ceilings, planes cruising and diving, and bombs, of course, falling peacefully through the sky as harmless as eggs or skittles before exploding in flashes of light and great clouds of smoke, while people cowered and suffocated and burnt in cellars and were pulled dust-covered and broken from the rubble of fallen buildings.

For a few moments I was paralysed, utterly without the strength or energy to move or even breathe. The dead of the past months clutched onto my core and wrapped their cold dead fingers around my bladder. I stared at the words and felt the presence of those who'd gone, not as warm, living, breathing, pulsing things, but as they were now, rotting and putrid, dead in the ground, worm-eaten and stinking, yellow and grey, animated only by their slow disintegration. Then all the dead of Lyttleton, from all its springs and summers and autumns and winters, its rotting generations in its graveyards, its dead mothers, fathers, brothers and sisters, all trapped in the eternal limbo of death, all envious of warm life, their tortured souls apparent for a moment or two, clamouring to be heard in the silent wail of the siren, like a choir of lunatics or zombies, baying soundlessly to the skies.

My lighter burnt my thumb, and I nearly fell as I dropped it. It ricocheted off some branches, then skidded down the post. I began to climb down to find it but then stopped as I heard the racing of a car engine and saw headlights bouncing over the rough ground towards the edge of the wood. I climbed back up to the siren, where I could see through the branches and remain hidden. I held onto the post to watch as the car skidded to a halt in the dry dirt not more than thirty feet from my hiding place. When the snarl of the engine stopped, I could hear my breathing, the fairground in the distance, and the booming sound in my right ear getting louder.

For a few moments the car just sat there, ticking and cooling in the gathering dust and darkness. I stayed motionless in the tree, watching through the leaves and branches, transfixed, wide-eyed and petrified like prey for some nearby nocturnal beast. At first, nothing happened. I felt myself becoming part of the scene, the grainy iron post against the skin of my hand, the mottled dark of the tree, the smell of the car's cooling engine consuming me. Then one of the back doors opened and a man staggered out and stood, swaying a little and leaning on the open door. I could hear his breathing, heavy and laboured, but could barely make him out in the gloom. A voice from inside the car said something, hard and angry, and the man began to walk, very slowly, dragging his feet through the dirt and leaves towards the woods. The headlights flicked on, and the man turned and brought his hand up in front of his face. When he took it away and squinted into the light, I saw that he was beaten and bloody, and his shirt was torn and stained.

His thin hair stood on end in shocked disarray. I recognised him with a short gasp. Mr Pettifer, the optician. I was rigid again but the jolt of fear and recognition caused a warm trickle of cidery piss to run down my right leg, soaking my sock and dribbling from the sole of my shoe into the dark below.

Pettifer stood in the headlights and put his hands out in front of him. His legs buckled once, but he managed to stay upright. The engine started with one loud rev and the car reversed and stopped. I expected it to turn and drive away, but for a few seconds it idled with its headlights on full while Pettifer stood and wobbled and shielded his eyes from the blinding light. Then the wheels spun in the dirt and the car roared and pounced like a lion and hit Pettifer at the tops of his thighs. He flipped forward, his face denting the bonnet as the car stopped with a jerk and he slid off the hood onto the ground and lay moaning in the headlights, his face buried in the dirt.

Another man got out of the driver's side and went to the boot. He opened it and looked around. I flinched in the tree and almost fell. Neil Terridge, his face gaunt and stark, black shadows where his eyes should have been. He took a fuel can from the boot and walked to where Pettifer lay grasping at the ground with his fingers. Terridge knelt and bent his head close to Pettifer's, whispering words I couldn't hear. Pettifer groaned a desperate, incoherent protest. Terridge stood up, unscrewed the lid, and began emptying the can, starting at Pettifer's head and moving all the way down his body to his feet, shaking the liquid free in big dousing splashes. The smell of petrol began to cloy the warm night air. Pettifer began to drag himself across the grass, his smashed legs trailing behind him like limp entrails. Terridge watched him for a moment, then struck a match. The surrounding night was sucked into the small glow he held just a few inches from his face, as if he'd caught a firefly to watch it die in front of him. Then he dropped the match, and I watched as the tiny flame fell in slow motion to the ground and whooshed into a blue-and-yellow fire that chased and engulfed Pettifer, who screamed as he erupted into flame, dragging himself faster, then shaking violently before stopping and burning in the grass like a log that had rolled from a bonfire. Terridge looked at the smouldering mess in the dark grass, then threw the fuel can into the boot and slammed it. He got back into the car, then reversed and drove away, all spinning tyres, dust and flying twigs and stones, leaving Pettifer prone and smoking in the blackened dirt. The meaty smell of his roasted skin and the acrid fumes of his burnt clothes and hair filled the night amongst the trees around the swing. I pressed and pressed the *RED FOR ALERT* button and heard the same rising wail and falling moan and clamouring dead, over and over until there was nothing but silence and the sensation of falling into darkness.

LISA

The morning after Lyttleton Fair, I got another visit from Dreek. This time it was later and I was already up. My ability to go back to sleep after waking in the early hours had long gone, and there was little pleasure to be had lying in bed at the mercy of my own thoughts and memories. I opened the door and found Dreek on his own this time with his hat in his hands and a pained expression that told me everything I needed to know bar the details.

Neil's chocolate brown Ford Cortina had been found in the gravel car park by the beach huts, the floor and seats strewn with empty cans and bottles. His body had been discovered at daybreak by an early dog walker. He had filled his pockets full of stones and staggered into the sea, reaching far enough from shore to succeed in drowning. The current had dragged him along the coast a few hundred yards until the tide had receded and revealed him in the first light of morning, out on the black sand of the seabed, half covered with crabs and seaweed, the centrepiece of an almighty scrap amongst the seagulls.

I asked Dreek if there had been any kind of note on his body or in the car. He said that no note had been found but there had been several photographs in his wallet. They were being treated as evidence, so he could not yet release them or talk about them.

From time to time, Dreek would visit to inform me of any development in the investigation. And after the case was closed, he'd find other excuses to visit, seeing if I needed any shopping or anything done around the house, until he gave up the pretence and would just come with a bottle of wine. One evening, he came with Neil's wallet and said it was no longer needed by the police. After he'd gone the next morning, I took out the pictures and laid them on the table. There was one of Neil, Stacy and the kids, one of Shaun about fourteen, hands on hips in muddy football kit, post-match sweaty grin, the one with the dead Argentinian soldiers, Alessandro visible in the foreground, one of him and me as kids, holding hands and smiling into blinding white sunlight, and one passport photograph of me, cut from the strip in the kitchen drawer, his handwriting on the back, *Leece x*.

EPILOGUE

Autumn into Winter

KEVIN

I spent a night and day in hospital, under observation. The police were prohibited from questioning me. But soon after returning home, Dreek visited with a tired-looking detective who smelt strongly of coffee and cigarettes. He asked me what I'd seen, and I told him I didn't remember anything after the siren.

"Siren?" the detective asked. "What siren?"

"The one in the tree," I told him. "The air raid siren."

The detective glanced at Dreek, then looked at me like I was stupid or still concussed. The same detective visited several more times over the next few weeks, each time asking me if I remembered anything further from that night. And each time I told him the same thing. I remembered nothing after the siren. Fortunately for me, there had been another witness, a neighbour who'd seen Pettifer bundled into a car by men whose description fitted that of Neil Terridge and two of his friends. The body at the beach meant the police were tying loose ends rather than building a case.

My memories of winter, spring and summer that year are clear and detailed, while those of the autumn that followed are less so. There are few sharp edges of occurrence and almost no days that stand out in colour in the slow fade of time, as if the letters and numbers of the calendar during those months blotted and blurred into one another.

I was kept off school for the whole autumn term. This had never been the plan. But in the weeks after Lyttleton Hall, I woke every night shouting and sweating with the sweet chickeny smell of Pettifer's burning flesh cloying the darkness of my room. When I closed my eyes to sleep, I would see a dreadful procession of the whole year at once: the dead white bodies of Shaun Terridge and Paula Werth, Alan Mitchell with his broken neck and head back to front, the hollow-eyed maggoty tabby cat dragging itself through dead leaves, Emma's mouth giggling beneath shotgun nostrils, Chivers smirking at me on the Chair-O-Plane while fingering a flick-knife, Walks white with anger, standing in the hole with the shovel, Jase lisping obscene threats into my ear, Eddie Rinch with bloody nose and accusing eyes, Pettifer burning on the ground with his skin bubbling and popping, and the siren behind Lyttleton Hall, grey and rusted like an old dustbin, wailing and moaning in the dark crown of the tree.

Mum made it her business to heal me. Only knowing half of what had happened, she was convinced of what I needed. And as it transpired, she was right. She sensed my fear of school and all its pockets of dread and humiliation, and somehow understood that lying in bed for hours each day, drinking Lucozade and reading old comics, and eating soup in front of the telly were the most effective remedies for my adolescent mind and body.

I watched the changing of the seasons through my bedroom window, blank with exhaustion and sedation, brought low by the nightly horrors of sleep. Outside, the street turned from green to gold to brown to colourless grey. The hours of light shortened until the days seemed like anomalies, dull and dirty offences to the long, crisp, cold nights. By midwinter, my enuresis was cured. Mum's determination, the bedside alarm and many small-hours trips to the bathroom had all done their work, aided by a more fitful and restless sleep habit that would never leave me.

Amidst my convalescence, Dad returned. He was there more and more and then all the time. Later, when the light of my brain was fully on again, without the fug of medicine and fatigue, I wondered if their reunion had been because of me, if Mum and Dad had buried their problems for the good of mine. At first this worried me. I listened through the floorboards at night for the return of a hostile tone to their muffled voices, like the one that had been there just before Dad had left. But soon the selfishness of mid-teens ran its normal course, and I took for granted again their happiness and found it less bothersome to presume it would always be so or pay it no attention at all.

On the Sunday morning before Christmas 1982, a year on from meeting Dreek outside Colemans' in the fog and flashing lights, Mum said she was going to lay flowers for Shaun and Paula. So after breakfast, we set off on the short walk from our house to the Old Church Road. On the way, we were both quiet. Mum was lost in her thoughts, perhaps inside herself somewhere, repeating a prayer for the dead and thinking about Shaun's mum, Lisa. I worried that we were walking towards the source of my nightmares. I was fearful I might see Shaun or Paula, mangled from the accident and rotten from a year in the ground, or Alan with his head all skew-whiff and his eyeballs half-eaten by worms, waving from the gate of the old churchyard. But when we arrived at the site of the accident, the bright winter sunshine had chased all traces of ghosts away. Fresh flowers and tributes and football scarves had been laid at the base of a new road sign. LYTTLETON. Please drive carefully through village.

ACKNOWLEDGEMENTS

I would like to thank Dianne Armstrong for all the reading, editing, feedback and unwavering support. Mark and Philip Armstrong for their reading, views and comments. Matthew Walker for his sustained interest, reading and opinions. Dexter Petley for his encouragement and forensic critique of the first draft. Rosie Lowe, Holly Porter, Daniel Burchmore and Emily Gett of The Book Guild for their clarity and support throughout the publishing process, and Kathy Waghorn, Chelsea Taylor and Fern Bushnell for their work on the production of the novel.